Two tortured souls will find rapture in each other's arms . . .

Captive of Sin

Sir Gideon lounged on a carved wooden settee near the blazing grate. His dark eyes rested upon her with fierce concentration as she rose from her chair. On trembling legs, she moved to the center of the room where Akash waited.

She unwrapped the thick shawl from her head and pulled the coat from her shoulders. She dropped both to the floor. It was absurd, but she felt as though she undressed for Sir Gideon's pleasure. The wanton notion came from nowhere. It shocked her, but she couldn't dismiss it.

How had this happened? In ballrooms and salons, she'd met so many men—attractive men, sophisticated men, attentive men. None had affected her like this taciturn, black-haired Adonis, with his glittering eyes and troubled air. The sensations scared the life out of her.

By Anna Campbell

CAPTIVE OF SIN
TEMPT THE DEVIL
UNTOUCHED
CLAIMING THE COURTESAN

Anna Campbell

Captive of Sin

AVON

An Imprint of HarperCollinsPublishers

AVON BOOKS
An Imprint of HarperCollins*Publishers*
10 East 53rd Street
New York, New York 10022-5299

Copyright © 2009 by Anna Campbell
Excerpts from *With Seduction in Mind* copyright © 2009 by Laura Lee Guhrke; *The Most Wicked of Sins* copyright © 2009 by Kathryn Caskie; *Captive of Sin* copyright © 2009 by Anna Campbell; *True Confessions* copyright © 2001 by Rachel Gibson
ISBN 978-0-06-168428-9
www.avonromance.com

First Avon Books paperback printing: November 2009

Avon Trademark Reg. U.S. Pat. Off. and in Other Countries, Marca Registrada, Hecho en U.S.A.
HarperCollins® is a registered trademark of HarperCollins Publishers.

Printed in the U.S.A.

10 9 8 7 6 5 4 3 2

For my beloved mother, Dagmar.

Acknowledgments

I always love writing the acknowledgments page, where I get to thank everyone who helped me along the way with a book.

As always, my deepest gratitude goes to everyone at Avon Books in New York. I'd particularly like to thank May Chen, my fabulous editor, the brilliant art department, and Pam Spengler-Jaffee and her amazing team in marketing. I'd also like to thank the great people at Avon Australia, especially Linda Funnell, Shona Martyn, Cassie Marsden, Christine Farmer, and Jordan Weaver.

Special thanks to my wonderful agent, Nancy Yost. Nancy, I love working with you!

This book involved some tricky research questions. I'd particularly like to thank Brenda Ross from the Société Jersiaise's Lord Coutanche Library on Jersey in the Channel Islands, who rushed to save me when all other avenues of investigation had come to an end.

Thanks, as ever, to my wonderful critique partner, Annie West. I'd also like to express my heartfelt gratitude to Sharon Archer and Christine Wells, who came to my rescue at a difficult moment in this book.

I'd like to thank all my friends at the Romance Bandits, Romance Writers of Australia, and Romance Writers of America. You're an unfailing source of inspiration. Thanks also to Michelle Buonfiglio, Kim Castillo, Maria Lokken, and Marisa O'Neill for your stalwart support.

Finally, a big thank-you to all those readers who have enjoyed my books! I can't tell you what a thrill it is to know that my stories have touched your hearts.

One

G ood God, what have we here?"

The man's deep voice pierced Charis's pain-ridden doze. She flinched, stirring from her cramped position. For one dazed moment, she wondered why she was shivering in fetid straw instead of snuggled in her bed at Holcombe Hall.

Blazing agony struck, and she stifled an involuntary moan. And a curse for her rank stupidity.

How could she forget the danger long enough to fall asleep?

But she'd been blind with exhaustion when she'd stumbled into the stable behind the sprawling inn. Unable to manage another step, even though she hadn't come far enough to be safe.

Now she wasn't safe at all.

The light from the man's lantern dazzled her bleary eyes. She discerned little more than a tall shape looming outside the stall. Choking with panic, she clawed upright until she huddled against the rough planking. Blood pulsed like thunder in her ears.

Muffling a whimper as she moved her injured left arm, Charis crossed shaking hands over her torn bodice. Scenting her terror, the big chestnut horse that filled most of the space shifted restively.

As the man lifted the lantern to illuminate Charis's corner, she shied away. Beyond the ring of yellow light that surrounded him, menacing shadows thickened and multiplied up to the high-pitched ceiling.

"Please don't be frightened." The stranger made a curiously truncated gesture with one black-gloved hand. "I mean you no harm."

The rich baritone was sheathed in warm concern. He made no overt movement toward her. Charis's crippling fear didn't subside. Men, she'd learned from cruel experience, lied. Even men with velvet voices, smooth and cultured.

A sharp twinge in her chest reminded her she hadn't drawn breath since he'd found her. The air she sucked into her starved lungs reeked of horse manure, hay dust, and the sour stink of her own fear.

She turned her head and really looked at the man. Her throat jammed with shock.

He was utterly beautiful.

Beautiful. A word she'd never before associated with a male. In this case, no other description sprang to her churning mind.

Beauty as stark and perfect as this only stoked her alarm. He embodied the elegant world she must relinquish to survive.

Despite her terror, her attention clung to the slashing planes of forehead and cheekbones and jaw, the straight arrogant prow of his nose. He was tanned, unusual in February.

With his intense, compelling features and ruffled hair, black as a gypsy's, he looked like a prince from a fairy tale.

Charis no longer believed in fairy tales.

Her eyes darted around the narrow stall. But he blocked the only exit. Again, she cursed her idiocy. With her good hand, she fumbled beneath her for a rock, a rusty nail, anything she could use to defend herself. Her trembling fingers met nothing but prickly straw.

Unblinking, she watched him set the lantern on the ground. His movements were slow and easy, openly reassuring. But if he wanted to snatch her, he now had both hands free. Her sinews tautened as she prepared to scratch and punch her way out.

In the charged silence, the rattle of her breathing deafened her. It even masked the wind's constant wail. The powerful horse shifted again and gave a worried whicker, tossing its head against the rope that tied it facing toward the corridor.

What if the nervous beast started to kick or buck in this confined space? The horse's hooves looked huge, sharp, deadly. Dread settled like a stone in her empty belly. With every moment, her refuge's unsuitability became more apparent.

Why, oh, why hadn't she kept going, no matter how tired and hurt? Even sheltering in a hedgerow, she'd be safer than here.

The man stepped into the stall, his black greatcoat swirling around his booted ankles. Shrinking back, Charis prepared to wrench free of grabbing hands. Fresh sweat chilled her already icy skin. He was so much bigger and stronger than she.

But he merely snagged the animal's halter with a firm grip that brooked no rebellion. "Hush, Khan." He stroked the gelding's nose as his voice softened into alluring music. The man's tall body conveyed an assured confidence that was almost tangible. "There's nothing to worry about."

The complex mixture of authority and care in his tone should have calmed Charis. Instead, it slipped down her spine like glacial ice. She knew all about men who believed they ruled the universe. She knew how they reacted when their wishes were thwarted. Her furtive search for a weapon grew more frantic.

Khan, foolish, trusting creature, quieted under his master's murmured promises. For the man must own the beast if he knew its name. Nobody could mistake the stranger for a groom. His manner was too effortlessly aristocratic, his clothing too fine.

She found no weapon.

She'd have to make a dash for freedom and hope her stiff, tired legs carried her. Surreptitiously, she pushed upward. Even this small movement sparked agony. Every muscle ached, and her arm felt like it was on fire. She locked her teeth to muffle her whimpers.

"There's no need to run away." He didn't glance up from the now docile horse.

"Yes, there is," she surprised herself by saying, although she'd resolved not to address him. Her swollen face thickened her voice into unfamiliarity. But her upper-class diction marked her as an object of interest. Memorable. Noticeable.

A target.

Clumsily, she struggled to her feet. She felt less vulnerable standing. In her awkward rise, she bumped the wall and bit back a sharp cry. Battling dizzying pain, she cradled her throbbing arm against her.

Her ungainly lurch spooked Khan, who sidled and snorted. Her father had been a connoisseur of horseflesh. Charis had immediately recognized Khan for the highbred aristocrat he was.

Much like the man holding the beast's head.

"I know you're afraid." At first, she thought he spoke to Khan. His attention remained on the horse. "I know you need help."

Help to hand her over to the law, she thought bitterly. "Why should you care? You're a stranger."

"That's true. Although when you chose my horse's stall, you also chose me."

"That was just chance."

At last, he looked directly at her. Surely it was only a trick of the lamplight that his eyes shone so dark and brilliant above those dramatic cheekbones. "All things in life are chance."

Charis shivered under that appraising ebony gaze. The moment seemed to hold a significance it couldn't possibly have. Shaking off the strange preternatural sensation, she raised her chin. She had enough problems in the here and now without taking on the metaphysical.

"Kindly step aside, sir. I must be on my way."

"It's not safe for a lady to travel by herself." He didn't budge, and while his voice remained quiet, it was implacable.

To underline his warning, a burst of carousing came from the inn across the yard. On such a cold night, the taproom must be packed. The freezing weather was one of her few strokes of luck—the grooms had left their posts to seek the fire's warmth. Otherwise, they'd have discovered her hiding place immediately. Why wasn't this stranger equally eager to stay inside like any sensible man instead of wandering around this cavernous stable?

"That is none of your concern." How on earth could she escape? Again, she berated herself for not struggling on.

"Won't you trust me with your story?" His voice dropped into sweet persuasion. The tone wasn't far different from the one he'd used to settle Khan. And like Khan, she felt the insidious lure of that mellifluous baritone. "I can see you're in trouble. I swear . . ."

He broke off abruptly and tilted his head toward the main doors, far down the long corridor. Then Charis caught the shuffle of approaching footsteps. What inhumanly acute hearing he must possess to discern anyone's arrival over the creaking roof and the whistle of the wind.

"Aught amiss here, my lord?" a rough male voice, she guessed belonging to a groom, asked from several yards away.

My lord? She'd been right about his social status. With a frightened whimper, Charis shrank into the shadows as the man shifted the lantern so darkness shrouded her. As she retreated, each rustle of straw sounded loud as a gunshot.

"Just seeing to my horse, my good man." With a casual air, he wandered out of sight toward the newcomer.

"Can I aid thee?" The groom's voice grew clearer as he approached.

Charis's breath caught in her throat and she hunched as far from the light as she could. Her arm protested the movement, but she ignored the shooting pain.

"No. All's well."

Charis buried damp palms in the tattered, stained skirts of her once-elegant day gown and silently prayed that she remain undetected. Her heart banged so frenetically against her ribs, she was surprised the groom didn't hear it and come to investigate.

"It's a cold night for man and beast, that's for certain sure."

"Too cold to be out and about." For all the ring of authority in his voice, the lord sounded relaxed, unworried. "Find your place by the hearth and have a drink on me."

Charis edged as far behind Khan's rump as she dared, keeping a wary eye on those lethal hind legs.

"Very kind of your lordship, I'm sure. I don't mind if I do." The groom's reply rang with surprised gratitude. "Sure I can't assist?"

"Quite sure." The lord's voice indicated dismissal, and whatever coin changed hands ensured immediate compliance.

"Good e'en to your lordship."

With excruciating slowness, the groom shambled away. It seemed to take forever before his lordship appeared at the stall's entrance. He raised the lantern to reveal her trembling form against the back wall.

"He's gone."

"Thank heaven." In a relieved gasp, Charis released the breath she'd held for what felt like an hour. She didn't know why the man had helped conceal her. All that mattered right now was that he had.

He surveyed her with a troubled expression on his striking features. "You can't stay here. The inn is crawling with people. You've been lucky to stay undisturbed this long. At least come out where I can see you."

"I don't . . ." she started uncertainly. Although the man made no attempt to drag her out, she pressed against the boards. The movement cramped her aching muscles with fresh pain.

The man stepped away to indicate he presented no danger. At last she saw her way clear to take to her heels.

She hesitated.

She bit her lower lip, then wished she hadn't when the torn flesh stung. The stranger was right. What chance her making it past the inn yard? This close to home, someone would surely recognize her.

As if he read her thoughts, the watchfulness faded from his eyes. "My name is Gideon."

Even as Charis limped past Khan into the aisle, she remained poised for flight if the man—Gideon—made a move. But his stance was relaxed, and he left her space. She sucked in a shuddering breath that tested her bruised ribs. With every second he didn't touch her, she felt safer.

"You're hurt." He sounded tranquil, but anger sparked his eyes to black fire as one comprehensive glance swept her from head to toe.

She could imagine what a disreputable slattern she looked. Humiliated heat crawled up her neck, and she lifted her right hand to clutch her ragged bodice. Her stepbrother Hubert had ripped it when he'd held her down. Now the neckline gaped to reveal the lacy edge of her shift.

Her face felt as though a thousand wasps stung it. Her blue dress was torn and filthy and pitifully inadequate on this arctic night. Under capped sleeves, scratches and bruises covered her arms, legacy of the beating and her frantic flight through fields and woods. Her hair was a matted bird's nest. Most of its pins had shaken loose as she'd fought her way through the hedgerows around Holcombe.

Before Gideon could question her or, worse, express the

pity that lurked like a ghost under his outrage, she launched into the story she'd prepared. "I was traveling to my aunt in Portsmouth when . . . when footpads set upon me."

Curse that telltale falter. Lying never came easily. He wouldn't believe her. Which meant her game was up.

She waited in breathless suspense for him to brand her a sham and a runaway. But he merely whipped off his heavy black coat and stepped closer.

Fear had her backing away at a stumbling run until she slammed into a thick post. She strangled a scream as the impact shot jagged lightning along her arm. Automatically, she jerked forward, and he seized the opportunity to drop the coat around her trembling shoulders.

"Here." He stepped away again.

Gradually, panic ebbed, and she straightened under the coat's weight. Its warmth made her feel slightly more human. The garment swamped her, trailing on the ground. The fabric smelled pleasantly of fresh air and something clean and musky that must be its owner.

He was clever enough not to crowd her. Even so, she remained nervously aware of his commanding height and leanly muscled body, now revealed in black jacket, white shirt, and brown breeches that clung lovingly to long, strong legs. From his highly polished boots to his plain white neckcloth, his clothing was simple but of the highest quality.

"Th . . . thank you," she said through chattering teeth.

She blinked back stinging tears and clutched the deliciously cozy woolen folds around her like a shield. Strange, but his kindness proved the greatest threat to her fraying control.

"What is your name?"

The loan of the coat seemed to require some gesture of trust in return. "Sarah Watson," she said in a grudging voice, stealing the identity of her great-aunt's dour companion in Bath. Remembering her manners, she dropped into a stiff curtsy.

He forestalled her with another of those odd, incomplete

gestures. His intent dark eyes didn't waver. "May I escort you to some friend or relation in Winchester, Miss Watson? This stable isn't safe."

She wasn't safe anywhere, heaven help her. Fear stirred low in her belly as she remembered what would happen if her stepbrothers caught her.

"I'm . . . I'm a stranger in this part of the country, sir. I'm from Carlisle." The most distant town she could think of without actually crossing the border into Scotland. She stiffened the wobbly legs that threatened to buckle beneath her and glared at him, daring him to challenge her story.

His expression remained neutral, but she knew he sifted her responses for truth and falsehood. "A long journey for a lady on her own. Didn't you have a maid to accompany you, at least?"

With every moment, she sank further into an abyss of lies. But what choice did she have? If she revealed her identity, any law-abiding citizen would immediately hand her over to the authorities.

Nonetheless, her unruly tongue tripped over her answer. "My maid ran off when we changed coaches in London."

"You have indeed suffered a series of misfortunes, Miss Watson."

Did his response contain a hint of irony? His expression remained all polite interest. She decided to accept his comment at face value. "It's been a terrible day." At least that much was true. "Now all I wish is to reach my aunt's house."

"You're a long way from Portsmouth."

Didn't she know it? She'd barely covered a few miles and already tested the edge of her endurance. She had no money to pay for a seat on a coach, and even if she had, she couldn't risk someone seeing her and remembering her. Yet again, the insurmountable task she set herself struck her. Then she recalled what awaited back at Holcombe. "I'll manage."

"How?" he asked with the first trace of sharpness. "You're dead on your feet."

Hearing her own doubts voiced with such emphasis made her belly clench with sick despair. "Needs must."

His lips flattened. Clearly he found her sullen answer as unimpressive as she did herself. "I offer you transport if you care to accept."

Charis jerked back as if he tried to touch her. This seemed too good to be true. Transport to Portsmouth was a godsend. Her stepbrothers would already be on her trail. If she went with this stranger, she'd cover more ground. Not only that, her stepbrothers would ask after a girl traveling alone.

"I couldn't inconvenience you so." She intended the words to sound final, but her injuries slurred her speech.

"I'm traveling south anyway." His expression became somber. "Chivalry forbids me to abandon a woman to the mercy of any blackguard she meets on the road."

In spite of physical misery and encroaching fear, a grim laugh escaped Charis. She made a dismissive gesture with her good hand. "Chivalry is an unreliable quality at the best of times."

"You have my word as a gentleman that your virtue is safe, Miss Watson." He didn't smile.

She'd heard so many lies recently, she just assumed anything a man said must be falsehood. But strangely, she believed him when he pledged his word.

Good Lord, if this man meant to rape her, surely he'd have made a move by now. Every scrap of sense prompted her to credit him as that most chimerical of creatures.

A genuine man of honor.

Or was she just dazzled by his remarkable looks? She was vulnerable and exhausted. Ceaseless pain turned her mind hazy. She was frightened for her life.

The pause extended, stretched into taut silence. If he'd tried to persuade her, she would have insisted on going on alone. But he let her make up her mind. Only the tension straightening the powerful shoulders under his superbly cut jacket indicated he awaited her answer with more than indifference.

Finally, she sighed. It was a sound of acquiescence. Fear clogged her veins, but desperation was stronger. Wondering if she cast her lot with the devil, she gave a brief nod. "Then I accept your help with gratitude."

"First we'll take you to a doctor."

For an instant, her terror had faded to a distant thrum. The chance of escape had beckoned like a lifeboat to a drowning man. Now his words reminded her she'd found no sanctuary yet.

Perhaps ever, unless she was very clever and very lucky.

Any doctor in Winchester would recognize her immediately. She shook her head in swift denial, cradling her arm. "I don't need a doctor. My injuries aren't as bad as they look."

She waited for argument. None came. "All right. No doctor."

Relief made her sag, although she tried to mask her overwhelming reaction. Apparently she'd fallen in with the most credulous gentleman in the county. So far, he accepted her story without a moment's doubt.

Odd, she wouldn't have considered him a stupid man. Intelligence sizzled in those perceptive dark eyes.

Perhaps he was just naïve. More reason to go with him. Evading him in Portsmouth should present no trouble.

What she'd do then was a complete blank. She had no money and no friends. Or no friends she could put at risk of prosecution. Her stepbrothers had already terrified her one close relative, her great-aunt, into handing her over to them. She wore a gold locket and her mother's pearl ring, neither of great value. Somehow she had to hide for three weeks. Her crushing dilemma made her shudder.

One step at a time. She chivied her flagging courage. Getting out of Winchester undetected was her first goal.

"Gideon."

A man spoke from the stable doorway. Charis started, again testing her injuries, and felt the blood drain from her face. Her rescuer reached out but cut the gesture short of making contact. "Don't worry. He's a friend."

Such was his natural authority, Charis curtailed her retreat, although her heart pounded like a hammer and cold sweat broke out on her skin.

"I'm here," Gideon called, without taking his eyes off her.

Another man, as tall as her rescuer, slender, dark, obviously foreign for all his fine London tailoring, strolled into view. "What have you found?"

"Miss Watson, this is Akash. Akash, may I present Miss Sarah Watson? She's been set upon by ruffians and requires aid."

The newcomer's liquid brown eyes rested upon Charis. She waited for him to question her threadbare tale. But after a pause, he merely quirked one elegant black eyebrow at Gideon.

"I'm guessing we're not staying here tonight?" His voice was pure England, although he looked like he inhabited some Arabian fantasy.

"You know I'm in a hurry to get to Penrhyn."

"Indeed," he said neutrally.

"Yes, via Portsmouth."

"I've always had a violent desire to visit Portsmouth." Akash sounded perfectly undisturbed at the prospect of braving the cold to assist a stranger. Too undisturbed.

Suddenly, Charis didn't feel safe after all. Putting herself into the care of two unfamiliar men was the height of foolishness. Their quick acceptance of her paper-thin story seemed suspicious rather than reassuring.

On trembling legs, she backed toward Khan, who whickered softly in her ear. "I can't impose on your good natures. I shall make my own way to my aunt."

"No man of honor would countenance such a plan, Miss Watson." Gideon sounded immovable.

She could sound immovable too. "Nonetheless, it is what I must do."

Gideon sent a quick smile to his companion. For one dazzling moment, amusement lit his face to brilliance. Glittering dark eyes, creases in his cheeks and around his eyes, a flash of straight white teeth.

Charis's heart lurched to a halt, then broke into a wayward

race. Foolishly, in spite of fear and pain and mistrust, she longed for nothing more than to see him smile again.

Smile at her.

"I believe you've terrified the chit, Akash."

She ignored Akash's soft laugh and frowned at Gideon. "Pray, sir, I'm no chit."

"Would you feel happier if I gave you this?"

She looked down to see him extending a small dueling pistol. She hadn't noticed him reaching into his jacket. Tiredness made her stupid. Tiredness and the effects of a vicious beating.

And most unwelcome admission of all, a man's unguarded smile.

She stared at the gun as though she didn't recognize what it was. The room receded in dark waves. The thunder in her ears rose to blanket all other sound.

"Akash!"

Gideon's shout came from a long way off, then the world spun as strong arms swept her off her feet.

But not the strong arms she wanted to close around her. Even through her near faint, she recognized that bone-deep and mortifying fact.

Gideon stared at the half-unconscious girl Akash clutched to him. She was a tumble of slender arms and legs and frothy blue skirts. Her bright bronze hair trailed across Akash's black sleeve like a flag. Her hem was torn and wet, and her pale blue half boots were caked in mud.

His hands fisted at his sides, and anger cannoned through him. Who the devil had abused her? Even before this last year, he'd abhorred cruelty. And some bastard had beaten this girl to within an inch of her life.

Gideon was too familiar with violence to misjudge how badly she was hurt. Damn it, he wanted a doctor to look at her.

But the chit was so frightened. Gideon knew too what desperate fear looked like, and he couldn't mistake it in the girl's wide hazel eyes, lovely even in her ruined face. If he pushed her too far, she'd scarper and meet God knew what dangers.

What in Hades had happened to her? He'd immediately recognized her pathetic lies. He'd lay money no footpads had attacked her but, hell, someone had.

Futile rage, sickeningly familiar, flooded his mouth with a vile, rusty taste. He stepped back and breathed hard through his nose as he fought for composure. He needed to stay calm, or he'd frighten her.

The girl stirred in Akash's grip, and her pale hand clenched in his coat. Gideon's attention caught on an expensive, if old-fashioned pearl ring on one slender finger. Nor had he missed the pretty gold locket revealed under her tattered bodice. Whoever she was and whatever her current straitened circumstances, she came from money.

Her voice was thick with distress. "Please . . . please put me down. I can walk. Really."

Gideon's rage faded, replaced by piercing compassion. His anger couldn't help her. She was small, defenseless, heartbreakingly brave. And young. Impossible to tell exactly how old she was under the patchwork of bruising, but he'd guess not much more than her early twenties.

Add to her courage a pride that cut Gideon to the heart. Oh, he understood how she felt, all right. He guessed pride was all she had left.

Pride and two strangers who would see her safe, whether she trusted them or not.

He couldn't abandon her to her fate. He was too bitterly aware what it was like to stand against powerful foes with no hope of prevailing.

"Guvnor, is there a problem with the nag?"

Gideon turned toward the door with a surge of irritation. Akash had come out to check on him, although if challenged he'd never admit it. Now here was Tulliver, asking after his charge's health like a gruff and grizzled nursemaid.

The yearning for freedom was a crashing wave inside him. He'd give up his hope of heaven for one moment without eyes observing his every move. Fresh air in his face. A good mount beneath him. Nothing but clear open country.

And no people for a hundred bloody miles.

"Sir Gideon?"

The wild and glorious dream faded. How could he blame his companions for their concern? They were good men, both. He'd spent so long alone, it still struck him as remarkable that they pledged him their loyalty.

Surely they must recognize he was completely unworthy of the honor.

"We're not staying, Tulliver," he said to the brawny ex-soldier he'd hired as his servant after the fellow's untiring service on the ship from India. "We'll need a carriage, food for the journey. And a driver, I expect."

"No need, sir. I can handle a rig."

Tulliver, Gideon had learned, could handle almost anything, from a man out of his head with pain and shame right up to a duchess's comfort. The East India Company had lost a treasure when Tulliver resigned.

Tulliver's eyes flickered impassively over the woman in Akash's arms, but he asked no questions. He never did. Yet somehow he managed to know everything. He bowed and headed outside again.

"Please, sir," the girl said in a shaking voice.

Silently, Akash set her upon her feet. She staggered, and Gideon reached out before he remembered and snatched his hand back. The girl raised her chin and stared him down as if he'd made an improper remark at a debutante ball.

Again, her pride touched something deep within him. Something pure and fresh like a tender green shoot after the first snows melted. He was astounded any untainted feeling could survive what he'd endured.

"I put you to some inconvenience." Her attention still on Gideon, she stepped away from Akash. She held one arm awkwardly against her. "While I'm grateful, I can't allow you to discommode yourself on my account."

She spoke like a damned octogenarian duchess. A confounded haughty one, at that. In spite of the moment's seriousness, Gideon felt his lips twitch.

Of course she didn't miss it. "You're laughing at me."

He didn't deny it. Instead, he let an element of steel enter his tone. "Miss Watson, you need our help. I can't bundle you in the carriage and force you to come with me."

A lie. Of course he could. He would if he had to.

"I'd scream if you did," she said defiantly, even as her shoulders drooped under the weight of his coat. And the weight of her despair and fear, he guessed.

Why was he so determined on rescuing this prickly-tempered waif? She stood before him, trembling with pain, panic, and weariness. Her dark bronze hair was a tangle around her pale face. Her gown was ripped and stained. Bruising hid any beauty she possessed.

He bit back a caustic grunt of laughter.

Even if she was a beauty, what use was that beauty to him?

He quashed the acrid question and shot her a straight look. "It's February. It's cold. You're in no fit state to go on alone."

Tulliver appeared in the doorway. "I've arranged the carriage, guvnor. The landlord is chasing up the grooms."

Gideon watched terror flood the girl's eyes. She was definitely eager for nobody to see her. He needed to know why. "Go back into the stall, Miss Watson. Khan won't hurt you."

"I'm not frightened of your horse," she retorted. She tugged the coat around her slender body and withdrew into the darkness.

✣

The staff at Winchester's largest inn were used to arranging transport for patrons. The small closed carriage was ready for departure within minutes.

Gideon stepped into the stall. The girl huddled behind Khan. He tried to quell his automatic reaction to the crowded space and the darkness. But the gloved hand he placed on the rough wooden divider was unsteady.

Thank God the gloom hid his reaction. What confidence could she have in a rescuer who trembled like a willow at the merest shadow?

"We're ready."

She straightened and wrapped the coat around her like a cape. He supposed she couldn't bear to force her injured arm into a sleeve. As she looked up, he caught the shine of her eyes. "Why are you doing this?"

He shrugged, trying to appear as if aiding stray maidens was his everyday activity. "You need help."

"It doesn't seem enough when I see the trouble you've taken."

"It will earn me points in heaven," he said with a lightness he didn't feel. He extended the bundle he held. "I thought you might like this."

She didn't immediately take it. "What is it?"

"A shawl. The night is cold." And she'd need to cover that distinctive hair when she entered the carriage. Although if he told her that, she'd know he tagged her tale as a pack of lies.

"Where did you get it?" Her voice dripped suspicion.

He hid a smile. She was so wary, so defensive. Yet if he wanted, he could render her unconscious in the blink of an eye. That possibility had occurred to him, but he'd dismissed it. She'd had enough violence done to her.

"Tulliver bought it from a lady at the inn."

Good thick wool—he thought with a moment's regret of the shimmering, gorgeous fabrics he'd seen in India. He lifted the brown shawl briefly to his nose and sniffed. "It smells of pug, but you'll welcome its warmth."

To his surprise, she gave a short huff of laughter. "I've been sleeping in a stable. A whiff of *eau de chien* won't unsettle me in the least."

The chit had backbone. He'd always admired courage, and this girl had more than was good for her. Something tired and rusty and long unfamiliar stirred in his heart. He stifled the unwelcome sensation and offered the shawl once more. "Miss Watson?"

"Thank you."

As he'd known she would, she wrapped it around her head and shoulders. In his enveloping greatcoat and with her head covered, she looked almost anonymous. He couldn't miss how she favored her right arm. Was it broken? Again, he wished she'd let him take her to a sawbones.

"And take this, just in case." He passed her the pistol and watched her slip it into the coat's voluminous pockets. "Do you know how to use it?"

He already knew the answer. She handled the gun with an ease that indicated familiarity.

"Yes. My father was a marksman. He taught me to shoot."

Gideon shadowed her when they crossed the yard to the waiting carriage. Akash was already up on his temperamental gray.

As Gideon opened the door for Miss Watson, he caught his friend's eye. He wondered what Akash made of the night's events and the new addition to their party. He'd find out, he knew. Just because Akash had said nothing yet didn't mean he had nothing to say.

The girl paused, as if expecting Gideon to hand her up. Yet another clue to a privileged life, if she but knew it. When Gideon didn't respond, she climbed into the carriage.

Tulliver followed, leading his sturdy mount and Khan, and tied both horses to the back of the coach. Gideon cast a last look around the windswept yard. Ostensibly, nobody paid them any attention.

On a frosty night like this, anyone who didn't have to be outside sought what warmth they could. The few servants crossing the open area seemed to mind their own business. Still, old habits died hard, and Gideon took note of the scene's every detail.

Tulliver came up to his side. "All set, guvnor?"

"Yes." One last glance to make sure, but nobody appeared unduly interested in their little party. "Let's get under way."

"Very good."

Tulliver climbed into the driver's seat. Gideon entered the vehicle where the mysterious Miss Watson, with her sharp tongue and terrified eyes, awaited.

As he surveyed her unkempt figure perched stiffly on the leather-covered bench, he was suddenly aware that for the first time in a long while, he felt something other than weary self-disgust. She made him curious; she made him concerned; she made him care.

Miss Watson was an unlikely miracle worker. He'd lived with wretchedness so long, even this much emotion felt like spring thaw after endless winter.

Wondering what other unexpected results his impulsive actions might yield, he subsided on the seat opposite and closed his eyes in counterfeit slumber. The coach jerked into movement with a crack of the whip and a shout from Tulliver. They jolted out of the inn yard and into the freezing winter night.

Two

Horrific images haunted Charis's dreams. An endless replaying of Hubert's fists pounding into her while Felix watched with a gloating smile. The wrenching drag on her arm. The final blow to her head that sent her whirling into oblivion.

When she opened scratchy eyes to the lamplit confines of the shabby coach, she expected to hear the echo of her screams. The only sounds were the creaking of the carriage and the howl of the wind. Sir Gideon sprawled opposite, apparently asleep.

Cool, blessed relief flooded her, and she sucked in a shuddering breath that made her bruised ribs twinge. For the moment, she was safe from both Felix and Hubert.

She was shaking, not far from tears, curled into the corner as if she cowered away from the beating. Her jaw throbbed painfully in time with the vehicle's sway. Her injured arm had stiffened into agony, and she bit back a moan as she folded it against her heaving chest.

Long minutes passed while she fought dizzying pain.

But gradually her head cleared, and her breathing steadied. Using her good arm, she tugged the coat around her like a blanket and turned her attention to her companion. His lean body stretched out with an elegant abandon that made her foolish heart race.

To her shame, not with fear.

When the journey started, she'd braced for interrogation. But Sir Gideon had lounged on the bench, spread his arms along the back of the seat, extended his long booted legs into the corner, and closed his eyes. From the look of him, he'd hardly moved since.

Studying him like this felt like illicit intimacy. Although even now, his expression was guarded, closed. A lock of black hair fell across his brow. It should make him look vulnerable. It didn't.

As her gaze roamed his sculpted features, she realized with a shock that he was close to her age. His air of authority had made her assume he was in his thirties. But now, with his eyes shut, he didn't look much past twenty-five. Ashamed of her unseemly curiosity, she stared into the loose folds of the coat over her lap.

"Are we near Portsmouth?" she asked in a croaky voice, looking up.

He opened his eyes and regarded her assessingly. "No. We're not far out of Winchester."

The coach drew to a juddering stop. Charis reached forward to push the blinds aside. They were in a large field. The change from road to turf under the wheels must have disturbed her nightmares.

The grassy area was empty. No lights shone in the distance. They could be a thousand miles from anywhere.

Abruptly what had seemed an acceptable risk in Winchester became a terrifying threat. She was alone and defenseless in an isolated location with three men she didn't know. The hairs on the back of her neck prickled, and her throat closed with rising dread.

How could she be so naïve? How could she be so fatally

stupid? She scrabbled wildly for the door catch. Perhaps in the dark, she had a chance of escape.

"What are you doing?" Sir Gideon asked with what sounded like casual interest.

Was Gideon even his real name?

"Getting out," she muttered.

She tensed, waiting for him to grab her, but he only straightened against the worn upholstery. She sucked a shaky breath through her teeth and continued her panicked search for the latch.

"I gave you my word I wouldn't hurt you," he said quietly.

"I know what a man's word is worth."

Ah, at last!

The door banged open, and she tumbled forward. Only to land smack against her kidnapper's accomplice. A choked scream erupted as hard hands closed around her upper arms through the voluminous coat. A scream of pain as much as fear.

"Let me go!" She struggled against his firm hold. Her abused flesh protested the violent movements, but she fought on.

"Your pardon, Miss Watson."

To her astonishment, Akash carefully placed her on her feet and moved back. Behind her, she heard the carriage creak as Sir Gideon emerged into the night. He stood at her side, tall, urbane, his expression quizzical in the bright moonlight.

Tulliver came up, holding a lantern. "What's all this to-do?"

He stared at her as if she'd escaped Bedlam. Her hysteria ebbed on a sick tide, leaving behind humiliated awareness that she'd made a fool of herself.

"Miss Watson was under the impression we brought her here to have our wicked way."

Both the irony in Sir Gideon's voice and the irritated look Tulliver cast her made her more than ever certain she'd jumped to false conclusions. Fading panic bubbled through her blood and left her tottering with reaction. She pulled the thick greatcoat around her shivering body and suddenly realized her rescuer wore only a jacket over his shirt.

"You must be freezing." She plucked at the coat with her good hand.

"No," he said sharply, gesturing for her to stop, although he didn't touch her. Then more calmly, "I don't feel the cold."

"Miss Watson, we've stopped so I can examine your injuries," Akash said.

Her eyes went automatically to Sir Gideon. "You have medical knowledge?"

The carriage lamps glanced a sheen of gold across his glossy hair as he shook his head. "Akash and Tulliver between them make up a fair doctor. And we have supplies. Bandages. Ointments. Laudanum to dull the pain."

"I won't be drugged." On unsteady legs, she retreated until she bumped into the carriage.

Bad as the beating had been, it was Felix's threat to drug her and hand her over for Lord Desaye's rape that had finally made her flee Holcombe Hall. When her ordeal started, she'd considered escape, then decided to cling to the dubious security of life at Holcombe. It was only for a couple of weeks. She could endure whatever her stepbrothers did as long as she had the ultimate promise of freedom. On the road, she'd be at the mercy of anyone she met. Defenseless. Destitute. Helpless.

But when her stepbrothers threatened unspeakable degradation, the dangers of the road had paled in comparison.

How she loathed the Farrells. Her two stepbrothers provided a contrast in menace. Hubert, all bullying brute strength, and Felix, spite and intellect. Whatever damage Hubert inflicted, it was Felix she really feared.

In response to her vehement refusal, Akash shrugged, the movement subtly foreign. "Let me at least see what the damage is. If you'll permit?"

"Be careful. She's hurt her arm," Sir Gideon said urgently.

"My friend, you know you can trust me with her."

Reluctantly, Charis stepped forward. Akash carefully lifted the coat away from her shoulders and laid it inside the coach.

She stood before them in her wreck of a gown. The night was freezing. The needle-sharp wind carried a promise of snow. Her good hand rose shaking to close her bodice while she angled her chin with a pathetic attempt at pride. She was decent. Barely. But she knew she looked dirty and hurt and helpless. With moonlight, the carriage lamps and the lantern, her bruises and abrasions must show with humiliating clarity.

"Please sit down, Miss Watson." Sir Gideon slid a folding stool from the back of the carriage and set it behind her. He also passed her the pug-scented shawl.

She subsided with gratitude—her knees felt like rubber—and draped the shawl over her shoulders. Hesitantly, she extended her arm toward Akash. He frowned as he gently manipulated her wrist. Although his hold was skilled and sure, she winced.

"It's sprained but not broken," he said eventually.

Relief gushed through her. Life over the next three weeks would be tough if she was whole. A broken arm would be a disaster. Thank goodness Hubert's beating had ceased once he knocked her unconscious.

Akash tested her hands, arms, neck, then ran his fingers carefully over her face. His touch was so impersonal, she gradually relaxed and became aware of the activity around her. While Tulliver checked the horses, Gideon collected a leather bag strapped to the back of the carriage. Without speaking, he placed it beside Akash. He turned away and began to lay a fire.

Trying to distract herself from both the cold and the painful examination, she watched the graceful deftness of Gideon's gloved hands as he accomplished the workaday task. The breath caught in her throat when the crackling flames caught and lit his remarkable face to gold, gleaming along smooth cheekbone and angular jaw.

Beautiful. The word whispered through her like a *glissando* on a harp.

Looking at Sir Gideon made her restless, edgy. She shifted to ease a strange pressure in the pit of her stomach.

"I'm sorry, Miss Watson." Akash raised his hands from her shoulders.

She shook her head. "It's nothing."

She blushed when she realized he'd seen where her attention strayed. Straightening on the rickety stool, she strove to bring her unruly heartbeat under control.

As she looked up into Akash's face, the compassion in his eyes made her cringe. He was a handsome man. The recognition was as dispassionate as if she studied a fine portrait. His handsomeness didn't call to her the way Sir Gideon's did.

Sir Gideon disappeared into moonlit darkness and returned carrying a tin kettle, which he set on the blaze. She'd been so focused on watching him that she hadn't heard the stream bubbling in the distance. Behind her, Tulliver muttered softly as he fussed over the horses.

Once the water heated, Akash used a damp cloth to wash the blood and dirt from her swollen face. Even the lightest touch stung, and she tautened every muscle to stay still. She struggled not to glance at Gideon as she huddled in her shawl.

Eventually, she couldn't help herself. While she silently bore Akash's ministrations, she looked across to where Sir Gideon stood on the far side of the circle of firelight.

His febrile dark eyes were glued to her. Some deep turmoil she didn't understand stirred in his gaze. His gloved hands clenched at his sides. She read anger in his expression, the same anger he'd betrayed when he first saw her battered face. She shivered although she knew the rage was targeted at her abusers and not at her.

He stiffened as he noticed her attention and turned away to fetch more folding stools, which he set up around the fire.

She bent her head, knowing her unconcealed interest was unbecoming in a lady.

Akash opened the bag and located a small ceramic pot. When he opened it, a pungent herbal smell filled the air. She jerked back, then made herself sit as he stroked the ointment onto her cheeks. Her face felt like it had been whipped with nettles. She couldn't stifle a gasp of discomfort.

"Damn it, man. You're hurting her!" Gideon's protest was sharp, and he took an urgent step in their direction. "Be careful!"

Akash ignored his protective friend and spoke to Charis. "Where else are you hurt?"

Her ribs ached, and she had grazes on her knees from where she'd fallen in the dark. But her arm and face were by far the worst of it. "Nowhere."

Akash's stare was searching as he replaced the lid on the ointment. "Are you sure?"

"I'm sure." She wanted him to stop. She couldn't bear much more. Already her vision grew hazy as endurance faded.

"I'll wrap your arm to reduce the swelling." Akash opened another jar and smoothed the contents on her arm. It was as smelly as the first ointment, but when it touched her skin, she felt a spreading heat.

Surely this torture must soon be over. The shawl and her flimsy dress offered little protection from the biting wind. She drooped with exhaustion by the time Akash wrapped a bandage around her arm.

Gideon knelt and drew another length of linen from the bag that held their medical supplies. "A sling might be a good idea."

"Yes." Akash rigged the linen around her neck. Immediately, the painful pressure on her arm eased. "Does that feel better?"

"Yes, thank you." She looked up with a shaky smile. "You've been very kind."

He gave another of those exotic shrugs. "My pleasure.

I know you're sore and sorry, but I can't find any lasting damage. I'll need to check in the daylight, but from what I can see, your injuries are superficial. You'll be fighting fit in no time."

She was too tired to do much more than whisper another thank-you. Gideon fetched the greatcoat from the carriage and dropped it around her shoulders. As the heavy folds enveloped her, his already familiar scent teased her nostrils. The warmth was immediate and welcome. "Come and sit near the fire."

Already he'd moved out of reach. For a lost moment, she watched him stride away. Then crushing weariness hit, and she stumbled the short distance to the fire, where she collapsed onto a stool. Her frozen extremities tingled as restoring heat slowly seeped through her.

Sir Gideon lifted a heavy wicker basket packed with food from the back of the carriage. To her embarrassment, her belly rumbled. Her stepbrothers had kept her on minimal rations, hoping hunger would sap her resistance.

It was a silent meal. As the four of them sat around the merrily burning little fire, Charis prepared for more questions. Any questions. But her companions seemed astoundingly ready to accept her lies at face value. Guilt settled like a stone in her now-full belly, and she pushed away the pork pie she'd barely nibbled at.

"Are you feeling better?" Sir Gideon asked, noticing her sudden stillness. Of course he noticed. Throughout the meal, he'd studied her across the flames. He sat directly opposite her, with Tulliver and Akash on either side.

"Yes, thank you."

With surprise, she realized it was true. Her face didn't sting so badly, and the pain in her arm was a distant throb rather than fiery agony.

She sipped fine claret from the traveler's cup Sir Gideon passed her. The men had made do with drinking from the bottle. It was oddly intimate to place her lips where Gideon's had once been, however long ago. Almost like a kiss. The thought made her blush even while her lips tingled as though they indeed brushed his.

After supper, Tulliver returned to the horses, and Akash and Sir Gideon cleared up. Charis frowned. Could Gideon really be a man of her own class if he accepted such mundane tasks? He was strangely comfortable with his rough surroundings. Her stepbrothers wouldn't dream of dirtying their hands with rinsing a plate or setting a fire. Servants were there to serve. The landed classes were there to be served.

The relationship between the men was puzzling too. Tulliver seemed on friendly terms with his masters. Akash was surely also an employee, yet he and Sir Gideon treated each other as equals.

Gideon opened the carriage door for her. Again, he didn't assist her inside. The easy, automatic action of a gentleman. Yet he didn't do it. Instead, Akash stepped forward and helped her into the carriage. Wearing the greatcoat loose around her shoulders and with her sling, she couldn't have managed otherwise.

"Miss Watson."

"Thank you, Akash," she murmured, and was hardly aware when he moved away.

Instead, her eyes fastened on Sir Gideon, who waited outside. A cloud covered the moon, and the striking face became a mixture of shadows and light. Still beautiful but sinister.

She shivered. "Who are you?" she whispered, subsiding onto her seat.

"Who are you?" His dark gaze didn't waver from her as he resumed his place opposite, his back to the horses, as a gentleman would.

Charis wrapped the coat around her against the sharp early-morning chill and settled her injured arm more comfortably. "I asked first."

It was a childish response, and she knew he recognized it

as such from the twitch of his firm mouth. Like the rest of his face, his mouth was perfect. Sharply cut upper lip indicating character and integrity. A fuller lower lip indicating . . .

Something stirred and smoldered in her belly as she stared at him in the electric silence. What a time to realize she'd never before been alone with a man who wasn't a relative. The moment seemed dangerous in a way that had nothing to do with her quest to escape Felix and Hubert.

"My name is Gideon Trevithick." He paused as if expecting a response but the name meant nothing to her. "Of Penrhyn in Cornwall."

"Is that a famous house?" Perhaps that explained his watchful reaction.

Another wry smile. "No. That's two questions. My turn."

She stiffened although she should have expected this. And long before now.

"I'm tired." It was true, although a good meal and Akash's skills meant she didn't feel nearly as low as she had.

"It's a long journey to Portsmouth. Surely you can stay awake a few moments to entertain your fellow traveler."

She sighed. Her deceit made her sick with self-loathing. But what could she do? If she told the truth, he'd hand her over to the nearest magistrate.

"I've told you my name and where I live. I've told you the disaster that befell me today. I seek my aunt in Portsmouth." Her uninjured hand fiddled at the sling and betrayed her nervousness. With a shuddering breath, she pressed her palm flat on her lap. "We're chance-met travelers. What else can you need to know?" She knew she sounded churlish, but she hated telling lies.

In the uncertain light, his face was a gorgeous mask. She had no idea if he believed her or not. He paused as if winnowing her answers, then spoke in a somber voice. "I need to know why you're so frightened."

"The footpads . . ."

He made a slashing gesture with his gloved hand, silencing her. "If you truly had been set upon by thieves, you wouldn't have hidden in the stable. Won't you trust me, Sarah?" His soft request vibrated deep in her bones, and for one yearning moment, she almost told him the truth. Before she remembered what was at stake.

"I . . . I have trusted you," she said huskily. She swallowed nervously. His use of her Christian name, even a false one, established a new intimacy. It made her lies more heinous.

Disappointment shadowed his face as he sat back against the worn leather. "I can't help you if I don't know what trouble you flee."

"You are helping me." Charis blinked back the mist that appeared in front of her eyes. He deserved better return for his generosity than deceit.

She tried to tell herself he was a man, and, for that reason alone, she couldn't trust him. The insistence rang hollow. Her father had been a good man. Everything told her Sir Gideon Trevithick was a good man too.

She forced a stronger tone. "It's my turn for a question."

He folded his arms across his powerful chest and surveyed her from under lowered black brows. "Ask away."

It frightened her how much she yearned to know about him. Curiosity raged like a fever. But to her utter mortification, the first question that emerged was, "Are you married?"

His laugh held a harsh edge. "Good God, no."

Shock at his emphatic answer overwhelmed her embarrassment. "You make it sound an impossibility."

"Believe me, it is." He looked out the window at the dark landscape.

Helpless to resist, she stared at his profile, perfect as a cameo or a face on a coin. Thick dark hair sprang back from a high forehead. The straight, commanding nose. The proud chin and angular jaw. His physical splendor struck her like a blow.

He turned and caught her studying him. Her color mounted higher. Thank goodness the dim light and her bruises hid her blush.

For a long moment, she stared into turbulent dark eyes. He

was in turmoil, and she wasn't vain enough to imagine she was the cause. No, her little drama briefly intersected with his life and would just as quickly veer away. She stifled the pang of senseless regret that knowledge aroused.

The thick dark eyelashes that veiled his eyes were the only remotely feminine feature on his face. Yes, he was beautiful, but he was also uncompromisingly male.

"My turn. Where are your parents?"

"Dead," she said starkly before she thought to lie.

"I'm sorry."

She looked down at where her good hand clenched in her lap. "My father died when I was sixteen. My mother died three years ago."

"How old are you now?" She was grateful he didn't pursue the subject. After all this time, it still hurt to talk about her parents.

"Twenty. Almost twenty-one." Just saying the words reminded her that on the first day of March, she reached her majority. And safety. If she stayed free for the next three weeks, her stepbrothers couldn't touch her. Or her fortune. "That's two questions."

The conversation was odd, prickly. Like a dangerous game. "You can have two now."

"Tulliver calls you Sir Gideon. Were you knighted by the King?"

"Yes."

She waited for him to elaborate, perhaps boast of whatever feats brought about his elevation. But he remained silent.

"So it's not an old title?"

"That too. I'm a baronet for my sins. Although I wasn't expected to inherit."

"Penrhyn is the family seat?"

"Yes."

"Why aren't you there now?"

"I was in London." He paused. "My turn well and truly. Carlisle to Portsmouth is a long journey. Especially for a woman on her own. What prompted it?"

"My circumstances changed." That at least was the truth.

"So your aunt expects you?"

"Aunt . . . Aunt Mary desires a companion. She's . . . she's a rich spinster." Close enough to the truth about her real great-aunt in Bath except her name was Georgiana. How Charis wished she could apply to that wonderful woman for help now. But her great-aunt, for all her fortune, was powerless against the law and the Farrells' bullying.

"Miss Mary Watson of Portsmouth." Did she hear skepticism in his deep voice, rich as vintage wine?

"Yes, that's right."

"So you can direct us to her house."

Oh, Lord, no. She should have thought of that complication. She'd chosen Portsmouth as her destination because she imagined there she'd be part of a transient population, as unremarkable as a grain of sand in a gale. But she'd never visited the town, knew nothing about it.

"Of course." She spoke hurriedly, before he quizzed her further on her mythical aunt. "Why were you in London?"

Did she mistake the haunted look that darkened his eyes? "Cornwall is isolated, especially in winter."

Except he was tanned. His answers puzzled her. He mightn't be lying like she was, but he wasn't completely honest. "Does Akash work for you?"

He gave a surprised laugh. It was the first time she'd heard him laugh properly. His face lit with amusement, and her heart crashed to a trembling stop in her chest. He was the most breathtakingly attractive man she'd ever seen.

"Of course not. He's my friend."

"But . . ." She stopped for fear of causing offense.

"You shouldn't make simple judgments, Miss Watson." He reached into the pocket of his jacket and withdrew a flat silver flask. She waited for him to drink, but he held it out to her. "It's brandy."

"I don't take strong spirits."

"It will help you sleep and dull your aches."

"Akash's treatment did that."

"Once you've been on the road a few hours, his magic will wear thin." Sir Gideon's voice lowered to velvet persuasion. "Drink it, Sarah. I promise it won't hurt."

She found herself reaching out, taking the flask and drinking. All under the power of fathomless dark eyes. As the liquor hit her throat, she coughed. Her bruised ribs protested the abrupt pressure even as comforting warmth spread through her veins.

She passed back the flask. Her brief vitality faded. Exhaustion weighted her aching limbs. Her swollen jaw protested as she fought back a yawn.

She wouldn't sleep. She didn't trust her companions enough to fall into unconsciousness. And she needed to be alert to seize her chance to escape.

She wouldn't sleep. She wouldn't . . .

The carriage rolled into Portsmouth the next morning. Gideon had dozed in snatches. That was all he managed these days, whether in a speeding coach or the most luxurious feather bed. Sometimes he thought he'd sell his soul for an uninterrupted night's sleep. Other days he recognized he didn't have a soul to sell.

At least his fear of closed-in spaces wasn't as overwhelming as it had been when he first left India. His confinement in this coach had been uncomfortable, but he'd managed, thank God.

From the bench opposite, Akash studied him in silence. It had started to snow before dawn, and his friend had sought refuge in the vehicle. They'd suggested to Tulliver that they stop at a wayside inn. But Tulliver had proven as immune to English cold as he had to blistering heat on the boat back from India.

Gideon's eyes alighted on the slumbering bundle at Akash's

side. Sarah lay curled in the corner, pressed against the upholstery as if even asleep she remained wary.

Gideon's belly knotted with coruscating anger at whoever had hurt her. The craven deserved to rot in hell.

He slid back the blind and caught his first glimpse of Miss Sarah Watson in daylight. The bruising on her face was worse this morning, for all Akash's arcane skills. Her hair was a rat's nest. One scratched hand clutched his thick greatcoat around her, hiding the slender curves he recalled with such unwelcome clarity from last night. The other dangled loosely against her breast, suspended from Akash's makeshift sling.

"Shall I wake her?" Akash murmured.

Gideon nodded. Gently, Akash touched her hand where it clenched in the coat's thick black wool. Not for the first time, Gideon envied his friend the ease of contact.

He remained still, watching the girl stir. Her eyes—a cloudy hazel in the bright light reflected off the snow outside—opened and slowly focused on him. With accusation.

"You drugged me." Her voice was slurred. With sleep or her swollen face. Or the opium.

"You needed rest. It was only a drop of laudanum." More than that. But he'd had no idea how else to grant her the blessing of rest.

"Don't do it again," she spat out, sounding more alert by the second. Her remarkable eyes cleared to a deep green, flecked with scattered gold like broken sunlight. Her eyes were the only trace of beauty in her battered face.

He bent his head in acknowledgment. "I won't." He paused. "How do you feel?"

Her lips quirked, then she winced as the smile tested her torn lip. Nonetheless, her voice held a trace of dry humor. "Like a mule has kicked me. A big angry mule."

She confronted her fate with her head held high. No whining or cowering. Her spirit took his breath away. Made him want more than he had a right to ask.

As she'd said, they were chance-met strangers. Useless to

rage against inevitable fate. She was not for him. She could never be for him. No woman could be.

He'd faced that damnable truth months ago.

He hoped she didn't hear the betraying roughness in his voice when he forced a dry reply. "You're feeling much better, then?"

She gave a choked giggle at his attempt at a joke and raised one hand to her bruised cheek. "It hurts to laugh."

"I'm sure it does." Only the bravest woman would laugh in such circumstances.

"Where does your aunt live, Miss Watson?" Akash asked.

His friend had cast him a searching look and now concentrated on the girl. Heat crawled up the back of Gideon's neck as he realized Akash must guess his admiration for Miss Watson. And Akash would pity him, which stung Gideon's pride like acid.

The lilt faded from the girl's voice, and she sounded stiff as she always did when she lied. "Not far. If you drop me in the center of town, I can find my own way. I've imposed enough."

Gideon's lips crooked in grim amusement as she avoided his eyes. "We cannot abandon a lady to her own devices."

She looked down to where her uninjured hand fisted in her lap. Her discomfort was palpable. "My . . . my aunt is a maiden lady of reclusive habits. It would frighten her if I arrived on her doorstep in the company of three unknown gentlemen."

"And she'd be perfectly undisturbed to see you arrive hurt, ragged, and alone?"

She cast him a resentful glance under her thick gold-tipped lashes. "When I explain, she'll understand."

The carriage pulled, as arranged during the night, into Portsmouth's best inn. The girl's hands tightened until the knuckles shone white. "Where are we?"

"We're changing horses and stopping for breakfast. After that, Akash and I will escort you to your aunt's."

"No."

"No to breakfast or no to our company?"

She had the grace to look a little shamefaced at her bald reply. "I must admit breakfast appeals."

He guessed she meant to take advantage of one last meal before escaping. It was what he'd do if destitute and in danger. "Breakfast it is," he said neutrally.

The carriage stopped. Akash turned to her. "I'll carry you in."

The girl's eyes darted to meet Gideon's. He had the oddest feeling she wanted him to volunteer. He was such a poor specimen that even this simple service was beyond him. Clenching his hands, he told himself he'd long ago come to terms with bleak reality. Today, consigning this wonderful girl to someone else's arms, that sounded more than ever like a hollow lie.

"Thank you, but I can walk."

"Your injuries will attract less attention if I carry you." Akash said, closely watching the interplay between them.

"It will be better this way, Miss Watson," Gideon said.

Fleeting disappointment shadowed her features. Strange how even with her injuries, her face was so expressive. She raised her chin as if girding herself to face a challenge.

"As you will," she said quietly.

Akash carried Charis up the stairs with an impersonal aplomb that saved her any embarrassment. She couldn't imagine lying in Sir Gideon's arms with quite this coolness. The thought of Gideon holding her close to his broad chest brought a blush to her cheeks, and she bent her head to hide the flood of color.

What was this strange attraction she felt toward Sir Gideon? His physical presence filled her mind in a way she'd never before experienced.

It was astonishing how he occupied her attention, attention that should be devoted purely to escape and her safety over the next three weeks. From the first moment she'd seen him, he'd become the lodestone for every thought, every feeling. With each moment that passed, her obsession grew. Was it just because he'd rescued her from discovery and disaster? Or was this turbulent feeling something else entirely?

Thank goodness her reckless heart had settled by the time Akash placed her on her feet in the large private room Sir Gideon had requested upon their arrival. Then her pulse set off on its wild jig again as the object of her ridiculous fantasy strode in behind them. She fought to suppress her surprising, unwelcome reaction, but nothing stemmed her tingling awareness of him as he crossed toward the fire.

Once they'd sent Tulliver to order a substantial breakfast, Akash turned to Charis with what she already recognized as his characteristic seriousness. "Can I see your injuries, Miss Watson? There was only so much I could do in the dark."

"Thank you. You're very kind." In truth, Charis felt much improved apart from a bitter taste lingering from the much-resented laudanum. The room's warmth thawed some of the stiffness from her muscles.

Sir Gideon lounged on a carved wooden settle near the blazing grate. His dark eyes rested upon her with fierce concentration as she rose from her chair. On trembling legs, she moved to the center of the room, where Akash waited.

She unwrapped the thick shawl from her head and pulled the coat from her shoulders. She dropped both to the floor. It was absurd, but she felt as though she undressed for Sir Gideon's pleasure. The wanton notion came from nowhere. It shocked her, but she couldn't dismiss it.

Sir Gideon's unwavering regard looked like desire. Which made no sense when she knew she was a veritable monster. But heat prickled her skin, and she licked suddenly dry lips.

His eyes flickered at the movement.

Her heart slammed against her ribs. Something about Gideon's unblinking stare pierced her to the bone. It was like he read her soul.

She shifted under Akash's hands.

"Did I hurt you?" he asked, frowning.

"No," she murmured.

Akash's medical skills must be why he assumed responsibility for her care. Whatever he'd put on her bruises last night had certainly helped. She was sore but nothing like yesterday.

Strange. This handsome, considerate gentleman touched her yet it meant nothing. Sir Gideon was halfway across the room, and he owned her every breath.

How had this happened? Her head whirled as she tried to make sense of her unprecedented reactions. In ballrooms and salons, she'd met so many men, attractive men, sophisticated men, attentive men. None had affected her like this taciturn, black-haired Adonis, with his glittering eyes and troubled air. The sensations stirring in her veins scared the life out of her.

As she answered Akash's questions about her injuries, her gaze dropped to where Sir Gideon's gloved hands encircled an untouched tankard of ale. Wicked excitement shivered through her as she imagined those hands touching her. So far, he hadn't so much as taken her arm.

Avidly, she drank in his features. His face was grave and pure like the stone effigy of a crusading knight. His cheekbones and jaw were cut at perfect angles. His mouth was stern, firm, beautiful, but with a hint of softness in the curve of the lower lip. He looked like a carved saint until one met his burning eyes.

No sanctity there.

They were so dark, almost black. Intense. Glittering. Full of suppressed passion and pain.

And anger.

Because someone had dared to hurt her.

Warmth seeped into a heart that had been cold for so long. She couldn't entrust herself to these men. Too much hung upon her keeping her identity secret. She still had to escape.

But knowing that such a remarkable being as Sir Gideon

Trevithick placed himself so firmly on her side bolstered courage that came shamefully close to faltering.

Gideon's eyes met hers and flashed a warning. He surged to his feet and strode over to gaze out the window.

Helplessly, Charis studied his straight back in its perfectly fitted black jacket. He hadn't had to say the words aloud. That last glare from his brilliant eyes had all but shouted *keep out*.

Akash manipulated her wrist. Its tenderness was a mere echo of last night's agony. Even her ribs didn't feel as though an elephant had trampled them anymore. She had a sudden memory of the dark stall where Gideon had found her. Without his help to escape and Akash's treatment for her injuries, she'd be in a bad way indeed.

The instincts that insisted Sir Gideon was her dauntless champion urged her to tell him everything and throw herself upon his mercy.

No, he was a stranger. She couldn't risk the consequences of ill-advised confidences. If Sir Gideon handed her over to the law as duty demanded, her stepbrothers would have her back in their custody as soon as they rode to Portsmouth.

Or worse, perhaps Gideon and Akash would be as blinded by her gold as every other suitor. Her heart screamed that these were good men. Experience urged caution. Even good men abandoned principle when they learned of her massive fortune.

Safer by far to rely on her own resources, meager as they were. Still, she couldn't suppress a pang of guilt at how she deceived and used people who tried to aid her. Her experiences with her stepbrothers should make it impossible to place herself willingly into any man's care. But still her heart insisted she made a huge mistake when she rejected Sir Gideon's help.

"Thank you for everything you've both done," she said softly, knowing it was sinfully inadequate when measured against her lies.

"You're welcome." Akash bound her arm, then left the sling off.

She bent to pick up her shawl and stumbled to her chair. Standing so long had tested her strength. Across the room, Gideon didn't say a word, just watched the snow drift past the window. She told herself she had no right to feel slighted by his indifference.

The arrival of breakfast interrupted her dour thoughts. Charis kept her head down and shrouded in the shawl. She couldn't help her ill-matched costume, but if the servants saw her hair and bruised face, they'd identify her immediately if her stepbrothers asked about her.

Feverishly, she tried to plan her escape even while Sir Gideon's nearness was a persistent tug on her senses. The bad weather was both savior and pest. If she could get away, it would hide her. But she wasn't dressed for such cold. She resigned herself to stealing the greatcoat. It was a loan rather than a theft, she assured her howling conscience. In a few weeks, she'd return it and repay Sir Gideon for his kindness.

Surely tracing Sir Gideon Trevithick of Penrhyn in Cornwall wouldn't be difficult. If they made contact again . . .

She put a brake on foolish dreams.

First she had to survive the next three weeks and stay out of her stepbrothers' clutches. She had to find shelter and food and some way of supporting herself, all without revealing her identity. Or the identity of the powerful men who sought her. Hubert was Lord Burkett and Felix was a rising figure in Parliament.

Gideon, Akash, and she settled down to another silent meal. Tulliver must have retreated to the taproom. Charis was grateful for the lack of conversation. She'd choke on any more lies. And she had a foolish desire to cry at the thought of leaving Sir Gideon. How had he gained this astounding power over her emotions in such a short time? It was like a strange madness possessed her.

After the servants cleared the plates, she managed to inject an appropriate note of feminine embarrassment into her voice. "Would it be all right if I had a few moments of privacy?"

A look passed between Gideon and Akash but both stood readily enough. "We'll send someone to assist you," Gideon said.

"No need," Charis said hurriedly, her chance at escape evaporating before her eyes.

"I insist." Gideon, curse him, waited while Akash left to summon the servants.

A parade of maids brought hot water and towels and a range of grooming articles. She couldn't help sighing with pleasure when the last item laid out before her was a cheap brown cotton gown. She was desperate to change her ragged, dirty dress.

Goodness knows where Sir Gideon found the frock at such short notice. Yet another sign of his thoughtfulness. Again, she suppressed that rebel urge to confess everything and beg him to help her. Men changed when they saw the chance of filling their pockets with gold.

Gideon stood by the door and dismissed the staff. "Tulliver's outside if you need anything."

"Thank you." How she wished she could say more, say good-bye, express her gratitude, tell him she wished she could know him better.

But it was impossible.

For a long moment, she stared at him, drinking in his physical magnificence, the strength and intelligence in his compelling features. Already she knew she'd never forget him. She turned away and pretended interest in the items on the tray. If she kept looking at Gideon, she'd start to cry.

The door closed softly. At last Charis was alone. She let out the breath she'd been holding. Yet she didn't immediately put her plan into action. Instead she slowly approached the cheval mirror in the corner.

Ridiculous, really, given her legion of troubles, that the mere act of checking her reflection needed every ounce of courage.

She braced to confront the woman in the mirror. When she did, she couldn't stem a broken peal of laughter.

Had she read desire in Sir Gideon's eyes? What a vain, deluded fool she was. No man could look at her now with anything but pity. Or revulsion.

She'd expected to be shocked. What she saw was worse than her wildest imaginings. Her face was a mottled mixture of purple and yellow. Her jaw was grotesquely distorted. Above the bruising, familiar hazel eyes stared back with a dazed expression.

She bit down hard on her quivering lip, but the jab of pain couldn't dam her tears. She was a monstrosity, a hobgoblin, a gorgon. So stupid to mourn what would mend, but she had to lift her good hand to dash the moisture from her streaming eyes. Akash had assured her the damage was superficial, but the words seemed meaningless when she looked at the woman in the mirror.

The once-elegant blue dress was streaked with dirt and torn beyond repair. Her shaking hand shifted to touch the matted hair that tumbled around her shoulders.

She drew in a breath that was close to a sob and met her watery gaze in the glass. This wouldn't do. She straightened her spine. She was Lady Charis Weston, the last of a long line of warriors. No daughter of Hugh Davenport Weston would admit defeat to a pair of poltroons like Hubert and Felix.

The horrors she saw in the mirror would pass. Right now, she needed to concentrate on escape.

Hurriedly, she washed and changed out of the ruined gown. The cheap dress was scratchy on her sensitive skin and too big, but at least it was clean and whole. Fastening the frock took too long, and she panted with pain before she finished.

She spent valuable minutes struggling with the knots in her hair. Eventually, she managed to bundle it away from her face. The girl in the mirror started to look moderately respectable. As long as nobody noticed her bruised face.

With shaking hands, she drew the greatcoat on. Her sore arm twinged as she gingerly slid it into the sleeve, but, thanks to Akash, the pain was bearable. The huge coat looked absurd on her small body, but she couldn't manage without its warmth.

She patted the pocket to check for the pistol. Once she'd found somewhere safe to stay, she'd pawn it. She told herself taking it wasn't theft. When she could, she'd redeem the weapon and return it. She'd already steeled herself to pawning her mother's ring and locket although her heart ached at the prospect.

How long had she been in here? Were Gideon or Akash likely to return and demand to know what she was up to? She mustn't linger. Dressing had taken too long already.

Her mouth was dry with nerves as she darted to the window. Beneath the sill, she knew a flat roof extended over the rear yard. Climbing about in the snow with a sprained wrist was risky. But less so than waiting for her stepbrothers to find her, or for her rescuers to discover her identity and hand her over to the local magistrate.

Carefully, she raised the sash window and eased herself out. Her bruised ribs protested, but she gritted her teeth and continued. Any pain now would be as nothing if her stepbrothers caught her.

Three weeks to freedom, she promised herself grimly.

Stifling the alluring memory of black eyes burning into hers, she found her footing on the slippery roof.

Three

"Guvnor, we got trouble."

Gideon looked up from the dregs of his ale to meet Tulliver's worried eyes. A shock to see him anything but imperturbable.

"What is it, Tulliver?" He set his tankard on the table. He sat in the darkest corner of the inn. And the coldest. The benches around him were empty. On this frigid day, the occupants of the long room crowded around the fire blazing at the other end. But even so, all these people sharing his space, his air, left him jumpy, on edge.

Of course, he knew what Tulliver would say before the man spoke.

"The lass. She's gone."

Tulliver had been on watch outside the room. Gideon didn't need to ask whether she'd got out that way. "How in Hades did she go across the roof? She's got a sprained wrist."

"Aye. But it didn't stop her." Tulliver's voice held a trace of grudging admiration.

"Damn." Gideon surged to his feet and strode toward the taproom's rear door.

Stupid, stupid girl. Didn't she realize the risks? But he reserved his sharpest castigation for himself. Careless bastard he was. How could he let her escape? It wasn't as if he hadn't guessed her plans. Although given her injuries, he'd never imagined she'd clamber out an upstairs window and make it across an icy roof.

"How long ago?" he grated out.

Tulliver kept up with his rapid pace. "Seconds, I reckon. The room wasn't cold enough for the window to be open long."

"She could be anywhere." He ducked under the low lintel and entered a long, flagstoned corridor. "Damn," he said again with more emphasis.

"Damn what?" Akash emerged from a side hallway.

"Miss Watson's gone," Gideon said sharply.

Akash grabbed his arm. Immediately Gideon stiffened, and Akash snatched his hand away with a gesture of apology. But his eyes didn't waver in the gloom. The stare was calm, perceptive, compassionate.

"She can't give you back what you've lost. No one can."

Gideon flinched as if he'd been struck. Had anyone else but Akash said it, they'd be nursing a broken jaw.

"You think I don't know that?" he asked through tight lips.

"Then let her follow her own destiny."

He owed this man so much. His health. His sanity. His very life. But now he had no time to explain what he barely understood himself. "If I help her, it might wash some of the black from my soul."

"She's a stranger."

"She's in trouble. We have to find her."

For a moment they couldn't afford to waste, Akash studied him. Finally, he gave an abrupt nod. "She has an aunt in town?"

"A lie. She's on the run from someone or something. My guess is she means to take her chances on the streets."

"She's a lady. She won't survive."

"She will if we find her." The idea of the girl's pride and courage coming to disaster made Gideon's gut cramp. Without another word, he set off down the hallway toward the back door.

They emerged into a bleak snow-covered yard behind the kitchens. The freezing wind smelled of thousands of coal fires and salt from the sea. Directly above was the room the girl had escaped. The day was gray and grim, but there was plenty of light to show a line of small footprints leading to the back gate.

Thank God it had stopped snowing, although it was perishing cold. Gideon hoped Sarah had had the sense to take his greatcoat. He shoved his gloved hands into his jacket pockets and set out along the trail. Akash and Tulliver were a reassuring presence behind him.

The high wooden gate led into a dingy alley sheltered from the weather by brick walls. No more footprints. It didn't matter. One end of the alley ended in a blank wall. She could only have taken the other direction, toward the busy street that passed the front of the inn.

Cursing, Gideon set out at a run and burst onto the packed thoroughfare. Even on a bitter day, Portsmouth thronged with people. Sailors of many nations. Respectable burghers. Militia in their bright scarlet uniforms. Roughly dressed farmworkers from the surrounding countryside.

But no slight bright-haired girl weaved her way through the pulsing, noisy crowd. Gideon scanned the street while dread beat a remorseless tattoo in his heart. She was small and too easy to miss.

She was small and too easy to hurt.

"Do you see her?" Akash asked beside him.

"No. But she can't have gone far. Tulliver only just missed her. Those footprints are fresh. And she doesn't know the

town. We'll split up and meet back here in half an hour."
Without waiting for a reply, Gideon launched himself down
the street.

Leaden fear settled in his belly as he realized he headed
toward the docks. For all his burning need to find Sarah, he
hoped to hell she'd chosen a different route. Portsmouth was
a navy town and full of press-ganged sailors, brutish men not
far removed from criminals. Every step closer to the water-
front was a step closer to peril.

The press of people chafed, but compared to those overwhelming weeks in London, it was bearable. He forced
himself to breathe deeply, evenly, concentrating on each in-
halation and exhalation. He could control his discomfort in a
crowd. He couldn't quell the tension that tightened his shoulders as his fear for Sarah rose. At least he'd given her the
pistol although heaven knew if she had the spirit to use it.

He recalled her reckless courage. She'd use it, all right. He
just prayed he found her before she needed to.

Devil take her, why hadn't the chit trusted him?

He tried desperately not to think what might happen to
her. She'd already suffered so much. He'd promised her help,
and he'd failed miserably.

He'd failed so often. Damn it, he wasn't going to fail this
time, not when the girl's life was at stake.

Swiftly but purposefully, he moved down the street,
checking doorways and side passages. He doubted she'd go
into one of the shops lining the road, crowded as they were
with people avoiding the weather. She'd be too conspicuous,
with her bruised face and bandaged wrist.

Dear Lord, keep her safe until I get to her.

He repeated the silent plea with every thud of his heart
until the words lost meaning, and all he knew was his over-
powering need to find her. Still he searched. Every nook,
every recess, every corner. By God, he wouldn't let her
escape him.

He nearly missed her.

A group of rowdy men crowded into a narrow alley. Sailors by the look of them, with their dirty calico smocks. Drunk, seeking trouble.

Something about their concentrated menace alerted instincts honed in a thousand dusty Indian byways. Then one of the roughly dressed men shifted, and Gideon glimpsed a familiar black greatcoat.

Sarah.

Seeing her trapped, he yielded to a deep, gut-churning anger. The will to kill coiled in his belly like a cobra. With a low growl, he reached into his pocket for his pistol, twin to the one he'd given her.

As his fingers curled securely around the handle, he strode up behind the bastards. None of them noticed his approach although he made no attempt at subterfuge. They were too focused on their terrified bounty.

Shaking and trying to stifle panic, Charis backed into the damp stonework. Her good hand fumbled for her gun in the coat's generous pockets. The four burly men stank of liquor, rotten fish, and pungent male sweat. She sucked in a shuddering breath, then gagged on the foul stench.

Why hadn't she listened to that persistent voice insisting she trust Sir Gideon? Now it was too late. She was a woman alone, fair game for any stranger.

The largest man ripped the shawl off her head and flung it into the sludge on the ground. As she choked back a futile protest, her insecurely fastened hair collapsed around her face.

"Eh, lookee, Jack! She got lady's hair," one of the men cried in delight.

"All the better to hold her with, shipmates." The big man twined one meaty paw in a tangled hank while he ripped at his coarse trousers with his other hand. The tang of male excitement was ripe on the cold air and made Charis's muscles knot with revulsion.

When she strained to break free, agony shot through her scalp. Bile rose as she read unmistakable intent in her captor's sunken, bloodshot eyes.

"She's been fair knocked around," another of the sailors said doubtfully.

"I ain't bothered with her sodding face," the man snarled. "I reckon the bits I want are in fine working order." He laughed salaciously. He was close enough for the alcohol on his breath to make her recoil.

"Leave me alone." Her voice sounded raw.

"You don't mean that, hinny." His croon was more frightening than anger. Her stomach roiled with icy terror.

"Have at her, Jack," one of the men urged in a guttural voice.

Frantically, she fought for a grip on the little gun but it kept sliding out of reach. She stretched after it, but the slightest movement ripped unbearably at her trapped hair.

"I'll scream if you touch me." Her voice cracked.

The man's leering grin reeked confidence. His brutal hold tightened until hot tears rose to sting her eyes. "You'd have hollered afore now if you reckoned it'd do you a mite of good."

On the street, she'd hesitated one fatal instant before calling for help. Time enough for them to crowd her into this alley, stinking of urine and rotting refuse.

Charis opened her mouth to scream but only a whimper emerged when the man wrenched at her hair. "Shut your gob, bitch."

"Let me go," she croaked, still scrabbling for the gun, but her trembling, damp hand couldn't find purchase on the pearl handle. Her heart pounded so furiously against her ribs, she thought it must burst.

"I'll let you go, all right." The beefy sailor smacked his thick lips together as if contemplating a hearty meal. "Once

I've got my fill. And if you cut the ruddy backchat. Otherwise, I'll wring your neck, my bonny."

Desolation froze the blood in Charis's veins. Death was a cold, tangible presence. There was no hope. All her struggles, all her suffering, all her defiance led to this. Lady Charis Weston violated and murdered in a port city's backstreet.

"Get away from her."

Like a honed saber, the command sliced through Charis's blind horror. *Sir Gideon is here. I'm safe. I'm safe.*

Her galloping pulse slowed to a joyous hymn of gratitude. She dragged in her first unfettered breath since she'd escaped the inn, then gasped as her bruised ribs protested. Abruptly, she became aware of aches lingering from yesterday's beating. Her sprained arm throbbed painfully.

The ringleader relinquished his grip on her hair. The burning pressure on her scalp eased. She slumped against the wall as a dizzying wave of relief washed over her.

He stepped to one side to face the man at the mouth of the alley. Charis at last got a clear view of Gideon. She shivered as she stared into that perfect, ruthless face. Fury blazed in his eyes. He looked strong, brave, in control. *Lethal.*

"Move along, chum." The sailor folded his arms across his bulging chest. He was much broader than Gideon and stocky with muscle. The blackguard's cohorts set up a solid barrier around him.

"Leave her be." As Gideon approached, he sounded completely undaunted by the array of masculine strength. His voice was colder than the wind whistling through the alley.

The ringleader gave a contemptuous grunt of laughter. "Who's going to make me, pretty boy? You?"

Gideon raised a completely steady hand. Clear wintry light gleamed on the polished barrel of his pistol.

"Aye, very nice." The ringleader cast a derisive glance at the gun even as his cronies sidled out of the way. "You forget there's four of us."

"If I kill you, I imagine your friends will lose their thirst for blood." He sounded careless, unafraid. Charis's heart leaped at his reckless bravery. "Make no mistake, if you don't let the lady go, I will shoot."

Her paralysis faded as she sucked reviving air into her lungs. At last her fingers closed firmly on her gun.

"Not if I get a chance first," she said hoarsely. She brought her weapon up. The gun was perfectly balanced and sat in her hand like an extension of her arm. "Step aside."

"Shit, where did that come from?" one of the sailors muttered, backing farther off.

"Is the girl worth the risk?" Gideon asked almost casually, keeping his gun raised.

For one horrible instant, Charis glanced between the ring-leader and Gideon. The sailor's expression warred between bravado and self-preservation, and his Adam's apple moved up and down in his thick throat. Gideon's shoulders tensed, and his jaw firmed with purpose. His aim didn't waver. She couldn't doubt he'd shoot if he had to.

The brute must have reached the same conclusion. His pig-like eyes flickered, and the tension drained from his heavy body. "Oh, bugger it, take the slut and welcome you are to her. Her slice isn't worth a friggin' bullet."

"Sarah, come here." Through the buzzing in her ears, she heard the ice in Gideon's voice. "You're safe now."

Her gun suddenly seemed heavier than stone. Her hand wobbled as she lowered it. On legs that felt no firmer than jelly, she stumbled up the alley to stand beside Gideon. She desperately wanted to reach out and touch him, but his powerful self-containment kept her hands by her sides.

"We're going to walk out of this alley and go our way un-molested." Gideon didn't glance at her. His pistol remained pointed squarely at the leader's chest.

The effortless tone of authority took effect. Not one of the ruffians shifted to stop them as she and Gideon backed off. The few yards to safety felt like a thousand miles. Charis's heart lodged in her throat, and her skin tightened with every step. Could they really emerge unscathed?

They'd almost made it, had turned to face the street when

Charis heard an angry shout behind them. "Hell's bells, mates! There's four of us and only bleedin' one of him. Let's give the bastard what for!"

A crash of booted feet behind them.

"Run!" Gideon shouted. "I've got the gun. I'll be all right!"

Charis lifted handfuls of greatcoat and sprang into a wild dash. She ignored the way her body screamed agony at the sudden dash.

But they'd left their escape too late. The thugs surrounded them at the mouth of the alley. Charis came to a juddering stop, her heart jamming in her throat.

"Stay behind me," Gideon snapped, stepping between her and the closing circle of brawny sailors. The rough, flushed faces promised retribution, violence and pain.

Shaking, she pressed against the wall. Her blood pounded so loudly, she hardly heard the bustle from the crowded street so close.

"You're making a mistake." Gideon sounded as if the men posed no threat at all. He still held the pistol, but she guessed he was reluctant to shoot in case he hit someone in the street.

"No mistake, my hearty." The ringleader's swaggering confidence returned. "We'll take our fun with you, then it's the wench's turn."

"I think not." Although she couldn't see his face, she knew he smiled.

She opened her mouth and shrieked as loudly as she could. The shrill sound bounced between the narrow walls.

"Gideon."

She strained upward to see. Akash loomed at the entrance to the alley. Next to him, Tulliver. Thank God. They must have been close enough to hear her.

The sailors dived at the newcomers. The world exploded into a fury of hard fists and boots and grunts of pain.

The violence transported her to the horrific afternoon when Hubert had hit her. She ducked her head and cowered against the clammy bricks. Black edged her vision as the battle raged around her. Trembling, she clutched her sprained wrist to her chest and prayed for the nightmare to pass. She squeezed her eyes shut and fought a powerful urge to vomit.

Bodies hurtled close, then lurched away in the fight's chaotic dance. Gideon brushed against her. She recognized his scent before she opened her eyes and saw him swing into the fray again.

The shouting crescendoed, became more confused. The brawl spilled out into the street. At a distance, she heard someone yell for the town watch.

"Miss Watson, let me get you out of here." The calm voice emerged from the pandemonium.

With dazed eyes, she turned to look into Akash's face. He was disheveled but had suffered no obvious injuries.

Disappointment scourged her that it wasn't Sir Gideon. She blinked to dispel the foolish reaction and managed a brief nod. Akash took her uninjured arm and, shielding her with his body, drew her onto the street.

The scene was a wild melee. Difficult even to spot the original combatants in the milling crowd.

"Sir Gideon?" she gasped, digging her fingers into Akash's sleeve.

He glanced down quickly with a smile so carefree, it astonished her. "He's fine. Never better."

She scanned the heaving mob and spotted Gideon. With his height, he was hard to miss. He swung punches with an abandon that left his opponents staggering. His face was brilliant with elation, a dazzling exhilaration she'd never seen in him before.

She staggered to an astonished halt.

He'd shown her nothing but gentleness. Yet the man she watched now took a savage delight in violence. She desperately wanted to despise him—she'd always loathed brute force, even before Hubert's assault. But looking at Gideon, she couldn't help but respond to the display of unfettered male power. He moved with a smooth beauty that was almost mechanical, like a perfectly calibrated engine doing what it was designed for.

Her breath caught in her throat at how glorious he was. Every drop of moisture dried from her mouth, and her blood ran hot in her veins.

This new Gideon frightened her. But she couldn't deny he thrilled her too.

The brief awareness shattered as Akash lunged forward to deflect someone who grabbed at her. For a horrified second, she stared into the reddened eyes of one of the sailors. The man faltered under Akash's blow and fell cursing.

"Miss Watson, don't just stand there," Akash snapped, and wrenched her through the heaving crowd.

She stumbled and just avoided another blow aimed at her head. She couldn't see Tulliver in the throng. Pray God he was all right. To her left, Sir Gideon dispatched with casual competence anyone who dared approach.

A man snatched at her injured wrist. She choked back a scream. Pain shot a red-hot blast up her arm. She screamed again as Akash struck her assailant down without a moment's compunction, his aquiline face severe and expressionless.

Akash turned back to her and spoke almost roughly. "Are you all right?"

"Yes," she said, although her wrist burned with fiery agony. She pressed it to her breast and let Akash tug her toward the edge of the crowd. He dragged her into a deeply recessed doorway, where the cacophony marginally diminished.

"Are you sure you're unharmed?" He was breathing heavily as he gave her a hard look.

"Yes." She stared out at the street with utter dismay. "This is all my fault."

Akash's silence signaled agreement. The doorway was wide enough to accommodate both of them without touching. He released her and leaned against the stone doorframe, studying her with unfathomable brown eyes.

She frowned in confusion. "Don't you want to help Sir Gideon?"

Akash shook his dark head. "He'd prefer I kept an eye on you."

Her bruised ribs twinged as she made a convulsive movement toward the street. "He could be killed."

A smile curved Akash's mouth. "The man who can kill Gideon Trevithick hasn't been born. Don't worry, Miss Watson. He'll live to chastise you for your rashness in running away."

Something in his easy confidence settled her choking panic. "I had to go," she said sullenly, guilt twisting her belly.

"Utter rot," Akash said amiably. He darted a look outside. "Ah. At last. The watch has arrived. Peace will soon descend upon the streets of Portsmouth."

It took surprisingly little effort to quell the brawl. Most participants just melted away into the alleys. Gradually, Charis's heartbeat slowed. Heady relief bubbled in her veins.

Until she observed Gideon speaking to a well-dressed man, who clearly counted as the authority in town.

She shrank behind Akash. Renewed fear ate at her. Dear God, had she come so far only to fail now? If the authorities took her in charge, she'd be on a direct path back to her stepbrothers.

Akash glanced at her briefly. Gideon didn't look at them at all. He was once again the contained, courteous man she'd first met. The fight's wild berserker might never have existed. In a fever of nerves, she watched as Gideon pressed a wad of banknotes into the man's hand, then turned away.

A few curious onlookers hung around, but everyone else had gone on their way. Charis still couldn't see Tulliver. She'd faced rape and death, yet no trace remained of her ordeal apart from the blood and mud on the street.

"Wait a moment," Akash said when she made to leave the doorway.

Three well-dressed men strolled toward Gideon. One stopped, stared, and let out an exclamation of delighted surprise. "By gum! It's the Hero of Rangy whatsit."

Gideon paused at the first loud hail. Charis had a clear view of his face. So often, the sheer beauty of his features made it difficult to read his expression. Now she couldn't mistake how the blood drained from his cheeks and his brows contracted. He looked annoyed and on edge.

Hunted.

"Oh, hell," Akash breathed at her side, tensing.

The man who greeted Gideon turned in open excitement to his two companions. "You know who he is. The cove the King just knighted. Lasted a year in some filthy hole in India. Bravest fellow in the empire, Wellington called him."

His mouth stern with displeasure, Gideon retreated along the street toward Charis and Akash. He was close enough for her to hear him say in a forbidding voice, "I'm afraid you've made an error, sir."

The man advanced, his hand extended. "Dash it, man! There's no error. Your sketch is in every newspaper from here to John O'Groats, I'll warrant. Anyway, I cheered you in Pall Mall when you and the cavalry rode by on your parade of honor."

"You don't . . ."

"Let me shake the hand of the Hero of. . . What was that heathen place they had you locked up? Some benighted name no Christian can get his tongue around."

"Rangapindhi," one of his companions said with audible enthusiasm. "By George, it's a privilege to meet you, sir. By George, it is!"

The fuss attracted notice and quickly another crowd built up. But this time, it clamored with approval.

Wearing a coldly aloof expression, Gideon stood stock-still in the midst of the noisy mob. He looked like he had nothing but contempt for the congratulatory throng. His jaw was set, his lips thinned, his eyes veiled. He could never be less than handsome, but his frigid demeanor and stilted gestures repelled human warmth.

"Where in God's name is Tulliver?" Akash muttered beside Charis.

"I haven't seen him." Charis craned her neck to observe Gideon. Curiosity and confusion warred in her mind. She thought she'd begun to understand the man who rescued her in Winchester. It turned out he was as unknown as the wastes of Greenland.

His admirers didn't seem to mind Gideon's lack of welcome. They shook his hand and clapped him on the shoulders. All to a man looked at him as if he'd just stepped off Mount Olympus.

Wheels clattered on cobblestones. A moving carriage forced people out of the way.

A familiar carriage with a familiar driver.

"About bloody time," Akash said savagely, and wrapped an arm around Charis. "Come on. Run. And keep your head down."

He didn't need to tell her. She had no wish for anyone to see her face. She scuttled at his side, floundering to keep up with a man who made no allowance for her shorter legs or her injuries. The mad dash stirred all her fading aches into sharp agony, so her head rang when she finally reached the carriage.

Akash flung open the door and tossed her inside. She landed against the seat with a jolt that sent pain slicing through her. She stifled a cry and fisted her hands as she fought the giddiness. A breath hissed through her teeth. Another.

The worst of her dizziness ebbed. Ignoring her discomfort, she slid across the seat to press her face to the carriage window.

Both men were so tall, it was easy to locate them. Through the joyful hordes, Akash pushed his way toward his friend. Gideon retained that frozen, remote expression, but he didn't break away from his devotees.

She couldn't hear what Akash said to Gideon over the hubbub. She saw Gideon turn and head with jerkily precise movements toward the carriage. With visible reluctance, the crowd parted before him. Voracious hands stretched out to pluck at his clothing, delay his departure, compel his attention. Doggedly he continued his automaton-like progress.

He climbed in and sat opposite. He didn't speak. He didn't look at her. He didn't appear to know she was there at all.

Akash slammed the door on them.

"Aren't you coming with us?" she asked frantically. Suddenly, Gideon seemed a frightening stranger.

He shook his head. "I'm staying to see to the horses. I'll follow in my own time."

There was a burst of patriotic cheering outside. Someone started to sing "God Save the King." Clearly the locals were still stirred up at having a celebrity in their midst.

The celebrity straightened and shot Akash an angry glare. "For Christ's sake, let us go."

"God keep you, my friend. I'll see you soon." He stepped back and sent Charis an elegant bow. "Miss Watson. Your servant."

Before Charis could respond, Tulliver whipped the horses to a pace dangerous in town streets. The lurch of the carriage nearly threw Charis from her seat. She clutched at the strap and stared bewildered at her companion.

He looked ill. As though he suffered intolerable pain. With a shock, she realized the set expression was endurance, not disdain.

Automatically, she stretched out to take his gloved hand. "Sir Gideon . . ."

"Curse you, don't touch me!"

He wrenched out of reach. But not before she felt his desperate, uncontrollable shaking.

Four

Through the suffocating miasma, Gideon knew he'd frightened the girl. But conscience was a dim whisper against the screaming demons in his skull. He clutched his head with shaking hands to silence the howling devils. It didn't help.

Nothing ever helped.

His sight failed, turning the girl's face into a pale blur. His throat was so tight, he choked. He sucked a shuddering breath into lungs starved of air.

She said something. He missed everything apart from the end. ". . . get Tulliver."

He forced himself to concentrate, pressed words to stiff lips until sound emerged. He didn't want Tulliver. Tulliver would drug him, trapping the monsters inside his head.

"No."

He sucked another breath through grinding teeth, even as thick darkness closed in.

"No Tulliver." Then what he prayed wasn't a lie. "This will pass."

Words worn threadbare with repetition.

Perhaps one day the nightmare wouldn't pass. The constant terror of that prospect made fear congeal like greasy soup in his belly.

I'm not insane. I'm not insane.

His gloved hands clawed at the worn leather seat as he battled for clarity. For control. For calm.

The demons were too strong. Horrible, shrieking phantom images rioted in his mind.

I'm in England.

I'm safe.

I'm free.

The litany failed. What freedom could he claim when grisly specters haunted his every moment?

"Please let me get Tulliver." The girl swam toward him through murky water. At the last minute, he realized she meant to rap on the roof and stop the coach.

"No!" The word emerged as a croak.

Speech was so damned difficult. He wished he was alone. But what couldn't be cured must be endured. The old aphorism, his nurse's favorite, helped him to cobble together an explanation. Even if every word cut his throat like broken glass.

"Tulliver will give . . . laudanum."

Opium hurled him into whirling oblivion. The dreams the drug brought threatened to send him mad indeed.

She frowned. "If it eases you . . ."

"No!" he all but screamed.

The girl recoiled. Good God, let him muster some control. He snatched another breath and fought to calm the frantic gallop of his heart.

She stared at him out of great, wide, terrified eyes. He loathed it when his personal . . . idiosyncrasies inconvenienced others.

Vaguely he told himself to assure her she shouldn't be afraid. He wasn't dangerous in this state. Unless she touched him. Thank Christ, after that first tentative attempt to offer comfort, she'd kept her hands to herself.

What had he meant to say? Thought was elusive and fleeting as wisps of mist.

That's right. Tulliver. He set his jaw and spoke in a low, harsh tone. Quickly, before will failed.

"There's nothing anyone can do. The best . . ." He stopped to fight back the caterwauling devils. "Please ignore me."

"That won't help." Even through swirling chaos, he heard the firmness in her voice.

Every joint tensed into quivering spasms. His stomach heaved like a stormy sea. Waves of hot and cold washed over him. He lashed his arms around his chest, but nothing eased the agonizing cramps. This attack was one of the crippling ones.

On his own, he'd bear the pain until it passed. But he couldn't distress the chit by vomiting all over her.

He'd have to accept opium's poisonous boon.

"Can you stop the coach?" he managed to force through chattering teeth.

Mercifully, she didn't question his change of mind. She banged hard on the roof. The carriage lurched to a halt. The abrupt movement set off jangling cymbals in his head, dimmed his sight.

The door wrenched open. Voices were a buzz in his ears. Tulliver passed in a tin basin.

"It's a bad one this time, lad," he said impassively, as Gideon's shaking hands curled around the dish.

Gideon's gut tangled into knots. He was seconds from losing control. He managed to snarl, "Take the girl."

His world turned to violent black as he began to retch. He was lost on a hideous sea, lit by brief crimson flashes where pain flared into agony.

He had no idea how long it was before awareness returned. Opening bleary eyes, he realized someone else's hands held the basin steady.

His mouth tasted foul. A hundred mallets battered his skull. Just the simple act of breathing threatened to split his chest in two.

Efficient hands removed the disgusting bowl. The same hands, soft and gentle, pressed a damp cloth to his burning forehead. He closed his eyes and groaned at the bliss of that coolness on his burning skin.

His belly was still rebellious. He concentrated on breathing. In. Out. In. Out.

"Akash?" he rasped across a raw throat. Although he knew the hands didn't belong to his friend.

"He's back in Portsmouth."

The girl. Miss Watson. Sarah.

With difficulty, Gideon cracked his eyes open. His blinding headache built with every second. Soon, he wouldn't be able to sit upright.

His clothes were rank and dripping with sweat. Acrid shame for his animal filth assailed him. "I told Tulliver to take you outside."

Her smile was dry as the deserts of Rajasthan. She knelt on the bench at his side. Her surprisingly competent hands supported his head. He was so sick and weak, her touch didn't make his skin crawl with familiar revulsion. He had a vague thought that helping him couldn't be easy with her sprained wrist, but the notion drifted off like a will-o'-the-wisp.

"Tulliver had his hands full." Her voice softened into compassion. "Are you feeling better?"

"He'll have the devil's own headache. He always does after one of his takings," Tulliver said calmly.

Gideon hadn't seen anything beyond the girl. Now he looked past her to where Tulliver waited, holding the bowl.

"He has these attacks often?" The girl's clear gaze rested on him with curiosity and concern.

Even in this state, his pride revolted at her pity. "I'm not an ailing puppy, Miss Watson. I can speak for myself."

Her lips turned down at his childish response. Which he

regretted as soon as it emerged. Helping him couldn't have been pleasant. She deserved gratitude, not pique.

The pounding in his head made rational, connected thought increasingly difficult. He closed his eyes and stifled renewed nausea.

"I'll get the laudanum, lad." Tulliver's voice came from a long way off, masked by the painful throb of Gideon's blood.

"The sickness has passed," he forced out.

"The laudanum makes you sleep. You know sleep is all that brings you through. Do you want to stop at an inn? A bed might be better than rattling around in this rig."

A bed. Cool sheets. Quiet. A cessation of movement. All beckoned like the promise of heaven.

He hesitated. He had to reach Penrhyn. Something urgent.

He opened his eyes and saw the girl's worried face above him in the gloomy carriage interior. Of course. If they stopped, she might run.

They had to keep going. He'd have to accept the despised laudanum. And endure the harrowing visions.

"No . . . inn." He shook his head. Even so much movement made his stomach revolt. "Get the laudanum, Tulliver."

"Aye, guvnor."

As the coach rattled on through the day and into the night, Sir Gideon slept like the dead.

At first his unconsciousness perturbed Charis. His illness had been so violent, she'd feared for his life.

He stretched awkwardly over a bench that was too short for his height. She studied his face, pale, drawn, handsome still. The muscles around his eyes were tight, and his mouth was white with strain. The certainty built that while he might lie motionless as a stone effigy, his dreams brought no peace.

She turned away and stared unseeingly out into the darkness. Who were these men she'd cast her lot with? Tulliver, who faced trouble with such stoic competence. Akash, clever, enigmatic like a strange foreign idol.

Sir Gideon . . .

She commanded her wayward heart not to flutter at the thought of her rescuer. It was like telling the sun not to rise. Every moment she spent with him only drew the net of fascination tighter.

He was famous, a celebrity. The crowd in Portsmouth had pressed about him, bristling with excitement. They'd hailed him as the Hero of somewhere called Rangapindhi. Was he home after some daring patriotic action overseas?

Her stepbrothers had kept her isolated for months. She hadn't seen a newspaper or received any letters. Recent events in the wider world were a complete mystery.

If Sir Gideon was newly returned from India, it suggested a few explanations to things that puzzled her. His tan. Akash. Even his illness. Perhaps some tropical disease attacked him.

His horrific sufferings had cut her to the quick. Gideon Trevithick, her only bulwark against her stepbrothers, was unquestionably ill. But the nature of his sickness was an enigma. What ailment turned a man so quickly from invincible avenging angel to shivering wreck?

At dawn, Sir Gideon stirred from his deathlike sleep. The movement was slight but enough to disturb Charis's restless doze. She opened bleary eyes, excruciatingly aware of her own aches and exhaustion. The carriage's endless jolting had punctuated her erratic dreams. She'd checked him periodically through the night, but his sickness hadn't returned.

Without looking at her, he groaned and swung his feet to the floor as he sat up. He rubbed his hands across his face in a weary gesture. Granting him a moment's privacy, she opened the blinds and looked out the window onto a wild and unpopulated world. There was a charged intimacy in sharing this tiny space after she'd seen him at his extremity. It made her nervy, shy, unsure.

The view didn't help to restore her courage. They'd abandoned civilization miles past. The lonely, windswept scene was depressing, frightening to a woman with only strangers to rely upon. Staunchly, she reminded herself that her stepbrothers would have difficulty tracking her through this wasteland.

She wondered how much farther Sir Gideon meant to go. Since they'd left Portsmouth, the only punctuation to eternal travel was stopping to change horses. Hurried, efficient movement, a flare of torches, Tulliver rebinding her arm if the bandage had loosened, a hot drink shoved into her hands. Then away they went again. The beef broth from the last stop, a poor place in the middle of desolate moorland, had left a nasty taste in her mouth. Luckily, she had a cast-iron stomach.

She turned back to her companion, and an involuntary gasp escaped. "You look awful."

He gave a surprised grunt of laughter and scraped his hand across the stubble darkening his angular jaw. "Thank you."

She blushed. "I'm sorry. I had no right . . ."

"No harm done. I'm sure your observation, if not polite, was accurate." He sounded like the man who had found her in the stable. Ironic. Distant. In command of himself.

Except now she knew his composure was a veneer.

He might sound like master of all he surveyed. But he didn't look much better than he had last night when he'd shivered in her arms. Dark circles surrounded sunken, dull eyes. His tan held a sickly hue in the pale sunlight penetrating the windows. He badly needed a shave, and his hair was a tousled mess.

His eyes sharpened on her. With every moment, he looked more alert. "How is your arm, Miss Watson?"

She didn't immediately recognize her false identity. Dear

Lord, let him not notice her hesitation. She needed to remember the danger she faced if he discovered who she was. Difficult when the last day had only built the affinity she'd so quickly felt for him.

Carefully she flexed her fingers. Hardly a twinge. "Much better, thank you." She studied him as he sprawled against the worn leather upholstery. His long legs extended across the well between the two seats. The shabby carriage wasn't built for a man of his height. "How are you?"

He stretched and winced, then leaned his head back. "It was just a passing inconvenience."

His expression indicated movement was painful. After lying still for so long, he'd be stiff as a board. The continual rolling and jolting of the vehicle must be agonizing. She ignored his unconvincing lie and dropped to her knees on the rocking floor.

"Let me take your boots off and rub your legs. I nursed my father in his last illness. This helped him when he'd had a bad night."

She'd forgotten no decent young lady offered to touch a gentleman who wasn't a close relative. She remembered only when he tensed, and his dark eyes flashed with horror. "Miss Watson, please return to your seat. I assure you my slight troubles don't warrant your concern."

Clumsily, her cheeks flaming with mortification, she scrambled back onto her seat. "I'm . . . I'm not usually so rag-mannered."

Yesterday he'd suffered her touch. He'd turned his face into her hand as she'd wiped his brow. But yesterday he'd been victim to his mysterious illness.

"It was a generous offer," he said kindly.

She hated his kindness. Because clearly it wasn't based on anything personal, like regard or respect. She hated owing her safety to that disinterested kindness.

Hiding a wince as the movement tested her sore arm, she fumbled to open a flask of water Tulliver had given her last night. "Are you thirsty?"

"Dry as sand." He accepted the flask without touching her fingers.

Charis berated herself for noticing. And minding. Did she want to fend off a Lothario? She should commend Sir Gideon as a man of honor.

Sourly, she recognized her hypocrisy.

Fascinated, she watched the movement of his powerful throat as he tipped his head to drink. Nor did she miss the tightness around his eyes as he returned the flask and subsided against the upholstery.

"Does your head hurt?" she asked before she reminded herself he wouldn't appreciate her solicitude.

A fleeting smile curved his lips. "Like the very devil." He sighed heavily. "All of this must frighten you. I'm sorry."

"I don't frighten easily," she said flatly.

He didn't argue although he must know she'd been terrified in Winchester. More of his cursed kindness. She wouldn't resent it nearly so much if he didn't use it as defense against her curiosity.

"Your face seems better this morning," he said.

"Oh." She'd forgotten what a horror she must look. She raised a tentative hand to her sore jaw. It didn't feel as distended. Speaking was certainly easier. Whatever heathen potions Akash had slathered on her, they'd worked. "Yes."

Sir Gideon's regard was steady as it rested upon her. Steady and implacable. "Will you trust me with the truth now? You have no aunt in Portsmouth. You're on the run from someone. Someone who threatens your very life if the state I found you in is any indication."

She stiffened under his probing gaze. Briefly she considered persisting with her lies. But as she looked into his face, she knew denial was useless. She sucked in a breath that contained a heady mixture of relief and uncertainty. "How long have you known?"

"From the beginning."

He sat up carefully and stared at her. If his face had held an ounce of anger or censure, she'd have kept silent. But he looked interested, calm, capable. He looked like a man she could trust with her life.

She shifted uncomfortably, her conscience flinching at the lies she'd told. "I don't see why you want to help. I've caused nothing but trouble. You should consign me to perdition."

Another of those faint smiles. "True."

"Well?"

He shrugged. "I've been alone against the world in my time. I'd hate you to come to grief because you had no champion."

Again, she thought of a medieval knight. A lonely, gallant figure on an impossible quest. "What happened to you?"

He laughed softly. "Oh, no, my lady. This is my interrogation. Who hurt you?"

Lingering caution insisted she conceal the precise details of her plight. She'd seen how greed changed men. She couldn't risk that happening to Sir Gideon if she told him who she really was. But his gallantry toward her meant she owed him more than the shabby falsehoods she'd produced so far.

"My brothers. They're trying to force me to marry a wastrel. I cannot . . . will not stomach the match." Her hands fisted in her skirts. It seemed odd, uncomfortable to trust a man even a little after all she'd been through. "When they realized my opposition was more than a girlish whim, they resorted to stronger persuasion." Close to the truth. Close enough to salve her stinging conscience, anyway.

Sir Gideon's face remained expressionless as he listened. What did he make of this tale that belonged in a gothic novel? Did he even believe her? At least he showed no skepticism.

"Why are your brothers so eager for you to marry this man?"

His lack of histrionics calmed her. Her hands slowly uncurled until they lay flat upon her lap. Her voice emerged almost normally. "They owe him money. My inheritance becomes my husband's if I marry or mine if I turn twenty-one unwed."

"When do you turn twenty-one?"

"The first of March."

"That's only three weeks away."

"You perceive my brothers' need for urgency," she said dryly.

"Self-serving maggots," he bit out with sudden savagery.

She'd misjudged his calmness. Looking closer, she realized he was furiously angry. His voice was quiet, his manner unthreatening. But she had a sudden vivid memory of the man who overcame every adversary in the Portsmouth brawl. Foreboding tinged with satisfaction shivered through her. She wouldn't like to be Felix or Hubert if Sir Gideon got his hands on them.

"I'm so sorry for telling lies," she whispered, guilt twisting her stomach into knots. She twined her hands together and gazed down, unwilling to meet his searching eyes. Eyes clever enough to discern she still wasn't completely honest.

"You were in danger. You had no reason to trust me."

"Except you saved my life," she said almost soundlessly.

Except you're fine and handsome and brave. And I've held you while you were sick and unaware. And watched you sleep through a long dark night. You make my heart beat like a drum, and I can hardly breathe when I look into your eyes.

She glanced up in time to catch the annoyance that crossed his face. "It was nothing."

"It wasn't nothing to me." She raised her chin and stared unflinchingly at him.

"Miss Watson, I don't want your gratitude," he snapped.

She hid the pang of hurt his response provoked. And refrained from insisting that she'd be grateful to him until the day she died.

An awkward pause fell.

When eventually he resumed his questions, his expression didn't lighten. "Presumably someone other than your brothers has custody of your fortune while you're a minor. Why didn't you appeal to them?"

"My trustees claim they're powerless to intervene." Her voice was husky with chagrin she couldn't help feeling when Gideon refused her thanks. "My brothers convinced them I'm wild and flighty and need a man's guidance."

She'd spent many a night cursing the spineless solicitors at Spencer, Spencer and Crosshill. Old Mr. Crosshill had been her father's friend, but he'd been dead four years. His egregious nephew had advised her to accept her stepbrothers' plans with suitable female obedience.

"No relative offered you shelter?"

"None with the power to stand up to my brothers." Charis's voice flattened into grimness. "Believe me, Sir Gideon, I've assessed all options. Only one remains. Will you put me down at the next substantial town we come to?"

"What do you intend?"

To survive the next three weeks without surrendering either to privation or my stepbrothers.

"I only have to avoid my brothers until the first of March." Heat climbed in her cheeks. Her pride abhorred what she was about to ask. But she must conquer pride for survival's sake. "If you lend me a few shillings, I'll repay you when I come into my inheritance. I couldn't find any money to take with me. Which must seem hen-witted, but . . ."

"Miss Watson."

"I'm not solvent right . . ."

"Miss Watson." His voice was sharper.

She relapsed into silence, embarrassed at her nervous babbling. Tears of humiliation rose to her eyes. She didn't want to set out alone. More than that, she didn't want to leave Sir Gideon, which was just too pathetic to admit. How had he so quickly become the most important person in her life? It seemed absurd. Unreal. Dangerous.

He appeared displeased. Again. "Confound you, I'm not going to slip you some blunt and put you down defenseless and alone in a strange place. If any town between here and Penrhyn was big enough to offer a hiding place. Haven't you looked out the window, girl? We're well into the wilds of Cornwall."

She gulped back the lump in her throat while fugitive hope stirred in her heart. "Oh."

He looked in better health, more like the man she'd met than last night's invalid. He looked clever and purposeful and invincible. He looked like he would keep her safe forever.

His deep voice was firm. "We aren't far from my home. I hope you'll accept my offer of sanctuary."

Five

Gideon expected Miss Watson to demur. After all, only yesterday she'd been so desperate to escape that she'd risked her life to run away. But she turned a solemn hazel gaze in his direction and, after a moment, nodded.

He couldn't help noting her beautiful eyes, remarkable even in her bruised face. A striking mixture of green and gold, they were the shifting, fascinating color of the tarns he remembered from the woods near Penrhyn.

"I accept, Sir Gideon. Thank you." Her lush lashes lowered to shade her eyes to malachite. "I just hope your many kindnesses to me don't bring you trouble."

More damned gratitude. He dismissed her remark with a grunt. "I'm not sure how kind you'll think I am when you see the house. I haven't been back since I was sixteen. Even then, it was far from luxurious. Lord knows what state the place is in now."

According to his father's solicitors, the old manor still stood as it had stood through four hundred years of wild Cornish weather. They hadn't, however, been able to vouchsafe the property's condition. Ramshackle, Gideon guessed, reading between the lines of legal nonsense.

Neither his father nor his older brother had been much of a manager. No reason that should change because Sir Barker Trevithick's despised younger son vanished into Asia. Before breaking his neck in a drunken hunting accident, Sir Barker hadn't known whether his second son was alive or dead. Nor, Gideon grimly knew, had he much cared. But then, he'd thought the succession rested safely in Harry's plate-size hands.

Like so much about Gideon's return to England, the deaths of his father and brother aroused conflicting reactions. Neither had ever evinced an ounce of affection for him, and he wasn't hypocritical enough to pretend to mourn their passing. Nonetheless, there was a . . . regret when he thought of two lives so close to his own wasted in debauchery and drunkenness.

Curiosity lit Sarah's face, and she leaned forward, bracing herself against the jolting carriage. "Has the house been unoccupied since you left?"

"No. My older brother lived there until last winter, when a fever took him."

He kept his voice steady and unemotional. Still, the girl's expression filled with compassion. "I'm so sorry," she whispered.

Her ready sympathy made him uncomfortable. "We weren't close." To say the least. Wild beasts received a more tender upbringing than the two young Trevithicks.

"Then I'm sorry for that too," she said. "Family is important."

"Not to me," he said tersely. "And I hardly think your experience is any improvement on mine."

Her jaw firmed. "My brothers' brutality can't destroy my faith in human relations. That would give them too great a victory."

Again, he couldn't stifle his admiration for her indomitable spirit. "You're a brave young woman." And she'd need every scrap of that bravery before she was done. He paused and forced himself to set before her a factor she should consider. "It will be a bachelor establishment, Miss Watson. Me. Tulliver. A few servants. Akash when he arrives in a couple of days."

Briefly, she raised her good hand to touch her mottled cheek. The gesture indicated uncertainty and drew his unwilling attention to her face. This morning both the bruising and the swelling had subsided. A hint of her true features emerged like a shadowy reflection in a mirror. With a doomed sinking in his gut, Gideon recognized that Miss Watson promised to prove a beauty under her injuries.

When he'd rescued her, he hadn't spared a thought for her physical attractions. She was just a woman needing help. The last thing he wanted to deal with was a winsome female. She would only be a blistering reminder of everything he'd never have.

Fate clearly was in a mood to torment him.

"No ladies at all?" She sounded hesitant. He couldn't blame her. For a gently bred girl, the prospect of moving into a masculine household must be daunting. "No aged spinster aunts or widowed cousins?"

"I'm afraid not." He wished he could reassure her that his aid came without risk of consequences. He wished to God he had some alternative plan for her safety. "We may get away with it. I've been abroad a long time, and I have no plans to join local society. The house is remote, and the villagers distrust outsiders."

Nervously, she plucked at the bandage on her arm, her fingers long, pale, and graceful. He noticed she held her arm more easily against the swaying carriage. Clearly Akash's potions had relieved the worst of her pain.

There was a troubled silence before Sarah spoke. "My safety is more important than my name." She sounded as though she reached that conclusion reluctantly. As she looked up, she managed a shaky smile. "I still can't see why you take this trouble. Your generosity to a stranger does you credit."

Gideon shifted uncomfortably under her wholehearted approbation. He desperately needed to shatter the encroaching intimacy, fine as spider's web, strong as steel, but something in her unblinking regard forced the truth from him.

"I abhor injustice. I abhor bullies. Everything in me resists allowing men who treat a woman as you've been treated to profit from their evil." His voice roughened with emotion. "While there is breath in my body, Miss Watson, I'll do my utmost to ensure your freedom and security."

Immediately he repented his impulsive declaration.

Her eyes glowed gold as a streak of sunlight striking a forest pool. Her lips parted, but no words emerged. She leaned toward him but, thank God, didn't touch him. Even so, his skin itched as though she reached for him.

Damn, damn, damn. He should have recognized the looming danger before this. He needed to destroy this building affinity, not encourage it. Why hadn't he kept his blasted mouth shut?

At last he interpreted exactly what her expression portended. His inescapable conclusions made his stomach lurch with nausea.

Miss Watson regarded him with unstinting, uncritical, and completely unwarranted hero worship.

Following his moving declaration of unconditional protection, Sir Gideon's withdrawal was tangible. She stifled a prickle of hurt she had no right to feel.

He spent most of the day asleep. Or feigning sleep. She couldn't be sure. What she could be sure of was that he wouldn't welcome her curiosity. Even though curiosity about him gnawed at her mind like hungry rats.

His apparent oblivion provided her with uninterrupted hours to study her companion. The mysterious ailment had passed although he was still pale and gaunt. Charis was guiltily aware that her reckless escape had prompted his attack although she had no idea why. His suffering had been so extreme, she could hardly bear witnessing it. The agonizing frustration was that she could do so little to help.

She gathered he endured these awful spells on a regular basis. What on earth was wrong with him? She hadn't seen anything like his illness before although she'd nursed her father and her mother and ministered to many sick tenants on the estate.

Gideon Trevithick puzzled her. He fascinated her. She'd never known anyone to compare to him. She'd never known anyone who affected her the way he did. He was such a compelling mixture of strength and vulnerability. Every time she looked at him, her heart launched into a tipsy dance. This breathless excitement was unfamiliar and frightening. None of her suitors had stirred this hunger for their merest presence.

Perhaps she felt this way because he'd saved her. First in Winchester, then from those vile miscreants in the alley. A shudder rippled through her as she imagined what would have happened in Portsmouth if Gideon hadn't appeared like a guardian angel. Degradation and death had edged so close.

But as her eyes traced Sir Gideon's dark features, she knew her interest went beyond gratitude. Deep and sincere as that gratitude was. He was beautiful, he was brave, he was damaged, he was frighteningly clever. And the briefest sight of him made her breath jam in her throat.

Dear Lord, she'd known him little more than a day, and already she brimmed with giddy, irrational longings. What state would she be in after three weeks in his company?

At least the continuing silence served one good purpose. He didn't question her further, saving her from dredging up more lies to prick her conscience. Ingrained habits of mistrust and caution urged her to keep her identity secret, although if anyone deserved her honesty, it was Sir Gideon.

Now she was about to move into his house. A forbidden thrill raced through her at the prospect. A thrill mixed with apprehension. If the world discovered she lived under his roof without a chaperone, she'd be ruined. Another good reason to keep her identity secret.

She glanced across at her sleeping rescuer and couldn't help thinking that ruin had never looked so alluring.

Oh, Charis, wicked, wicked. The angels weep for you.

Charis's endlessly circling thoughts eventually took on the carriage's rocking rhythm and lulled her into a half-waking state. Each lurch of the coach worsened her aches and reminded her she was far from recovered after Hubert's beating.

For most of the day, they traversed rough moorland. In the late afternoon, Charis was awake to notice they passed between two gateposts, worn and covered in ivy. Rampant lions held carved stone shields so old and moss-encrusted, any detail was long obliterated. Rusted gates hung drunkenly, smothered in weeds that had died last summer and never been cut back. Soon after, they entered a thick wood.

Charis stirred to mark the change in the landscape but was too tired to ponder its significance. She stretched stiff muscles and bit back a moan as the movement tested her injuries. With a sigh she couldn't restrain, she leaned her head back against the seat, hoping to heaven there wasn't another night of travel ahead. She was heartily sick of the rattling, bumping coach.

They continued for another half hour or so. Interlacing branches above the rutted track turned the interior of the carriage into shadowy mystery. In his corner, Sir Gideon was a silent, magnetic presence, his long legs stretched across the well between the benches, his arms crossed over his hard chest. She had no idea whether he was asleep or pretending.

To her regret, Charis knew she looked like she'd been dragged through a bush. She'd been a fright yesterday, and the day's traveling would only worsen her appearance. Since he'd changed his clothes, Gideon had regained his louche elegance. Even the faint beard darkening his jaw enhanced his masculine appeal, adding a rakish air to his chiseled features. She closed her eyes and told herself to think of something other than Sir Gideon. A command impossible to obey.

Through her fog of discomfort and exhaustion, Charis heard Tulliver shout and felt the carriage shudder to a halt. She opened dazed eyes. They'd left the wood, and late sunlight flooded through the windows.

She leaned her head out the window and looked up at the grizzled figure in the driver's seat. "Why have we stopped, Tulliver?"

"Look, miss." He gestured with his whip. "Penrhyn."

With a glance at Sir Gideon's motionless figure, she forced her tired muscles into ungainly movement. She scrambled from the coach and turned in the direction Tulliver indicated.

And fell in love at first sight.

They were on a slight rise. Behind stretched the woods they'd just driven through. In front, the land sloped gently down to the cliffs. Beyond was the glory of the sea, deep blue in the fading light.

Part of sky, sea, wild landscape was the house perched on the edge of the cliffs, looking westward. Centuries old. Worn. Welcoming, even at this distance. Its soft golden stone glowed in the long rays of sunlight. Penrhyn called to Charis across the pale winter grass that trembled in the fresh sea breeze.

"It takes your breath away, doesn't it?"

Reluctantly, she tore her gaze from the house to look at Gideon, who emerged from the carriage behind her. He'd been nurtured in this glorious place. No wonder he was so remarkable. She swallowed to shift the lump of emotion that lodged in her throat at the house's perfect beauty. "It's magnificent."

He stopped beside her, close enough for her to be aware

of his commanding height. She wasn't an especially short woman, but he made her feel small and fragile. Her heart did its usual dip and leap at his nearness. How she wished she could control her foolish reactions.

"Yes, it is." His voice was calm. Artificially so, she guessed. Although his striking face was impassive, she couldn't mistake the tension in his lean frame. "I wondered if it had changed. It hasn't."

Charis frowned, confused by the currents swirling beneath his calm surface. For someone who had left his home many years ago, he appeared less than overjoyed to be back. "How could you bear to stay away for so long?"

Sudden emotion darkened his face, and his eyes burned as they met hers. The searing look lasted barely a second before he returned his attention to the old house. "How can I bear to come back?" he muttered, seemingly against his will.

"You sound like you hate it," she said, aghast.

He shook his head, and a lock of black hair fell across his forehead. "No, I love it. That's what makes everything so impossible."

The corrosive honesty of his response flooded her with astonishment. Sir Gideon didn't strike her as a confiding man. That he revealed as much as he did indicated his turmoil.

With an abrupt movement, he turned on his heel and climbed back into the carriage. Shocked, bewildered, Charis watched him go. It was as though he couldn't bear to look on his inheritance any longer. But for a moment, the hardness in his gaze had shattered, and she'd glimpsed a longing that made her heart stutter.

She wished to the depths of her being that she understood him. She wished to the depths of her being that he considered her worthy of his confidence. More than either, she wished she could do something to ease his unspoken anguish.

But she was a stranger. A brief visitor to his life. She had no significance for him beyond the present moment.

She glanced up at Tulliver, who had witnessed the whole

exchange with his usual sangfroid. There was a light in his eyes that might have been understanding and was certainly pity.

For whom? Sir Gideon? Or the pathetically infatuated Miss Watson?

His voice was kind. "You might as well get back in, miss. We've got a mile or so to go."

Charis's shoulders sagged with weariness, and she limped after Gideon into the vehicle. Tulliver whipped the horses to a canter as they turned for the house. Gideon settled into his corner and stared out the window.

The sun plunged toward the sea in flaming glory by the time they passed through a crumbling stone arch and into the paved courtyard in front of Penrhyn. A closer viewing revealed the house was shabby and unkempt, but nothing could destroy the enchantment it laid over Charis. An enchantment indelibly part of the yearning she felt for its master.

"Parts stretch back to the fifteenth century, although most of it is Elizabethan." They were the first words Gideon had spoken since that tense, revealing moment on the rise.

"It's beautiful."

He gave a short, caustic laugh. Through the dimness, she read the derision on his face. "Believe me, your enthusiasm will wane when you get inside to a cold house and damp sheets and a makeshift supper—if we manage any supper at all."

"I don't care." His cynicism couldn't damp her pleasure in Penrhyn. The ancient stones breathed warmth. The house had been loved, and it would be loved again. It was old and knew how to wait.

Holcombe Hall was a cold white Palladian pile. Architecturally perfect. Built for a Marquess of Burkett last century when the Farrell family still had money and prestige. She'd hated it from the moment she'd arrived there after her mother's marriage to the late Lord Burkett. God rot his miserable soul.

As the coach slowed, two men dashed out to hold the tired horses. Four women hurriedly lined worn steps rising to a heavy door.

"Let the circus begin," Gideon said bleakly. With a savage movement, he opened the door and leaped to the ground before the carriage reached a complete stop.

Gideon sucked air into lungs constricted with an anger he didn't understand. He hadn't expected his return to his boyhood home to be so fraught with emotion. But at the first sight of the old house, he'd felt crushed between the urge to escape and the yearning to stay forever.

Another deep breath in a futile attempt to calm his galloping pulse. The essence of Penrhyn overwhelmed his senses, cleared the last sour traces of yesterday's laudanum. And brought back a thousand agonizing memories.

Still he drank in the air—tangy with salt and wild thyme and sun on old stone and good Cornish earth. He was home and the sweet, fragrant reality split his heart in two.

"Sir Gideon, welcome home!"

The familiar voice wrenched him from distraction. He straightened and fought to mask his tumultuous reactions. He met a shrewd blue gaze in a lined face. A face he knew. Behind the tall, rake-thin old man, the staff bowed and curtsied.

Surprise and something approaching pleasure stirred. "Pollett? Elias Pollett?"

The man's eyes shone bright with welcome. "Aye, lad . . . Sir Gideon."

Pollett had been his father's head groom. Even when Gideon was a boy, Pollett had seemed old. Gideon's memories of his family were unfailingly desolate. His memories of the local people less so. Mostly they'd ignored him. Which was kinder than any treatment he'd received from his father. But Pollett had been an ally as far as he was able. He'd secretly taught Gideon to ride after Sir Barker abandoned his son as a hopeless case.

"How did the solicitors know to give you a position?"

"I never left, sir. A few of us stayed to see the house secure until you got back from furrin parts and took charge."

Took charge? What a joke. Gideon wasn't even sure he intended to remain. Although the scents of sea and wild herbs insisted he belonged here. Demanded he accepted he was a Trevithick to the bone. Like all Trevithicks, born at Penrhyn and fated to die at Penrhyn. As much part of this place as the cliffs and the waves and the wheeling, crying gulls.

"Before that, I was Sir Harold's bailiff." The slow, deep roll of Pollett's Cornish accent fell on Gideon's ears like music. "Didn't anyone tell you?"

They might have. He hadn't been interested enough to pay attention to much beyond the basics of his solicitor's correspondence. Difficult as it was, he summoned a smile. "I can't think of any man better suited to run the estate, Pollett."

It was true. Unexpected his brother had seen it too. He wouldn't have credited Harry with such good sense.

Pollett's face creased in concern. "The estate isn't as it should be. I did my best, but . . ."

Gideon made a dismissive gesture. "It doesn't matter." The house stood, and anything else could be fixed. If he could summon heart for the task.

"We've been short-staffed. And Sir Harold . . ."

Gideon met Pollett's eyes and a silent message of understanding passed between them. Harry had already been a hopeless drunkard when Gideon left, for all he'd only been nineteen.

Sir Barker had been a man of stubborn opinions. He'd considered drinking, like hard riding and ceaseless womanizing, an essential manly attribute. Gideon's open contempt for his sire's swinish pursuits was just one of many conflicts between them.

A memory of Harry before the liquor got to him assailed Gideon and aroused a pang of genuine sorrow. His brother had been tall and gold like a Norse god. Strong. Hearty. Stupid as an ox but not vicious.

Any viciousness in the family had been his father's.

Pollett swallowed visibly as Harry's bluff ghost hovered, then vanished. "All will be well now there's a real Trevithick holding the reins."

Dear God, how much more of this could he take? The hope and joy in Pollett's face made Gideon flinch. He didn't deserve this unconditional welcome.

To avoid the old man's gaze, Gideon turned back to the carriage. He looked inside to where Sarah shrank into the shadows. "Come out, Miss Watson."

He stood back as she reluctantly obeyed. When she emerged, Pollett's face lit with curiosity and the beginnings of speculation. "Are felicitations in order, Sir Gideon?"

If a man traveled alone with a woman, she could fill few roles in his life. A relative, and Pollett intimately knew the sparseness of the Trevithick family tree. A wife. A mistress.

Gideon stifled grim laughter. He wished to hell he was normal enough to have a mistress. If he did, she'd be a damned sight better turned out than Miss Watson. However low the Trevithicks sank, they always dressed their lady-birds *comme il faut*.

The girl hovered at his side with visible uncertainty. She'd raised the greatcoat's collar around her face, and her shoulders hunched.

Shame was so familiar, he had no trouble recognizing it in another. He hated seeing such a proud spirit brought low. She hid her injuries, as though they marked her unclean, contagious. More than that, she must know her virtue was in question.

She waited silently, gazing at the ground. Poor Sarah. Hurt. Alone. Helpless.

Her brothers' violence cast her into an unforgiving world. How she must loathe relying so totally on strangers. In this isolated place, she had nowhere to run, nowhere to hide.

His glance swept the small crowd arrayed before him.

Generations of service tied these men and women to the Trevithicks. He drew himself up to his full height, and his voice rang with authority. "Miss Watson is an acquaintance who needs somewhere to stay." He ignored her muffled gasp of horror as he used her name. "It's imperative nobody knows of her presence. I entrust her safety to your good sense and discretion."

Sarah mightn't realize it, but he'd just claimed her as a denizen of his private kingdom. Penrhyn had always been a realm unto itself, loyal to those who belonged, suspicious of incomers. He waited as first one maid dropped into a curtsy, then another, and the men bowed acknowledgment.

Gideon gestured for her to precede him up the stairs and into the cavernous hall. But as he followed her into the house, reluctance weighted his tread.

The day's last sunlight poured in dusty rays through tall mullioned windows. Inside, the shabbiness evidenced outside was overwhelming. Sparse furniture littered the vast space. There were signs of a hurried cleaning, but the elaborately carved moldings were unpolished, the curtains dusty, the fires unlit. The servants trailed in and lined up against the dark paneling.

"We put on extra staff when we heard you were coming, Sir Gideon. But I awaited your orders before I did too much. For the last year, it's just been me and Mrs. Pollett in the house." For a moment, Pollett's formality faded. "I'm sorry, lad. It's not much of a homecoming."

Gideon looked around the unprepared, dirty room. Memories of his childhood were colder than the winter air. His father had conducted punishments here, usually before the staff. Gideon's refusal to cry under the whip should have pleased the old tartar. After all, Sir Barker's constant carp was that he'd spawned a puling weakling in his second son. But Gideon's sullen obstinacy had only incited greater violence.

"Sir Gideon?"

The girl's soft voice shattered his painful reminiscences.

He turned to look at her. The collar folded back from her face, and as luck would have it, she stood in a pool of sunlight. Lit like a saint in a religious painting.

Her features were clearly discernible. A pointed chin, full lips, large eyes as changeable as the Cornish weather. Her hands tangled in the black folds of the coat, he guessed to hide their unsteadiness.

"You must be tired." Now he looked more closely, there were dark crescents beneath her eyes, visible even under the bruising. "The travel has been difficult."

When she met his stare, she raised her chin and summoned a fleeting smile. She was alone, afraid, defenseless, but she dared fate to defeat her. Something shifted in the farthest reaches of his heart, and the house's sounds receded to a hushed murmur. Sarah Watson drew him as no other woman ever had. If circumstances weren't so tragically askew, he might aspire to offer for her hand.

Instead, she'd do better to run a thousand miles from him. He was no use to himself. He was no use to the world. He could be no use to a wife.

That knowledge didn't stop him yearning for joys other men took for granted.

He'd had months to count the agonizing toll of his years in India. He thought he'd measured the price of his experiences. But only now, when the phantom life he might have led beckoned like a desert mirage, did he truly comprehend all that had been stolen.

Grim reality dictated that Sarah remained an unfulfilled promise of everything he'd never have.

He tamped down the poignant longing, the regret, the sadness. She'd be gone in three weeks. He could endure that, surely. He'd endured a year of unspeakable suffering in Rangapindhi and survived.

"I'm all right." She hesitated and bit her lip. "I'd love a bath, if that's possible."

"I'm sure it is." Gideon glanced at Pollett, who waited nearby. "Are any bedrooms ready?"

"Aye, Sir Gideon." The man stumbled every time he spoke the title. "The master suite is prepared."

"That will not be suitable for Miss Watson," he said curtly. The glare he shot Pollett made it clear Miss Watson was not and never would be his mistress. "Have the maids make up the Chinese room. You'll need to make preparations for my man Tulliver too. And I'm expecting another guest, an Indian colleague, in the next few days. He'll use the ivy room."

Pollett bowed and spoke in a subdued voice. "Yes, Sir Gideon."

Gideon desperately needed to escape this room with its hordes of unhappy ghosts. He gestured Sarah toward one end of the hall. "In the meantime, Miss Watson and I will take tea in the library. If it's habitable."

Pollett bowed again as he passed. When he lifted his head, he spoke softly and with a sincerity that made Gideon cringe. "I'm glad you lived to come home, lad."

"Thank you," he muttered, wishing he felt a shred of gratitude for his survival into the hellish present.

At Sir Gideon's side, Charis crossed a dark corridor and entered an even darker room. She drew her first unconstricted breath since she'd arrived. Thank goodness she was no longer the cynosure of all eyes. She loathed knowing the servants thought she was no better than she ought to be. In spite of Sir Gideon's gallant efforts to insist she wasn't his mistress. Her bruised face only increased speculation.

She waited uncertainly as he flung aside a heavy set of blue velvet curtains. Choking dust flew into the air. Sudden light dazzled her. She closed her eyes and opened them on a wall of windows facing an overgrown terrace poised above the sea.

For a long moment, Gideon stared at the magnificent

view. Charis sensed sadness and curiously, for a man who returned home, a deep loneliness.

Was he grieving for his dead brother and father? Or did something else trouble him?

His essential isolation prompted her to touch him, offer comfort, remind him he was part of the human race. She curled her hands into the coat and stifled the impulse. The journey had taught her he wouldn't welcome her overtures.

His rejections hurt, but not as much as it hurt to witness his brooding unhappiness. More sign that she was dangerously vulnerable to this man who was little more than a stranger. But she'd already fallen off the precipice. It was too late to try to save herself.

Eventually, he turned, brushing dust from his hands. His expression was neutral, the brief vulnerability hidden.

"I've brought you to a hovel, I'm sorry." He moved across to help her take the coat off. He draped it over a set of mahogany library stairs. Like everything in the room, they were covered in thick dust. But no amount of dirt could conceal the impressive walls of leather-bound books or the elaborately carved furniture and plasterwork. This was a beautiful room, but nobody had cared for it in years.

"Hardly a hovel." Gingerly she perched on an upholstered chair, sending up a puff of dust that made her sneeze. She was weary to the bone, and every muscle ached from the beating and the hours in the coach. She'd sell her soul for a hot bath and a bed and the chance to sleep for a month. She'd sell her soul twice over to see a glimmer of joy in Sir Gideon's dark face.

"How are you feeling?" He surveyed her with an impersonal concern that made her want to shrivel up in the corner.

"I'll be glad to stay put for a little while," she said. "How are you?"

He frowned as if the reminder of his illness rankled. "I'm perfectly well, thank you." He swung away, discouraging further inquiries after his health. "You should rest and regain your strength. I'll send Mrs. Pollett to you after we've eaten. She's not Akash, but she knows most of the country remedies."

"Thank you." She had no right to mind his eagerness to consign her to other people's care. Frightening how much power a glance or a word from him had over her emotions. She tried to set up self-protective barriers, but they crumbled to rubble the moment she looked at him.

She sneezed again and muttered her thanks as she accepted the handkerchief Gideon extended in her direction. Through watery eyes, she watched him prowl the room, lifting items seemingly at random and inspecting them.

How curious he was so ill at ease in his own house. Why was his homecoming so strained? He'd dropped hints of a clouded family history. Did old memories torment him? Something did. Tension stiffened his back, and deep lines bracketed his expressive mouth.

The door opened to a girl carrying a tray. The cups didn't match. One was Meissen, one was Sèvres. Both were exquisite. Once, someone at Penrhyn had had taste and money to indulge it.

Sharing the tray was a plate of roughly hewn cheese sandwiches. To Charis's embarrassment, her stomach growled. She flushed. Great-aunt Georgiana would be mortified at such a faux pas.

Sir Gideon replaced a small marble bust of Plato on the windowsill and turned to the maid. "What's your name, lass?"

The musical baritone worked its usual magic. Even Charis, who should by now be inured to its allure, shivered in sensual reaction to that deep, musical sound. The girl's thin shoulders relaxed, and she sent Sir Gideon a shy smile as she slid the tray onto a dusty rosewood side table.

"Dorcas, Sir Gideon." She curtsied. "I be Pollett's granddaughter. Ee mightn't remember me, sir, but I remember ee, though I were only a ween of five when ee left."

"You used to churn the butter for your mother."

"Aye, sir." The girl flushed with surprised pleasure. "Fancy ee remembering that."

Gideon tilted his head toward Charis. "Miss Watson needs a maid. Would you be interested in helping, Dorcas?"

The girl curtsied to Charis. "Oh, aye, miss. But I bain't never been a lady's maid afore."

"I'm sure you'll be splendid, Dorcas," Charis said. Again, she had reason to be grateful for Gideon's thoughtfulness. She was wicked to want more than he offered.

The girl grinned with gap-toothed delight. "Thank ee, miss. Thank ee."

When Dorcas had gone, Gideon glanced across at Charis. "She'll be clumsy at first, but she was a quick child. I imagine she'll learn fast."

"There's no need to make excuses. You're kind to think of my convenience. My step . . . my brothers . . ." Dear heaven, the false intimacy of being alone with Sir Gideon in this beautiful, neglected room made her forget she lived a lie. She needed to watch her tongue, or she'd reveal her true identity. "My brothers deprived me of my maid over the last weeks."

It infuriated her to recall Felix and Hubert's petty tyrannies. As though lacking a servant's attentions would convince her to marry the foul Lord Desaye.

Gideon strolled across to the table. He lifted the plate of sandwiches and extended it toward her. "You're hungry after your journey."

She stood, ignoring a yelp of discomfort from her abused body. This at least she knew how to do. Something familiar in the sea of unfamiliarity. "Shall I pour your tea?"

"Thank you." Gideon put down the plate as Pollett entered the room. Charis concentrated on fiddling with the tea things, her color rising as she recalled Pollett's quick assumption that she was Sir Gideon's mistress.

"Is all in order, sir?"

"We need a fire," Gideon said, taking a seat near the table.

As Pollett left, Charis passed Gideon his tea and a plate with two sandwiches arranged upon it. Her left arm made the simple duty more trouble than usual, but she managed. Such a small achievement, but enough to revive her spirit.

He smiled almost naturally. "So this is what it's like to be under a lady's dominion."

She frowned with puzzlement. "Surely you've taken tea with a female before."

"Never alone. Never in my own house." He swallowed a mouthful of tea and lifted his chunky sandwich for a healthy bite. Whatever his illness of yesterday, it seemed to have passed.

"What about your mother?" She took the chair opposite. As she sipped from her cup, she stifled a sigh of pleasure. It was a small luxury, yet one she'd missed.

His face became expressionless. "My mother died at my birth. My father didn't remarry, having already sired two sons and seeing no need to submit himself again to the yoke of matrimony."

"I'm sorry about your mother." Had his mother bought the pretty china and chosen the delicate, faded fabrics that upholstered the furniture? So much death marred his life. Was this what darkened his soul? Sadness thickened her throat, and the tea abruptly lost its flavor. "No feminine influence at all in the house?"

His lips quirked. "No *ladies* at any rate."

"Oh."

She couldn't control a blush although her heart beat faster at the idea of him with a woman. He wouldn't sit across the table, drinking tea. He'd snatch her up in his arms and kiss her and . . . She tamped down the wanton images before she made more of a fool of herself than she had already. Her face felt like it was on fire.

The smile became a smirk. "Indeed."

She dragged her mind kicking and screaming back to reality and looked around the room. Anything to avoid his knowing glance. Now she thought about it, the house shrieked its lack of chatelaine. Penrhyn badly needed a woman to take charge and restore its former glory.

Perhaps the absence of early feminine influence explained Sir Gideon's awkwardness with her. Although he didn't strike her as an innately shy man. Again, she wondered if he disliked her. The possibility made her belly tighten with denial. She dearly wanted Sir Gideon's approval.

Surely he must like her just a little. His manner at times such as this was almost intimate. Certainly more intimate than she could remember encountering in other gentlemen. Every time he turned that warm regard on her, she felt like a sunflower opening to the sun. She knew the reaction was improper, dizzying, perilous, but she couldn't help it.

He broke the tense silence and spoke with a polite formality that chilled the already icy air. "I hope you'll treat the house as your own, Miss Watson. Go where you please. Read anything in the library. There's a pianoforte in the morning room—or there used to be. I wouldn't advise you to stray too far from the grounds in case you're seen. Although I suspect your injuries put anything too energetic out of reach at present."

"Thank you," Charis said dully. Stupid to long for Sir Gideon's arms to close around her. She forced herself to remember they were chance-met strangers. This silly wayward lilt of the heart was purely one-sided.

All this emotional turmoil on top of the beating and the long days of travel conspired to sap her last ounce of energy. With a tired gesture, she set her cup in its saucer. Every second intensified her multitude of aches. Her head thickened with weariness.

He rose from his chair and moved across to a sideboard, where he splashed some brandy into a glass. "The house and estate will demand my attention for the next few days. Penrhyn's been too long without a master." She recognized his tone as a deliberate attempt to put her at a distance.

"You don't have to entertain me or neglect your duties on my behalf." Her voice was flat with disappointment. But what had she expected? That he'd devote his attention to her? Much as she wanted his company as a buffer against the unfamiliarity.

Charis, don't pretend that's the reason.

She forced an even tone. "You've already done so much for me."

"Don't be absurd." He emptied the glass in a single swallow and set it down with a crack. "I did what anyone would have."

"You're too modest, Sir Gideon."

"Don't make me out to be more than I am, Miss Watson." His eyes glittered like obsidian as they focused on her. The tension that extended between them like a thin golden wire tightened to breaking point. "I'm as miserable a sinner as ever walked this earth. Pray remember that."

The invisible wire linking them snapped. He turned and stalked from the room, leaving her to stare after him in hopeless, hurt bewilderment. The sun turned away from her, and she shivered in the sudden, biting cold.

Six

Over the next days, Gideon saw little of Sarah. With his guest recuperating in her room, avoiding her proved a surprisingly simple matter.

They shared dinner under the curious eyes of his servants. Occasionally, they crossed paths in a corridor, and he'd inquire after her health. All perfectly polite, two strangers passing the time of day. Thankfully, there was no hint of the burgeoning, dangerous intimacy that had hovered on the journey to Penrhyn.

With every encounter, he couldn't help noticing the remarkable beauty that emerged from beneath the disfiguring bruises. It was yet another of fate's cruel jokes that the desperate, injured girl turned into a woman of spectacular attractions who stirred his sluggish blood.

It was unlikely her brothers would track her this far, but Gideon wasn't taking chances. He made sure someone always knew where she was. A pack of brawny villagers boosted the household staff, and shifts of men patrolled the approaches to the house.

Even if he'd wanted to play nursemaid, he wouldn't have had time. He was frantically busy. Mostly he was absent from the house, fielding endless requests and questions, and making decisions about the estate. After years of neglect, there were a thousand matters, small and large, to address.

What became abundantly clear during his first day as its reluctant master was that Penrhyn was in his blood. He was home to stay.

He could no more abandon the place than he could fly to Constantinople. When he'd seen the old house again, a sullen, unwelcome love had flooded him, a bone-deep sense that Penrhyn was meant to be his. Illogical, inconvenient, but undeniable. He couldn't relinquish this windswept corner of the kingdom to anyone else's stewardship. Although God knew who he kept it for. He was the last Trevithick. There would be no sons to inherit.

That sad fact haunted him, a mournful threnody beneath his activity. And if the memory of one delicate woman also haunted him, he was too occupied to brood on the fact. At least during daylight hours. Nights were a different matter. He'd throw himself exhausted on his bed, only to lie awake listening to the endless crash of the waves and thinking about Sarah. Or worse, drifting into restless dreams where he was free to touch her as he never could in the harsh light of reality.

With every hour, that hankering to touch her intensified. With every hour, the pain of knowing that he never would lacerated him.

On the morning of his third day at Penrhyn, Gideon shut himself in his library, determined to tame the chaos his predecessors had left of the accounts.

He'd been at work for about an hour when Sarah wandered into view through the tall windows facing the overgrown parterre. The dusty ledger in front of him immediately lost what small interest it held. He watched for Dorcas or one of the men set to guarding Sarah. But his visitor remained alone in the dewy, sunlit garden.

For a forbidden, secret moment, he stared, drinking in her beauty. The bruises were barely noticeable now, and her face resumed its natural shape. Since yesterday she'd discarded her bandage, and she no longer moved as if every step hurt. To his relief, Akash's assessment of her injuries as looking worse than they were had proven accurate.

Sarah paused in a patch of light and turned her face to the pale February sun. Her lips curved with a natural sensuality.

Gideon's heart battered his ribs. His breath jammed in his chest. She was glorious. None of the fabled courtesans of India held a candle to her uniquely English loveliness.

Was he so shallow that her pretty face made him want her?

If only the truth were so uncomplicated. He could resist the lure of beauty if beauty alone attracted him. But the waif he'd rescued in Winchester had become a woman of endless allure. Strong. Brave. Tender. Sweet.

Ah, so sweet.

A long plait fell down the supple line of Sarah's back. Gideon's hand, lying idle on the desk, flexed as if it tangled in that silky bronze mane. He locked his teeth and cursed himself for a fool. Such fantasies were futile.

Knowing he tormented himself to no purpose, he hungrily watched the subtle sway of her hips as she started walking again. The way the ill-fitting cotton frock skimmed her lissome waist. He frowned. Why was she still wearing the cheap dress from Portsmouth? He'd asked Mrs. Pollett to find her fresh clothing.

He'd sort it out later. He bent to his work, determined to punish himself no further with impossible yearnings. Then, helplessly, he raised his gaze as Sarah strolled through a morning more like April than February and disappeared behind a hedge of overgrown camellias.

A page of figures his eyes failed to register. Another. Another.

From here, the grounds sloped down to the cliffs. Given the decrepitude of the rest of the estate, Gideon guessed the paths were unstable, falling to pieces. There was danger for someone who didn't know Penrhyn. Devil take them, where were the people supposed to be watching her?

"Damn it," he muttered, and shoved the thick ledgers aside. He snatched his gloves from the desk and leaped into a run.

Charis was sitting on a worn stone bench when she heard Gideon's purposeful footsteps. He was in a tearing hurry. She couldn't imagine why. Especially as he'd worked so hard to stay out of her way since they'd arrived. She tried to tell herself he was busy, and she had no right to feel slighted, but some instinct insisted the lack of contact wasn't accidental.

He broke into the cleared space and paused, breathing heavily. He appeared to be searching for something.

Although she'd sworn she'd behave with circumspection in his presence, although she'd preserved a polite façade when encountering him in the house, her heart beat so fast, her greeting stuck in her throat. She hadn't expected to see him this morning, and his arrival threw her good intentions into disarray.

He looked toward the cliff edge, scanned the clearing, then finally turned in her direction. His face flooded with visible relief. "There you are."

Every time she saw him, it was like the first time. As she experienced anew the shock of his male beauty, the world seemed to tumble away from her feet, leaving her suspended in space. The sensation was dizzying, scary, overwhelming.

Today, his onyx eyes were clear, and he moved with an easy freedom that fitted his long-limbed body. He'd spent the recent days outdoors, and the exercise suited him.

She swallowed to dislodge the lump in her throat, but her voice still emerged as a croak. "Sir Gideon, what's wrong?"

"I saw you heading down here." He ran his hand through his hair, ruffling it into beguiling untidiness. "I wasn't sure of the state of the cliff edge."

It hardly hurt to smile now. Just a slight ache. A glimpse in her bedroom mirror before she'd come outside had revealed a face she finally recognized as hers. "So you rushed to my rescue again." She tamped down a twinge of forbidden pleasure that he'd come seeking her.

He made a noncommittal noise in his throat. "You're looking better."

"I'm feeling better." She fiddled nervously with her mother's pearl ring and tried to think of something clever to say. Nothing came to mind. Hard to recall she'd been the toast of Bath society. Sir Gideon made her act like a gauche schoolgirl.

"I'm glad." That half smile appeared. Odd—disturbing— how familiar and dear it was.

A charged silence fell. She knew she devoured him with her eyes. What made no sense was that he seemed to devour her in return. Then it was as if he recalled his resolve to keep his distance.

"Well, my apologies for disturbing you." He sounded stiff, awkward. "As you're in no immediate danger . . ."

"I'll be careful."

She wished she could make him stay. Absurd when they were strangers, but she'd missed him in the last days. To her chagrin, Sarah found herself blushing, as though she spoke her foolish yearning aloud.

She waited in tense misery for him to forsake her to loneliness. But he took a step closer and gestured to the glorious view. The sea was blue and calm today. The waves played like soft music under their conversation. "It looks gentle, but don't mistake its peril."

"I can hardly resist exploring. I hope you don't mind. Penrhyn has such fairy-tale charm." Her instant affinity for this place had only strengthened. Each night, she went to sleep in her paneled corner bedroom listening to the sea. "Like *La Belle au Bois Dormant*."

Again that half smile. Her poor, longing heart skipped a beat every time she saw it. "On my honor, there are no sleeping princesses here, Miss Watson."

"Perhaps a prince?" she asked lightly, then regretted not keeping her mouth shut.

His expression closed, became remote. "No princes either."

She waited for him to storm off as he had from the library the last time she'd attempted to share more than platitudes. But he remained where he was, frowning down at the ground.

Eventually, she broke the uncomfortable silence. "What are your plans for the property?"

His eyes were guarded as they focused on her, but to her surprise, he answered readily enough. "There's potential for the estate to be profitable. It was once. The woods contain good timber and while the land isn't much use for crops, it will support sheep. Most of the skilled men have gone, but we could set up a fishing fleet again. First I mean to reopen the tin mines."

"Tin?" She leaned back on her arms. She still wasn't used to having the full use of both arms. Her wrist gave the occasional twinge, but it was almost back to full working order.

"Yes." He moved close enough to raise one booted foot onto the far end of her bench. He rested one arm on his thigh and bent toward her. Her skin prickled with awareness, and her breath became shallow and choppy. She prayed he didn't notice. "The land is littered with worked-out diggings, but there's still ore to be found. The sea and tin have always kept the Trevithicks."

He spoke with an odd lack of involvement, but she wasn't convinced he was as unemotional about his home as he wanted her to believe. She'd seen his face when he glimpsed it for the first time upon his return. "Will you restore the house?"

To her astonishment, a glint lit his dark eyes. "I'll demolish it and build a modern villa."

Shocked, she jumped to her feet. "That would be an act of unforgivable vandalism."

He laughed softly. "Just teasing you, Miss Watson." To

her regret, he straightened and shifted out of reach. "I've remarked your predilection for Penrhyn."

Her color rose, and she curled her hands at her sides. "I can't believe you don't care. The house needs to be loved."

The more she saw of Penrhyn's master, the more she believed that was true of him too. How she wished she could restore him to joy. But the last days had made it apparent that he regarded her as a duty and nothing more.

"It's only bricks and mortar," he said mildly.

"You'll feel differently when you have children," she said fiercely, even as she flinched to contemplate him marrying another woman.

The brief moment of levity evaporated. His voice was terse. "I have no plans to marry."

"Of course you'll marry. You're young, you're handsome, you're . . ."

He silenced her with a cutting gesture of one hand. "Spare my blushes, Miss Watson."

His sarcasm stung, although she knew she deserved the set-down. Her cheeks stung with humiliated heat. She wished she could keep her impulsive comments to herself, but something about Sir Gideon made her burst into ill-considered speech at the very worst of moments. The merest sight of him, and any pretensions of poise flew into the ether.

"I'm sorry," she said in a subdued voice. "I had no right to say those things. You must think I'm a rag-mannered hoyden."

"No."

Just "no"? What was she to make of that? What *did* he think of her? She stifled the needy, desperate questions that struggled to the surface. She'd already embarrassed him— and herself—sufficiently. Frantically, she cast around for some neutral topic. "When I came out, I was looking for the path to the beach."

His mouth lengthened with disapproval. "It's steep and not easy for a lady. That's how I remember it nine years ago.

I suspect it's in worse repair now. You'd be better staying in the grounds."

Lady Charis Weston would have stepped aside, let him return to his work as he clearly wished. Sarah Watson was a more demanding creature and desperate for a few more minutes of his company. "Can't we at least try?"

Sudden amusement flashed across his face, banishing the sternness, making him look years younger. "You're a stubborn scrap of a thing, aren't you?"

Even more astonishingly, his black eyes swept her body, subjecting her to a thorough, masculine inspection. Instant agonizing tension extended between them. Heat crawled over her skin, and her heart bucked and plunged in her chest. Her nipples puckered with painful swiftness, and something warmed and melted in the pit of her stomach.

The powerful, unfamiliar sensations frightened Charis. It was as if the body she'd known for twenty years suddenly belonged to a stranger. With every ragged breath, the hard points of her nipples rubbed against her shift. The friction was maddening, unstoppable, infuriating.

She lifted a shaking hand to her breast to ease the ache, then realized what she did. Her face became hotter. He couldn't miss her discomfort. She wished the ground would open up and swallow her like the whale had swallowed Jonah.

She lowered her head to hide her mortifying reaction, to break that scorching connection with his eyes. "Not exactly a scrap," she muttered, turning away to rip at the leaves of a camellia.

"No, perhaps not." He released a harsh laugh, bitter and without amusement. She didn't have the courage to check his expression. "Let's show you our fine beach."

She sucked in a shuddering breath while delight and self-consciousness vied within her. Now that she wasn't looking at him, she gained some small control over herself.

"I'd like that," she said almost inaudibly.

Feeling like the greatest fool in Creation, she scattered

the shreds of greenery on the ground and nerved herself to glance at him under her lashes. She'd expected to see anger or contempt or disgust, but his expression was, as so often, inscrutable. Was there a chance he hadn't noticed how flustered she was?

At least he was still here. More, he planned to escort her to the beach. Breathlessly, she waited for him to take her arm, but he merely gestured her toward the overgrown path and fell into step behind her.

He went ahead once they had to fight their way through a mass of untidy rhododendrons. Like everything else at Penrhyn, the garden reeked of neglect. Charis knew it was insane but she felt that the house cried out to her to save it, to make it a home.

Stupid fancy. She was only a temporary visitor to this beautiful place. She'd leave soon, to be quickly forgotten by Penrhyn and its owner.

The bleak knowledge set like concrete in her belly.

Her host was as unkempt as the manor. She studied his tall figure as he forged a path for her. He wore breeches and shirtsleeves, and his boots were old and scuffed. Still, he was utterly splendid. Her pulse, which had started to steady, kicked into a gallop again. She pictured him standing on the prow of a ship. A gold ring glinting in one ear. A cutlass at his waist. A knife clenched between his teeth.

He stopped to lift a prickly bramble high over her head. "What are you smiling about?"

She hadn't realized she was smiling. "Were any of your ancestors pirates?"

"Black Jack Trevithick was one of Bess's Sea Hawks." As she passed him, he flashed her a grin that was devilment personified. Her unruly heart somersaulted. Heaven help her. "His portrait's in the long gallery. At least it was. Black Jack looks like me, so my father may have retired it. My father and brother took after my grandmother's family, the St. Ledgers. But I'm all Black Trevithick."

"Is that because of your hair color?"

"Partly. Also black temper, black nature, black sheep, black heart."

She couldn't restrain a startled laugh as she pushed her way through the shrubbery ahead of him. "Goodness. I find myself quite terrified to be in your presence."

Of course it wasn't true. Gideon Trevithick's company was as intoxicating as champagne. He unsettled her more than anybody she'd ever met. He confused and troubled her. But she could hardly countenance that once she left, she'd never hear his voice again.

Although of course it wasn't just his conversation that made her head swim with excitement. He was handsome. More than handsome. He was beautiful, like some being sent down from heaven to illuminate dull earth. And strong and virile and manly. No woman with blood in her veins could fail to respond to his attractions.

Perhaps when he knew who she really was, he'd consider courting her. She saw no evidence of huge riches at Penrhyn. Could he overcome his disinterest in her person if he knew he married the greatest heiress in England? The Earl of Marley's title had lapsed along with the entail upon her father's death. Every penny, every acre, of the massive Weston inheritance devolved upon the earl's one direct descendant, his daughter.

Dear Lord, was she so lacking in pride, she'd trade gold to gain the man she wanted even if he didn't want her? Her belly clenched in sick shame. She needed to leash her foolish imagination before it brought her to grief.

They emerged from the bushes onto the cliff edge. Below, the sea spread like shining blue silk. Gideon paused behind her. She was so attuned to him, she felt his every breath. An unwelcome premonition brushed across her skin and made her shiver. This preternatural awareness seemed more significant than mere physical reaction.

"This is such a beautiful place," she said softly.

With an unwillingness she immediately recognized, he moved closer. A light wind played with his thick hair.

Lucky breeze to take liberties with him that she couldn't.
She closed her fists at her sides to stop herself smoothing the
disheveled locks. It disturbed and frightened her, this continual, frustrated need for physical contact. It left her jumpy
and awkward.

She watched him draw in a deep breath of crystalline air.
The tension seeped from his broad shoulders as if the view
fed his soul.

"I didn't realize how much I'd missed it. The sea. The
wind. How . . . clean it all feels." His eyes remained fixed
on the horizon, but she had the strangest impression he
saw something else entirely. Something that haunted him.
"When I was in Rangapindhi, I remembered this view. It
made me want to live."

She must have made some sound of protest or surprise
because he stiffened and turned his head, fastening those
glittering eyes upon her.

"Why wouldn't you want to live?" she echoed, shocked.

He frowned. "Do you truly not know? My story has been
in all the papers. Quite the sensation of the season." He
spoke with a biting sarcasm she didn't understand.

"My brothers kept me prisoner. I'd never heard your name
until we met." She curled her arms around herself, although
the chill she felt was more spiritual than physical. "Those
men in Portsmouth called you the Hero of Rangapindhi.
Were you a soldier?"

"No." He bit the word out like a bullet fired from a gun.
His unspoken pain was a vivid, twisting, tangible entity.

Charis tightened her arms to stop herself reaching out.
A stinging mixture of compassion and desire lodged in her
throat. She forced her question past the constriction although
she was sure he'd dismiss her curiosity. "Did you hate India
so much?"

His regard was unwavering, and his voice deepened with
emotion. "No, I loved it."

It was the same answer he'd given her when she asked
whether he hated Penrhyn. Gideon Trevithick seemed to

have an ambiguous relationship with love. Again, she wondered at the despair that shadowed him, closer to the surface today than she'd ever seen it.

He sighed, and his shoulders slumped. "I wish I was the man you think I am." His voice was so sad, it made her want to cry. "But I'm not worth an ounce of your regard."

She sensed the acrid shame beneath his words. He was dauntingly complex, and he drew her more powerfully than anyone else ever had. After a long silence, she dared to ask, "Will you tell me why?"

"No. I don't want you to share my nightmares." His smile festered with bitterness. He lifted his gloved hand. For one breathless moment, she imagined he meant to touch her cheek. Her eyes fluttered shut as she waited to feel the brush of his fingers.

Nothing happened. She opened her eyes slowly to catch poignant sorrow on his face. His hand fell to his side. "But believe me when I say I'm no hero."

She swallowed, and her voice shook as she spoke. "You're a hero to me."

The regret drained from his expression, leaving comprehension and a pity that stabbed her like a knife. "Miss Watson . . ."

Intent on silencing him, she made a gesture of denial. She didn't want comforting platitudes. The pity in his eyes indicated he divined her unseemly hunger for him. How could he not? The feeling was too overwhelming to hide, and he was a perceptive man.

She blushed with mortification, and spoke quickly, before he could. "Aren't . . . aren't we going to the beach?"

He straightened, his mouth firming. But he didn't argue with her abrupt change of subject, for which she was grateful. "The path is just here."

He walked past, and she realized the ground dipped away sharply. A few steps after him, and she saw a thin track snaking down the cliff.

Charis looked down, and her stomach lurched. Far below,

rows of jagged rocks awaited. Resolutely, she lifted her head and stared at Gideon's straight back in his loose white shirt. As he began to descend, he was utterly at ease in this rough, dangerous terrain. Not hard to imagine a gangly, intense, dark-eyed boy seeking refuge from a troubled home life among these cliffs.

Charis stepped carefully after him, not surprised at his silence. Now he'd guessed how besotted she was, he must wonder what he could say. Humiliation added its sour tang to the poisonous brew of unhappiness and longing stewing inside her.

At first the going was easy, the slope gradual. The path was in surprisingly good repair. But soon the track narrowed, became steeper. She placed a hand on the rock face as the descent grew more precipitous.

For one fatal second too long, her eyes dwelt on the tall man ahead. Every scrap of information she gleaned about him only fed her curiosity to know more.

The path dipped. Her foot slid on a loose stone. She clutched wildly at the rock wall, but her fingers slid uselessly across the cold, smooth surface.

"Gideon!" she screamed.

Dear God, she didn't want to die. She wanted to live and make Gideon love her.

The thought, bright and burning like lightning, seared her mind as she tumbled helplessly toward the edge.

Seven

Sarah!" Gideon whirled and lashed out to grab her before she plummeted to her death.

His hands closed like manacles around her slender wrists. There wasn't time to think or feel. There wasn't time to recoil from the shock of physical contact. He pivoted and slammed her back hard into the wall.

She screamed again, with pain this time, as her head banged against the rock. Then she closed her eyes and sagged, trembling and gasping from his hold.

He slumped over her, silently protecting her with his body from the drop behind him. His gut churned, and terror tasted rusty on his tongue. His chest heaved as he fought for breath, and his shoulders ached with the strain of snatching her to safety. He didn't relax his punishing grip although he shifted to press her hands flat into the rock on either side of her.

Hell, he'd come so close to losing her.

He leaned his forehead on the rock above her head, waiting for the wildly careening world to slow and stop. Dizzying relief thundered through him. Cold sweat chilled his skin as his mind replayed over and over the few seconds when Sarah slid uncontrollably.

They remained unmoving, her facing him, his hands clutching hers, mere inches separating their bodies.

Gradually, Gideon's suffocating fear ebbed. Reality returned, his mind started to function. He heard the crash of the waves on the rocks below. He felt the cool breeze on his damp skin. He felt the path's unevenness under his booted feet.

Sarah lifted her chin with a curiously jerky movement and stared unblinking at him as if he provided her one sure compass point. Her pupils were dilated, and her face was haggard with shock and pain. Her lips parted as she drew a ragged breath.

With a spurt of guilt, he realized his unyielding grip must hurt her sprained wrist. Logic indicated she was safe. Even so, it was only with the utmost difficulty that he forced himself to release her left hand.

Biting her lip to smother a sob, she gingerly bent her arm against her chest. The fingers of her other hand twisted to twine convulsively around his.

"Sarah, dear God . . ." His choked whisper ruffled the soft hair on the top of her head. "Are you all right?"

She gave an unsteady nod. "Yes."

His heart still raced, and he shook like a dog in a thunderstorm. "What about your wrist?"

"I jolted it, but I don't think there's any damage." Wincing, she stretched her arm and carefully moved it. Her earlier bruises had faded to yellow, so the impression of Gideon's fingers was red and stark on her pale skin.

He cursed himself for a blundering brute. He hadn't had time to be gentle. All that mattered was keeping her alive. He sucked in a shuddering breath.

Suddenly he was aware how close they stood. He only needed to shift a fraction, and her body would brush his.

What the devil was wrong with him, standing over her

like this? He knew better. He had to stop touching Sarah now. *Now.*

Familiar, unstoppable nausea rose. Blackness filled his head. With a roughness he couldn't help, he wrenched his gloved hand away from her. Blindly, he turned to press his back to the rock wall beside her. His gloved hands splayed against the stone as he struggled to mask his reaction. She was too close, but he couldn't bear to have her out of reach just yet.

For a long, taut moment, the only sounds were the mournful cries of the gulls, the pounding waves, and his hoarse panting.

Eventually, she shifted toward him. He didn't look at her, but he felt her study him. He was guiltily aware that he must frighten and confuse her. Explanations, apologies gushed up, but he furiously bit them back. His pride revolted at putting his humiliating state into words.

When she didn't immediately speak, he steeled himself to look into her ashen face. In a gesture that poignantly reminded him of the lost waif in Winchester, she cradled her wrist upon her breast.

Her voice emerged almost normally. "You saved my life again. How can I ever repay you?"

Oh, damnation. This was the last thing he needed. She stared at him as if he was St. George, and he'd just rescued her from the dragon. The unfettered admiration and gratitude in her hazel eyes sliced at his conscience. If he'd planned to discourage her interest, what had just happened beggared good intentions.

"You can repay me by being more careful in future," he said harshly. And hated himself as he watched the radiance dim from her eyes. In truth, he wasn't angry at her as much as at the whole bloody impossible situation. He had no right to bask in a beautiful woman's approbation, even if he had just saved her life.

Her cheeks, which had been pale as paper, flushed with

color. Her response was muted. "I'm sorry. I wasn't paying attention. Yet again, my foolishness put you at risk."

His tone softened. "No harm done."

Which, damn it, wasn't true. With every second he spent in her company, the insidious bond between them tightened like drawn silk cords. His recent efforts to avoid Sarah had achieved precisely nothing. He was as irrevocably connected to her as he'd ever been.

She straightened and winced at the movement. This morning's tidy plait had loosened into a mass of bright flying tendrils around her face. He fought the urge to smooth that wild halo.

For one intense moment, she met his eyes, then her thick lashes fluttered to her cheeks. White teeth worried at her plump lower lip, and her breath audibly caught.

Just like that, in a blazing instant, sexual need kicked into fierce life. He hardened. His heart broke into a savage rhythm. Every drop of moisture dried from his mouth.

His sickness at touching her passed in a bright flash. What possessed him instead was worse. Because he couldn't do one damned thing to relieve his hunger.

The startling rush of desire left him reeling, light-headed. He'd accepted his lack of interest in women since Rangapindhi as a blessing. The only blessing. He'd assumed his indifference was permanent. What was the point of wanting what he could no longer have? Better not to want.

Dear Lord, let her not look down. Let her not see how aroused he was. He tried to edge away, but the narrow path gave him little room.

How the hell was he going to survive three weeks of this?

He couldn't touch her. Every dictate of ethics and morality and chivalry insisted he couldn't touch her.

If only principle was all that made him hesitate.

He *couldn't* touch her. That was the sodding tragedy of it.

She was still speaking. He fought back the clamor in his head and tried to concentrate on what she said.

". . . few bruises."

Confound it, he needed to get a grip on his reactions. Through the buzzing in his ears, he battled to focus. He realized her good hand plucked unhappily at the sleeve of her plain gown. ". . . mend it."

He tore his gaze from her mouth. So soft. So moist. So tempting. And glanced down to her dress. He must have ripped the sleeve when he dragged her back from the brink. There was a gaping rent in the threadbare brown material.

That was one problem he could solve, surely. He sucked in a tattered breath and spoke over her stumbling explanations. "I'll take you back to the house. One of the servants must have something you can wear."

She sent him an odd look. He hoped to Hades she had been talking about clothes. "As you wish."

He frowned. She sounded disappointed. "Are you sure you're not injured?"

Her restless hand tangled in her skirts, and she looked away. "Of course I feel a little knocked around. But, no, I'm not seriously hurt. Thanks to you."

"Miss Watson, there's no call to harp on your totally unnecessary gratitude," he said repressively.

He flushed as he realized he barked like a displeased sergeant dressing down a recruit. She cast him a resentful glance that scorched him to his soles. He needed to get away. Fast. But his feet were welded to the path.

"I hardly think it's unnecessary." Her tone was soft but firm.

"Sarah . . ." He knew it was a mistake using her Christian name the moment the word emerged. He needed to resist further closeness, not reinforce it.

"I won't refer to it again." She still sounded subdued.

"Shall we go?" He gestured her past him, but she hesitated.

"Sarah?" Damn, he'd said it again. Every second in her presence extended his torture. If he didn't put some distance between them soon, he'd grab her. Then the shaking would start, and the sickness and the humiliation.

"Can't we go down to the beach? Only for a minute?" She sounded wistful, like a child denied a treat. "I've been cooped up for so long. I'd love to see the sea. I've never been so close to the ocean before."

He desperately tried to ignore the plea in her hazel eyes. Curling his hands into fists, he strove to steady his tone. "You need to rest."

Her lips—Lucifer himself must have created those moist, red lips—turned down in a dismissive quirk. "I'll be careful on the way down. I'm not such a fragile vessel as you imagine. I've had a shock, but I'm perfectly all right. What sort of girls have you been talking to?"

"I haven't been talking with many girls at all," he said before he could remind himself that swapping confidences with his gorgeous tormentor was unlikely to ease his predicament.

With every second, she looked more like her usual self. "You surprise me."

Curse her, why did he feel the urge to explain? "I told you Penrhyn was a masculine province."

Apart from his father's blowsy mistresses, who occasionally took up residence. His father's taste had run to the overblown, the obvious. None of those women had been remotely interested in a studious stripling, for which Gideon had been heartily grateful.

"Surely when you left home . . ."

"I went to Cambridge at sixteen and immersed myself in study."

Frowning thoughtfully, she laced her hands at her waist. A sign he hadn't done her wrist serious injury, he was relieved to note. "The university men I know caroused their way through their education."

His smile was grim. "I suspect the men who paid court to you weren't second sons with no prospects. I was much younger, not to mention poorer, than most of my fellow students."

If he were another man with another life, he'd surely have

been among those men who courted her. He straightened as if physically resisting the forbidden idea. A stray strand of windblown hair briefly clung to her lush lips. Another blast of sensual awareness shook him. He fleetingly closed his eyes and told himself he mustn't under any circumstances kiss her.

He breathed deeply, struggling for composure. When he could see straight, he stepped past so he could precede her down the cliff, in case they struck any more unstable patches. Against his every instinct, he'd take Sarah to the beach. He knew when he was beaten. "Watch your step. It's steep, and you've used up at least three of your nine lives today."

"Thank you," she said softly to his back. "I know I'm a trial."

She had no idea just what a trial she was. Pray God she never found out. Craving to seize her in his arms tightened his skin and made his heart gallop as it had galloped when she teetered toward the edge. Except this time with lust rather than terror.

The reminder of her fall made him slow his pace. His hand itched to reach back and grab hers, in case she stumbled. Such a natural action, yet completely outside his capability. He couldn't risk another of his attacks. He cursed himself and his affliction.

On the way down, he frequently glanced back to check on her. Her near disaster had obviously convinced her to treat the path with respect, and she negotiated it with visible concentration. Thank God. At least it checked her questions.

When he reached the base of the cliff, he jumped from the rocks to the beach. He landed hard on the firm sand and turned to watch Sarah carefully climbing from boulder to boulder.

Guilt bit at him as he remembered how he'd shoved her against the rock wall. For all her brave words, he recognized the stiffness in her movements as discomfort. He bit back a demand that they return to the house. After his experiences in Rangapindhi, he understood better than most her need for freedom.

She crossed to stand at his side just past the high-water mark. The bruises on her face were mere shadows now. In the bright clear light, her beauty was flamboyant, heartbreaking. She made him feel as close to alive as he ever expected to again.

The errant breeze flirted with her hair, teasing it around her face as she turned to him. "So you went to India to make your fortune?"

More blasted questions. He wished he had the heart to tell her to mind her own business. But he couldn't resist the honest interest shining in her eyes.

His voice was stilted as he replied. He wasn't used to talking about himself, and every time she pried a confidence out of him, it was an acknowledgment that they were more than just chance-met strangers. "An opportunity arose."

Gideon began to walk along the coarse yellow sand, and she fell into step beside him. She flattened her hands on her skirts to stop the wind lifting them, but still he caught a breathtaking glimpse of slender ankles and shapely calves. He closed his eyes briefly and prayed for strength.

She was going to kill him before she was done.

"With the East India Company?"

He dragged himself back to the conversation and tried to ignore how lovely she was. He made himself go on, partly to distract himself from the pale flash of Sarah's stockings.

"My talent for languages attracted the attention of powerful people." He spoke without vanity. He had a freak facility for picking up foreign tongues. Some strange tic in how his mind worked. "They thought I could be useful."

"As a trader?" She bent to pick up a scallop shell, the movement hitching up the back of her dress. He stopped to watch her, then wished he hadn't. His hands flexed at his sides as he fought the urge to toss those skirts up to a more pleasurable purpose.

Because to his eternal regret, there could never be pleasure.

"More as native liaison." The answer was strained. He didn't want to tell her the truth, that he'd been a spy. Of course, if she cared to investigate, she'd find out. His life had been sensationalized in every newspaper in Britain. In the world, for all he knew.

Elements of the press coverage were true, at least superficially. The papers had invented the rest, each story more lurid than the last. In the public mind, he'd become a bizarre mixture of Robin Hood, Casanova, and Sir Galahad.

The cruel farce of his celebrity made him cringe.

She straightened and ran a thoughtful finger along the edge of the hard white shell. He already knew enough to guess another question percolated. "Were the Indian girls beautiful?"

"Yes."

She glanced quickly up at him, then away, a delicate pink washing her cheeks. "Were you in love with someone there?"

Dear Lord, were all women so fixated on love? He'd heard more on the subject today than he remembered hearing in all his twenty-five years. Against his will, he found himself answering. "No."

The man who stepped off the ship in Calcutta seven years ago had never known a lover. But Gideon's fascination with Indian language and art, nurtured in the dusty library of his college, became a fascination with the living, breathing culture. And soon the living, breathing female embodiments of that culture.

That first six months as he traveled around the Company's offices and residences, he'd succumbed to hedonistic license. The women were beautiful and generous and adept at pleasure. He'd never imagined a world like it. Sex became a drug.

His hedonistic existence came to an abrupt end once he entered the field. The dangers of betrayal were too great.

He swung away from further questions and strode along the beach, his long legs eating up the stretch of sand. The gulls cried overhead. The loneliest sound in the world.

He should have known she wouldn't let him escape. Run-

ning footsteps crunched behind him, then he felt the soft
touch of her hand on his arm.

Through his shirtsleeve, that contact scorched. Rapacious
hunger jolted him even as his flesh crawled. He jerked free.
"Don't touch me!"

She recoiled, her eyes darkening with such pain that he
flinched. "I'm sorry," she said huskily.

He fought to speak normally, but his voice emerged dull
and flat. "No matter. I don't like to be touched."

Her mouth straightened into an unhappy line. "By me, at
any rate."

God in heaven, how much of this could he take? He sucked
in a lungful of salty air and floundered for control. "It's not
you."

She shook her head and raised a hand to keep her wind-
tossed hair from her eyes. He couldn't mistake the anguish
in her face. "Don't spare my feelings. I've noticed your revulsion for my presence."

He let his breath out in a despairing hiss. "That's not true."

Sarah's slender throat moved as if she stifled a protest.
Hell, he hated to hurt her. He felt like the lowest bastard
in Creation, even though he acted for her sake as much as
his own.

*Don't be a blockhead, Trevithick. The girl isn't suffer-
ing from genuine love but from a bad case of hero worship.
She'll survive without ill effects.*

"Miss Watson . . . Sarah . . ." He stopped, struck silent by
her vibrating misery.

"You must consider me a foolish creature." The breeze
whipped at her low words, so he had to lean closer to hear. A
dizzying waft of her scent mixed with the salt air and made
his nostrils flare in masculine response.

A torrent of words fought to escape, words that told her
how exquisite she was, how brave, how wonderful. He stifled them all. He had no right to pay compliments to innocent young girls.

"I have a great-aunt who would be horrified at my behavior. She worked hard to turn me into a lady." Sarah hesitated, sucked in a breath, then went on in an artificially bright voice. Gideon knew she desperately strove to ease the prickling tension between them. "I was quite the tomboy when she took me in hand. My father raised me much as he'd raise a son. You see, the estates would all be mine one day."

Even through the wild tumult in his head, Gideon knew this didn't make sense. He frowned. "Wasn't your oldest brother the heir?"

Guilt flooded her vivid features. "The entail had come to an end. My father . . ."

Her shoulders sagged as she relapsed into troubled silence. Gideon had noticed before that she wasn't a good liar. He was an excellent liar—he'd learned to be as defense against a violent father. He'd perfected the skill, playing a role where discovery of his identity meant death.

"They're my stepbrothers," she said in a subdued voice. "My father died when I was sixteen . . ." The sunlight shone stark on her expression of naked grief. "My mother remarried. Her husband had two adult sons who hated me on sight."

Gideon shifted closer as if even on this deserted beach, he protected her from her rapacious family. His mind flared with a fierce, relentless urge to kill anyone who threatened her. His voice roughened with the power of his anger. At last he discovered her secrets. At last he came to grips with the forces ranged against them. "Those are the swine who beat you?"

"Yes." Sarah paused, then continued with a reluctance he could hear. "My mother passed away not long after she married my stepfather. Her choice hadn't been a happy one. Her new husband was a drunkard, a gambler, and a wastrel. From the first, he was openly unfaithful."

Gideon's gut clenched as he read the pain she tried so hard to hide. If he was any sort of man, he'd take her in his arms and offer comfort. But of course, he was no man at all. "Have you lived in that bears' den since you were sixteen?"

Sarah shook her head and tossed the scallop shell to the

ground with a disgusted gesture. "To them, I was just another useless mouth to feed. After my mother's death, I went to a great-aunt in Bath. She's the one who tried to instill some manners." The desolation faded from her face, and real affection tinged her smile. "Great-aunt Georgiana was determined to find me a brilliant match. Bath in the season is a social whirl."

"I'm sure you didn't lack for suitors." Absurd to be jealous of these unknown men who had flirted and danced with her.

She shrugged and looked toward the waves, her color rising. He studied her profile. Those men had seen exactly what he saw now. Innocence. Generosity. Beauty. And a fresh and fragrant sensuality that drew him like a bee to honeysuckle.

Gideon had believed himself immune to female allure. Good God, the merest contact with anyone's skin set him shaking like a windblown leaf. Yet this girl promised such passion, even he couldn't resist.

She began to walk up the beach. Silently, he joined her, pleased to note she moved more easily now she was on flat ground.

"My stepfather fell down the stairs in a drunken stupor and broke his neck." Her tone deepened with contempt, and her hands tangled in her skirts. "My stepbrothers inherited nothing but crippling debts. And whatever they could wring out of being named my guardians in the will."

Ah, this was the crux of the problem. As her legal guardians, her stepbrothers had every right to compel Sarah back into their custody. No wonder she'd been so reluctant to confide the details of her dilemma to a stranger. Gideon broke the law by sheltering her. That fact alone would cause many people to hand her over to the authorities, whatever the personal issues involved.

Gideon kept his voice even, much as he wanted to rage and curse the mongrels who had hurt her. "So legally you're at their mercy."

"Yes, unfortunately. After they took me from my great-aunt, they launched the scheme to marry me off." A wayward gust blew a long strand of hair across her face, and she absently brushed it back. Her tone developed an edge. "When they realized I wasn't so gullible, they tried to put me completely in their power. No letters in or out of the house. No newspapers. If I tried to visit the village, they stopped me. At first with excuses. Later with threats."

Poor chit, relying on spirit and cleverness, in a situation where only brute strength counted. "Couldn't you bribe a servant to take a message?"

She shook her head. "The servants knew any chance of wages relied on my marriage."

A scorching need to smash her stepbrothers into jelly filled him. Almost as scorching as his urge to sweep this girl into his arms and kiss her senseless. And what a damned disaster that would be. "I suppose as your birthday approached, they became desperate."

She stopped and sent him a stark look. With one hand, she held her hair away from her face. The freshening breeze finished the destruction of her plait. In her thin gown, she must be cold although she showed no sign of it.

"Naïvely, I thought some code of gentlemanly behavior would constrain them." She went on in a curiously flat tone as though she distanced herself from what she said. "They cut back my meals. They locked me in my room. At first the violence was casual, and they made sure the bruises wouldn't show. I can't imagine why they troubled. It wasn't as though the servants didn't know. And I saw nobody else."

She paused as if waiting for Gideon to comment. But he was too angry to trust himself to speak.

"At least the violence was honest." Her voice scraped into rage and her fists curled at her sides. "It was worse when they insisted the marriage was for my own good. That made me sick to the stomach." She looked over the waves again but not before he caught a flash of fury in her eyes.

"Damned curs," Gideon muttered under his breath. An

inadequate response. But everything was inadequate against what she'd been through.

"That last day was the first time they set out to beat me into obedience. Before Hubert started hitting me, Felix said I should save everyone trouble and give in before they made things really tough."

Gideon could imagine how she'd responded to that. "Of course you sent them to the devil."

"Yes. But then . . ." For the first time, she faltered and stared down at the sand in front of her. "Felix said . . ."

Nausea knotted Gideon's gut. He could imagine what came next. No wonder she'd been frightened out of her mind in Winchester. "You don't have to tell me."

He shrank from the trust he read in her gaze as she turned to him. She looked as if she believed he could move mountains. With bone-deep sorrow, he wished to God he was the man she thought he was.

Her color rose in a tide of shame. "Felix said they'd drug me and let my suitor take my maidenhead. I said they could do what they liked. Nothing would ever make me marry him."

His eagerness to murder her stepbrothers ramped higher, blocked his throat. "That was foolhardy."

She swallowed and continued in a toneless voice. "I knew they wouldn't kill me. If I die, the money goes to my second cousin, a bluestocking spinster who's lived all her life in Italy. I've never met her."

She spoke almost expressionlessly. Gideon's belly knotted with horror as he contemplated what she'd been through. He could hardly bear to formulate his question. "Did they force you?"

"No." Except for two hectic flags of color along her slanted cheekbones, she was pale. "But Felix said all three of them would take turns. Hubert wasn't in favor of the plan, but Felix always gets his way." She sucked in a shaky breath and spoke quickly as if that was the only way she could get the words out. "The idea of the three of them raping me, it was . . ."

"Intolerable." Bile filled Gideon's mouth as he imagined what would have happened if she hadn't fled. She'd survived a purgatory he understood better than most.

Her hands twisted more tightly in her skirts. "During the beating, Hubert knocked me out. Only for a few seconds. When I woke up, they started badgering me again. I wouldn't relent, so Felix slammed out in a temper, taking Hubert with him. It was the first time they forgot to lock the door. Perhaps because I'd made no attempt to escape, they believed I wouldn't or couldn't try to get out. While they were arguing downstairs, I crept into another room and climbed out a window that opened onto an oak tree. Thank goodness I knew the countryside enough to reach the Winchester Road."

"Thank goodness we found you in that inn." Nightmare images filled his mind of Sarah's rape and abuse. He had no doubt her stepbrothers would have carried out their threats. But now she was with him, and nobody would hurt her again. The determination to keep her safe stiffened every sinew.

Her voice became concerned. "I meant just to travel to Portsmouth with you, then disappear. By helping me, you're in danger too."

"I can handle your stepbrothers." He looked forward with bloodthirsty enthusiasm to exiling such scum to the lowest circle of hell.

His confident response drained some of the tension from her face. "You were amazing in that fight in Portsmouth."

Heat mottled his cheeks. He abhorred that only the spilling of blood made him a whole man. Violence dissipated the fog that possessed his mind, gifted him with clarity of purpose and unhesitating action. "I was a thug."

"You were a hero," she said with a conviction that made him wince. Dear God, what was he going to do about her misplaced admiration? He needed to scotch it now, but nothing he said made any difference. Knowing she wouldn't listen, he bit back arguments about his unworthiness.

Her head bent in apparent thought, she walked farther

along the beach. He didn't follow. The wind lashed at him as he watched her retreat.

It was time they returned to the house. She must be freezing. Still, he didn't move to fetch her. He needed a moment of privacy to rein in his blistering rage at her stepbrothers.

Long ago he'd guessed she came from a good family, but her fortune must be enormous to provoke this frenzy of greed. Gideon recalled no great families called Watson, but then he'd never moved in high society. The Trevithicks were only minor gentry. His experience of the haut ton was limited to his recent sojourn in the capital. Those weeks were a painful blur. Concealing his illness from the avid mob had been almost impossible. Mostly he'd just felt an overwhelming desire to escape.

And, of course, Sarah's stepbrothers would have a different last name. It hardly mattered. Duke's daughter or shopkeeper's daughter, Sarah was utterly out of reach. A man like him couldn't start to think about taking a wife.

His hungry gaze fastened on her as she paused to pick up a pebble and pitch it into the sea. Her stepbrothers assumed their ward lacked powerful friends. Perhaps at last, being the Hero of Rangapindhi might prove of some use. Those bastards would pay for their crimes before he was done.

It would be his parting gift to Sarah.

He'd see her safe and happy. Then the kindest thing he could do was forsake her forever. With a grim knell in his heart, he trudged up the beach to where she silently stared across the waves.

Eight

After so many hours in Sarah's company, Gideon inevitably dreamt of her. Such cruel fantasies to torment him when he couldn't lay a hand on her in the real world. At dawn he woke, sweating and restless and painfully aroused. He desperately needed to escape the house, partly because he couldn't bear to meet Sarah's clear gaze and recall what an insatiable satyr he was.

At least in his dreams.

After an early breakfast, he set out for a long ride along the cliffs on an unfamiliar mount. Akash hadn't yet arrived with Khan and the other horses. Now he strode along the gallery, heading for his rooms and a quick wash before he settled to the estate papers. And hopefully no intrusive thoughts of hazel-eyed houris.

From either side, his ancestors stared down. He didn't count on their approval. How could he? His forebears must resent knowing all their labor, all their ambition, all their hopes ended with him.

God knows what would happen to the estate once he was

gone. In the meantime, he'd devote his life to restoring it. Not for the sake of these louring faces but for the people who lived here. Dark, secretive, taciturn. And loyal to death to the Trevithicks.

He hadn't expected to survive to see his homeland again. But he had—to return to news that Harry was dead. How ironic that his father and his brother perished too young in safe, peaceful England. While Gideon had come through untold dangers.

With such somber thoughts for company, Gideon rounded the bend in the gallery and almost ran Sarah down.

"Sir Gideon!"

He reached out as she stumbled. Then he remembered and snatched his gloved hands back. Blood pumped through his veins in primitive demand. He hardened with uncontrollable swiftness. Untrammeled images from his dreams swamped his mind. His body moving in hers. Her bronze hair flowing about them like wild silk. Her soft moans of pleasure.

For one burning instant, he stood close enough to catch her scent. A hint of carnation soap. The essence of Sarah herself. Then she found her balance and shifted away, thank God.

Sucking in a deep breath, he retreated a step. The extra distance did nothing to curb the storm inside him. "Sarah . . ."

At his withdrawal, her eyes darkened with hurt. He wanted to tell her again it wasn't her, but he stopped himself. Better by far she never learned his filthy secrets. He couldn't burden her so.

She bit her lip and glanced at the painting she'd been studying. "He could be your twin."

"What?" Gideon struggled to focus on what she said.

"The man in the portrait."

He blinked to clear his vision and realized she stood looking at Black Jack Trevithick. For a long moment, Gideon stared into painted eyes so similar to his own. Black Jack wasn't smiling, but the long, sensual mouth quirked on the verge of laughter.

"That's Black Jack. An altogether more dashing fellow than I."

"He certainly has the devil in his eyes."

"Not just in his eyes if the stories are true."

"Women, you mean? If looks are anything to go by, I suspect the stories are true." She glanced directly at Gideon. "You'll have to tell me."

He shifted uncomfortably. A discussion of his disreputable forebear's amorous conquests. Just what he needed when he struggled to rein in his own unruly sexual appetites. "Most aren't fit for a lady's ears."

She laughed softly and flashed him a smile. Her full lips curved bewitchingly, and he caught a glimpse of small white teeth. Another bolt of arousal left him staggering. Her warmth beckoned, more enticing than a fire on a winter's night.

He tilted his chin in Black Jack's direction. "Actually, there's one story you might like."

"Only one?"

"Well, the only one I mean to tell."

"Spoilsport." Her lips twitched in a way that sent another frisson down his spine.

He strove to sound as if he weren't about to combust into ashes. "Black Jack was the local wild boy. He could sail anything that floated, ride any horse that galloped, seduce any maiden into compliance. The family legend is he charmed Queen Bess out of her chastity."

The enchanting smile still hovered around Sarah's lips. "What a man."

"Precisely." He struggled to concentrate on his story rather than Sarah's attractions. An impossible task when her attractions were so compelling. "On one of his raids along the Spanish Main, he captured a galleon."

Her face was alight with interest. "Packed with treasure, so the Trevithicks were set up forever?"

"Who's telling this tale?"

"You are. Pray, go on."

"Packed with treasure, so Black Jack came back to Cornwall and rebuilt the house as it stands today."

"If he built this house, he had an artist's spirit. What else was on the galleon?"

He fell into the familiar tale, telling it as he'd heard it as a child from his nurse, one of Pollett's sisters. "A grandee's daughter called Donna Ana, the most beautiful woman in King Philip's empire."

"She fell in love with Black Jack at first sight?"

"No, she fought him tooth and nail. But Jack wanted her and brought her back to Penrhyn as his bride."

"Don't tell me she pined for Spain and died a melancholy death far from everything she loved?"

"Now what sort of romantic legend is that?"

"The sort I don't like to hear."

An amused sound emerged from his throat. So dangerous, letting himself relax with her. But sweeter than the rich Indian confectionery he remembered from the bazaars. "After a battle royal, she fell in love with her Cornish pirate and gave him ten healthy children. He lived into old age as a faithful and devoted husband."

Sarah's smile filled with unguarded delight. He felt as though he stood in a shaft of summer sunlight, for all it was a cold February day. "That's lovely."

Her response didn't surprise him. He knew she was a romantic. Look at how she romanticized him.

"I suspect in reality their marriage was much like anyone else's." Gideon stifled his own boyish fascination with his swashbuckling ancestor. Misguided romanticism had already cost him everything that made life worthwhile.

Her smile faded. "No. It was a grand passion, so their life together was a grand adventure." She must have guessed he meant to argue for a more prosaic interpretation because she rushed into speech. "Is there a picture of Donna Ana?"

Gideon gestured to the opposite wall. The small panel on wood depicted a dumpy woman wearing an unflattering black gown from the reign of James Stuart. "There."

Sarah spent some time staring into the woman's plump, lined face. He moved to stand behind her, not close enough to touch. "Are you disappointed?"

Of course she must be. The most beautiful girl in the Spanish Empire had turned into a middle-aged frump. If Donna Ana ever was beautiful. Perhaps family mythology embroidered that part of the tale. Perhaps Jack just married this little hen to secure her Spanish gold. The wealth he seized from the galleon was real enough. The proof was all around them in Penrhyn's faded glory.

"No, I'm not disappointed," Sarah said softly, turning to face him. "She looks like she led a happy life even though she was far from home and family. She must have loved her wild husband and her brood of children."

In this dusty room with its beautiful parquetry floor, dark paneling, and elaborate plaster ceiling, Sarah was the only thing truly alive. She burned like a flame. His eyes feverishly drank her in. Satiny hair pulled back in a plait. Great, glowing eyes. Her cheap gown hinted at the untold riches of her body beneath.

Her cheap, torn, dirty gown.

He scowled. "Good God, woman, what are you wearing?"

A flush rose in her cheeks, and she self-consciously tweaked her faded skirts. "It was all I had."

"I asked the housekeeper to find you something."

She made a face. "Mrs. Pollett is three times my size. She lent me a couple of dresses, but they were hopeless. The nightdress was so big, it wouldn't stay up."

He stiffened. All over. Darkness edged his vision. His mind burned with scorching images of Sarah's shift sliding to the ground with a sensual whisper. Leaving her bare and beautiful and ready for him.

He cleared his throat, clenched his fists, and battled for control.

Her color became more hectic, and her hands rose to her cheeks. "I shouldn't have said that."

Gideon swallowed and strove to concentrate on the least

arousing objects he could think of. Radishes. Turnips. Cabbages. Carrots.

No, not carrots.

"No . . ." He cleared his throat again. "No, you shouldn't."

"You won't believe this, but I wasn't dragged up under a bush," she mumbled.

He knew what he'd like to do with her under a bush. Or what he'd like to do if he was a whole man and able to turn his desire into action.

He struggled for a normal tone as wanton images of Sarah naked and eager rocketed through his mind. "My mother's clothing is packed in the attics. Would you like to see if any is suitable? You can't run around in that rag for the next three weeks."

Sarah pointed to a gold-framed picture along the same wall as Black Jack's. "Is that your mother?"

"Yes."

As he'd known she would, she wandered down to stand in front of the exquisite Lawrence. The woman in the portrait wore one of the diaphanous gowns popular at the end of the last century. Blond hair curled softly around her delicate face.

"She's very pretty."

"In her first season, she was considered a diamond of the first water. She was only eighteen when she married my father."

"Is he the rather florid man in the next picture?"

"Yes. And my brother Harry is the fellow next to him, who looks like a younger version of his sire."

His gut tightened with the usual contradictory emotions as he studied Sir Barker and Harry. Regret, certainly. A complex brew of grief and anger. The futile wish that at least a trace of warmth had marked his interactions with his family.

"You don't look like either of your parents."

"My father might have wanted to proclaim me bastard, but the proof of my mother's fidelity is in this gallery."

Interspersed with more conventional-looking faces, Black Jack's piratical features looked out at the world, sometimes in daughters of the house, more often in sons. Black Trevithicks were usually male. Their faces were everywhere, under cavalier curls or bag wigs. Intelligent, knowing black eyes. Lazy, confident smiles.

Sarah tipped her head to the side, surveying his mother. "She looks sad."

Gideon was surprised Sarah sensed the picture's melancholy. He found himself telling her what he'd never told another person. "My father wasn't an easy man. What little I've learned of their union indicates an infelicitous match. My brother's delivery was difficult, and the doctors advised separate bedrooms. But my father insisted on his rights, so three years and four miscarriages later, I arrived."

"And she slipped away." Sarah returned her attention to the portrait. "How tragic."

"Yes, it was."

Would his childhood have been different if his mother had lived? She'd been a gentle woman with intellectual tastes. He'd always believed he inherited his love of learning from her.

"You don't mind if I wear her clothes?"

He shrugged. "She was unfailingly kind. Everyone who knew her agreed on that. My father viewed her generous nature as a sign of weakness. The villagers, though, loved her and still speak of her fondly. She'd be the first to offer her wardrobe to a lady in distress."

"I would have liked your mother." Sarah's smile was tinged with compassion.

He tensed. His pride revolted at her pity.

"Come up to the attics," he said sharply, and tried to ignore the way her eyes once more darkened with hurt.

He turned on his heel to stalk out of the gallery and along the dim corridor that ran through the back of the house. She scurried to keep pace with his long stride. Without speaking, they climbed a series of ever-narrowing stairways lit by dirty mullioned windows.

Outside the last door, Gideon lifted two candlesticks from a niche. He lit the candles and passed one to Sarah, who waited slightly breathless at his side. He stifled a pang of guilt. It wasn't long since she'd endured a savage beating, and yesterday she'd nearly fallen off a cliff. He should have more consideration than to rush her through the house at top speed.

Still, his tone was brusque. "Here. It's dark up there."

"Thank you."

Silently, she followed him up the final precipitous staircase. He entered the attics ahead of her and halted abruptly as a thousand memories overwhelmed him.

The smell was exactly the same. Dust. Old dry wood. Fusty air. Painfully reminding him of boyhood misery.

"Heavens, you could fit a village up here." Sarah stepped closer but thank God, didn't touch him. Still her vibrant presence stirred his blood to turbulence.

Against his will, he looked at her. Flickering candlelight transformed her into a creature of dark mystery. Turned her great hazel eyes into bottomless pools. Gilded a cheekbone as she tilted her head with open curiosity to survey the cavernous area.

"It's where I studied when I was a boy." He raised his candle to illuminate a corner under the sloping roof. "Nobody's touched it since I was last here. Look."

Sarah moved closer to the untidy pile of books stacked near the ragged blanket he'd used in winter. In January, the attics had been as cold as an ice cave in hell. "You wanted to get away from your father."

He cast her a sharp glance. "He hated having a bookish son. But no number of beatings changed me. I was stubborn."

"You were strong. You *are* strong."

He could have argued but didn't. "Luckily, most of the year I was away at school."

"Do you know where your mother's belongings are?"

He pointed to some trunks against the wall. "They haven't been shifted either. My father's and brother's things are downstairs. It's such a big house, I hardly need the room."

"It's a house meant for children," she said quietly. "Lots of them."

He tensed, wondering if she meant to pursue the subject of marriage again but she said no more. Relief trickled through his veins.

"Let's hope the mice haven't got to everything." He strode across to unlatch the first trunk. Anything to break the web of intimacy slowly spinning between them.

"I can't smell mice. Your cats must be ferocious hunters."

"Under my father's and brother's careless regime, they had to be to keep their bellies full." He flung back the heavy lid with a bang. Immediately faded scents crammed his senses. Lavender to keep the clothes fresh. A faint echo of rose fragrance that must have belonged to his mother.

Sarah stepped softly to his side. "I feel like she's here."

"So do I." His voice was flat with control. He placed his candle on the trunk behind. Sarah must see how his hands shook. She couldn't miss the way the flame wavered in the airless room.

Reluctantly, he began to sift through the trunk's contents. Bonnets. Hats. Scarves. Handkerchiefs. Stockings. Shoes. Soft kidskin gloves that had shaped themselves to his mother's hands. Hands he'd never touched.

Finally, at the bottom, he found neatly folded clothing. His gloved hand brushed heavy silk, and he carefully lifted what proved to be an evening cloak. As the shining blue fabric unfurled, a gust of rose perfume drifted into the still room.

He'd never touched his mother's things before. It had seemed somehow wrong to pry into her private possessions. Although he'd always known which trunks were hers.

Carefully, he laid the cloak aside. Behind him he was vaguely aware of Sarah's footfall as she explored the attic. Then suddenly light bloomed around him.

"This might help." She set the lantern down near him.

"It's the one I used to read by."

"I found it with your books." She knelt, her shoulder inches from his.

He desperately wanted to tell her to move away. She was close enough for little eddies of scent to tease him, her peppery carnation fragrance mingling with the evocative rose. She was close enough for him to hear the uneven rhythm of her breathing.

Did his proximity disturb her as hers disturbed him? Sweet God, this became more impossible with every second. Briefly he shut his eyes and prayed for strength. When he opened them again, Sarah pored over the items he'd discarded on the floor.

"Everything is so delicate," she said softly. "Like it was made by angels. Look." She held up a filmy shawl of lace fragile as a spider's web.

He reached out to touch the fabric, then jerked back. All his life, his mother's gentle ghost had haunted him. Touching her clothing made her tragedy poignantly immediate.

He struggled to inject a prosaic element into his voice. "Not exactly suitable for late winter."

He had to get this over with quickly, before he made an utter fool of himself. He drew out a satin ball gown. Its rich peach color gleamed in the candlelight.

"Nor is that." Sarah's voice sounded huskier than usual. As if she'd just got out of bed, God help him. His hands curled in the slippery material.

"These must have come from her London season." Still, he strove to sound casual, unconcerned. The last thing he needed was Sarah to discover her interest in him was reciprocated. "My father never socialized. Or not with people he'd introduce to his wife. She'd have little call for a dress like this at Penrhyn."

All the gowns were too elaborate for Sarah to wear around the house. Gideon repacked the trunk, his hands lingering on the fine materials. He knew it was only imagination, but a hint of warmth from that pretty laughing girl, the toast of London, still remained. He shut the lid and turned to the next trunk.

As with the other one, accessories lay on top. He quickly riffled through them. He passed Sarah a sturdy pair of half boots. "See if those fit."

The first gown he pulled out was a sprigged muslin day dress. He stood and turned around, then wished to God he'd stayed put.

Sarah sat on the trunk they'd already checked, sliding on the shoe. Her skirts hiked to reveal two trim ankles. Petticoats frothed, white and alluring, around her shapely calves. Her thick braid tumbled over one shoulder to dangle between her breasts. As she leaned forward, her bodice gaped to reveal the pale skin of her cleavage.

His mouth went dry as sand. His heart slammed hard against his ribs. Hunger to tumble this girl on the dusty floor made him giddy. The urge to escape rose to choke him.

He must have made a noise because she turned startled eyes in his direction. "Gideon?"

Just his name. A low question. Just as he'd started calling her Sarah, somewhere she'd started calling him Gideon. He whipped around and dropped to his knees before the open trunk. His breath rattled loud in his ears as he fought to rein in the agonizing conflict inside him.

He couldn't touch her. No matter how much he wanted to. He knew what would happen. He'd frighten and disgust her.

He fumbled in the trunk, roughly pushing aside the first gown. Without looking, he grabbed something and shoved it in Sarah's direction.

"What about this?" he bit out, still not glancing at her.

"I think . . ." She paused, and he felt her take the garment from his hands. "I think if I'm not to shock the servants, I might need something a little more substantial."

He sucked in a deep breath and blinked to clear the haze from his eyes. Carefully he turned. She stood watching him with a complex mixture of hunger and trepidation. The boot had toppled over and lay on the floor near the trunk. She clutched a filmy chemise in front of her.

God give him strength. He refused to picture that sheer scrap of cream silk clinging to Sarah's lissome body. He straight-out refused.

Gideon gritted his teeth until his jaw ached and tried to quash the bawdy images filling his mind. His face itched as hot color rose in an unstoppable tide. He was acting like a damned fool.

Her voice had been light, amused. Perhaps she hadn't noticed his turmoil. Then he looked into her eyes and read secret knowledge in the hazel depths. She sensed he responded to her as a man responded to a woman. It frightened her—fear lurked in her gaze too—but not enough to send her fleeing back downstairs.

"Your pardon." His voice sounded rusty. "I meant to give you this."

Clumsily, he handed her the muslin. She ventured closer to drop the chemise back into the trunk, then she studied the dress.

"What do you think?" She held it up for his consideration.

Good Lord, she couldn't torment him deliberately, could she? She looked so utterly innocent and unconcerned. Which, now his brain returned to something approximating working order, struck him as cursed suspicious.

"It doesn't matter what I think," he said in a clipped tone. "Will it fit you?"

"It looks like it might. The shoes didn't. Your mother had much daintier feet than I." She lifted her skirt a few inches and circled her bare foot in demonstration.

The witch! She tortured him for her own amusement. If he could bear to touch her, he'd bloody well strangle her.

If he could bear to touch her, he wouldn't strangle her. He'd ravish her within an inch of her life.

It suddenly struck him, as it should have struck him long before, that being up here alone with Sarah was a very bad idea indeed. He'd thought to find her a couple of things to wear and escape with no consequences. That now seemed an absurdly optimistic plan.

Hell, he had to get out of here. Now.

The attics had appeared so spacious when he first set foot in them. Now they felt oppressive, crowded, closing in on him.

When all the time he knew what closed in on him was insatiable desire.

He stumbled to his feet with clumsy haste. Tension formed a painful line across his shoulders. "Everything you need is in this trunk. I'll get the servants to bring it to your room."

She flinched at his tone, then leaned near to replace the items they'd removed. Near enough for her skirts to brush his legs with a subtle sensual whisper. Sarah's warm, womanly scent momentarily submerged his mother's rose perfume.

In spite of his best intentions, he closed his eyes and inhaled. It was the fragrance of paradise. And he, poor sinner, was locked in perpetual agony outside the gates.

He shouldn't have hesitated. He should have made a run for it while he could. Blast her, he shouldn't have come up here in the first place. Mrs. Pollett could just as easily have shown her the trunks.

When he opened his eyes, she stood before him, her face uplifted, her lips parted, her arms outstretched. Her face was stark with need and vulnerability and a desperate, hard-won courage.

He couldn't mistake what she wanted.

Even that recognition didn't shift him. Every limb was heavy as lead. Denial jammed in his throat and emerged as a groan. He staggered back, but she'd already begun her forward momentum.

He twisted awkwardly to evade her but she grabbed his arms. Her fingers curled into his flesh in inescapable talons. Blind horror held him paralyzed.

"Gideon, please," she said in a broken voice that made his gut cramp with guilt and sinful longing.

Her slim, tender body slammed into his. Her slender arms,

surprisingly strong, wrapped around his neck. Her heady scent rocked his brain, scattering rational thought.

Shaking, he clutched her waist, crazy with the need to push her off him. But his will failed at the final moment.

She tensed as she stretched up. The damp, seeking heat of her mouth pressed against his.

He stood motionless under her clumsy, passionate assault. Fiery pleasure streaked through him like summer lightning. Automatically his hands tightened around her waist, and he tugged her closer.

For one blazing second, he lost himself in the sizzling kiss. Darkness. Pleasure. Sweetness. Heat.

His blood pumped, his skin burned. His mouth moved in cautious answer to her furious, unpracticed ardor. He couldn't mistake her inexperience, or her passion. He guessed she had no idea what she invited when she launched herself at him.

If he'd been a normal man.

Although right now, he damn well felt like a normal man. He felt like a man overcome with lust. A man who kissed the woman he wanted more than his life.

Clamoring questions exploded in his mind. Had a miracle occurred? Had incendiary desire at last vanquished the ghosts of Rangapindhi?

His starved senses filled with the glory of her. The clinging pressure of her grip around his neck. Her soft breasts crushed to his chest. The carnation scent. The taste of her mouth. Fresh like the sea. Hot like fire.

The warmth was delicious. Astonishing.

He moved his lips in a more purposeful response. A shudder of excitement rippled through her, and she pressed closer. He surrendered to overwhelming pleasure.

It was too late.

Savage, rending wraiths clawed to the surface. The firm youthful flesh under his palms turned cold and slimy. The lush mouth pressed against his stretched into a rictus grin. The sweet scents of flowers and the sea drowned in stinking decay.

Frantically, he fought the suffocating blackness. *Don't let this happen now. Dear God, not now. Not when he had her in his arms at last.*

His muscles spasmed into pain. The nightmare images stole awareness. He wrenched his mouth from hers. He shook like a rabid dog. "Let me go," he choked out.

She didn't seem to hear. Instead, she moved closer.

He couldn't endure this. He had to stop it.

"Damn it, I said let me go," he snarled. With unsteady hands, he ruthlessly dragged her arms from around his neck.

She resisted, though it must hurt her. "No. Please, Gideon, no."

His voice broke with desperation. "For God's sake, Sarah, leave me be!"

Through the devils screeching in his head, he felt her sudden stillness. She pulled back far enough for him to catch the bright agony in her eyes. And the gradually dawning realization that he was in earnest.

Still, she didn't release him.

With sudden roughness, he heaved her out of his way and headed for the stairs. He needed air. He needed solitude. His gut heaved with acrid nausea. His hands shook so badly, he couldn't trust himself to pick up the candles.

"Wait."

He tried to ignore her ragged plea. Every particle of his being craved escape.

"Please don't go like this." Through the buzzing in his ears, he heard her rush after him. Against his will he stopped, hunching his shoulders against her.

"Never do that again." His voice was hoarse and raw. His fists opened and closed in an idiot rhythm at his sides.

"I don't understand."

The bewildered despair in her words harrowed his heart. He wounded her and he regretted it to the base of his soul.

Oh, Sarah, Sarah, what have you done with your recklessness?

"I know you don't." He still couldn't bear to look at her.

He could hardly bear to breathe the same air. "I don't either, not really."

He ached all over as if he had a fever. Only the last remnants of stubborn Trevithick pride kept him upright. At least now she didn't touch him, he gained some control over his nausea. It would be the ultimate defeat if he lost his breakfast in front of her.

"Is it me?" Her voice shook with anguish. "You keep saying it's not."

He wished to heaven she were another woman, one who would blush and scuttle away to hide her humiliation. But another woman wouldn't set herself so impulsively after what she wanted.

However misguided that wanting was.

"No," he forced out. His blood pounded like heavy surf after a wild storm, blocking out everything else.

Except Sarah.

He was agonizingly conscious of her standing behind him. Of every jagged breath she drew. Of how close she was to tears.

"I don't believe you. I disgust you."

"No!" Turning his head in her direction was harder than turning back the tide.

For the first time, he saw her clearly. She was haggard, and silent tears ran down her white cheeks. The trails shimmered in the uncertain gold light.

He wanted to say so much, tell her everything. Explain, excuse, soothe, comfort.

None of it would do any good. None of it would change him into a man worthy to call her his.

So he said again the only thing he could. "No."

"Then why . . ." She made a helpless gesture with one trembling hand.

"Sarah . . ."

The thunder in his ears became louder. He closed his eyes and prayed he'd dredge up the right words. Though he knew there were no right words to be found.

Then he realized the thunder wasn't entirely in his imagination. Someone clattered up the stairs to the attic. Someone heavy and wearing boots.

"Sir Gideon!"

"Tulliver?" The intrusion came from another world.

The usually impassive Tulliver reached the top of the staircase and stood panting. "Strangers riding up the drive. The local magistrate is with them."

Nine

W hat the devil happened to the men watching the road?" Gideon snapped.

Charis flinched at Gideon's anger, then realized just what Tulliver said. Terror locked every muscle. Her stepbrothers had found her. Because who else would visit Penrhyn with an officer of the law? She braced herself to run. But where could she go?

Dear Lord, could this vile day get any worse? In her belly, fear, humiliation, and, to her disgust, frustrated desire stewed in a bilious mixture. Despair, heavy, draining, black and thick as tar, leaked into her soul.

"They came to warn us quick smart enough." She knew Tulliver noted her tears but with his usual consideration, after the first glance, he kept his attention on Gideon. "But nobody could find you or the lass. We searched high and low to no avail."

"Hell," Gideon breathed. "I'm sorry, Tulliver. I should have told someone where I was. This disaster is my blasted fault."

"What do you want to do?" Tulliver was back to sounding his imperturbable self.

Gideon straightened and sent his henchman a flashing grin that reminded Charis of Black Jack. Just thus must the reckless privateer have faced down the Spanish galleon that carried his destiny. The shaking, distraught man of seconds ago might never have existed.

Black Jack had prevailed. So would Gideon.

Courage leached back, stiffening her backbone. Gideon might reject her, but her faith in him remained unshaken. He was her Percival, her Galahad, her Lancelot. From the first moment she'd seen him, he'd been her bulwark. After all they'd been through, he wouldn't let her fall into her stepbrothers' hands.

"Why, I'll greet them like the gentlemen they are."

He turned to Charis, and she couldn't mistake the searching inspection he gave her. As if checking whether her mettle was up to this.

She raised her chin and sent him a straight look. She was mortally afraid, but she refused to succumb to fear. "That means tossing them in the cesspit."

Gideon gave a curiously lighthearted laugh. She could only interpret the spark in his dark eyes as admiration. "That's my girl."

He waited for her to put her shoe on, then blew out the candles and gestured her toward the steps. It cut her to the bone that he still couldn't bear to lay a hand on her. After her antics today, he'd probably never touch her again.

Oh, Charis, you've got more important things to worry about right now than the fact you made a fool of yourself.

Gideon collected the lantern and followed her down to the gallery. He pressed an unremarkable plaster molding near the fireplace.

"Heavens," Charis breathed, as a secret latch clicked and what looked like an innocent section of paneling turned out to be a door. "A priest's hole."

"A smuggler's stash, more like. If you stay quietly here,

nobody will find you." His voice dropped. "I give you my word I'll keep you safe. Trust me."

She looked into his eyes. The pain and confusion and anger that had gripped him upstairs had vanished. Instead, he looked calm and determined and, most reassuring of all, completely confident.

"I trust you." She meant it from the depths of her soul. Odd to think she trusted him more than she'd trusted anyone since her father's death. Even after the way he'd recoiled from her kiss.

"Good." He gave her the lantern and watched her step into the recess. Except it wasn't a recess at all but a landing off steps leading downward.

The door closed behind her. For a moment, stark, illogical terror gripped her. What if something happened to Gideon and Tulliver and nobody knew she was here? What if she ended up trapped behind this wall forever?

A soft knock on the panel interrupted her flight into panic. "Are you all right?"

Just the sound of Gideon's deep voice calmed her galloping heart. She was a hopeless case to be so in love with a man who couldn't bear her merest touch. How she wished she could help what she felt, but she'd been utterly lost from the moment he'd rescued her in Winchester.

"Yes."

"You can listen to what happens in the drawing room if you go down a level. If you want to get out, the passage leads to a cave on the beach."

'Thank you." She didn't mean just for his reassuring information.

"It's nothing," he said, dismissing her gratitude as he always did.

She heard his boots click on the parquetry floor as he retreated. Then a more ominous sound. The great iron knocker on the oak front door pounded once, twice.

❧

"Shall I send the bastards on their way?" Tulliver cracked his knuckles.

Gideon laughed softly. "No. Let's play these hyenas the civilized way. At least at first. Show them into the drawing room and say I'll be there presently."

"What are your plans? The lass is safe enough where she is."

"I think it's about time I got some benefit from being the bloody Hero of Rangapindhi."

Tulliver's eyes glinted with his rare humor. "Aye, guvnor. It is about time and all."

Downstairs, Mrs. Pollett opened the door. Gideon didn't wait to watch her greet the arrivals but scaled the steps to his bedroom two at a time. In his heart, savage satisfaction beat like a drum.

At last his enemies would have faces. Sarah's stepbrothers were foes he could fight and defeat. After that vile debacle in the attics, he welcomed an unambiguous purpose. The kiss changed everything between him and Sarah, yet it changed nothing. He grimly recognized that stark reality, yet still the physical aftermath lingered to torment him. His lips tingled, his skin itched, his gut cramped. And rapacious desire was a roiling eddy in his blood.

He left his unwelcome guests cooling their heels long enough to put them on edge. He had no fears they'd take it into their heads to search for Sarah on their own. Tulliver guarded the door from the hallway. So Gideon's insouciant air as he sauntered into the drawing room twenty minutes later wasn't entirely pretense. Sir John Holland, the local magistrate, turned to greet him with barely concealed relief.

"Sir John, pleased to see you." Gideon stepped forward and forced himself to accept the middle-aged fellow's brief handshake. His flesh crawled at the contact but with an effort, he concealed the reaction.

Sir John looked irritated but not overly worried, which meant this visit was more reconnoiter than hostile raid. "Sir Gideon. I haven't seen you since you were a stripling. Now you've set the world on its ear, begad. You must come to dinner and tell Lady Susan and me all about your adventures." He suddenly sobered. "Sorry to hear about your pater and Sir Harold, of course. Mustn't forget the sad circumstances that brought you back to us."

"Sir John, is this a social call?" The game commenced. Gideon intended to reveal nothing he didn't have to.

The man straightened and cast an annoyed glance at his two companions. "Not entirely, although been meaning to pay my respects."

There was an awkward pause. In his best rake-of-the-ton manner, Gideon arched his eyebrows at the two strangers, who stood in silent menace behind Sir John.

Of course, he'd studied them from the moment he'd entered the room. Just as they'd studied him.

He noted their surprise at his elegance. Thank God for the London tailors he'd patronized upon his return from Rangapindhi. He wanted these wretches to realize they dealt with a man of standing.

Sir John cleared his throat uncomfortably. "Sir Gideon Trevithick, may I present Hubert Farrell, Lord Burkett, and his brother, Lord Felix Farrell?"

Lord Burkett? Good God, the older brother was a bloody marquess. Sarah had kept that salient piece of information to herself.

Gideon had known a large amount of money was in question, and he'd guessed she must come from the gentry at the very least. Until now, he hadn't realized he tangled with the aristocracy's upper echelons.

"Delighted, I'm sure, " Gideon said with deliberate boredom, returning the Farrells' chilly bows with a dismissive bow of his own.

Lord Burkett was in his late twenties, large, powerful, brutish, although already his heavily muscled frame turned to fat. Gideon bit back his sick fury as he pictured those thick hands pummeling Sarah's tender flesh. Lord Felix, younger by a year or two, was slight, fair, and handsome.

Burkett looked confused. Felix looked suspicious. Even on such short acquaintance, Gideon recognized Lord Felix as the more dangerous of the two.

"Get to the meat of the matter, Holland," Burkett demanded.

"As I said, I'm sure Sir Gideon doesn't know . . ."

Burkett glared at Gideon and spoke over the magistrate. "We've lost our sister, Lady Charis Weston."

Gideon sat with a show of nonchalance and gestured to his visitors to do the same. Although his impulse was to throw the brothers out on their blue-blooded rumps once he'd delivered a well-deserved beating. After that agonizing scene upstairs with Sarah, he itched to work his turmoil out in violence. Nobody deserved a pasting more than these bastards.

Sir John took the sofa near the fireplace. Lord Felix selected a chair nearby. Burkett remained standing in the center of the room, a bullish, aggressive presence. How in the name of all that was holy had Sarah survived the rough guardianship of these villains?

Then he realized what Burkett had said. Sarah apparently wasn't his charge's real name.

Charis Weston.

Lord Felix's attention fixed on his face, seeking guilt or fear. *Keep looking, hellspawn,* Gideon told him silently. Compared to the Nawab of Rangapindhi, Felix was a toy.

Without difficulty, he maintained his disinterested drawl. "Commiserations. Although I'm not sure how that's my concern."

"You were seen with her in Winchester and Portsmouth," Felix said sharply. He tried to hide it, but desperation to lay his hands on Charis seeped from his tense frame. "I imagine she told you a pack of lies about needing help. She's a flighty piece, almost feebleminded, who ran off in a fit of pique. We seek her for her own good before she comes to harm. Is she here?"

Damn, their departure from Winchester must have been observed although he'd been so careful. Gideon kept his voice even. "Ah, you mean the poor waif I gave transport to on her way to her aunt in Portsmouth?"

"She has no aunt in Portsmouth," Burkett growled, taking a step closer. He was clearly accustomed to using his bulk to intimidate.

Gideon shrugged. "That was her story in Winchester. Chit claimed she'd been set upon by footpads. She was in a bad way. Knocked about."

Burkett shifted uncomfortably, but Felix's eyes remained cold and intent. Gideon retained his bland expression as he privately consigned them both to Hades.

"I grieve to hear that. A lone woman on the road faces many dangers. That's why we're eager to return her to her loving family." Felix made a creditable attempt at sounding concerned.

"Commendable," Gideon murmured, cursing the oily bastard for a liar and a fraud. The bruises on Sarah's—no, Charis's—face were testament to how *loving* her family was.

"As we haven't found her on the road to Penrhyn, we can only surmise she's staying with you. Pray send for her. We'll end this lamentable episode and any inconvenience you suffer, Sir Gideon." As he stood, Lord Felix's tone became if anything more unctuous. Gideon suppressed a shudder of loathing. "Clearly you're a man of honor, and a lady is safe in your company. But the world may not be so kind in its assessment. Our sister's reputation is at stake, so we'd appreciate your keeping details of this unfortunate incident mum."

Gideon struggled not to plant his fist in Felix's smug face. But he'd learned self-control in the hardest school. His response gave no indication of his abhorrence for these men. "I'd love to help you, my dear fellow. If indeed this girl is your sister." He let his tone descend into regret. "But she ran off after the ruckus in Portsmouth. My man and I tried to find her but with no success. I suspect she's still there."

"You expect us to believe you abandoned a defenseless woman?" Felix hissed, clenching his fists by his sides.

Gideon shrugged again although he already knew his careless act didn't convince the younger Farrell. "I assumed she'd gone to her aunt."

"But she hasn't got an aunt in Portsmouth," Burkett repeated, as if the fact made some difference.

"She told me she did. She was most adamant that Portsmouth was her destination."

"Because she thought to disappear there," Felix said between his teeth. "It's a port city. Nobody would pay her attention."

Gideon raised his eyebrows again. "That's a clever scheme for someone who's feebleminded. Devil take me if it's not."

"That's not at issue," Felix snapped. "What is at issue is that we are her legal guardians, and if you harbor her, Sir Gideon, you break the law and will pay the penalty."

"Steady on, Lord Felix!" Sir John protested, rising from his seat.

Gideon ignored the slur on his honor. His voice turned silky. "Which I'm sure is why I have the inestimable pleasure not only of your company but of the magistrate's. I'm surprised you didn't invite the militia along to infest the front hall."

"If circumstances compel us to use force, we will," Felix said steadily. He sent a meaningful glance to Sir John, who looked increasingly uncomfortable at the conversation's prickly turn. "As a representative of the law, you'll back us, Sir John."

Sir John cleared his throat and cast a nervous glance at Gideon. Gideon guessed what went through his mind. He'd known the Trevithicks all his life and recognized their local influence. The Farrells might be powerful men on the nation's stage, but they didn't live on his doorstep.

"There's no need for unpleasantness, gentlemen." Sir John directed a pleading stare at Gideon. "If Sir Gideon gives us his word that the girl you believe to be Lady Charis ran away in Portsmouth, we must be satisfied."

"Be damned to that," Burkett objected, taking a threatening step in Gideon's direction. His hands opened and closed at his sides as if he restrained himself from grabbing Gideon and beating the truth from him. *Poor Charis, at this brute's mercy.* Gideon could hardly bear imagining it. "She's the richest heiress in England. He's keeping her for his own gain."

The richest heiress in England? Hell and damnation, what had he got himself mixed up with?

The blasted girl had hidden a lot from him. None of which shook his determination to help her. He wouldn't hand a stray cat over to the Farrells, let alone a woman he admired and . . . cared for.

"Do you doubt my bond, sir?" Gideon rose to his full height.

Burkett was big and brawny, but Gideon topped him by several inches. Gideon also had the steel lent by years of living with endless danger. Burkett didn't frighten him in the least. He could break the overweening bully without a thought.

As Gideon had expected, Burkett backed down. "You haven't given us your word." He sounded sulky.

Gideon's voice was firm. "I give you my word the girl I knew as Sarah Watson ran away in Portsmouth. There's no guarantee the chit I encountered is even your sister."

"What did she look like?" Lord Felix asked.

"Small. Skinny. Bruised. Light brown hair. Spoke with a rough accent." It was possible someone had got a close look at Charis. He couldn't stray too far from the truth without awakening suspicion. "I can't for the life of me imagine she's an heiress. Her clothing was poor and her manners deplorable."

"She played a part," Felix insisted.

"I have no idea. What I do know is she took off after the brawl, and I haven't seen her since. If you believe this girl really is your sister—which I take leave to doubt—you'd be better concentrating your search in Portsmouth."

"Can we check the house?" Burkett asked stubbornly.

"No, by God," Gideon snapped. "I'll be damned if I let a

pair of strangers march through my private rooms on a wild-goose chase after some featherbrained bit of muslin."

Burkett puffed out his impressive chest. "You insult my sister, sir."

"I do no such thing. Confound it, I don't know your sister. The world has come to a pretty pass when a man is harassed on his own property for offering aid to a distressed maid-servant."

"Sir Gideon has given us his word," Sir John said placat-ingly. "Surely that's good enough."

Felix spread his hands to indicate his benevolent inten-tions. "Sir John, we act purely from brotherly concern. If we satisfy ourselves she's never been in this house, we'll leave Sir Gideon in peace, with our gratitude and apologies."

Good God, but the younger Farrell was a slimy customer. He sounded so reasonable. If Gideon hadn't seen the marks on Charis's face, he'd almost believe the weasel's protesta-tions.

"Sir Gideon, surely under the circumstances . . ." Sir John looked across at him hopefully.

Time to play the hero card. Gideon straightened and let outrage infuse his reply. "When I left this country to risk my life in its service, an Englishman's home was his castle. Unless you intend to invoke the full power of the law, Sir John, I must on principle refuse this monstrous imposition on my rights. I have returned after years of danger and depri-vation beyond mortal imagination. Was it to face tyranny in my own homeland? Surely not. If so, His Majesty will hear of it. When he knighted me for my services to the Crown, he was most effusive about his gratitude and favor."

"So you refuse?" Felix's voice was dangerous. His eyes didn't waver from Gideon.

"Look here, Lord Felix," Sir John said. "Sir Gideon is a national hero. You can't barge into his house unannounced and insist on turning the place upside down. Good Lord, man, we're not even sure the girl he picked up in Winchester is Lady Charis. Sir Gideon's description leads me to believe she can't possibly be a lady. He's a man of great perspicacity. If he says she was a serving wench, my bet is that's exactly what she was."

"We only seek to confirm your story," Lord Burkett said sullenly.

"A gentleman's statement should suffice." Gideon turned toward the door. "Now I am no longer at leisure."

"You haven't heard the end of this, Sir Gideon." Felix spoke as if addressing a minion.

The urge to knock Felix to the ground was so strong, Gideon could taste it. With difficulty, he maintained his lordly tone and kept his hands to himself. "I suggest you return to Portsmouth and pursue more fruitful leads there, my lords. You've come a long way for nothing."

"Topping idea." Sir John rubbed his hands together nervously as he stepped up to Gideon, obviously eager to end this encounter. "I'm sure the lady is in Portsmouth. Or safe at home, now she's discovered life away from her family is no picnic."

Felix pulled on his leather gloves with a slow deliberation Gideon knew was meant to constitute a threat. His tone was deliberate too. "We'll return to Portsmouth to pick up the trail. But if it leads us back here, my dear Sir Gideon, your renown won't save you from the consequences. Good day, sir." After an insolent bow, he strode out, his older brother shambling in his wake.

Sir John stayed behind and muttered under his breath. "Sir Gideon, most regrettable incident. Two unpleasant young men. I pray they find their troublesome sister and don't bother us again. The Farrells always were a thoroughly bad lot. Father was a drunkard and gambler. Left the sons nothing but a mountain of debts and the wardship of young Lady Charis, the Earl of Marley's heiress. Hope the poor chit is safe."

"You're very well informed, Sir John."

"The late Lord Burkett was notorious. The sons are chips off the old block. I wouldn't trouble you, except they have their rights. They're the chit's legal guardians. Lord Felix was correct. Anyone keeping her from them breaks the law." He paused and frowned. "Of course, I knew a gentleman such as yourself couldn't possibly be involved. Good God, you've hardly been back in the country a month. Barely time to unpack, let alone get entangled with a runaway heiress. That's what I told those two braggarts. But they wouldn't take the word of a mere country squire." He put on his hat with a disgruntled gesture and collected his stick from near the mantel. "Come to dinner once you've settled in."

"I'll look forward to it," Gideon said, showing Sir John the door.

Outside in the foyer, Tulliver stood stolidly guarding the two Farrells, who looked annoyed. Gideon guessed they'd tried to take advantage of his conversation with Sir John to do some reconnaissance.

"Good day, Sir Gideon. Our apologies for disturbing you." Sir John ushered his companions outside. Gideon followed and stood on the steps to make sure the Farrells left. He sent a groom after them to confirm they didn't return. He trusted Charis's stepbrothers as little as they trusted him.

"Get the girl out of her hiding place," he said to Tulliver, when they were alone.

"Do you want to see her, guvnor?"

"Not immediately. Tell her I'll talk to her in the library before dinner. In the meantime, have my mother's trunks brought down to her room and tell the maids to burn that rag she's wearing."

"What do I say about yon smarmy buggers?"

Gideon stared down the drive, empty now of Felix and Hubert and the reluctantly involved Sir John. When he replied to Tulliver, his voice was steady and very sure. "Tell her I've pledged myself to her safety. She has nothing to worry about."

With a sudden spurt of energy, he leaped down the steps to the courtyard. He turned left through the stone arch and headed for the windswept cliffs.

Ten

Her stomach somersaulting with nerves, Charis approached the library. This afternoon from behind the wall, she'd listened to Gideon keep Felix and Hubert at bay. She'd silently cheered his cleverness and bravery. But how would he greet her this evening? He'd discovered she was the richest heiress in England. Would she glimpse greed in his eyes as she'd glimpsed greed in so many men's eyes?

Or worse, would she see disgust as he recalled the way she'd flung herself into his arms?

Sick humiliation made her hesitate, trembling outside the closed door. For one blazing moment in the attic, she'd believed he felt the ineffable connection between them. It had been a mistake she'd bitterly repented since.

Courage, Charis.

Stiffening her shoulders, she wiped her damp palms on her skirts and quietly let herself into the dimly lit library.

Gideon didn't immediately notice her arrival. He stood near the grate, staring down at the fire with a somber expression. From the shadows on the edge of the room, her gaze hungrily traced the flame-gilded angles of his face, the lean power of his body. He was dressed more formally than usual, in a dark blue superfine coat and biscuit trousers. He looked like the elegant man she'd met rather than the dashing, disheveled pirate she'd come to know at Penrhyn.

The memory of the brief, dazzling heat of his mouth overwhelmed thought. Then she recalled how he'd wrenched away as if she carried some contagious disease.

Shame choked her. She could hardly believe she'd launched herself at him like that. But he'd been so close, and she'd longed so keenly to feel his embrace. And for one doomed, misguided instant, she'd imagined he wanted her as much as she wanted him.

Poor pathetic fool she was.

Slowly, Gideon looked up, as though reluctant to abandon his reflections. He must also be reluctant to face the woman who had forced herself on him.

She braced to confront anger or scorn, but his serious black gaze focused on her without a hint of condemnation. Or covetousness.

"Good evening, Lady Charis," he said calmly.

She was heart-stoppingly aware this was the first time he'd used her real name. In spite of all her stern lectures to herself, she shivered with pleasure when that dark velvet voice said *Charis*.

"Good evening." On unsteady legs, she inched farther into the room. She was torn by painful longing to be with him and a cowardly desire to flee.

Gideon's eyes widened as she entered the circle of light cast by the candelabra, and he at last took in her appearance. Because she'd felt like she faced an executioner, pride prompted her to dress in her best. Or in his mother's best. A wide blue silk ribbon fastened the filmy white gown under her breasts. With Dorcas's help, she'd put her hair up in a loose mass, leaving strands to curl around her shoulders.

A flame lit Gideon's dark gaze, kindling answering fire

inside her. Familiar tension extended between them. A tension she'd learned in the most painful fashion not to trust.

How could he stare at her as if she took his breath away when he found her nearness unbearable? It was cruel.

She straightened, fighting the insidious yearning his presence invariably aroused, and spread her hands in apology. "I'm sorry I didn't tell you who I was. My inheritance makes men greedy." She should have long ago recognized Gideon was the exception to that rule.

"No matter." He laid one gloved hand on the carved marble mantelpiece. The misleading flash of desire had vanished, and his expression was cool, uninvolved. "And while I admit it's an unpleasant surprise to discover my adversaries are a marquess and his younger brother, I'd do little differently if I had the chance again."

"I nearly told you the truth so many times." Guilt was a sour taste in her mouth. What had seemed so imperative at the time now struck her as a childish, dangerous deception. Still, she tried to make him understand. "It wasn't just fear of how you'd react to who I was. I liked being Sarah Watson. She had more freedom than Lady Charis Weston ever enjoyed."

"Believe me, I understand the lure of freedom." He bent his head in thought, then glanced up to focus unwaveringly on her. "You have my word I'll do my best to keep Lady Charis at liberty too. Then in a few weeks, Lady Charis will have all the freedom she wants."

The irony was Lady Charis wanted only to stay here with Gideon. She was miserably aware that once she reached twenty-one, he had no further reason to keep her at Penrhyn. The prospect of leaving tore her heart to bleeding pieces.

"If my stepbrothers don't get me first." Fear thickened her throat, turning her voice husky. She tangled her trembling hands in her filmy skirts. "I heard you send them away, but . . ."

"They'll return. With full legal backing. I know."

"Your generosity to a stranger might cost you dear." Like a moth lured to a candle, she ventured closer. Not too close. She'd learned her lesson on that front. "You could go to prison for helping me."

"Didn't you hear Sir John? I'm a national hero." His voice was caustic and his expression bleak. "I doubt I'll be carted off to the clink. The public outcry would be deafening."

"I still shouldn't have involved you in this mess."

He sent her an uncompromising look under his marked black brows. "I despise bullies, Charis. Your stepbrothers deserve to lose."

She clenched her hands at her sides. "I can't stand the thought of your being harmed," she said fiercely. "If you come to disaster because of me, I'll never forgive myself."

His face contorted with sorrow, and he took a step toward her. "I'm not worth your pain."

"Of course you are." His constant self-abnegation infuriated her, made her ache with angry pity. He was so brave and strong and good, yet he seemed completely unaware of his true quality.

Impulsive, unstoppable words bubbled to the surface. Words she'd come close to saying so many times before. She spoke in a heated torrent before she thought to censor herself. "You're the best man I've ever known. You're magnificent. Unlike anyone else. You must know I fell in love with you the moment I saw you. I've only come to love you more every day since."

The headlong admission scorched the air from the room. Her heart slammed to a stop against her ribs. Her cheeks burned with shock and humiliation. She stood stock-still, as if her slightest movement might shatter her into a million pieces.

Dear heaven, what have I said? What have I done?

Hadn't she learned her lesson that afternoon? Her awful, awful gaucheness made her want to vanish into the floor. She'd give every penny she possessed to take back what she'd just done. But the declaration had been made. It was too late to deny it, even if she could bring herself to speak such a lie.

She did love him. She always would. He didn't love her. He couldn't even bear to touch her. But nothing changed the ineluctable truth of what she'd said.

Gideon recoiled and stared at her with what she could only interpret as horror. "Hell," he breathed.

Blindly, he fumbled toward a leather armchair and dropped into it, burying his head in his hands.

Charis felt like she suffocated. At best, she might expect her impulsive declaration to evoke understanding, at worst pity. But this broken desolation was beyond comprehension.

"Hell, hell, hell." His quiet despair reached far inside her like a hand closing around her heart and crushing it.

She was paralyzed with embarrassment. She had to keep reminding herself to breathe. Remorse, concern, self-castigation, all tangled like hissing snakes in her breast.

If he hadn't seemed so lost and tormented when he claimed his essential unworthiness, she'd never have made the reckless declaration. But the sight of him looking as if he didn't have a friend in the world had made her want to die. "I shouldn't have spoken," she said in a raw voice.

His shoulders tensed, and he raised dull eyes to look at her. "Your honesty does you credit."

Her mouth compressed as she fought not to cry. Tears wouldn't help her through this agonizing moment. "Well, I suppose that's one response to a declaration of love." Her tone was flat with control.

A muscle flickered in his cheek. "I can't give you what you want. I'm sorry."

The lump in her throat was like a great, jagged boulder. It hurt to force words past it. " 'Sorry' doesn't help."

As compassion filled his eyes, she realized she'd been right to fear his pity. She loathed the way he looked at her right now. It made her want to curl up in a dark corner and never emerge into the light again.

"You'll hate hearing this. And I know you won't believe

me. At least now." The kindness in his voice made her cringe. This was even worse than she'd expected. She guessed what he meant to tell her before he spoke.

"Charis . . ." He paused and closed his eyes as if struggling to find the words. "I'm touched and flattered by what you've said. Any man would be. You're a remarkable girl. You're . . ."

She felt sick. He lied to spare her feelings, and every false word flayed another strip from her soul. She took a step back and raised her hands to fend off his words. Why, oh, why had she let her foolish tongue run away with her? "Please, don't say any more."

Gideon's jaw firmed, and he leaned forward. Pain flared in his dark eyes and his voice was urgent. "I must. I hate to see you hurt. But what you feel, it will pass. You hardly know me. You can't love me. Not really. The way we met, it's given you a false impression. You've barely had a chance to catch breath since. When you return to a normal life, you'll . . ."

"What? Forget you?" Resentment at the futility of her dreams frayed the question.

"No." Drawing an unsteady breath, he made one of his familiar truncated gestures. "But you'll see more clearly. Right now you imagine I'm some sort of hero, but you're wrong."

"You *are* a hero." Her rubbery knees threatened to collapse under her as she ventured closer. She knew he hated that she argued, but she had to make him see himself as she saw him. "You're the famous Hero of Rangapindhi. Even my stepbrothers know who you are."

He flinched against the chair as if she struck him. "The reality of Rangapindhi was far from heroic, Sarah." He paused. "Charis. I'm sorry. You've always been Sarah to me."

She swallowed more useless tears. Her response emerged as a cracked whisper even as she knew nothing she said would convince him she wasn't victim to a childish fancy. "Call me what you like. But don't mistake my sincerity. That's cruel and unjust."

He rose, the muscle still dancing erratically in his cheek. "It's cruel and unjust to let you eat your heart out over a cardboard imitation of a man."

"You're not a cardboard imitation of a man," she said in a low, shaking voice. "And I love you."

He curled his gloved hands tightly around the back of the chair. Grief ravaged his black gaze. "Never say that again, Charis. For both our sakes."

"That won't make it less true." She brushed stinging moisture from her eyes. She refused to break down in front of him. He already thought she was immature and impulsive. A loss of control would only prove that beyond all doubt. He didn't believe her love, and she was fatalistically aware that nothing she said would change his mind.

"I know this is painful." The aching pity in his voice made her want to die. "But one day you'll see . . ."

She glared at him from burning eyes. At this moment, she hated him almost as much as she loved him. "Don't!"

He drew himself up to his full impressive height, and his hands flexed on the chair. She read his withdrawal as though he wrote it on the air in letters of fire. "Very well."

A turbulent silence fell. He released the chair and began to pace, settling near the desk, where he picked up the bust of Plato and pretended to examine it. Eventually, she couldn't bear to look at him anymore. She turned to stare at the bookcases, although her blurry eyes couldn't read the gilt titles on the leather spines. She raised shaking hands to catch her tears before they fell.

She could no longer tolerate the tension. "I'll go upstairs. I'm not . . . not hungry tonight."

He sighed with a heaviness she felt in her bones. "I know you wish me to the devil right now. But before you go, there's something we need to discuss."

Still, she didn't look at him. If she didn't escape soon, she'd start bawling and make more of a fool of herself than she had already. "Can't it wait?"

"No."

The uncompromising negative made her turn in surprise. He leaned against the front of the desk, his hands curled over the rim on either side. Strain tautened his body, and his face was more serious than she'd ever seen it. Foreboding clanged like a tocsin, overwhelmed even her embarrassment and chagrin.

"What is it?" She thought she'd clawed back a measure of calm until she met his fathomless black gaze, and hurt and humiliation washed over her again.

"Please sit down."

He gestured to the chair he'd vacated. Silently she obeyed, trying not to notice the trace of warmth lingering from his body.

"I saw immediately what your stepbrothers are," he said heavily. "Swine in fine clothing."

She wanted to tell him how wonderful he'd been this afternoon but he wouldn't welcome her praise. Instead, she raised her chin and spoke in a hard voice. "We can beat swine."

"Yes." He paused. "But I'm afraid the measures will be more drastic than either of us imagined."

She tilted forward, her hands fisting on the chair arms. "Do you intend to kill them?"

In spite of the fraught atmosphere, that startled a soft laugh from him. "What a bloodthirsty wench you are. No, I don't intend to kill them. Or only as a last resort. I have no wish to dangle from the hangman's rope when this is over."

She spoke from the quaking depths of her heart. "Will it ever be over?"

"Yes." He paused again, sending her an unreadable glance. "And no."

She frowned. She didn't know where he went with this. His expression told her nothing. "You speak in riddles."

With sudden restless energy, Gideon swung away from the desk. A few long strides, and he reached the windows. The night outside was dark, haunted by the sea's eternal thunder. Although they no longer spoke of it, her declaration of love lay heavily in the air between them. She supposed it always would. Again, she cursed herself for her impulsiveness.

After a few taut moments, he turned to her, his face terrifyingly grave. "There's only one way I can keep you safe."

She straightened against the chair. One hand clutched her mother's locket like a talisman against evil. "Are you going to take me away?"

"If they tracked you to the wild edge of England, they'll find you wherever we go. We can run if that's your choice, but I don't fancy our chances if every magistrate in the country is after us." He watched her steadily, and she caught the ghost of his earlier devastation beneath his purposeful manner.

"And people will recognize you." Her voice was husky, although for his sake, she tried to sound practical, unemotional.

"My celebrity is a blasted nuisance."

"Your celebrity saved us from a house search today."

"True."

"If we can't outrun them, what can we do? I could go alone." She paused and spoke with difficulty. She hated to beg. Worse, she hated to contemplate leaving Gideon. "If I had some money, I could find a room somewhere—London even. It's only a couple of weeks."

His face darkened in swift rejection. "Over my dead body."

She swallowed the dread that clogged her throat. For all her seething unhappiness, his statement filled her with relieved gratitude. "I can't see an alternative. Apart from the smugglers' hole."

"There is one alternative." His tone was neutral, artificially so, she thought. His eyes didn't waver from her face. "We could get married.

For one radiant moment, joy flared inside her.

Married . . .

She rose and took an unsteady step toward him. "Gideon . . ." she began as wild happiness exploded in her breast.

His troubled expression halted her in her tracks and reminded her of his pain when she'd told him she loved him. She sucked in a tremulous breath and looked at him properly.

Her glittering palace of hope disintegrated. The hands that had risen toward him fell back to her sides and formed fists of anguish.

"What's this about?" she asked in a flinty voice.

He shifted away from the windows, back toward the fire. He stopped before her, still too far away to touch. Of course.

"It's the obvious solution, Charis." An unexpected moment to realize he'd started to use her real name naturally. He spread his gloved hands as if appealing to her to see things his way. "If we're wed, I have a husband's legal rights."

Since she'd met him, becoming his wife had been a hopeless dream. Now he proposed, and she wanted to run away and cry her eyes out. Because he married her to save her, not because he wanted her as his life companion, the woman in his bed, the mother of his children.

"You said you'd never marry. Never have a family." Her lips felt as if they were made of wood. "That's changed?"

"No." He held himself rigid as a soldier on parade. His voice was implacable. "It will be a marriage in name only."

She shook her head. "That's not what I want." Then flinched as she saw pity seep back into his eyes.

"It's all I can give you. That and a chance to lead your own life once we see your stepbrothers off."

"I want to spend my life with you."

It was the cry of the spoilt girl, her father's darling, the indulged aristocrat. As she spoke, she cringed. He offered so much for her sake. She had no right to carp at the price she paid in return.

Even if she knew that price would destroy her.

He sighed again and ran his hand through his hair in a gesture of despair. "Perhaps the scheme is doomed after all. I can't bear to hurt you."

Sightlessly, she stared into the grate while her fantasies of a fulfilled life with Gideon scorched away to ash. She'd have a life with Gideon, but they'd be two polite strangers. Duty would sustain them, not mutual love. She wanted to scream her denial to the skies.

Now she understood his appalled reaction to her declaration of love. Marriage to a woman eating her heart out for him promised him eternal torment.

She forced herself to answer. "You said we have no option."

"We could run."

"I'll be safer as your wife."

"This is your whole life we're talking about."

"And yours." He sounded like he cherished no hopes of happiness for himself. The thought cut her like a razor. "I can't ask this sacrifice of you. It's too much."

His face was pale, set, as if he contemplated a death sentence. "Charis, there's no sacrifice on my part. My life is over. In any meaningful sense. Let me help you."

He spoke with such a complete absence of self-pity, it stole her breath. How could he say such things? Yet again, she realized so much here was beyond her comprehension.

Before she could summon a protest at his brutal assessment of his future, he went on, his tone abruptly becoming cool and businesslike. She guessed he resented how much he'd revealed in that last dour statement.

"One of the local men will sail us to Jersey. We can't board the packet in case your stepbrothers have people watching the ports. We'll marry as soon as we can. Certainly within a day of arrival. Two of the villagers will dress as you and me and take the road to Scotland. They'll leave in a fast carriage the moment I have your agreement."

"So Felix and Hubert will think we've eloped to Gretna," she said dully. The extent of Gideon's planning indicated he assumed she'd fall in with his scheme. Of course she would. What choice did she have?

She stiffened her spine. He did this for her. She owed it to him to make everything as smooth as she could.

"It's the more usual route, and the ruse should give us breathing space." He paused, studying her reaction. "We won't return from Jersey until you're twenty-one. Then what happens is up to you. For the sake of appearances, I suggest we live under the same roof for at least a year."

"As you wish." She had no right to resent his generosity. She should be on her knees in gratitude.

He frowned at her lifeless response. "Are you worried I'm a fortune hunter?"

She hadn't thought about the money. Odd when it had colored her relationship with every previous suitor. "No."

"Upon our marriage, your property becomes mine, but I swear I have no intention of keeping it. After the wedding, we'll have papers drawn up returning your fortune to you after a time, I suggest three months, just in case your stepbrothers try something."

"You don't know how much money you give up."

"I don't care."

Strangely, she believed him. Yet again, she thought how remarkable he was. Why in the name of all that was holy couldn't he see that?

"We can settle legalities before the wedding, if you insist. But the sooner you're my wife, the safer you'll be."

Gideon's wife. That was all she wanted to be. But not like this. Never like this.

"I trust you," she said flatly.

He sent her a searching look, then crossed to fill two glasses from the decanter of claret on the coffered sideboard. Like most of the furniture at Penrhyn, it was old and beautiful and completely out of fashion with its heavy seventeenth-century carvings of satyrs and nymphs.

In a day or so, she'd be mistress of this house and all it contained. What a bizarre thought. She'd loved Penrhyn from the first moment she saw it. At the moment, she'd willingly consign it to the sea.

"I know this is difficult for you." He passed her the heavy

crystal glass. As if she pressed on a bruise, she noted his care that his fingers didn't brush hers. "I wish I could make it easier."

You could love me, she silently told him. She stared mutely at him while her hand tightened around the glass until her knuckles shone white. "It's not your fault," she said through stiff lips. "My stepbrothers' greed instigated this disaster."

He sipped his wine, then placed it back on the sideboard as if it weren't to his liking. She knew what wasn't to his liking—tying himself to a woman he could never care for. And who cared for him too much.

He faced her, his eyes like black stones. "What you do after the marriage is completely your choice. If you take a lover, I'll acknowledge any children as legitimate. Within my power, I'll ensure your happiness."

She summoned some last shred of resistance although her strongest impulse was to run from the room and cower from the fate that closed around her. "What if I ask you to live as my husband in reality?"

His expression remained somber, implacable. "That's not within my power."

Bitterness surged. She thought her heart broke now. How would she survive endless years of this? "And you? Will you take lovers?"

"No. I pledge my fidelity." His voice contained an undertone of irony that perplexed her. "You needn't fear gossip about an unfaithful husband."

Charis drank some wine, needing the courage, however spurious. If only she embarked on a future of love and hope instead of this arid bargain.

"Yet you're prepared to play the cuckold yourself." Despite her best intentions, sharpness edged her response. "That seems uncommonly generous."

His face was stark with tension. This couldn't be easy for him. Yet again, she reminded herself he put himself through this for her benefit.

"Charis, you're too warm and vital to endure life without love. With your money and freedom, in fact if not under law, you'll be the envy of every woman in the ton."

Her lips tightened against the pain that shafted through her. "I doubt it. I'll be that most pitiable of creatures, a woman in love with a man who can't bear her."

His brows drew together, more in regret than anger, she thought. "I hold you in the greatest esteem. If things were different, I'd . . ." He stopped and dragged in a shuddering breath as he straightened.

"You esteem me so much, you consign me to a future of deceit and adultery."

She had no right to berate him. Guilt cramped her belly. An apology hovered, but she couldn't quite squeeze it out. She swung away to stand near the fire, but its warmth couldn't thaw the ice inside her.

"If this course is repugnant, we needn't pursue it," he said steadily. How she wished he'd be angry instead of endlessly understanding. She didn't deserve him. She didn't deserve this astonishingly heroic act he made on her behalf.

She turned back to him. "What choice do we have?"

"We run. We hide. We hope to blazes your stepbrothers don't find us." He picked up his wine and stared at it as if it held the answer to all the universe's questions. "Or we stay here, and I bluff them into thinking I'm not involved in your disappearance. I doubt they'd find you in the smugglers' hole."

"If I'm discovered, you'll be arrested."

As he glanced at her, his expression was grim. "It's not the plan I'd choose. But the decision is yours."

She clutched her wineglass like she'd clutched his hands when she'd stumbled on the cliffs. He'd saved her then. She knew he'd save her now.

But at what cost?

"How can I bear marrying you in such a coldhearted arrangement?" she asked rawly.

She waited for another patronizing comment about her

love not being real. Instead, he sent her a smile of surpassing tenderness. "You're the bravest person I know. A pair of nodcocks like the Farrells can't defeat a girl of your spirit." His smile faded. "Charis, there's something else."

Her lips compressed in a grimace, and she slumped back into her chair. "I don't think I want to know. Can you tell me tomorrow?"

"The truth will be no easier tomorrow. It never is."

"What a bleak statement."

She noticed he looked uncomfortable. He hadn't looked uncomfortable when he'd informed her he expected her to seek another man's bed. Or when she'd told him she loved him. No, he'd looked devastated then. As if every hope he'd ever cherished came to nothing.

"Although nonconsummation isn't grounds for annulment, your stepbrothers will challenge the marriage on any basis they can. You're a minor and acting against their wishes."

"Surely if we marry in Jersey, the wedding is legal."

"Yes. But your stepbrothers will seek or manufacture evidence of collusion or coercion or fraud. We're safer if we preserve appearances."

She swallowed. "Spend the days together?"

"And at least one night."

For a confused moment, she didn't understand. The statement seemed to contradict everything else he'd said.

It took her a few moments to speak, and she stumbled over the words. "You mean to share my bed."

"As your husband." Gideon paused, and the betraying muscle jerked in his cheek as he visibly strove for composure. "Charis, you can't return to Penrhyn a virgin."

Eleven

Charis stood in the prow of the sleek little boat as it slid into the harbor at St. Helier. Passing a castle on a causeway, they cut through green water toward the dock.

Ordinarily, she'd be excited to visit the island.

Ordinarily? What in her life had been ordinary since her stepbrothers had forced her to leave her great-aunt? And these last days had piled bizarre circumstance upon bizarre circumstance until her head felt ready to explode.

Yesterday she'd accepted a marriage proposal from the man she loved. Who categorically didn't love her. Who intended to set her free to fill another man's bed. After he'd made use of her body.

Once.

Tonight.

She placed a shaking hand over her roiling belly. Her queasy stomach wasn't the result of seasickness but of crippling nerves.

Dorcas had lent her a rough gown and a thick red woolen

cloak more practical than decorative. The village girl who had set out for Gretna in disguise wore a gorgeous emerald velvet cape that had belonged to Gideon's mother. She and the tall, heavily muffled man who accompanied her had departed with great clatter the evening before.

After that, dinner had been strained and silent. Gideon then sent her upstairs to sleep for a few hours before they left under cover of darkness. But she'd lain awake, struggling to come to terms with her desolate future.

Fate granted her dearest wish and blighted her hopes. All in one stroke.

Before midnight, she and Gideon took the secret passage to the beach. He rowed a small boat past the breakers to where Tulliver and William, one of the villagers, waited to sail them to Jersey.

Since then, their journey's speed had astonished Charis. The elements conspired to ensure that her wedding met no delay. A cowardly part of her wanted the voyage to last forever.

She brushed aside windblown strands from her tightly coiled braids and glanced back at Gideon. He stood at the helm like a pirate. Like Black Jack. His hair blew wildly around his face. His gaze was fixed on the horizon, and his white shirt billowed in the breeze. He looked happier and more at home than she'd ever seen him.

At his side stood Tulliver; William sat near the open vessel's stern. The two men would take the boat back to Penrhyn after the wedding.

Gideon's ease with the ship had surprised her. Although of course it shouldn't have. He'd grown up on the coast, and the blood of Black Jack Trevithick flowed in his veins.

Was there anything he couldn't do?

Oh, yes, he couldn't bring himself to live with his wife, could he?

The rancorous thought made her turn to watch the approach of the dock. It should pour with rain to match her mood. But the sky was blue, and the waves sparkled and danced in the sunlight. It was still afternoon. Plenty of time left to get married today.

Then she'd have to make sense of the rest of her life.

God help her.

Charis stood dazedly beside Gideon while a plump-cheeked vicar droned the words of the marriage service.

Gideon was dressed in the height of fashion in his dark blue coat. He looked like any girl's dream prince. Tall, handsome, openly solicitous for his young bride's welfare. Next to him, Charis felt like a beggar maid in Dorcas's cheap pink gown and straw bonnet with its matching ribbons. Heaven knew what the clergyman made of such an ill-matched pair.

In her gloved hands, she clutched a ragged bunch of flowers. To her astonishment, Tulliver had pressed the bouquet on her just before the vicar arrived at their hotel rooms.

The unexpected kindness had come close to shattering the numbness that had possessed her since she'd stepped off the boat. She'd acted like an automaton all afternoon, hardly speaking while Gideon found lodgings and arranged the wedding. If such a sad, shabby event deserved that festive name.

She couldn't let herself think or feel. If she did, she'd break down and cry. She refused to humiliate herself. Nor, more importantly, would she humiliate the man who made her his wife so much against his inclination.

"The ring?"

Would Gideon have remembered a ring? What they did today made a mockery of such a symbol of eternal love.

"Charis?" Gideon prompted.

She raised her eyes from her bouquet, sweet freesias that wouldn't grow on the mainland for weeks yet. Gideon extended his hand. Automatically, she shifted her flowers to her right hand and offered her left.

"Your glove?" he said.

She looked around for someone to hold her flowers, but neither William nor Tulliver noticed. Gideon's lips took on a flat line, then with quick efficiency she could only read as distaste, he stripped away the white lace glove that had belonged to his mother.

His hands shook as he roughly shoved a plain gold ring onto her finger.

It was done. She was married.

Forever linked to this difficult, brilliant, enigmatic, *wonderful* man.

If only he cared for her, this would be the happiest day of her life. It wouldn't matter that her only witnesses were as close to strangers as made no difference. Or that she was dressed like a milkmaid.

But he didn't care for her.

The knowledge pressed down on her heart like a huge stone.

"You may kiss the bride, Sir Gideon," the vicar said with a heartiness that grated. Everything grated at this moment. Even her own hopeless longing. Especially her own hopeless longing. "A bonny bride she is at that. Felicitations to you both and wishing you many bouncing babes, Lady Trevithick."

Charis bit the side of her cheek to stop herself snapping at the man. His good wishes made her want to scream. If she had any bouncing babes, they wouldn't be Gideon's. They'd be a betrayal of every word she'd just spoken.

She waited for Gideon to give the man the set-down he invited. Instead, her new husband caught her arm before she turned away. "I'll be delighted to kiss my bride."

Shocked, trembling, Charis couldn't have protested even if she wanted to. For one agonized instant, she remembered how he'd reacted yesterday. If he treated her like that now, she'd lose control of the scream building at the back of her throat.

Unsure, frightened, yearning, she raised her gaze to meet

his. The black eyes were glassy. The hand on her arm was stiff. Not even the vainest woman could think he wanted to kiss her.

Then she remembered they needed to make a show of affection in front of their sparse audience in case Hubert and Felix challenged the match. She also remembered Gideon did this for her sake, and temper was poor repayment.

She summoned her courage and plastered a smile on her face. It felt like the rictus grin on a skull, but a glance at the jovial vicar indicated it convinced him.

"I'll be delighted to kiss my beloved husband." At least she didn't have to lie about that.

Admiration lit Gideon's eyes before he leaned down and pressed his mouth to hers. The shock of the contact made her drop her bouquet. A host of sensations overwhelmed her, vividly familiar even though they'd kissed only once before.

His clean scent. Lemon soap. Beneath that, the fresh, salty tang of his skin. He'd washed and changed. But still he smelt like the sea. His height. Occasionally, she forgot how long and lean he was. He was as hot as a furnace. Standing next to him was like standing next to a great blazing hearth. When she'd been cold forever.

His mouth moved on hers with subtle pressure. Instinctively, she parted her lips and drew his breath into her lungs.

The intimacy was astonishing. By far the most intimate moment she'd ever shared with anyone.

She closed her eyes. Tingling warmth seeped from his kiss. Down, down, to settle at the base of her belly. She sighed and leaned forward, lifting her arms.

She opened hazy eyes to see him step away. He looked pale but composed as he briefly shook the vicar's hand. She realized she still reached out like a mendicant. Blushing, she folded her arms before her to hide their trembling.

Gideon only kissed her for show. Still, she'd clung to him like ivy clung to the walls of Marley Place. If she wasn't careful, he'd grow to despise her for this endless need she couldn't conquer.

"What a beautiful couple," the vicar was saying. "I'm happy to be of service to such a gallant gentleman, a hero of the nation."

Of necessity, Gideon had revealed their true identities to the man who married them. They'd booked into the hotel under false names. Mr. and Mrs. John Holloway.

Gideon's expression didn't change although Charis guessed the fulsome praise chafed. "Reverend Briggs, remember there's twenty guineas if you keep my identity to yourself for the next fortnight. My wife and I seek privacy."

"Of course. Of course. It's an honor for my island to host your nuptials. The Hero of Rangapindhi here. Now that's a tale I can tell my grandchildren."

"Tell them in two weeks." No mistaking the threat in Gideon's voice. The trace of menace pierced even the vicar's rapture.

"You have my word as a gentleman and a man of the cloth, Sir Gideon. No whisper of what passed today until you leave Jersey."

"Good."

Gideon turned to Charis and crooked his arm. Another action to convince their guests this was a normal wedding. Hesitantly, she rested her hand on his fine woolen sleeve. Beneath the expensive material, she felt his body's latent power. She fought the urge to curl her fingers into his coat. Goodness, she'd touched him more in the last ten minutes than she had since he'd been insensible with illness.

"Thank you for your assistance." As Gideon addressed the clergyman, he sounded lordly and cool, not at all the man who shrank from the brush of her hand.

The vicar closed his prayer book. "Will you and your bride join Mrs. Briggs and myself for a glass of madeira at the vicarage?"

Gideon's expression became more remote. "I'm afraid

that's impossible although your invitation is kind. Do we need to sign further documents?"

The vicar shook his head, his face almost comical with disappointment. "No. You're married right and tight."

"Capital. We'll wish you good day, then." The arm under Charis's hand was rock-hard with tension, but to any observer, Gideon appeared completely in control of himself and his surroundings. "Remember, not a word."

Tulliver and William approached them as the vicar left.

"God grant you every happiness, Lady Charis," Tulliver said quietly.

"Aye, my lady," William said behind her.

Such simple wishes. Such impossible wishes. Furiously, she blinked away tears. She couldn't cry now. She had to stay strong for what awaited.

"Thank you," she said in a choked voice.

"Are you all right?" Gideon murmured, leaning toward her as they stood near the grate. It made her wince to hear him sounding like any new groom, mindful of his wife's comfort.

"Yes," she said almost inaudibly, concealing her unhappiness by tilting her head, so her bonnet shaded her face.

But, of course, he must guess how she felt.

Her fingers clutched at his sleeve, then she realized what she did and snatched her hand away. "I'm sorry," she gasped.

He loathed her touching him. That much she knew.

He caught her hand in a ruthless grip and dragged it back. "We need to appear like any happy couple," he growled under his breath, even though she felt him shaking with disgust.

"Then smile," she hissed.

His lips curved upward, but no warmth entered his eyes. He looked drawn and distant as though his essential self hid away.

He turned to the men. "It's time to head home. If there's

sign of trouble in Penrhyn, send word under the names of John and Mary Holloway here at the Port Hotel. We'll make our own way back next month."

Tulliver bent his head in acknowledgment. "Aye, guvnor. And congratulations. You've snagged yourself a fine lass there, make no mistake."

For the first time, Gideon's smile looked natural. "I have at that. She got much the worst of the bargain."

His lies sliced at Charis. She bit back an acid retort.

Tulliver and William left Charis alone with Gideon. Suddenly, the luxurious parlor seemed cavernous, echoing. Across the floor, the door to the equally luxurious bedroom loomed like the gates of hell. She felt ill at ease with him now as she never had before. Even after that desperate kiss at Penrhyn.

"I've arranged dinner." Her husband leaned one arm on the mantelpiece. He'd wasted no time putting distance between them once their onlookers departed. His gloved hand fisted against the ledge, and he looked as if he braced for disaster.

"I'm not hungry," she said tonelessly.

"Appearances . . ."

"Must be maintained. I know."

Charis knew she behaved badly, but she couldn't help it. She was torn between desperate gratitude and frustrated longing. And slashing guilt because there should only be gratitude.

Lines of tension framed his mouth, and his eyes glittered with stress. Again, she reminded herself he put himself through this suffering for her. Sick shame left a vile taste in her mouth.

If she had a shred of decency, she'd ask nothing further of him.

But she couldn't silence her wayward heart, which shrieked and clamored and demanded. She longed for him to love her more than she wanted to take her next breath. Nor could anything shake her bone-deep certainty that if he let himself love her, he'd find his own salvation.

Self-serving justification for her hunger? Or truth? She couldn't say. But he was worth more than this barren bargain they'd struck. *She* was worth more.

Night had fallen, and she moved around the room lighting candles. There was some relief in the workaday action. As light bloomed, she became conscious of Gideon's shallow breathing.

"Are you ill?" she asked with deliberate calm, carefully lighting each branch of the candelabra on the sideboard.

"No," he said hoarsely. His face was paper white. He looked like a man approaching the limits of endurance.

She knew what set that haunted look in his eyes. The prospect of bedding her. She tensed her throat against the agony of that awareness.

Compassion as much as conscience provoked her to speak. "Gideon, we don't have to do this. The vicar said we're married right and tight. You've already gone to extraordinary lengths to keep me safe." She extended one hand in a wordless plea for him to lay aside his burdens. If only for one night. "I can never find words to express my thanks. Nothing could repay what your championship of me has cost you. You needn't make further sacrifices."

He sucked in a deep breath, then, to her complete shock, he laughed. His dark eyes glinted with self-derisive humor as he straightened away from the hearth.

"Good God, anyone who knew me in my salad days would roll around the floor laughing himself sick to hear you. You'd think I was some shivering virgin." A cynical expression crossed his face, and he suddenly looked eons older than his twenty-five years. "I have done this before, you know."

Yes, with his skilled and spectacular Indian *bibis*. The statement didn't ease her uncertainty. It just made her jealous and insecure. "I'm well aware of that," she said starkly.

How she wished she had an ounce of those women's sensual skills. She'd captivate her husband with such pleasure, he couldn't help falling in love.

His face filled with sorrow. "I'll try my best not to hurt you."

"I know." She'd trust him with her life. She already had. Just as she'd trusted him with her heart. Even if he didn't want it.

"With a first time, there can be pain."

The subject made him uncomfortable. Or perhaps he was merely uncomfortable talking about this with his troublesome bride. His exotic Indian lovers, she was sure, hadn't made him feel awkward.

Stop it, Charis.

"I know what takes place." Heat flooded her face. She wasn't easy with this conversation either. She raised her chin, although the hand holding the taper trembled. "I grew up in the country, and my mother told me what to expect."

He raised his eyebrows, and his lips curved in another ironic smile. "Quite the expert then."

She shook her head as nerves set her belly to cramping. "I never kissed anyone until . . . until yesterday."

His face hardened in anger. "You must think you've married the clumsiest oaf in Christendom."

Her voice was muted. "You know I don't think that. I'm prepared for what's going to happen."

"Well, that reassures a man." In an abrupt gesture, he ran a hand through his hair.

"I don't know what else to say," she said helplessly, fighting the urge to smooth that unruly dark mass. The need to touch him was a constant fever in her blood. Fighting it left her exhausted, jumpy, nervous. "It's hardly a normal marriage, is it?"

"No, it's hardly that." His voice thickened with regret. "You've missed out on so much. There's nothing I can do to make it up to you."

Stay with me. Love me.

She stifled the words. Things were difficult enough without her nagging him for what he couldn't give. She blew out the taper and set it in its holder.

"None of this is your fault," she said despondently, turning away and slumping into a chair. She was weary, although most of her tiredness was emotional rather than physical.

She went on in the same austere voice. "It's not my fault either. Hubert and Felix are greedy and corrupt. Lord Desaye is desperate and deceitful. But the amount of money my father left me is obscene. It turns men into monsters." She paused. "Every man except you."

He grimaced. "I'm already a monster." He continued before she could protest. "Lord Desaye, I take it, is the suitor."

She shuddered. "He gambled away his own fortune and his first wife's. A shadow hangs over her fate. He was the only witness to the carriage accident that killed her."

"How did he and your stepbrothers link up?" Gideon seemed relieved to discuss something other than her imminent deflowering.

"Money, of course." Her voice was flat. She fiddled with her wedding ring. It was old and heavy and sat loose on her finger. A symbol of the weak bond between her and Gideon? "They gambled together. I'm sure Hubert or Felix would have tried to marry me if the church didn't frown upon unions between stepsiblings."

"Did they tell you this?"

"On that last day. I'd worked it out already." She released the ring, and her fingers curled into claws in her lap. "I sometimes wish I'd been born poor. My fortune has only caused misery."

"You'll grow into your station. At least as my wife, you're safe from fortune hunters."

She looked at him curiously. "Doesn't the idea of keeping my wealth appeal? You haven't asked how much I'm worth."

"I know what you're worth," he said sharply, stepping

toward her. "It has nothing to do with pounds, shillings, and pence."

She fought back the traitorous warmth that seeped into her heart at his response. "Few people would agree."

"The rest have fewer brains than God gave a flea."

As she gazed into his blazing black eyes, she couldn't look away, and the breath caught in her throat. Heat flooded her and settled like lava in her belly. The overwhelming emotion that flooded her was heady, uncontrollable . . . terrifying. He had such power over her, and she was helpless to resist.

He stared at her as if he thought she was a princess. It was cruel. He didn't want her. She opened her mouth to speak but had no idea what she meant to say.

Someone knocked softly on the door. The charged silence shattered.

She sucked breath into starved lungs. Gideon gave permission for the servants to enter. Everything turned to movement as waiters set out dinner.

She'd seen Gideon leave a substantial tip when they'd registered. He'd explained he and his bride insisted upon privacy. If they left Jersey without undue disturbance, he'd see the staff were suitably rewarded.

With a flourish, one waiter produced a bottle of champagne. "The compliments of the house, Mr. Holloway. To you and the new Mrs. Holloway, our very best wishes for a long and happy life together."

Charis finally had some idea how Gideon felt when people hailed him as a hero. That he existed in two realities operating side by side but forever disconnected. She kept forgetting that as far as the outside world was concerned, this was the happiest day of her life.

The strain of reconciling the contradictions left her disoriented, sick, detached from any reality at all.

The waiter opened the champagne and poured it into two heavy crystal glasses befitting St. Helier's finest hostelry. There was more bustle as servants pulled out chairs and unfolded napkins and served the first course, a fish soup fragrant with garlic and herbs.

Finally, she and Gideon were alone. A painful tension tightened around them like a steel net.

"It looks delicious." She lifted her spoon, then put it down again, the soup untouched.

"Yes."

There was a pause while they both stared at their plates.

He looked up. "Perhaps I should see what's next."

"Perhaps you should," she murmured, although she knew she wouldn't eat that either. She felt like a boulder blocked her throat.

He lifted the covers and rich savory aromas drifted into the air. "*Poulet à la persane. Boeuf en daube.* Lobster. It's a feast."

"Didn't you order it?"

"I said to send up whatever they recommended. What would you like?"

"Anything."

She watched as he filled two plates from the serving dishes.

"You know, I used to dream of dinners like this when I was in India." He slid her plate in front of her and took his place opposite, shaking out his napkin with an elegance that made her breath catch. Even such a simple gesture left her aching with desire.

Could she endure a lifetime of this relentless longing?

"What did you eat there?" It was a neutral enough topic. Would she spend her years making meaningless conversation with the man she'd married? The cold unhappy future stretched before her like an endless steppe.

He shrugged, his hand playing with the stem of his glass. He still wore gloves. "Curry. Delicacies fit for a rajah. Cold rice with weevils."

Painful memories she couldn't hope to understand shadowed his face. Before she could inquire further, he raised his glass. "I'm remiss in my husbandly duty. To my lovely bride."

It was more than she could bear. She shoved her plate away and rose on wobbly legs. "Please don't."

He put down the champagne, like his dinner, untasted. "I too find my appetite lacking." He stood. "I'll take a walk. There's a bath coming. No hurry. I'll be away for several hours."

Snatching privacy to fortify himself for the onerous task ahead, she guessed with another stab of pain. "I wish you a pleasant stroll," she said lifelessly.

He bent his head in a courtly salute. "Thank you."

Only when he'd gone did she realize it was the first time he'd left her unprotected since he'd met her.

Twelve

Gideon held himself together until he closed the door behind him and stood in the deserted corridor. He collapsed, gasping, against the wall. Shivers combed through him like breakers up the beach at Penrhyn.

He couldn't go through with this.

He *had* to go through with this.

He closed his eyes and banged his head several times against the wood. But nothing could banish the vivid images in his mind.

Charis watching him across the table, her beautiful hazel eyes brilliant with anguish and a longing he shared but couldn't fulfill.

Charis standing beside him saying words that made her his wife.

Charis telling him she loved him.

Ah, the forbidden sweetness of that moment.

And the desolation.

She had such courage. What a consort she'd make for the man worthy of her.

Damn it, he could never be that man.

His rejection might hurt now, but she'd get over her infatuation. She'd emerge from this stronger, better, bright as a star. The real tragedy was that she tied herself so irrevocably to a wreck like him.

He groaned through clenched teeth. He'd endured unspeakable pain in India. Already he knew that the hell of watching his wife fall in love with another man would outstrip any devilish torture the Nawab devised.

Bear it, he must.

For Charis's sake.

The gods clearly laughed at his sufferings. They granted him the one woman he'd want for the rest of his days. Then they made it impossible for him to find joy with her.

He desired her to the depths of his being. His very skin ached for her touch. He'd exchange all the minutes remaining to him for one night of freedom in her arms. Instead, in his clumsiness, he was going to hurt her.

Not, by God, if he could help it.

With grim determination, he straightened from the wall. He turned up his collar and pulled down his hat to conceal his face.

He'd do what was necessary. Whatever it cost. His scheme might seem crack-brained, dangerous, but it was the only solution he had. He'd accept any pain if it saved Charis suffering.

He didn't deceive himself about the pain his plan promised.

As he trudged downstairs and out onto the street, his heart was heavy. It was cold on the seafront. The breeze from the sea had ice in it. Or perhaps the chill was in his grieving soul.

He knew where to find what he required. Behind the smart façades and bustling respectable thoroughfares, every town had its shadow. Despising what he did but seeing no alternative, he turned away from the lights and plunged into the old town's maze of streets.

The girl was even younger than Charis. Seventeen or eighteen. Although with the lives these women led, who could tell?

Standing on her corner, she retained a trace of country freshness. She was clean, and her dress hinted that some shred of spirit defiantly survived her profession.

Most of all, though, Gideon chose her because she bore absolutely no resemblance to the wife he'd left at the hotel.

"You, girl, do you have a room?"

She brightened as she looked at him, her light eyes, blue or gray, Gideon could hardly tell in the gloom, sparking as she took in his fine clothes. She patted her untidy blond chignon with a gesture designed to entice.

"Aye. But it will cost ye ten shillings, me handsome gent."

Ten shillings was a fortune for someone like her. He knew she cheated him, but he didn't have the heart to haggle. Given what was likely to happen when he came to the business, she'd earn her money before he finished.

"Done."

She frowned suspiciously. "I want to see yer blunt up front."

He fumbled in his pocket and withdrew a sovereign. The gold glinted evilly in the faint light. He dropped it into her outstretched hand.

His flesh crawled at the prospect of getting closer to her. God knew if he could go through with this. He hadn't even touched the chit yet, and already he was a trembling mess. The possibility of failure rose like a dark miasma.

"Let's go," he said roughly.

The girl stared at the coin, then glanced up with a smile that made her look older than she was. "An eager beaver, ain't ye, sir?

She waited for him to respond, but he was busy trying to keep his gorge down. God give him strength. He could do this. He could do this. He hadn't touched anyone since Rangapindhi. But surely he could perform with a stranger when it didn't matter if he made an utter disaster of the act. Surely he was man enough for that.

She shrugged. "Don't ye want to know my name?"

He closed his eyes in agony. Only the knowledge that Charis waited stopped him fleeing back to light and warmth.

"No," he managed to grit out, opening his eyes to shabby reality. "I don't want to know your name."

The girl looked at him strangely and pointed to the filthy stairway behind her. "It's up here, sir." She sounded subdued, or perhaps that was just the blood pounding in his ears.

Blindly, Gideon followed the plump blond tart upstairs to her room.

Charis didn't know what woke her. She couldn't remember falling asleep. It had been late, and she'd been alone. Just as she knew immediately she was alone in the bedroom now.

She cracked open a swollen eyelid. The room was pitch-dark. The servants had drawn the curtains when they came to collect the uneaten meal and take away the cold bath. But as her sight adjusted, she recognized the heavy furniture. Old French oak pieces like something from a prerevolutionary chateau.

As she shifted experimentally, she muffled a moan. Devils with hobnail boots blundered around her skull. She licked dry lips. Her mouth tasted sour and stale. She shifted again and realized her dress twisted around her as she lay awkwardly across the covers.

With a low groan, she sat up. She raised a trembling hand to her sticky face. She remembered now. Every last pathetic moment until she'd collapsed in a stupor.

She'd waited in a lather of nerves for Gideon to return from his walk. Nerves and genuine alarm. After all Gideon's subterfuges, it was unlikely Felix and Hubert would burst in on her the first night on Jersey. But she felt lost and defenseless now her Galahad abandoned her.

One hour passed. Two. Her apprehension turned to hurt defiance. She knew why he avoided her. Because he couldn't bear to touch her.

She wanted to send him to the devil. She wanted to beg him to love her the way she loved him.

With rankling hostility, she drank the champagne, as if the act somehow got back at him. Even after she started to feel sick, she kept drinking. She drank until the bottle was empty, and the room whirled in a wayward waltz.

Eventually, inevitably, her empty stomach rebelled, and she was vilely, painfully sick. By then it was past midnight and still no sign of her husband of mere hours.

Tears she'd dammed through the agonizing day welled up. Painful, humiliating, unstoppable tears. She clenched her fists, digging her nails into her palms as she battled for control. But nothing helped. Sobbing in ugly gulps, she'd curled up on the bed. Crying, she must have fallen asleep.

To wake with a headache, a rebellious stomach, and a heart brimming with shame.

Vaguely, she wondered what time it was. A heaviness in her limbs indicated she hadn't slept long enough to overcome her fatigue. Or perhaps the wine made her ache. She'd never had more than a glass or two at once before. The foul taste in her mouth made her swear one glass was too much in future.

The inn was silent, and no noise rose from the street. She felt suspended in some dark cocoon. Alone forever.

"Stop it," she whispered. Why she kept her voice down, she couldn't say. She was on her own.

Except something had disturbed her.

She held her breath and listened.

Not a sound.

Gideon obviously hadn't returned.

Curse him.

She should lie down. Rest her throbbing head. Still, she sat bristling with awareness, straining to discern the slightest sound through the enveloping darkness.

Very carefully, she edged off the bed.

Nothing stirred in the next room.

Icy fear trickled down her spine. What if Felix and Hubert lurked out there, ready to snatch her back to Holcombe Hall?

With shaking hands, she slid a large china jar from a chest of drawers. Its pale glimmer made it easy to locate. The jar wasn't much of a weapon, but, armed, she felt less vulnerable.

Crunching her toes against the chill, she padded on bare feet across the floor until she reached the door. The parlor beyond was quiet, empty. The fire had burned down, but its low glow revealed that nobody was there.

Except . . .

"I know you're here." Relief mixed with a fortifying dose of irritation trickled down her spine. Her voice sounded scratchy and unused. Speech made her sore head ache.

No answer.

She stepped farther into the room. The floor was cold against her soles. She took another step, so at least she stood on the rug and could curl her toes into the wool.

The silence continued.

Her lips thinned with annoyance. "It's no use pretending."

More silence.

She bent and placed the heavy jar on the floor. Unless she lost her temper and smashed it over Gideon's thick skull, she wouldn't need it.

Would he continue this foolish game?

She heard a shuddering sigh from the corner of deepest shadow. "How did you know?"

"I always know when you're near," she said wearily, and felt her way across to the sideboard.

"I'm sorry I woke you."

"It doesn't matter." Perhaps it was the desolate feeling attendant upon the early-morning hours, but right now, she felt that nothing in the world mattered.

The air was so still, she could hear the even susurration of Gideon's breath. His chair creaked as he shifted. The fire crackled in the background. The intimacy was intense, fraught, electric. At the same time Charis felt that a thousand miles of frozen sea separated her from Gideon.

Gooseflesh prickled her skin. She should have grabbed a blanket before leaving the bedroom. She picked up a candle, intending to light it in the coals.

His eyesight must be better than hers in this darkness because he spoke quickly. "Please don't light it."

She paused and faced him, leaning against the sideboard and shivering in the cold. "Why?"

He didn't answer. Or not in words anyway. "Go back to bed, Charis."

"Alone?"

"For God's sake, yes." His voice cracked. "We'll talk in the morning."

"What's the point?" She sucked in a deep breath and realized the sour alcohol smell didn't come from her or the empty champagne bottle. "You've been drinking."

It wasn't an accusation but of course it sounded like one. His chair creaked again as he straightened. "Yes. And I've been fighting." His voice sounded odd. Flat and unmusical as she'd never heard it.

With sudden determination, she stepped across to the hearth and lit the candle. A feeble glow bloomed. Her hand trembling, she turned and raised the candle in his direction. Against the back of her legs, the fire's warmth was welcome.

She expected him to jerk away but he sat unmoving as she illuminated the thick darkness around him. When she saw him, Charis couldn't contain a choked gasp.

"I take it I'm not too pretty?"

Her hand shook so badly, she had to slide the candlestick onto the mantel. But the uncertain light had revealed enough to make her feel sick all over again.

His lips lengthened in a grimace that she knew was meant to be a smile. He answered his own question. "Obviously not."

"You're unwell," she said in a raw voice, wrapping her arms around herself in an attempt to generate some warmth.

"No, just drunk and heartsick." He made a sudden savage gesture with one gloved hand. "For the love of Christ, Charis, *go back to bed.*"

"No," she said stubbornly, tightening her arms to hide her shaking.

"Not twelve hours ago, you promised to obey me."

"And you promised to love me," she snapped, then immediately regretted the words.

His face tautened with pain that made her flinch. He looked terrible. His clothes were torn and streaked with dirt. A graze marked his cheekbone, and blood stained the open collar of his shirt.

The elegant man she'd married was only a memory. He'd lost his neckcloth, his gloves were filthy, and his jaw was dark with bristle. Now she was closer, the reek of alcohol was unmistakable.

Worst by far was the expression in his eyes as he stared at her. He looked haggard and ill and as if he wished he were dead.

Still, his voice deepened into kindness. "Go back to bed, Charis. Everything will look better in the morning."

It was the facile, meaningless promise one offered a child. *There are no monsters under the bed. Let me kiss it better. There will be a happily ever after.*

Even though she quaked with nerves, her tone was firm. "No, everything won't. You need to tell me the truth, Gideon. I'm your wife. I deserve to know what's wrong." She paused, then made herself push on. She was tired of fighting imaginary horrors. The truth couldn't be worse than the phantoms in her mind. "Are you sick because . . . because of what you did with those women in India?"

He recoiled. For a horrible moment, she wondered if her guess was accurate.

"Venereal disease, you mean?" He shook his head. "No,

I'm clean. In fact, my body is in perfect working order. In *every* way."

The emphasis struck her as odd. "What do you . . . ?" Then she realized what he meant. "Oh."

"What's the point of lying? Close confines will soon make my condition plain." The words slurred slightly with drink as his control wavered. She doubted she'd get this much frankness out of him if he wasn't half-seas over. His deep voice vibrated with feeling. "I ache with desire for you."

The candle flame burned unflickering. Silence fell. Lengthened.

A coal exploded in the grate, snapping the tension. Charis's paralyzed brain began to work again. And harsh reality shone a stark light on his lie. How could she think him kind? He was crueler by far than her stepbrothers. They couldn't hurt her heart. Gideon could.

"Don't mock me, " she said sharply, rubbing her arms.

"If there's a joke, it's on me." Despair dripped from every word. His eyes sharpened on her. Abruptly he stood and ripped his coat off. "You're cold. At least put this on."

"Thank you." Her frozen hands took the garment. When she pulled it on, warmth and the subtle lemon scent of Gideon filled her senses. It was almost like he touched her. "You don't want me. You jump ten feet if I come near you."

He gave a short, unamused laugh as he dropped into his chair. He leaned his head back and studied the shadowy ceiling. "That's the vilest element of my affliction, dear wife. I can want to the point of insanity, but I can never have. A punishment worthy of a damned Greek myth."

She shook her head, ignoring the lingering twinges of headache. Perhaps the champagne had damaged her mind in some fundamental way. "You said you weren't sick."

"I said my body worked fine. The trouble, my love, is in my head. I should have warned you before you tied yourself to me for life. Your husband is possessed by devils."

My love? For a moment, the world faded to nothing. Had

she imagined that endearment? Surely she had. She wasn't his love. He could hardly bear sharing the same room as her.

She drew the scrambled remnants of her concentration together and addressed the immediate issue. "You're not mad," she said shakily. She believed that to her bones.

He clutched at the wooden arms of his chair as if they offered his only link to reality. "If I'm not mad already, our marriage will be the end of me."

What was he telling her? Her dazed mind struggled to sift fact from fantasy. She didn't understand what troubled him or what she could do to help. But it was astonishingly clear that what she'd always believed unassailable truth was categorically false.

"You want me?" she asked in dawning wonder.

His lips twisted in another of those grim smiles, and at last he looked at her. "Indubitably."

Letting her arms fall to her sides, she stepped nearer. "Surely that means . . ."

He surged to his feet and lurched toward the wall behind him. "Damn it, Charis, don't touch me."

He pressed against the wall. She heard the uneven rattle of his breath. She stopped and frowned. "I can't touch you, yet you say you . . . want me."

"I told you it was insane."

All of a sudden, a whole range of memories came into focus and made sense in a way they never had. If anything about this bizarre situation made sense. She spoke slowly. "You can't touch anyone. That's why you got sick after Portsmouth. All those people."

He was as tense as if she attacked him with a rapier instead of words. She expected him to lie or refuse to answer. But he gave an abrupt nod. "Yes."

She retreated carefully as if she tried to calm a wild animal. With one unsteady hand, she felt behind her until she gripped the back of a chair. "I won't come near you."

"Thank you," he said quietly, a world of relief in the words.

She kept her voice even, as if indeed he were an animal caught in a gamekeeper's trap. "Won't you sit down?"

He hesitated, then returned to his chair with jerky movements. In the feeble light, he looked tired but composed. Slowly she sank into the chair she held, curling her cold toes under her.

"Were you always like this?" She thought and answered her own question. "No, you can't have been. You've had lovers."

"Charis . . ."

Twining her hands together in her lap, she raised her chin. Her courage faltered, but she steeled herself. She was guiltily aware she took unfair advantage of his weariness, his inebriation, his wretchedness. But she had to seize her chance.

She forced out the question she'd always been afraid to ask. "What happened in Rangapindhi?"

Thirteen

Even in the dimness, Charis saw the blood drain from
Gideon's face. His eyes became opaque, as if he stared
at gruesome specters visible only to him. He gripped
the chair arms like a drowning sailor snatched at driftwood to
keep himself afloat.

Anyone with a scrap of sympathy would relent. Tell him
he was welcome to his secrets.

She remained silent and waited.

When she'd given up hope of an answer, he sucked in a
rasping breath and focused on her. "My tutor at Cambridge
recommended me to the East India Company."

"Your knack with languages." She kept her voice carefully neutral.

"Yes. And I was a rider and a cricketer and a marksman
and a swordsman. The Company always wanted men with
my peculiar skills."

As if the Company found many recruits with such talents,
Charis thought, noting again his lack of conceit in speaking of his abilities. She wasn't surprised he'd been both out-

standing scholar and outstanding sportsman. From the first, she'd recognized how remarkable he was. The tragedy was he could do so much out of the ordinary, yet something as simple and essential as sharing the touch of a human hand was denied him. Her belly cramped with a feeling more profound than pity.

"I was ripe for adventure, in need of a career, eager to find an outlet for my energies." His voice was husky but steady. Only his face, drawn and white, indicated the ordeal he found this recounting. "I set out to spread the light of European civilization to a benighted people."

"But it wasn't like that?" She hardly needed to ask. His tone reeked of shattered illusions.

"No. I encountered a sophisticated, exotic world beyond my wildest imaginings."

He'd told her he worked in native liaison, but that meant nothing to her. "So were you an administrator?"

Bleakness etched his expression. "Nothing so admirable, Charis. I was a spy."

Shock pinned her in her chair. So many elements that perplexed her about him came together at last. His cleverness and confidence against Hubert and Felix. His handiness in a street brawl. His secretiveness. His shame.

When she didn't speak, he went on, still in that calm voice so at odds with the torment in his black eyes. "I'm naturally swarthy, and my skin tans in the sun. I became Ahmal, a Muslim scribe. A scribe learns a kingdom's secrets, and few question his movements."

She clutched her hands together so tightly they hurt. It became near impossible to maintain her mask of composure. "It must have been difficult living a lie."

"Dirty, lonely, difficult." Still, he gazed at some far-off landscape she couldn't see. "But I thought I worked for the greater good against forces of barbarism. At least at first. In the end, I believed my masters' greed the greatest barbarism, far worse than anything I encountered among the natives." He paused, and his hands flexed convulsively on the chair arms. "Then, along with two of my colleagues, I was betrayed."

Finally, his unearthly self-command fragmented. The roughening of his voice told her he approached the worst part of his story. She tensed, and dread coalesced into a cold mass in her stomach. She already knew she'd loathe hearing what he told her.

"It was my last assignment." With every word, his tone became more austere. "The Nawab of Rangapindhi plotted to invade a neighboring kingdom, whose ruler favored the British. My superiors were desperate to learn what happened in Rangapindhi. But the Nawab was cunning and on his guard—worse, he had spies in the Company."

"This is a world I can hardly imagine," Charis said softly, forcing the words past her apprehension.

"For most of my adult life, it was my world, familiar as my own face in the mirror."

"But always dangerous."

"If you forgot that, you were as good as dead." Suddenly restless, he swung to his feet and crossed to stoke the fire with suppressed violence. The flames cast unforgiving light on the taut lines bracketing his mouth.

"I wasn't supposed to go to Rangapindhi." He set the poker down with exaggerated care, and his voice was flat with control. "I'd handed in my resignation and booked passage to England. But my masters wanted their best men, and I let myself be persuaded. Three of us—Charles Parsons, Robert Gerard, and I—went into Rangapindhi." The silence was longer this time and charged with Gideon's grief and anger. "Only I came out alive."

"What happened?" His expression told her it had been terrible beyond description.

"Gerard was careless. He'd been in the field ten years. Too long. He was a good, courageous man. But even the best make mistakes when pressure goes on too long."

She noted but didn't comment that he was ready to forgive a failing in another that he refused to forgive in himself. He

ran an unsteady hand through his hair, and his body sagged
with what she read as defeat. He was tired and hurt, and
she had no right to harangue him. But if she didn't catch
him now, when he was vulnerable, he'd retreat behind his
formidable defenses.

He sighed heavily. "Damn it, I've had too much to drink."

She rose on trembling legs, battling a dizzying mixture
of fear and overwhelming love. "Gideon, for pity's sake,
tell me."

Standing in the center of the shadowy room, his wife was as
beautiful as a carved alabaster angel in a cathedral. And just
as unrelenting.

Charis's unwavering gaze held such trust, such love. Both
pierced him with sorrow. Gideon couldn't rely on the love,
and he didn't deserve the trust.

He shut his eyes and fought for strength to deny her. Everything between them would change once she knew what had
happened in India. He couldn't burden her with the horrors
of his past. He couldn't enmesh her in the chaos of his life.

But simmering guilt and too much liquor played hell with
his principles.

Reluctantly, he opened his eyes and took a step closer.
"The Nawab had us chained and dragged into his audience
hall. I'd only seen him from a distance before. They called
him the Elephant of Rajasthan. Fat rolled off him in monstrous folds. He wore ropes of pearls as big as pigeon eggs.
They must have weighed a ton."

"He knew you were British in spite of your disguise?"

The memory made the skin on the back of his neck crawl,
and his hands fist at his sides. "He had us stripped in front
of his court."

He saw she didn't understand. Sometimes he forgot how
little his countrymen knew of the Subcontinent. "We posed
as Muslims, but none of us were circumcised."

Sweet pink flooded her cheeks, visible even in the flickering candlelight. "Oh."

"I'm surprised you know what I mean."

"I had the run of my father's library. He had some unusual books." She paused. "And anyway, it's in the Bible."

Again, he realized this woman was considerably more mysterious than anything he'd encountered in India.

"We provided an evening's diversion for the court." Gideon spoke quickly, hoping that would ease the telling. It didn't. "We were whipped."

He bit down hard, trying not to remember the cutting agony of the lash, the strangled groans and screams from Gerard and Parsons.

"He meant to humiliate you." Charis's composure was surprising, impressive, but he noticed the tremor in the hand she curled around the back of her chair.

"Us and the overweening British nation. He wanted information too, but that could wait until specialists got their hands on us. This was purely for His Highness's entertainment."

"You didn't beg for mercy." Her voice rang with certainty. The knuckles on her fine-boned hand shone white as she clutched the chair.

"I had too much stupid pride. It meant my beating went on considerably longer than the others'." Until he'd collapsed unconscious on the cold marble floor. He'd thought then he had tested the dregs of humiliation. How naïve he'd been. "Then they took us away and tortured us."

Dear Lord, don't let her ask about his torture in the Nawab's dungeons. The memories were so vivid, it was as though he still hung in chains from the seeping, fetid walls. Nothing this side of heaven could force him to tell her about that foul Gehenna. A place of neither night nor day, just darkness, lit by the flare of torches and reeking with blood and filth and terror.

The fiendish instruments. The endless torment. The inevitable knowledge that nothing could save them.

There would be pain. Then there would be death. No escape.

"Gideon . . ." She looked down and sucked in a shuddering breath. Not before he caught the shimmer of tears.

Her shaking distress wrenched him back from nightmare. "I should stop. I'm upsetting you."

As she looked up, her eyes glittered. He was astonished to recognize fury beneath her wretchedness. "Of course I'm upset. You describe your systematic degradation and torture." Her slender throat moved as she swallowed. "How long were you held?"

"A year. Mostly in a dark pit the size of a grave." His voice was still flat although his heart beat like a drum as he revisited the agonies of Rangapindhi. Not that they were ever far from his thoughts. But somehow putting what he'd endured into words revived all the vile reality.

Now he'd released the floodgates that dammed the memories, he couldn't stop. "Parsons died within the first week. Gerard, poor devil, hung on for over a month. God knows why I didn't die too. I should have. The jailers gave me just enough food to keep me alive. I've never been sure why. Just as I've never been sure why of the three of us, I survived."

She released the chair and wrapped her arms around herself. Standing there in her cheap, borrowed dress and a coat far too large for her, she should have looked absurd. But her beauty shone like a beacon, stole his breath.

"You wanted to die," she said bleakly.

His lips flattened. "Believe me, death would have been welcome. But I was too blasted stubborn to kill myself and give those bastards the satisfaction of besting me. And for all the pain they put me through, they never quite finished me off."

Raising her chin, she cast him a defiant look. Her voice emerged with unexpected ruthlessness. "So you were a hero."

He stiffened and stepped back. No hero he. A hero never begged for mercy from his torturers. A hero never longed for death to spare him another day's pain. A hero never succumbed to devils in his mind.

"No, I wasn't a bloody hero."

Her voice deepened into irony. "Because you told the Nawab what he wanted to know."

"Believe me, keeping my mouth shut was the extent of my courage. When the Company's men finally dragged me out of that pit, I was a babbling lunatic."

She made a sound in her throat that indicated disagreement, but mercifully she didn't argue. Strain marked her features. "And it's the torture that makes it impossible for you to . . . touch anyone?"

He met her perceptive gaze and decided he'd gone too far to prevaricate. He folded his arms in a futile attempt to hide his shaking. "We were chained together in the pit and left."

He thought at first she hadn't understood. Thank God.

Then he realized what scant color she retained leached from her face. "The three of you?"

He stiffened. Damnation, he should never have started this. Why didn't he make up some easy story about comfortable incarceration and eventual rescue?

But he couldn't look into her eyes and lie.

"Yes." The word was choked. He battered back memories of month after month chained to rotting corpses. Through the humid airless heat of an Indian summer. Through the savage cold of winter. The unrelenting stink, the decay of once-healthy flesh.

Horror dawned in her expression. And a compassion that stabbed at his pride.

Because he couldn't bear her to imagine even a hundredth of what he'd been through, he spoke quickly. "It was almost a relief when the Nawab exhibited me for general mockery. He loved having a captive sahib who stank like carrion and could hardly cover his nakedness. I was quite the highlight of his divans until the stench got so bad, even he couldn't stomach it."

"How did you escape?" she asked huskily.

"British troops ousted the Nawab. Akash entered Rangapindhi with the invading forces. He knew if I was alive, I must be in the palace. He found me in the lowest depths of the Nawab's prisons."

"Thank God for Akash," she whispered, closing her eyes briefly as if the words were a prayer.

"I was burning up with fever, barely able to walk, half-mad." More than half-mad. He'd spent a long time convinced his rescue was another sick fantasy.

Charis's brow creased in a thoughtful frown. Her voice was stronger, although still thick with emotion. "Your health has improved since."

"I can walk and talk without humiliating myself. Most of the time. Quite an achievement." He bit back the sarcastic edge. It wasn't her fault he was a wreck.

He crossed to stoke the fire again. The flaring flames revealed her somber, troubled expression. Unfamiliar shadows swam in her unblinking gaze. Shadows he'd put there. He cursed himself for a selfish swine. He should have found a room, slept off the drink, left her to innocent dreams.

Except he couldn't bear staying away from her.

"Charis, I've had months to recover." She was better facing the bleak truth than nurturing the smallest hope that he'd ever offer her a whole body and mind. "My physical health is as good as it will get. Nothing has shifted the devils in my mind. Nothing will."

She swallowed again. He expected a protest, but she spoke with perfect calm. "You believe you'll never touch another person?"

"Not without difficulty."

Her expression was unyielding. "Then how can you hope to consummate our marriage?"

He tensed. The attack was unexpected. He dredged his response from the deepest part of him. "I must. I will. I can."

Something in his face must have alerted her to the shame roiling in his gut. "Gideon, what is it?"

He swung away although she didn't approach him. Confound it, why didn't he hold his ground? He acted like he'd done something wrong. "Nothing."

Her voice was sharp. "Where were you tonight?"

Why did she have to be so damned acute? "I told you. Drinking. I got into an altercation with a couple of ruffians. They came out the worst, I'm pleased to say."

Then she did step closer, her skirts rustling. Christ, don't let her touch him. Not now. After telling her about Rangapindhi, he felt like he'd scraped off several layers of skin.

She exhaled in a long, impatient breath. "There's more."

Oh, she was damned right about that.

His guilt surged. Fought with the absurd urge to confess, to receive absolution. When he knew there was no real absolution for him ever, for this sin or his other, more heinous transgressions.

She waited for his answer. Strange how he'd withstood agonizing interrogations in Rangapindhi without cracking, but his wife's bristling silence made him frantic to spill his secrets.

Oh, hell, why shouldn't she know what he'd done tonight? Perhaps it was best she recognized what a craven she'd married. He'd tried to tell her so often, but she refused to heed him, devil take her foolish stubbornness.

He drew himself up to his full height, turned, and surveyed her down his long nose. "I paid for a tart," he said harshly.

As her expression darkened with hurt, his gut clenched in unwelcome remorse. She came to a trembling halt a few feet away. "What . . . what did you do with her?" she asked shakily.

Abruptly Gideon's guilty defiance evaporated. He felt utterly sickened. With himself. With the world. With every bloody thing in Creation.

Except the woman he'd married.

He avoided eyes that held no accusation, just tortured curiosity. Shame rose like bile. Sometimes his shame was so suffocating, he thought it would kill him.

His voice was toneless as he unleashed the mortifying truth. "Not one damned thing."

Even without watching, he knew the tension drained from her. He braced for a volley of questions. But she didn't speak. Which somehow forced him to explain.

"I couldn't. I thought . . ." God above, this was humiliating. His hands formed fists at his sides. He gulped for air, which seemed in short supply in the dark room. "I thought . . . I think I'll hurt you when I . . . when I bed you. I thought if I could take the edge off, it would go easier for you. I'd give up my life before I . . . I hurt you."

Good God, he stammered like an embarrassed schoolboy. Heat prickled his neck.

He risked a glance at her. Astonishingly, her lips curved in a faint smile although her eyes were still somber. "I'd rather you hurt me than you went to another woman."

He'd expected hysterics, rage, tears. Shock sent him tumbling headlong into speech. "I'd hoped to manage the act with a professional. I haven't willingly touched anyone since Rangapindhi. And you've seen what happens to me when I do touch someone. I'm in a damnable state to bed an inexperienced girl. I'd hoped . . . if I could touch a stranger, I'd be able to touch you, manage the act without too much pain or clumsiness." The final sour admission surged up. "But using that woman felt too much like betrayal."

Her smile widened as if he'd done something wonderful instead of shabby and sordid. Devil take her, what was wrong with the girl? Nothing he said or did, no matter how vile, made her despise him as he deserved.

He couldn't bear to look into her face any longer. Its beauty, its honesty, its *love* scourged his soul. On feet heavier than lead, he crossed the room to stare out the window.

The sky outside turned gray. His wedding night was over. And his bride was still a virgin.

She padded across to stand beside him. "It's a new day."

"We've got nothing but darkness ahead," he said grimly, glancing at her.

"I don't believe that." She sounded tired but sure as she looked at him. The honesty in her eyes always cut right through him.

"You will." He slumped onto the window seat. He felt empty, lost. He had no idea where they went from here. Not for the first time, he wondered if in marrying Charis, he'd inflicted worse harm on her than her stepbrothers ever could.

She stood too close, but at least she didn't touch him. "Do you want to come to bed?" she asked hesitantly.

"No." In the strengthening light, he saw her face more clearly. She looked exhausted, devastated. "You go."

She shook her head and knelt on the thick red-and-blue rug at his feet, pulling his coat more securely around her shoulders. "You've had less sleep than I."

"I'm used to it."

She drew her knees up and linked her hands around them. With her loose hair tumbled around her, she looked absurdly young. Except the expression in her eyes spoke of heartbreaking experience. She'd changed in the last hour, taken on some of his darkness.

What he'd dreaded had come to pass. The poison of Rangapindhi had infected her bright spirit. And there was no antidote.

Her gaze was somber as she stared across the room at the burning embers in the hearth. Instinctively, Gideon lifted his hand to stroke the soft fall of her thick hair, to offer a moment's comfort.

Then he remembered that such natural gestures were forever denied him. His heart contracted in agony as his hand dropped away from her.

Fourteen

Wearing only her shift, Charis waited alone in the big bed. It was late, past midnight, and the weather had turned colder during the day so a fire blazed in the grate.

No sound came from the parlor behind the closed door. She knew Gideon was in there, steeling himself for what he must do. She'd been steeling herself all day too. In her belly, huge ugly toads of fear somersaulted over each other. Her trembling fingers crushed the embroidered edge of the fine linen sheet.

Could consummating their marriage push him further into darkness?

Darkness hovered perilously close. She'd recognized that last night, when he'd told her about Rangapindhi. The magnitude of his suffering beggared belief.

Could she heal him? *Could anyone?*

And still they both had to get through tonight. She'd told Gideon she could do this. But every lonely second of delay made her bravado less and less convincing. If he didn't appear soon, her failing courage would desert her altogether.

Charis bit her lip and closed her eyes, whispering a silent prayer for strength. It didn't help.

When she opened her eyes, Gideon stood on the threshold. The doors in St. Helier's best hostelry were, of course, well oiled.

"Hello," she said stupidly, although she'd only left him to his brandy half an hour ago, and they'd spent an entire strained day together, carefully avoiding the subject of what happened tonight.

His beautiful mouth quirked in the wry smile that was indelibly imprinted on her poor yearning heart. "Hello to you too."

He was in shirtsleeves and trousers. The neck was open, slashing down to reveal a solid chest covered in curling dark hair. The sight shocked her. She'd imagined him hairless, like the marble statues in the hall at Marley Place. His long narrow feet were bare. He still wore his fine tan kid gloves.

All this she took in with one sweeping look, aware he studied her in his turn. What did he see? She kept the covers pulled to her shoulders as she sat against the carved oak bedhead. She'd plaited her hair as usual. It seemed inappropriate to leave it loose, too bridal when she didn't feel remotely like a bride.

She overcame her crippling shyness to glance into his face again. His fleeting amusement had evaporated. He was pale, and that telltale muscle flickered in his lean cheek.

"What . . . what do you want me to do?" she asked almost soundlessly.

Why, oh, why did this have to be so awkward? Surely people consummated marriages—or did this without legal niceties—all the time. Yet she was so nervous, she felt sick.

He stepped into the room and shut the door after him. "Lie down. Close your eyes," he said in a somber voice. "I'll try to be quick."

Charis's heart clenched with misery. She was sure when those other people came together, they said more than that. But those people wanted what was to occur. She bit back a protest at the bleak crudeness of it all.

He didn't come nearer. "Would you like me to blow out the candles?"

She started to shake her head, then nodded. "Yes, please." What happened was better done in shadow.

She watched him move around the room with his usual catlike grace. Soon the only light was the fire's flickering golden glow.

He stopped beside the bed. With his back to the hearth, she couldn't see his expression. He ran his hand through his hair, ruffling it. She itched to rise on her knees and smooth it. But, of course, she couldn't touch him.

The agony of that knowledge carved a crack in her heart as wide and deep as the sea they'd crossed to reach Jersey.

"Are . . . are you going to undress?" she asked uncertainly.

"No."

She bit her lip again. Her fingers tightened on the sheet until they ached. Gideon stood close enough for her to hear the uneven hiss of his breath. She looked at the superb man she'd married and wished with every particle of her being she was anywhere but here.

"Charis, I'll have to pull the covers away," he said with gentle insistence.

She realized she clutched the sheet like a shield. Absurd. She'd agreed to this. He was here for her sake and at great cost to himself. Too late to cavil at the bargain she'd made.

"Of course." With difficulty, she relaxed her clawlike grip.

Down, down the blankets went, until she lay revealed to her bare toes. She closed her eyes because she wasn't brave enough to look into Gideon's face. Uncontrollable heat rose in her cheeks. He'd see she was naked beneath her shift. A nauseating mixture of nerves and embarrassment kept her stiff and unmoving.

He was so still, standing next to the bed, that she couldn't even hear him breathing anymore.

He'd warned her he'd be clumsy. She was smart enough to believe him. She braced for him to grab her, but nothing happened.

What was he waiting for? Dear heaven, did the sight of her shatter his resolution? Now the moment of truth arrived, was he unable to go through with it?

"My God, but you're glorious," he whispered hoarsely.

Her eyes flew open with disbelieving shock. "What?"

His expression remained troubled, but his gaze was avid as it traced her body. "Charis, you're beautiful beyond a man's wildest dreams."

How could he say such things? It was too painful. She couldn't find pleasure in his praise when he shook with disgust at her slightest touch.

"Please . . ." She swallowed to dislodge the lump of distress in her throat. "Please get it over with."

His face contorted with sorrow. "I'm sorry, Charis."

"Don't say any more." She closed her eyes, partly to stem her foolish tears, and slid down in the bed. "Just . . . do what you must."

"As you wish." He sounded remote, as though he too retreated behind some inner bastion.

The mattress sagged with his weight, then she felt encroaching warmth as he straddled her legs. She knew the act would be less painful if she relaxed, but every muscle tensed in fearful expectation.

After a moment, he raised the hem of her shift. To her thighs. Then past her hips. The cold air on her skin made her shiver.

She placed shaking hands over her mound. Which was stupid. He'd do more than look at her before he was finished.

Reluctantly, she opened her eyes to find him staring at her . . . there. His face was taut with such anguish and longing, she couldn't bear it.

Hesitantly, he placed one gloved hand on the soft plain of her belly. Her breasts tightened, and restless heat settled between her legs. She was ashamed that she couldn't stifle her powerful and immediate reaction.

He snatched his hand back as if she scalded him. He was shaking. Of course he was. Touching her, even for such a short time, required every ounce of will.

She bit her lip so hard, she tasted blood. The urge to beg him to stop fought up through her closed throat. She could see in his strained, colorless face what this cost him.

She remained silent.

Still silent, she lifted her hands away from her sex.

Gideon stared at Charis in helpless wonder while his gut churned like a millwheel. She was the most exquisite creature he'd ever seen. His hunger was a raging storm.

The shift bunched under her breasts, but he clearly saw the rich pink of her nipples. Nipples that peaked like ripe raspberries the moment he touched her.

Her swift response was just another of fate's mockeries. She was formed for pleasure, but she'd find no pleasure with the man she married. Nonetheless, his eyes feasted on the treasures of her body. The delicious inward curve of her waist. The flare of her hips. The long, coltish legs.

His cock was hard and swollen and pulsed against the front of his trousers. If he took her now, he'd rip her to pieces. His mind might deem touching her as torture. His prick didn't care.

Dazedly, she stared into his face. She was white as new snow. She'd hardly looked at his body, although if she dropped her gaze, she couldn't miss his arousal.

He gritted his teeth and stroked the smooth skin of her thigh. For one heady moment, even through his glove, he felt her enticing warmth.

Then, as always, his mind went black. Screams echoed in his ears. Her flesh turned to rotting carrion. Her peppery carnation scent became the stink of death.

He fought back the shrieking demons. Wrestled them until they lay supine and silent. The battle left him shaking. He sucked in a breath that reeked of decay. Slowly, as if he pushed a massive weight up a steep and jagged path, he traced a tentative path to her hip.

He wasn't a small man. He needed to prepare her. But time was his enemy. The longer he waited, the more likely his demons would master him.

She was rigid with fear. The uncertainty in her beautiful eyes broke his heart. Her breath emerged in unsteady gasps. Not, he was grimly aware, of desire. The air bristled with tension.

He placed both hands on her thighs and carefully spread them. In a room lit only by firelight, her body's hollows were dark and mysterious. He knelt between her legs, and his nostrils flared as he caught her scent.

With clumsy fingers, he undid his trousers. His cock sprang free. When her eyes fastened on his organ, she made a muffled sound. Her hands curled into the sheet beneath as if she physically stopped herself leaping from the bed.

He hooked his hands under her hips and angled her up. Slowly, he pushed forward.

As he breached her body, she whimpered but didn't recoil. He pushed again, feeling the tissues give way.

To his grateful astonishment, she was damp. Damp enough to ease his entry.

Even so, she was damned tight.

He paused and sucked in a deep breath redolent of Charis. *She's alive, she's alive,* he chanted in his mind as he eased into her. *She's alive,* he told the ghosts in his head, blocking his ears to their panicked clamor.

She whimpered again and shifted, drawing him deeper.

The voices grew more insistent. He couldn't hold them

off. Cold sweat prickled his skin. His grip firmed on her hips. As his vision faded, he inhaled. The world shrank to one spark of light.

He had to do this now or fail utterly.

"Charis, forgive me," he said in a strangled voice. He tautened and thrust.

Pain shafted through Charis with the vivid, immediate brightness of lightning. A scream welled in her throat, but she bit it back.

Still, a choked moan escaped. She felt like she'd been split in half with a blunt ax. It was excruciating. Blinding.

She squeezed her eyes shut and prayed for it to be over.

Breathe. She needed to breathe.

She gasped for air, but Gideon's weight crushed her into the mattress. He was bigger and heavier than she'd realized. His height and superb coordination disguised how well muscled he was.

Frantically, she dug her fingers deeper into the sheets. He'd done what he needed to. Why didn't he pull out and leave her be?

Breathe, Charis, breathe.

The part he'd pushed into her chafed tender flesh. He was hard as granite. But unlike granite, he was hotter than a furnace. Stupidly, she'd imagined he'd feel cool, even cold, because of his reluctance to touch her.

His smell, familiar yet unfamiliar, surrounded her. She knew the clean scent of his soap and the essence of his skin. She guessed the extra spice in the air was male arousal.

His breathing was ragged, and he trembled. She raised her hands to grip his back, then remembered he hated to be touched. He wouldn't want her embrace, even as he lay buried inside her in the closest connection she'd ever known.

She sucked in another breath. An easier one. Where they joined, she still hurt, but the fierce agony faded.

He shifted with a soft grunt. The pressure changed, became less excruciating.

Charis waited for him to pull away. But his muscles tightened, and he thrust again. She bit back another moan and gripped the sheet to stop sliding up the bed.

She'd imagined this would be quick, over in seconds. But he was still inside her. He moved once more, and released a deep groan.

Another thrust. His hips pumped several times, and she felt a liquid heat deep inside her. He groaned again and slumped over her. In a cruel parody of tenderness, his head came to rest on her shoulder, his silky hair tickling her neck.

After all the hardness, the fleeting softness seemed alien, wrong.

After an endless time, Gideon withdrew and carefully pulled down her shift, hiding the tops of her thighs. Then he rolled onto his back to stare at the ceiling. His shirt was twisted and flapped free of his gaping trousers.

After one brief glance at him, Charis concentrated on the dark beams crossing the ceiling too. She didn't want to see the organ he'd pressed into her body.

She supposed she should say something, but she wasn't certain her voice would work. Her throat clenched so tight, it hurt. Although she was cold, she couldn't summon energy to reach for the covers.

Who knew how long they lay alongside each other? Not long, she guessed, although every second felt like an hour.

Where he'd taken her, she stung, although the piercing pain had subsided to a constant throbbing. She felt lost in a vast emptiness, as though the world had been destroyed in some unimaginable cataclysm. How odd that this most intimate act of all left her feeling like the only human left on earth.

Slowly, stiffly, he sat up. For one intense second, she felt him study her. She kept her eyes fixed on the ceiling.

Like distant thunder on a summer's day, devastation nudged at her awareness. But for the moment, exhaustion kept it at bay.

Jamming her eyes shut, she willed herself not to cry. She was much better hiding in this numbness. Given her way, she'd lie here forever.

Charis listened to him move about the room. Water splashed into a dish. Perhaps he meant to wash. Perhaps he was desperate to rid himself of every trace of her disgusting person.

She recognized she tortured herself and scotched the thought before it went any further. Instead, she sought that cold empty space in her heart where nothing could hurt her.

The rug muffled his footsteps as he moved closer. She couldn't help tensing at his approach. He stopped by the bed. Unthinkingly, she flinched.

Although he wouldn't touch her. He'd never touch her again, now she was his wife in fact as well as law.

He didn't say anything. There was a soft clink on the bedside cabinet. He shifted away, his footsteps deliberate but somehow defeated.

There was a click as he opened the door, then another as he closed it behind him.

She opened her eyes. The blazing fire still lit the room. The whole episode had probably taken less than half an hour.

Half an hour for her world to change.

She turned her head to see a blue-and-white china washbowl on the nightstand and a pile of towels. He'd seen to her comfort, then he'd left her in peace.

The tears she'd fought since he'd come to her bed overflowed.

Eventually Charis roused to go looking for her husband.

It wasn't in her nature to avoid difficulties. Lying in the rumpled bed, surrounded by the unfamiliar smell of sex, she had time to gather her courage.

And time to start worrying about Gideon.

As shock and discomfort receded, she began to think

what price that joyless coupling had exacted from him. She needed to see him, to reassure herself he was all right. She needed to see him because the moment when she'd wished him to Hades had been brief indeed. Now only his nearness could soothe her aching sadness.

She rolled out of bed, the abrupt movement setting up a host of unfamiliar twinges. Reminder, should she need it, that nothing would ever be the same after what had just happened.

Wrapping a blanket around her trembling shoulders, she trudged across the floor. She pushed the door open and stepped through. The parlor was quiet and dark except for the low glow of the fire.

Had he gone out? After what they'd done, sleep would elude him. She ventured closer to the Stygian corner where he'd sat last night. Then she realized he sprawled in a massive wooden armchair in front of the hearth.

"Gideon?" She hitched the blanket up and stepped around the chair's looming bulk to stand before him.

He didn't look at her. Instead, he stared at the fire. Something told her he'd stared into the fire for a long time. His gloved hand curled around a half-filled glass that dangled on the verge of spilling. Brandy, she guessed.

"Go back to bed, Charis."

The boneless curve of his long, lean body echoed the despair in his voice. His legs stretched toward the grate, and his shirt hung loose as it had in the bedroom. A frisson ran through her as she looked at his bare chest, gold in the flickering light.

A shiver, astonishingly, not of revulsion.

Charis beat back the cowardly urge to obey him and flee. Instead, she fixed an unwavering gaze upon him. "We need to talk."

His face tightened. With a savagery that made her wince, he lifted the glass and pitched it into the fire. There was the sharp tinkle of shattering glass and a brief flare as the brandy caught.

"Christ, no."

The eyes he focused on her glittered with anguish and a loathing that made her cringe.

"Do you hate me now, Gideon?" She didn't recognize the shaking voice as hers. She'd tried so hard to make the act easy for him, but to her shame, she hadn't succeeded in masking her discomfort.

His face contorted, and she stared aghast into naked torment. Only for a moment. He swiftly pulled the shutters over the turbulent depths.

"Of course I don't hate you," he said impatiently.

"But . . ."

"Go, Charis, now." His voice fractured.

She couldn't mistake his desperation to be alone. Although selfishly she wanted only to stay with him. The tumbled, lonely bed in the next room loomed like a gallows.

"Good night," she whispered, her shoulders drooping.

He didn't answer. Slowly, reluctantly, as if her feet were blocks of stone, she turned toward the door she'd left ajar.

One step. Two.

She didn't want to leave him. She never wanted to leave him.

She was almost at the door when she heard a muffled sound behind her. An unfamiliar sound although she immediately identified what it was.

Stifling a horrified cry, she turned. He pressed gloved hands to his eyes, and his broad, straight shoulders heaved as he struggled for air.

Hands that itched to comfort him curled into fists at her sides. She longed to succor the man she loved with the warmth of her body. But that was impossible. Touching her body had driven him to this extreme.

She darted across to him, and, as she had last night, she knelt on the floor beside him. Unfamiliar discomfort stabbed her as she curled her legs under her.

In painful suspense, she waited for him to send her away. He was a proud man. He'd hate to know she witnessed this.

But he didn't speak.

Perhaps he wasn't even aware of her presence. It was torture to listen to him struggle against his weeping. He hardly made a sound. Only the thick, uneven rasp of breath betrayed his agony.

The iron control that had sustained him through Rangapindhi and beyond disintegrated. How blind she'd been not to realize the universe of pain he contained. She should have known. She wasn't stupid. She claimed to love him. He'd told her about India. She'd seen what his ordeal cost his gallant spirit.

But only now did she truly understand the devastation that haunted him. His inhuman strength had delayed this moment too long. So when he finally broke, it was like a mountain cracked before her eyes.

From the first, she'd cherished a childish, flawless image of him. In this shadowy room, that image crumbled to dust. Gideon Trevithick wasn't Galahad or Lancelot or Percival. He wasn't an invincible guardian angel who appeared from nowhere to rescue her. He wasn't indestructible and powerful and immune from weakness.

Helpless, hurting, guilty, she listened to the sound of his heart breaking. This man who battled so hard to dam his tears was all too human. He could shatter and fall and fail. He was fragile flesh and blood, and he'd suffered more than any mortal should.

Wrapping her arms around her raised knees, she stared sightlessly at the fire, the only light in the dark room. This wordless vigil was all she could offer. She was guiltily aware that what they'd done had initiated this excruciating outpouring. Her penance was listening to him struggle to smother his sorrow as if it were shameful or unwarranted. She wanted to beg him to stop resisting, to give in, to let the horrors of his Indian years finally receive their due.

He'd fought so long and so hard, and still he fought. His valiant heart wouldn't surrender.

Slowly, the worst of his grief passed. Or at least the outward signs. His breath emerged more normally and not in broken, choked gasps.

After a long time, he spoke in a constricted voice. "This isn't fair on you."

She didn't look at him but continued to rest her cheek on her upraised knees. Weariness and sorrow weighed endlessly on her. "I can bear it."

They didn't speak again. She thought after a while he might have slept, exhausted by his travails. She didn't. Instead, she gazed dry-eyed at the dying fire.

Charis had loved Gideon Trevithick from the moment she'd first seen him. She'd loved his strength, his honor, his intelligence, his beauty. She still did.

But he'd been right to decry that love as a dazzled girl's emotion. It was a hothouse plant, green and lush but unable to withstand cold winds from the real world.

The last hour had changed that forever. The last hour had changed *her* forever.

The love she felt for Gideon now was more durable than stone.

Fifteen

The afternoon wind off the sea was so icy, even Gideon noticed its biting power. Unusual for this time of year, according to the porter at the hotel, who wished him and Charis well when they left on their walk.

Gideon wasn't sure appearing in public was a good idea. Someone might recognize him. After the last days, he couldn't bear fending off another crowd as he had in Portsmouth. More, there was a small but significant risk of word reaching Felix and Hubert that he and Charis were on Jersey.

But Gideon couldn't bear being confined in their rooms any longer. The acrid memories of last night's pain and disappointment weighted the air. Worse, that clumsy bedding had left a brooding sensual awareness in its wake. Living in close quarters with Charis and knowing he couldn't touch her, would never touch her again, was slowly driving him out of his mind.

As the day progressed, he'd watched his own strain increasingly reflected in his wife's pale face. The tension between them had stretched and stretched until it became intolerable. He'd heard her sigh of relief when he suggested going out.

Thankfully, it appeared the cold kept most people inside. The few hardy souls on the promenade paid Gideon and Charis no heed as they strolled along the seafront.

So far it had proven a mostly silent walk. As it had proven a mostly silent day.

Hell, what could he say after last night's emotional storms? His gut clenched with humiliation at his behavior, both during and after their bleak coupling. How could he bear to revisit the black ocean of anguish? Or perhaps even more harrowing, how could he discuss his inept use of her body?

The silence was heavy as lead with what remained studiously unspoken.

Charis turned into the wind and paused to look across the gray rolling waves. The stiff breeze snatched at her bonnet, and she raised one gloved hand to hold it firm.

At least she was dressed suitably. He'd called in a modiste that morning and ordered a wardrobe for his bride. The charming yellow ensemble Charis wore had been hurriedly altered to fit. Other garments would arrive over the next week.

It was the only time Charis had smiled all day, when she saw the designs for her dresses.

Gideon came up beside her as she leaned on the stone parapet. Beneath the bonnet's brim, her expression was pensive. Her lush, pink mouth drooped at the corners.

Ah, that soft mouth . . .

The continual low hum of desire made his head swim. Self-disgust followed fast.

Good God, he was a satyr of the vilest kind. After what he'd done last night, how could he think of touching her?

Turning, she caught his stare. From the color that invaded her pale cheeks, she guessed the heated direction of his thoughts.

She must despise him. She ought to despise him. He'd hurt her, then broken down and cried for the first time since his release from the Nawab's dungeons.

Her eyes darkened to green with some emotion he couldn't name. Although before last night's debacle, he might have called it interest. Her lips parted on a soundless sigh.

He jerked back as if she reached for him. But her yellow-gloved hands remained safely on the seawall.

His heart thudded like a drum. He rubbed the back of his neck with one hand. To his surprise, she laughed softly. Surprise and chagrin.

That low musical sound slid along his veins like honey and made him want what he could never have. He should be inured to frustration, but somehow the damned torture never ended.

"You look almost bashful." Her husky voice bubbled with warmth.

"Good God, Charis . . ." He struggled to express his shock. "You can't find our predicament amusing."

Her lips turned down. "I'd rather laugh than cry." She turned away and gazed across the choppy water. "You can see what everyone thinks when they look at us. That waiter this morning leered."

"We're newlyweds," he said somberly. "If your stepbrothers inquire, I want people to say we acted like any couple."

"Then perhaps you should touch me, " she said softly but implacably. She still stared over the restless iron gray sea.

Silence fell. While the waves rolled and the gulls cried and traffic clattered along the street behind them.

"Charis . . ."

She turned and the humor had fled. "You touched me last night."

He clenched his gloved hands by his sides. Clearly his sweet young wife was in the mood to torment him. "I didn't think you'd want to talk about what happened," he said in a tight voice. Christ, he didn't.

"Why would you think that?"

Because I hurt you. Because I made a tragic mess of something that should be wondrous. Because I can't stop thinking how it felt to be inside you.

"Because it's done."

An inadequate, cowardly answer. He knew it. So, blast her, did she.

"You're crossing a line through the subject of our . . . marital relations, never to revisit it?" Color still marked her high cheekbones. She wasn't as easy with this discussion as she wanted to appear.

"Don't you think that's best?"

She arched her elegant light brown eyebrows, a few shades darker than the bright glory of her hair under the neat chip bonnet. "No negotiation?"

He released a heavy sigh. "Revisiting last night should be as painful for you as it is for me."

She straightened from the wall and sent him a direct look. "You . . . you did what you had to."

"There was no joy." If only someone would approach so she'd abandon this conversation. But the promenade around them remained empty.

"Practice makes perfect," she said staunchly.

Every brave word gashed at him. "Not in this case."

He longed to tell her he'd give up his hope of heaven to change desolate reality. He longed to tell her she was more beautiful than the dawn. He longed to tell her he died of desire for her.

What good was any of that when, if he touched her, he'd only hurt her?

Her jaw set in a stubborn line. "I don't accept that."

"You have to." Why couldn't she see there was no hope? After how he'd botched things last night, she should shrink from him as if he had the plague.

"The Westons are fighters, Gideon," she said firmly. Her throat moved as she swallowed, another indication that beneath her determination, she was nervous. "I want a husband in my bed. I intend to do anything I can to achieve that end. Anything. I know you want me. I'll use it against you if I can."

Oh, dear Lord in heaven. He supposed he should admire her honesty in admitting her strategy, but all he could think of was the lacerating misery awaiting both of them. "We made a bargain . . ."

She shook her head. "No, you set ultimatums."

"You agreed." He couldn't keep a hint of temper from showing. It was difficult enough fighting for his own equilibrium without having to fight her as well.

"Yes, I did. Then." When she looked down, gold-tipped lashes fanned the hectic pink of her cheeks.

Need, primitive, uncontrollable, gnawed at him. How much easier this would be if she wasn't so beautiful.

Or would it?

He'd liked her from the start. His longing wasn't rooted in her appearance, spectacular as that was. He wanted her because of her pure, unquenchable spirit.

His voice roughened with urgency. He admired her courage, but she was tragically mistaken in what she wanted. "Charis, I beg of you, don't push this. I know what I ask seems cruel. But crueler by far to keep you clinging to futile hope. You'll end up destroying us both."

The fugitive color fled as quickly as it had arisen, and the eyes she raised were dull with misery. "It could save us too."

Regretfully he shook his head. "This isn't a fairy story, my wife."

Her lips flattened in displeasure. "No, it's a story where you consign me to another man's bed. Is that what you want?"

The prospect of her sharing last night's intimacies with another lover made him burn, like someone brushed his skin with naked flame. The idea of anyone but him touching her, hearing her sigh—God, pressing into that tight sheath— hurled him to the verge of murder.

"Yes."

"Liar."

She cast him a scornful look, turned, and marched back

toward the hotel, her boots clicking on the cobblestones. Helplessly Gideon stared after her. Unless he was very much mistaken, his wife had just declared war.

When he was younger, before Rangapindhi, he'd occasionally imagined taking a bride. The idea had seemed simple, inevitable, uncomplicated.

Hopelessly naïve.

He bit back a curse. He'd known when he came up with this plan to save her, it meant suffering. He'd known it required will and sacrifice.

But until his wife threatened to seduce him, he had no idea what hell awaited.

She was yards away, walking with a natural self-confidence that attracted more than one admiring glance from the few men braving the cold.

Impudent dogs.

Biting down his rage with her, with himself, with the whole damned world, he strode after her. His eyes never wavered from the saucy sway of her hips.

She didn't look at him when he caught up. For the sake of appearances, he grabbed her arm. Even through his glove and her merino sleeve, he felt the tingling warmth of her skin. The ineffable life force that had set his desire afire when he held her last night.

He wanted that heat and vitality.

Devil take it, he wanted her.

Even as another sizzling bolt of need hit, the old urge to snatch away fought to the surface.

She glanced sideways. "Are you all right?"

"Yes," he grated out, trying to control his inevitable shaking. He sucked in a breath and spoke with corrosive bitterness. "This is what you want? You've got bats in your belfry."

She looked straight ahead. "I want you."

Her voice was firm, sure, determined. And a little sad. Gideon had to remind himself she was a girl and couldn't know her own mind. After last night, the words rang hollow, false.

"Well, God help you," he said grimly, and tightened his reluctant hold on her slender arm.

Charis sat up in the bed where last night she'd lost her maidenhead. Rain slammed against the windows, and wind rattled the glass. The wild weather was nothing compared to the confused storm of emotions in her heart.

She'd hated what Gideon had done to her last night. More, she hated that he'd hated it. She was vain enough to want her husband to find pleasure in her.

There had been no pleasure.

Actually, that wasn't completely true. She'd felt pleasure when he touched her, even with him wearing those wretched gloves. When he'd stroked her bare flesh, a wanton heat had curled in her belly. Her breasts had ached for his caress, and her pulse had kicked into an unsteady race.

At last the body she'd longed to explore had been near enough to touch.

If he'd allowed her to touch him.

He'd been near enough for her to breathe his clean scent and feel the warmth radiating from his skin. She'd seen the hard planes of his chest, felt the brush of his hair against her neck.

All tantalizing hints of what they could find together, if only she could free him from Rangapindhi.

Her belly knotted as she recalled the unbearable intimacy of that moment when he pushed inside her. The pain had been overwhelming, but the act had bound her to him as nothing else could.

They were one flesh.

Only now did she understand what those words truly meant. Perhaps the anguish of the consummation made the joining so irrevocable. Perhaps if they'd embarked on married life in lighthearted hope, she wouldn't suffer this dark obsession with her husband.

She knew Gideon felt the connection too. For all he tried so staunchly to stay separate.

For the sake of that connection, she meant to take a huge risk. A risk not only for her and her bruised, longing heart. But also a risk for Gideon's grimly retained sanity and health. Heaven forfend she was wrong. The consequences would be tragic.

In the long dark watches of the night, she'd felt at the crossroads between two futures. The future Gideon planned—cold, divided, lonely. A future where she didn't resist his decision to give up on hope and love.

Or there was another future. A future where they grew together, confronted their challenges, created a family and a home.

Was there a chance she could make this second future reality?

Charis didn't fool herself about the magnitude of the obstacles. But last night as she'd witnessed his pain, something in her screamed denial at abandoning him to suffering. She yearned to cherish him. She wanted to restore his trust in life. More, his trust in himself. She wanted to give him back his capacity for happiness.

All huge tasks.

Impossible?

No. She refused to give up. Whatever it cost her.

Half an hour ago she'd left him in the parlor. He'd been drinking brandy, and the bleakness in his eyes had made her want to weep. The desolation had always been there, but now she knew his past, it cut her to the bone.

He'd already decided his life was over.

Well, the woman he'd married meant to shatter that resolution. She loved him so much, she couldn't lose.

Brave words. She wished she felt half as confident.

She looked up from her troubled thoughts to see Gideon

standing in the doorway. She hadn't heard him arrive. He always moved like a cat, so that was hardly surprising. His hair was ruffled, and one gloved hand negligently encircled a glass. He'd removed his neckcloth, and his shirt was open, giving her shadowy glimpses of his hard chest.

His masculine beauty was a constant goad. Sometimes, like now, it stopped her heart.

Her belly clenched as his half-dressed state inevitably reminded her of last night. His remorse at what he'd done that stabbed her like a blade. His sorrow afterward that made her want to die.

He didn't advance into the room. "I'll say good night, Charis."

"Aren't you coming to bed?" The question emerged as a husky invitation.

She licked lips dry with nerves. His gaze fastened feverishly on the movement. His gloved hand tautened on his brandy. The warm air swirled with sudden sensual turbulence.

He cleared his throat and shifted his gaze above her head. "I'm sleeping in the parlor. I think . . . I think it's best."

With unsteady hands, she grabbed a shawl and slid out of bed. Ignoring the resistance in his face, she stepped close enough to read ravaging torment in his dark eyes. "Don't be ridiculous, Gideon. It's cold and uncomfortable."

He looked at her. "After Rangapindhi, it's the height of luxury."

"Oh, my dear, Rangapindhi is over," she said in a low voice. It seemed a sign of progress that he mentioned his captivity without prompting. She extended one hand toward him, then let it drop to her side. "You're free."

His smile held no amusement. "I'll never be free."

This acceptance of his fate angered her. "If you don't fight, you won't."

His tall, lean body vibrating resentment, he stalked across to the fireplace. He tossed back his brandy and set the glass down sharply on the mantel. He focused a furious glare on her. "Don't talk about what you don't understand."

She mustered her fading courage. She couldn't fail at the first hurdle. Worse difficulties awaited before she gained what she wanted for him. A chance at happiness. Liberation from his past.

Her mind filled with a sudden memory of the stark desire in his face as he'd looked at her body last night. Had she nerve to use that weapon to break him?

With excruciating slowness, she let the beautiful shawl slide down. Her new nightdress was silk, and while far from immodest, had been designed by Madame Claire with a honeymoon in mind.

Color lined his slanted cheekbones as his eyes followed the slipping shawl, then returned to trace the dip of the neckline over her breasts. She shivered under that heated gaze and was suddenly overwhelmingly aware that sheer white material clung to hips and buttocks and swirled around her bare legs. The strange hot weight, familiar from last night, settled in her belly. Her heart set up a rapid tattoo of excitement.

"I understand you've decided to wallow in self-pity for the remainder of your days," she said, knowing she wasn't fair. But this wasn't about fairness. This was about ripping at his control until his memories lost their grip.

"You have no right to say that." A muscle jerked erratically in his cheek. He was close to losing patience.

"I'm your wife. I can say what I like," she said defiantly, standing straight, so her breasts pressed against the delicately embroidered bodice. The cool brush of silk on her nipples teased, built the damp heat between her legs. Her breasts swelled, yearning for his hands.

"This is a marriage of convenience," he said, sounding strangled. He was taut as a drawn bow. His gloved hands opened and closed convulsively at his sides.

"It's more like a marriage of inconvenience," she shot back, taking a step in his direction and tossing her thick plait behind one shoulder.

Feverishly, his eyes clung to her. "We had a bargain."

"Yes, my safety in return for a lifetime of unhappiness." She fought to keep her voice steady. Difficult when every reaction she achieved from him stoked the heat inside her. "Forgive me if I seek to renegotiate."

He turned away and closed his eyes as if he couldn't bear to look at her. One unsteady hand curled over the edge of the mantel.

"I won't forgive you if you make this more a nightmare than it already is." He flung his head up and glared at her like he hated her. His furious black eyes threatened to incinerate her where she stood. "Why the hell would you want to repeat last night's farrago? Damn it, Charis, I hurt you."

"It doesn't have to be like that," she said in a ghost of her usual voice.

"For us, it does." He sounded heartbreakingly sure.

Doubt frayed her resolution. What if she was wrong? What if her plan to help him only damaged him further? She lifted her chin and shored up her courage. "I'm not giving up, Gideon."

His mouth thinned with anger, but when he spoke, his voice was frigid. "You will. This is a war you can't win."

She spread her hands in helpless bewilderment. He had so much strength. Why didn't he enlist it in his own cause? "Don't you want a real life?"

His short laugh was so harsh, it flayed like flying shards of glass. "Of course I do."

She fought the impulse to retreat. She'd known when she chose this path that her greatest enemy would be Gideon himself. "Your memories aren't always in control," she said hoarsely. "I saw you in Portsmouth. You knocked down any man within reach. You weren't afraid to touch people then."

"Yes, I find relief in violence." His voice roughened into sarcasm. "Are you suggesting I beat you?"

She blinked back hot tears. How easy to make optimistic promises when she lay alone in her bed. Less so facing his stubborn intransigence.

He was so angry and lost, and he defended himself the

only way he could. She knew he acted for her sake. He firmly believed he wasn't worthy of her love. He believed living with him would destroy her. Limitless self-loathing was one of the toxic fruits of Rangapindhi.

Could she change his mind? Did she have the power to reach him? "Gideon . . ." she protested huskily.

He stiffened and glared at her. "Don't be a fool. I'd never hurt you."

She bent her head. "You're hurting me now."

She glanced up to see his face darken with remorse. He made one of those strange truncated gestures she'd noticed from the first. "Charis, don't."

She shook her head and twined her arms around herself. She was cold with a chill of the soul more than the body. If only he'd take her in his arms and warm her. "I can't help it," she whispered.

He stepped close enough for her to feel his living heat. How could he consign himself to a cold tomb of isolation?

"I've done you a great wrong," he said with a regret that made her want to cry.

"No."

"Yes, I have. I hoped to preserve your freedom by tying you to a man who made no demands. Instead, I've only brought you pain."

"I want to be your wife," she said obstinately.

"You are my wife."

"Not in any way that counts."

He sighed heavily and ran his hand through his hair. "Charis, you ask too much."

"Better than asking nothing at all," she snapped back.

His eyes flashed, and he swung away. She knew it was unjust to berate him over what he couldn't change.

Something women always said when they made less-than-satisfactory marriages.

He looked tired, discouraged. Her demands couldn't be easy. He'd come to an unknown woman's rescue and adopted responsibilities that took over his life.

Except she didn't believe he felt like that. In her heart, she believed he could love her. Sometimes, she caught him staring at her with such hunger, her heart skipped a beat.

"All I can promise is once we've established our marriage's legality, you can set up home anywhere," he said with a coldness she knew was meant to put her at a distance. "You need never see me again. This interlude will become only an unhappy memory."

"You think that's what I want?" she asked bitterly.

"You must make it what you want." He stepped away with an ironic gesture of one gloved hand. "Now go to bed."

Her temper had stirred distantly as she'd listened to his self-sacrificing statements. Now it sparked. Her jaw tensed. "Are you going to sleep by my side?" she asked in a dangerous tone.

He looked surprised. He needed to learn she wasn't an obedient hound to leap to his slightest command. He asked her to leave him alone to go to perdition. But she wasn't allowing him his way. The determination that had gripped her before he appeared returned full force. She wouldn't let him settle for this barren half-life he mapped out.

"No, of course not." He frowned. "Haven't you heard a word?"

"I've heard everything, and I agree with none of it."

"We'll talk in the morning."

Her lips tightened. "I'm sure we will."

"So good night." He turned toward the door, then must have realized she hadn't shifted. He confronted her with a frown of irritation. "Do you want something before I go?"

"I want you to come to bed."

His lips quirked in a sour grimace. "After what happened there, any normal woman would run shrieking."

She flinched at the *normal woman* remark but didn't budge. "I'm not asking you to do . . . that again." Hot color rushed into her cheeks.

"So you want a chaste bedmate?" His voice dripped derision.

She drew a harsh breath. "I want you with me, Gideon."

"No."

"All right. I'll sleep in the parlor." She folded her arms and stared at him implacably.

"Don't be absurd," he said with the beginnings of real anger. She realized until now he hadn't taken her seriously.

Of course he didn't. He thought she was a fragile young thing who needed protecting. Before they were done, he'd learn his wife possessed a will at least as strong as his. And a heart as valiant. She meant to fight for her marriage. She meant to fight for his future.

"Get into that bed now," he growled.

She shivered although the room wasn't cold. "Make me."

He straightened, and she watched rage war with frustration on his face. "You're acting like a child."

She shrugged and scooped the shawl from where it lay at her feet. "Shall I take the chair tonight?" She spoke with a nonchalance she didn't feel.

His jaw moved as he ground his teeth. Another shiver rippled through her. There was forbidden excitement in taunting him.

"Devil take you," he grated out, taking a step closer.

She wrapped the shawl around her shoulders and hoped to heaven he didn't take her at her word and make her sit up all night. The bedroom was warm, the parlor wasn't. She'd be blue within an hour, and after the last two nights, the prospect of stretching out in a soft bed was alluring.

She angled her chin and sent him the haughty stare she'd employed on a hundred importunate suitors. "Do you mean to herd me into the bed, Gideon?"

"You . . ."

She raised her eyebrows. "Yes?"

"You damned witch." His eyes glittered with fury.

Her belly quivered with nerves. And something far more powerful. "Hardly polite."

"Oh, hell!"

He lashed out and grabbed her around the waist. In one

furious movement, he swept her off her feet and bundled her against his chest.

She'd waited for this, prayed for it. Even so, the shock of his arms holding her high, the heat of his skin through his shirt, his sheer vibrating fury made her gasp.

His hands tightened, and he stared straight ahead. "You asked for this," he snarled, marching toward the bed.

Yes, she had. Thank the Lord, she'd got it. Tentatively, she slid one hand behind his neck, tangling her fingers in the silky hair at his nape. He didn't seem to notice.

"How dare you use brute force against me?" She wanted to sound outraged. The best she could manage was a dull sulkiness. While all the time, her heart danced.

"You should have thought of that before," he bit out.

The distant courtesy he cultivated before the world was gone. Instead, he was big, angry, commanding and breathtakingly male. A thrill sizzled through her right to her cold toes.

He reached the edge of the mattress. "Good night, Charis."

Unceremoniously, he dropped her to the tumbled sheets in a tangle of legs and arms and silky white nightgown.

For a moment, she lay winded, staring up at him. He'd had no difficulty carrying her. For all his leanness, he was very strong. The thought sent another thrill rocketing through her.

"How . . ." She paused and sucked in another breath. "How are you going to keep me here?"

"I could tie you up." He still sounded angry.

"You wouldn't."

"And gag you. Gagging seems a capital idea."

She pressed down into the mattress, wondering why the idea of her husband binding her made her belly tighten with excitement. "I'd bite you," she said breathlessly.

He closed his eyes as if praying for strength. "Devil take you, Charis . . ."

He turned away. Her heart sank as she waited for him to head for the door. After all her efforts, she'd lost. She ached with weariness. The day had been long and difficult for her as well as him. If she gave up tonight, would she have the will to fight again tomorrow?

Desperately, she scrambled for some argument to stop him retreating into the lonely fortress of the parlor. But she'd reached the limits of her persuasion. He'd touched her, and logic fled. All she knew was she'd do anything to make him touch her again.

He veered left before he exited the room and dropped onto a stool near the door. Violently he began to tug at his boots.

Relief welled. And wild rejoicing. She could hardly believe it. He stayed.

More, he confirmed her theory that at heights of emotion, he escaped his affliction. He'd touched her, carried her. He hadn't trembled or flinched. He'd been too furious to remember Rangapindhi.

Could a fever of desire achieve similar results?

The light was strong enough for her to see he was still annoyed. It was clear in his jerky movements and the flat line of his mouth.

"Do you want some help?" she asked in a shaky voice.

"Don't push it, Charis," he said grimly. He stood up on his bare feet and prowled across to the bed, umbrage bristling from every line of his long body.

She moved to give him room and snuggled under the blankets. The intimacy of his presence tonight seemed more intense than yesterday's reluctant consummation.

He slid into the bed and stretched out on his back. No part of his body touched hers.

"Aren't you going to undress?" she asked, although the question was inane. He lay next to her fully clothed. Clearly he meant to remain that way.

"No."

Heavens, he even kept his gloves on. She realized with a shock she'd never seen his naked hands.

That abruptly struck her as significant. Gentlemen wore gloves as a matter of course, and it was winter. But Gideon didn't feel the cold, and she'd seen him without neckcloth

and in his shirtsleeves, both far greater faux pas than forgetting his gloves. It seemed odd he was punctilious on this one
matter of dress.

Odd. Mysterious. *Important.*

He settled himself more comfortably. She was overwhelmingly aware of his physical presence. The way the mattress
tilted under him. His scent, so familiar now. The regular rise
and fall of his chest.

"Gideon . . ."

As he turned his head on the pillows to stare at her, she
caught the glint of his eyes. "Good night, Charis."

He sounded resentful. He'd hate being manipulated into
enforced proximity. She couldn't blame him.

But he was here. That was all she cared about.

She'd achieved her first victory. Now she had to work out
how to ignite his passion so the next time they shared this
bed, he touched her as her husband.

How she wished she knew more about men. All she had to
work on was instinct and last night's painful and embarrass-
ing joining. Surely the delicious feelings he aroused in her
weren't meant to end in desolation. There must be pleasure
in the act. Else why would people risk so much for passion?

Perhaps one day soon she'd find out.

"Good night, Gideon," she whispered, linking her hands
at her waist to stop them reaching for him.

Sixteen

Since Rangapindhi, horror and pain had poisoned Gideon's dreams. This dream belonged to a different, more benevolent world. Slender arms cradled him. A soft female breast curved under his cheek. A woman's breath sighed in time with his.

The piercing isolation that scored his every waking moment vanished. In this bewitching fantasy, he rejoined the human race.

Dear heaven, let him not wake.

Not yet.

Convulsively, he tightened the arms he curled around the woman's waist. He buried his face deeper in the lush bosom. A peppery floral fragrance teased his senses.

A familiar fragrance.

He knew who he dreamt about. He'd known from the first.

"Charis . . ." he whispered into the frail silk veiling her breast.

His dream wife stroked his hair back from his forehead.

The gesture's tenderness slashed his heart. Her fingers brushed his face, and he felt the breath stall in her lungs.

The dream's physical detail was so rich. So real.

Too real.

It was too late. He knew he wasn't asleep. The brief warmth was cruel mockery. Already he shrank from contact. Charis's scent became the oversweet stink of putrefying flesh. The touch of her hand, the grip of dead fingers.

His belly churning with nausea, he rolled away. As he sat up, he kept his back to her. He didn't want her to see the revulsion that he knew darkened his face.

"Hell," he groaned, burying his head in shaking hands. He tensed his throat against rising nausea.

"Gideon?" One word quivering with distress.

Of course she was distressed. She'd married a damned madman.

Through his agony, he was vaguely aware of how massively aroused he was. Hard as oak. Hot as Hades. It was a spiteful caprice of his affliction that his body continued to react like any virile twenty-five-year-old's.

"Gideon, are you all right?"

"Yes." He was lying.

Sunlight burned behind the closed curtains. Bedclothes rustled as she rose onto her knees. Damnably evocative sound. Desire became a hammering demand in his veins, so loud it drowned out the caterwauling in his skull. He wasn't sure whether desire or demons inflicted worse torture.

"I don't believe you." The mattress dipped as she shifted closer. Then—God help him—the insidious warmth of her hand on his tense back.

He went rigid, fighting the urge to wrench away. Fighting the urge to whirl around, fling her onto the sheets, and ravish her.

"Don't you know not to touch me?" he forced out through clenched teeth. Every breath strained his constricted lungs. His heart pounded so hard, he thought it must burst.

"I know you spent the night lying in my arms," she said quietly. Without, confound her, taking her hand away.

He'd broken into an icy sweat when he returned to full alertness. Now heat pooled where she touched him, making his blood simmer.

"I was asleep," he growled, loving her touch, hating her touch.

"I know," she said patiently, her palm rubbing in tantalizing, tormenting circles. He wore a shirt but the sensation of her touch was so intense, he might as well have been naked.

He was amazed steam didn't rise from his quivering flesh. His cock throbbed with the demand to be inside her. The memory of thrusting into her was so sharp, he could taste it.

"The difficulty is in your head. It's not in your body." She spoke slowly, as if trying to explain a mathematical problem to a dim student. How could she sound so calm when he was on the verge of exploding?

He could bear it no longer. He had to get away before he did something irrevocable, unforgivable. He lurched to his feet, spinning to confront her.

"I know that. It doesn't mean I'm making it up. God, Charis, if I could . . ."

He stopped and sucked in a shuddering breath. What use raging against fate? He couldn't do anything to alter his bleak future.

Although she must know his anger wasn't targeted at her, she paled under his onslaught. She knelt on the tumbled sheets in that sinful white nightdress. Gideon fought not to notice the provocative jut of her breasts against the transparent silk. He lost the battle. His eyes feasted on those luscious curves, and the moisture evaporated from his mouth. At his sides, his hands opened and closed as he struggled not to grab her.

"Don't you see what that means?" she asked earnestly, not seeming to register his seething restlessness.

Her voice was faint over the deafening crash of his heart. Had he missed something she said while he ogled her like a randy adolescent?

"Gideon?"

She clearly expected him to make coherent conversation. Didn't she realize the state he was in? But her eyes remained focused on his face with a sweet determination that only made him want her more.

He turned and snatched the armoire behind him open. He squeezed his eyes shut in an agony of desire as faint floral scent filled his nostrils.

Now that she wasn't touching him, hunger threatened to overpower him. Only the humiliating knowledge that touching her would unman him kept him from leaping on her.

Blindly, he fumbled in the dark cupboard until his hand fell on what he wanted. He turned and flung the yellow pelisse at Charis. "You're cold."

And I'm on fire.

She caught the coat and sent him a speculative look. To his frustration, she didn't cover her body.

Curse her, it was February. Didn't the woman have an ounce of sense? Through the buzzing in his ears, he tried to concentrate on what she said.

". . . and then you're free."

He shook his head to clear the fog from his eyes. "Free?"

Her soft pink mouth took on the tiniest of curves. "Are you listening?"

Itchy heat crawled up the back of his neck. He forced himself to stare at the undistinguished landscape on the wall behind her head. But the image of her perched on the bed, disheveled from sleep, was etched into his eyeballs.

"Of course I am."

She made a doubtful sound deep in her throat. He couldn't resist looking at her. Then he wished he hadn't surrendered to temptation. On her knees in front of him, she seemed all too available.

"It's important," she said.

"What?"

The hint of a smile faded, and her voice lowered into seriousness. "When you forget yourself, you're free."

He frowned. "I never forget myself."

"Yes, you do. You forget yourself in violence. You forget yourself in sleep. Perhaps if you wanted it enough, you could forget yourself in . . ."

"A good swiving?" he finished on a sarcastic note. Frustration sparked. "Every damned doctor in London poked and pried at me. None suggested the sex cure. Perhaps they should have. Even if the remedy doesn't work, their patients won't care." His voice roughened into urgency. "Will you bloody well cover yourself?"

She lifted the pelisse, inspected it with an unreadable expression. And deliberately tossed it to the floor.

"No." With a languor that in a more experienced woman he'd attribute to purposeful enticement, she leaned to one side and uncurled her legs.

He wouldn't look. He wouldn't look.

He looked.

The nightdress hiked up, revealing neat ankles and gracefully curved calves. The night before last, he'd slid between those slender legs and he'd . . .

His mind slammed shut on the memory. He'd hurt her and disgraced himself. He couldn't go through that again for all the gold in Guinea.

She slid her feet to the floor and stood. Still with that eye-catching slowness. To his regret, he watched her hem slither down to her bare feet. God help him, just the sight of her toes, rosy and perfect, made him think of bedsport.

Even during his wild early days in India, no woman had stirred him to this pitch of arousal. He swallowed the constriction in his throat and forced himself to say what he must. "Charis, we've been through this before. There's nothing to be done."

He strove to sound calm, sensible, resigned. Difficult

when his heart raced at triple time, and he couldn't rip his gaze from the girl standing only a few feet away. One step in her direction, and he'd be close enough to grab her.

What a damned disaster that would be.

"So you say," she said softly.

Was her voice always so husky? Or did his ears play tricks? He fisted his gloved hands by his sides and prayed for strength.

"What happened . . . changed me. I'm not a whole man."

Those sinfully thick eyelashes veiled her eyes. He couldn't remember seeing anyone in such minute detail before. It was like all the light in the world shone just on her.

"You looked whole the other night," she said evenly, although color rose in her cheeks.

Oh, dear merciful God in heaven. How could she remind him of that? It was meant to be the one time. It must be the one time.

His aching cock twitched as if to deny that assertion.

"You know what I mean," he snarled, nearly frantic with the painful heat sizzling through him. Heat that found no outlet. "You know . . . *What the devil are you doing?*"

"Unbinding my hair." She sounded unconcerned. Her deft fingers undid the long plait that curved sinuously across one shoulder.

"Don't." The command emerged as a croak.

"I need to brush it out and put it up for the day."

"Blast you, that's not why you're doing this."

He couldn't help but watch those busy fingers. Nor could he turn away when she buried her hands in the bronze mane and combed it loose so it fell like a shining curtain. Desire knotted every muscle in his body.

He lifted his hands to touch the glorious mass. Then hesitated midair. Feeling like the greatest fool in Christendom.

"Why do you think I'm doing it?" She shook her head so her hair slid around her in dark gold splendor.

"Your purpose is . . . seduction."

He stumbled over the last word like a prim spinster. Decadent images of that silky hair flowing about him as he pounded into her body fired his brain.

"You say you're impervious to the lure of the flesh."

"I never said that."

"Then what's stopping you?" She raised one hand and tugged at the ribbon holding her plunging neckline closed.

"Don't damn well do that." He should walk out the door right now.

"Why?"

He couldn't immediately think of an answer. All he could think of was how he would hurt her with his vile clumsiness if this scene reached the end she clearly wanted.

Why in Hades didn't she avoid him after that rough coupling? What was wrong with the chit?

His lips parted on a groan as her bodice gaped to reveal the valley between her breasts. He forced himself to concentrate on her face instead of her bosom. His heart slammed to a stop. The silent determination in her eyes shook him.

If he intended to retain a shred of honor, he needed to get out of here. Now. She didn't know what she invited. She couldn't.

"I'll wait outside while you dress."

"Coward," she said softly but distinctly.

"Charis, it's for the best." He tried to remember why he couldn't just jump on her and take what he wanted. His mind was a black, impenetrable jungle.

"Is the Hero of Rangapindhi running for cover?"

"I'm no hero," he snarled, cut to the quick. He *abhorred* the name the press bestowed on him. He turned to escape, unable any longer to bear the sight of what he wanted most in the world. Displayed for his delectation like a banquet. As unreachable as the stars. "I'll order breakfast."

He waited for argument, plea, protest. But she was silent. Clearly, she'd recognized her quest to seduce her oaf of a husband was futile.

He told himself that what trickled through his veins like

acid was relief. She must at last see he was no use to her. It was tragic but irrefutable.

He reached for the door. Through unfocused eyes, he noticed his hand was unsteady.

There was a sudden flurry of footsteps behind him. Then a blinding, exquisite moment when she hurled herself, every lovely inch, against his back.

The shock stopped his breath. His heart hitched, then crashed against his ribs. Her heat made him dizzy. The softness of her breasts and belly pressed into him. Her arms snaked around his waist.

"Don't go," she said in a broken voice.

She leaned her cheek upon his back. The fragrances of carnations and warm female flesh filled his senses like smoke. He closed his eyes and groaned. Swearing under his breath, he banged his head on the door. The sharp pain did nothing to clear his mind.

His skin prickled at the contact, but sexual hunger drowned out his screaming demons. He could touch her now, all right. But in this state, he wasn't safe with any woman, let alone this exquisite girl.

He sucked in more air. Speech was torture when every sense concentrated on Charis. "Please step away."

Her grip around his waist tightened, and he felt desperation in the clawing fingers. She strained so close, he felt her every breath. And her trembling. "You'll leave."

"I must." His voice cracked, and he clutched the doorknob so hard, his hand spasmed. "For God's sake, Charis, do as I ask."

For a long moment, she didn't budge. Then, with tangible reluctance, she slid her arms away and straightened.

His animal hunger spiked, insisted he seize her, toss her on her back. Grinding his teeth, he beat back the raging demands.

He released the doorknob. His hand ached with stiffness. Slowly, against his will, he turned to face her.

She stood a couple of feet away. Her chest heaved as she

fought for breath. He'd been terrified he'd made her cry. But for all her palpable, quaking misery, she remained dry-eyed. In a defiant gesture he recognized, she lifted her chin as if she stared down death itself.

Swiftly, she tugged the nightdress over her head and flung it into the corner.

"Damn you, Charis, " he breathed, stepping toward her before he recalled he couldn't touch her. "Don't do this."

Unclothed, she was . . . heavenly. Slender neck, straight shoulders, long graceful arms, high breasts with whorled pink crests. Flat belly punctuated by the sweet hollow of her navel.

Last, helplessly, his gaze focused on the delta between her legs. Blazing arousal flared. He swallowed and forced himself to breathe. He drank in the sight of her as he'd drink from an oasis after crossing a desert.

The desert still extended ahead.

Dry. Waterless. Barren. Deadly.

She glanced down at his trousers, then unflinchingly lifted her eyes. "You want me. I know it." Her voice broke.

He strove to deny his desire. But his throat closed and wouldn't permit that ultimate heresy.

His heart pumped out an inexorable rhythm. Two words. Over and over. *Take her. Take her. Take her.*

"Do I . . . do I please you?"

He fought to frame the lie, to tell her she meant nothing to him, to set her free.

Vibrating with tension, she stood before him. She stared back from steady hazel eyes, more brown than green. But her lips were soft with a vulnerability that mangled his gut.

He opened his mouth to speak.

She didn't flinch. Nor did her gaze waver.

She must guess what he meant to say.

Her mouth trembled. If he hadn't watched so closely, he'd have missed the tiny tensing of her lips. It was the reaction of someone braced for the killing blow, for pain past endurance.

He knew that feeling. Just so had he faced down his jailers in Rangapindhi.

That hint of vulnerability broke him.

Three strides, and he was at her side. He swung her high in his arms. Blood thundered in his ears. Two more strides, and he reached the bed. Without letting her go, he pushed her back onto the crumpled sheets.

Gideon was pure animal. Savage. Hungry. Desperate.

He knelt between her legs, his cock straining. Roughly, he brushed away the thick dark blond hair cascading across her bare breasts. The demons shrieked for him to stop, but roaring physical need trapped them behind a wall of glass.

He grabbed her hips with his gloved hands and pressed hard, openmouthed kisses across the white plain of her belly. She tasted like hot musky honey.

He suckled on her nipple, pressing it against his tongue, drawing the flavor deep into his mouth. She cried out and bucked.

He didn't linger. This moment poised on a knife edge. His lips closed on her other nipple, biting until she writhed. She lifted her hands to his shoulders.

Dear God, if she pushed him away, what would he do?

But her fingers dug into his damp shirt, clenching and unclenching in time with the rhythm of his mouth on her breast.

He ripped his trousers open. The pounding in his head was so loud, he hardly heard the material shredding.

With ruthless hands, he angled her hips up and plunged into her.

Heat.

Pressure.

One fragile, glowing moment that might have been peace.

Stray details overwhelmed starved senses. Her scent. The soft rattle of her breathing. The way she quivered under him.

He rose to look at her. Her eyes were closed, and her face was stark with tension. Damn it, he must be hurting her. Principle insisted he stop, withdraw, leave her be.

He began to pull out. Meaning to end this travesty. But the sensation of his tumescent flesh sliding free of her sleek passage nearly blew the top of his head off. Pleasure so intense it edged on pain incinerated him in a white-hot blast.

His scruples dissolved to ash. His heart tolled a despairing note as he thrust back inside her. Hard. Demanding. Pitiless.

She closed around him with what felt like welcome. This time he paused, luxuriating in the tightness. He shifted. Edged deeper.

Charis moaned, a low, guttural sound that resonated in his gut. The hands on his shoulders slid down to curl around his straining back. She tilted her hips higher.

Her eyes opened. The pupils were dilated, and the irises were rich gold. The skin on her face stretched tight. She tipped her head back, her thick lashes fluttered down, and she arched with a long, low, keening sound.

What frail restraints he'd imposed snapped. There was just the hot clasp of her body and his thundering need.

He changed the angle of penetration. Her body moved with him. He withdrew and thrust again. He needed the rhythm more than he needed breath.

Faster.

Harder.

The endless rocking of his hips against hers. The slide of his flesh into her slender body. The creak of the bed. The rustle of the sheets. The catch of her breath.

His body tensed. The pace became wilder.

His release built, knotting his spine, twisting his gut, tightening his balls to agony.

He lifted his head, and his throat clenched on a shout. Anguish. Shame. Possession.

Freedom.

One last thrust. His world ignited into fire.

He flooded her with his agony and his loss and his anger. His hips jerked as the crisis flung him into eternity.

For a long time, Gideon's mind closed down to anything but the volcanic release.

He slumped over her, gasping for breath. There was only his quivering body, the gallop of his heart, the warm embrace of darkness.

He was utterly exhausted. Weary to the point of torpor.

Vaguely, he heard her make a sound of discomfort.

He tried to shut it from his mind. He belonged in this darkness. He wanted to stay here.

He'd acted like a beast.

The unwelcome knowledge nibbled at the blanketing stillness.

Oh, merciful God, what have I done?

With a groan of utter desolation, he pulled free and rolled onto his back. If he could trust his legs to carry him, he'd walk out.

He stared at the ceiling, waiting for his breath to steady and his heartbeat to resume its usual rate. Waiting for the world to crash in on him.

In spite of his howling conscience, his physical self relished what he'd done. The sheer power of the experience eclipsed every previous sexual encounter the way the sun outshone a candle.

He stirred, turned his head to look at Charis. The movement cost the last of his depleted strength. She'd drained him to the lees.

"Are you all right?" he asked gruffly.

She was in profile. She licked her lips. The innocent movement sent a smoldering bolt to his loins. Suddenly, he wasn't quite as exhausted as he had been.

She made no attempt to cover her nakedness. Knowing she lay bare beside him piqued his desire. He, on the other hand, hadn't had the finesse to do more than tear his trousers open and have at her.

"Perfectly, thank you."

Gideon frowned. Her polite, detached tone worried him.

Perhaps he really had hurt her. He leaned up on one elbow to see into her face. "I fell on you like a hungry dog on a bone."

She stared upward. He wondered what her determinedly neutral expression concealed. Devastation? Fury? Pain? Oh, hell, don't let him have done her injury. He'd been passionately unrestrained, and until two nights ago, she'd been a virgin.

She glanced at him out the corner of her eye. "You're not shaking. You're not sick. You're not sweating."

He frowned. "I'm worried about you. Forget about me."

"*You* forgot about you."

She sat up, drawing her knees up. The girlish grace of the movement captured his attention, stirred his interest. Then he realized what she'd said.

"Was that an experiment?" Resentment stirred under his concern. "You've got a bloody cheek."

She bent so her thick hair fell forward, hiding her expression. "I couldn't see how else to test if what I guessed was true."

He scowled at her. "And got a right royal fucking in return."

She jerked her head up and stared at him. He sucked in a shuddering breath, ignoring the shock on her face. His tone bit. "I hope you're pleased with yourself, madam."

With a movement that shot another jolt of arousal through him, she shook back her untidy tumble of hair. A smile curved her lush pink lips. Lips which to his shame he hadn't kissed, even as he'd slammed into her like a hammer.

"Of course I'm pleased with myself. I drove my husband wild with desire."

He jackknifed onto his knees. If the habit of keeping his hands to himself weren't so ingrained, he'd shake her until her teeth rattled. "What the devil . . ."

Her smile faded. "Gideon, you touched me."

"Blast you, Charis, I did more than touch you. You deserve better."

She grabbed his arm. "I don't care what I deserve. I want you. However I can get you." The smile reappeared. "And it was exciting."

"Exciting?" He had trouble speaking. He felt like he'd entered a new universe, where nothing from the old one made sense.

"Of course it was exciting," she said urgently. "You looked as if you'd die unless you touched me. You'll do better next time."

"Are you sure there will be a next time?"

"I've discovered your weakness." Satisfaction warmed her voice. "When I'm naked, you're powerless."

The problem was the witch was right. Even now his cock stirred with interest.

She still regarded him with that faint enigmatic smile. "To think I ever doubted you wanted me."

Foolish woman. He gave an unamused laugh. "I always want you. Damn it, Charis, I'm in love with you."

Seventeen

Aghast, Gideon stiffened. *Bloody, bloody, bloody hell. Why in the name of all that was holy did I say that?* He'd give his left arm to take back the words. But it was too late.

Violently, he tugged away from Charis and surged to his feet. He stalked across to scoop the discarded nightdress from the floor. With an angry gesture, he tossed it across the end of the bed.

He should have kept his blasted mouth shut. But the wild, uncontrolled sex had broken some barrier within him. The declaration he'd fought back for so long had surged up unstoppable as a king tide.

She started as if emerging from a daze. "You love me," she whispered.

She stared at him with huge, shining eyes. Her lips parted. She looked so happy, he couldn't bear it. Clearly the damage was done, and there was no point in telling her he'd lied. Although it would be better for both of them if she believed he had.

The harsh facts that put a life with her completely out of reach hadn't changed, for all that every cell of his body ached with love for her. One bout of desperate passion didn't change the cruel reality of his existence. He wasn't a normal man. He'd never be a normal man. And if she pledged herself to him now, one day she'd regret that commitment.

He couldn't bear to contemplate her love turning to hatred and disgust when she realized just what she'd sacrificed by walling herself away with her half-insane wreck of a husband. Her best chance of happiness was to establish a future far away from Gideon and his demons. But he could see what he'd just said made it less likely than ever that he'd convince her of that incontrovertible truth anytime soon.

Again, he cursed the impetuous declaration that forever changed the landscape between him and his beautiful, misguided wife.

"It doesn't matter," he said with a carelessness that even in his own ears sounded false.

A tiny frown line appeared between her brows. "Oh, Gideon." She spoke his name with such deep compassion, he tensed with fuming resentment. He couldn't endure her pity.

So he didn't have to look at her, glowing, irresistible, he struggled to concentrate on doing up his trousers. His gloved hands shook so much that he fumbled hopelessly with the fastenings. It was like being in the grip of his affliction, except he trembled now not because he'd touched her but because he so badly wanted to.

During those dazzling moments in her arms, his world had come right. He could offer her a lifetime of misery while she was his only hope of happiness. That was his eternal burden. He couldn't make her share it.

"I'll ring for hot water," he said with a studied neutrality that cost him more than he wanted to admit. At last he managed to close his trousers. "You'll want to wash."

"That's it?" He still wasn't looking at her, but he heard the irritation in her voice. "You take me to bed. You tell me you love me. Then we just have breakfast as though nothing's happened?"

He glanced up and tried not to notice how very . . . naked she was. "Charis, I wish you'd put on your nightdress."

Her lips firmed with impatience. "That doesn't answer my question."

He sighed and ran his gloved hand through his hair. "Nothing should have happened."

"Why?"

"Will you put on the confounded nightdress?" he demanded in desperation.

She stretched out one slender arm, hooked up the silk garment, and slid it over her tousled head. "There. Is that better?"

"Not really." He breathed hard through his nostrils and fisted his hands at his sides. He burned to take her again. Her defiance only fed his incessant craving. He was an insatiable satyr. If the girl had any sense, she'd run a thousand miles to get away from him.

"I don't see why this is a problem," she said stubbornly. "You love me. I love you."

"You don't love me," he bit out.

She rolled her eyes. The sudden reversion to sulky schoolgirl would have summoned a smile if he didn't feel like she flayed his soul.

"No, of course I don't," she said sarcastically. "I'm a stupid sparrow of a female with hardly brains to feed myself. And you're so terrifically unworthy. The contemptible fellow dragged weeping out of a pit in India when any other man would have taken the trifles you'd endured in his stride."

"Charis . . ." he said in a dangerously low voice. Her mockery cut him to the bone. Especially as it held an unfortunate echo of his genuine concerns. "You go too far."

"Well, it's all so absurd, Gideon." She spread her hands in a frustrated gesture, the movement making her breasts jiggle enticingly under the sheer silk. His mouth dried, and his hands flexed as if they cupped those firm mounds.

"We love each other." Her cheeks flooded with pink. "Why are you standing half a room away?"

A glance under her eyelashes sent blood sizzling through his veins. Damn her, she could give Circe lessons. He braced his shoulders as if only physical restraint stopped him diving on her.

"Because I can't touch you without losing my mind," he snarled, need thundering through his body.

She slid her legs over the bed and stood straight before him. "I touched you before, and you didn't notice."

"You . . ."

He started back as if she touched him now. He'd vaguely noticed she'd taken his arm. When was the last time he'd vaguely noticed even the merest contact with anyone?

Good God, could she be right about sexual excitement offering a reprieve? None of the doctors had suggested it. Ever since his rescue from Rangapindhi, he'd assumed he faced a life of eternal celibacy. Had he been mistaken?

He compelled his lust-fogged mind to review the facts. He'd just maintained extremely intimate contact with his wife. He was far from composed—he was fuming and upset and randy as hell. But if he felt ill, it was his conscience that troubled him, not memories of Rangapindhi.

As if she knew he at last took her idea seriously, she stepped forward and placed one hand flat over his heart. Her cheeks were brilliant with color. "Gideon, what just happened was so lovely. Let's not spoil it by fighting."

He tensed for the familiar sick reaction. There was only the warmth of her hand and the hardening of his cock, which definitely approved of her plan for a normal marriage.

"Lovely?" he forced out in blank astonishment.

Lovely and exciting. His brain tried to make sense of what she said. Neither word seemed adequate to describe that earth-shattering sex. But he was human enough to be grateful she hadn't found his untrammeled passion completely distasteful.

She nodded and sent him a smile that made his gut tighten

with the same lust that had got him in trouble only a short while ago. "Yes, lovely."

Hope, so long a stranger in his life, inched into uncertain life. Was it possible he had changed? He could hardly bear to contemplate the idea. The sudden intrusion of light into the Stygian darkness of his life blinded him, left him bewildered.

Hardly believing he could, he lifted one gloved hand and placed it over hers. Through the fine kid, the heat of her skin was a distant echo of life and joy.

For a forbidden moment, he basked in the glow of her hazel eyes. His hand shook, but with emotion not physical weakness.

He found his voice, rusty, thick, unsteady. "Truce."

He loved her.

Charis could hardly believe it. But Gideon's quaking desperation as he clutched her hand to his chest convinced her it was true, perhaps more than actually hearing the words.

With that declaration, Gideon changed her world forever. Her heart rejoiced. She felt new, reborn, strong. At last there was a chance she could win what she wanted with all her soul for both of them. A life of happiness, a future at Penrhyn, children, contentment, peace.

She and Gideon spent the afternoon tooling around Jersey's lanes in a hired curricle. When he suggested the outing, she'd leaped at the chance to escape their rooms. In the cramped conveyance, awareness tautened between them, but movement and air made the bristling atmosphere bearable.

Almost.

With a flourish, Gideon drew the vehicle to a stop on the crest of a hill. Below spread a vista of fields, with the sea silver in the distance. A breeze teased strands of hair from under her bonnet. The gloomy weather had cleared, and the day was fragrant with coming spring.

He loved her.

The sun shone more brightly. The birds sang more fervently. The air brushed across her skin more sweetly.

"Oh, what a pretty place." She risked tucking her gloved hand around his arm.

When he didn't recoil, she leaned forward, deliberately rubbing the side of her breast against him. Surprised pleasure awoke as she heard his breath catch.

Those torrid moments in his arms had taught her so much. That she could drive him mad with need. That he could touch her with the deepest intimacy. That the sensation of her husband's body pumping into hers was the purest excitement she'd ever known.

Now she was familiar with the scent of his arousal, the sound he made in his throat when he penetrated her flesh, his hard strength as he pounded into her. The experience hadn't been entirely comfortable. He'd been rough, and she wasn't yet accustomed to a man's passion.

He'd thundered into her like a regiment of horses charging down an enemy position. She should have been terrified.

Instead, she'd loved every hot, sweaty minute.

She'd loved his body joining with hers. She'd loved seeing him a helpless slave to desire.

She wanted him to do it again. Soon.

His arm was rigid under her hold, but at least he didn't pull away. "It's good to get out of town." Did she hear a trace of huskiness in his comment?

"The press of people worries you?" She turned to study him. He'd been preoccupied most of the day but to her relief, he showed no signs of illness. What happened this morning had clearly unsettled him. She couldn't doubt he'd found physical satisfaction. But his mind was far from easy.

She curled her fingers around his arm, testing the unrelenting muscle. He was so strong and masculine. The heated memory of him surging into her filled her senses. She felt her color rise.

He sent her a brief, assessing glance. "A little."

It took her a moment to realize he answered her question. The problem with this plan to drive him out of his mind with lust was that she wasn't exactly immune to his touch either. So difficult to focus on a goal when his mere presence turned her into a steaming pool of desire.

She reminded herself to be patient. This would be a long, slow siege, but victory would be worth it. For Gideon and for her.

"London must have been a nightmare."

He looked over the horses' heads, and his gloved hands tightened on the reins. "Yes."

"How did you bear it?"

He shrugged. "I had no choice. The sovereign commanded. I obeyed. I drank. I took opium when liquor failed. I canceled what engagements I could. Tulliver and Akash helped."

"And now there's St. Helier."

He smiled. "Believe me, St. Helier is much easier than London."

"Don't worry. We'll soon be back at Penrhyn."

Amusement sparked his dark eyes to starlight as he glanced at her. "Good God, madam, you sound like a wife."

She met his gleaming gaze, shadowed under the curling brim of his stylish hat. He looked like a buck of the ton. Impossible to reconcile this elegance with the rumpled, satiated man from a few hours ago.

"I am a wife," she said softly. For the first time, she almost felt like one. His eyes changed, focused, and her heart shifted in her breast. "I wish you'd kiss me," she whispered before she reminded herself what trouble her propensity for blurting out her thoughts had already caused.

A taut silence fell. She waited for him to retreat as he had so often before.

The humor drained from his face, replaced by a concentrated sensuality. His gaze dropped to her mouth. Her breath escaped her parted lips on a sigh.

Her senses sharpened. The sounds around them suddenly seemed unusually loud. Birdsong. The sea's distant roar. The jangle of harness as one of the horses shifted.

Then her heart's furious pounding drowned out everything else.

Slowly, so slowly she thought she'd die with waiting, his face moved closer. His warm, moist breath feathered across her lips. She made a choked sound of yearning.

If he stopped now, she'd scream.

He closed his eyes and brushed his lips across hers. A glancing contact.

She growled with impatience and strained toward him. There was no sign of his usual reluctance for physical contact. She silently whispered a prayer of thankfulness.

"You're teasing," she said hoarsely.

Those lips she wanted on hers quirked. "A little. Take off your bonnet, so I can do this properly."

Even through her yearning, she recognized how promising that sounded. With shaking hands, she untied the yellow satin ribbons and ripped the hat from her head. It was new and very stylish. Without hesitation, she dropped it to the curricle's floor.

In a fever of anticipation, she watched him secure the reins, although the horses seemed happy to laze in the waning sun. He swept his hat from his head.

He must hear her heart's furious beat, it was so loud. Her palms were moist. Nervously, she wiped them on her skirts. "Hurry," she said in a shaking voice.

He laughed softly. The deep sound shivered through her. She squirmed restlessly on the seat.

Slowly—why, oh, why was he so slow? Couldn't he tell she was in a lather of desire?—he lifted one hand to cup the back of her head. His gloved fingers speared through the hair at her nape.

"You're so fierce," he murmured.

"Don't you like it?" She hardly knew what she said. All she knew was that he touched her as if nothing else in the entire world mattered.

"I didn't say that."

He lifted his other hand and placed it under her chin, holding her face angled up. Absurd when he must know evasion was the last thing on her mind.

"*Gideon . . .*"

An invitation. A protest. A plea.

"Shh." A tender smile hovered around his lips.

He dipped his head and gave her another fleeting kiss.

Still he played with her. In spite of his own need. An inferno of desire raged behind those black eyes. Heat radiated from him. She shifted, trying to get closer to that blaze.

Very gently he placed his lips on the corner of hers. A kiss on her nose. On her chin. Between her brows.

"Kiss me," she said almost tearfully. This delay was more than mortal flesh could stand.

"I am kissing you."

She shook with impatience. She wanted passion. She wanted to know he hungered for her. But this tenderness was sweeter than sugar. She felt her soul unfurl. He'd made love to her twice. Neither time had he been tender.

Now he treated her as if she were made of finest Venetian glass. Likely to shatter at the slightest touch.

She raised her hands. One hooked around his wrist. The other rested on his chest where she'd touched him this morning. Under her palm, his heart raced.

"Kiss me properly," she begged. "Or I'll go mad."

"We're both mad," he said with sudden determination. "God help us."

As abruptly as that, the world exploded into flame. His mouth covered hers with ferocious passion.

She gasped with shock. Then with astounded pleasure. He was all hot desire. But the ghost of earlier tenderness lingered like embers from a banked fire. Like stars fading at sunrise.

She surrendered, parting her lips.

His relentless physical onslaught gave no quarter. He slipped his tongue across her lips. Then flicked it inside. She stiffened at the unfamiliar intrusion.

Abruptly he lifted his head.

Oh, don't let him stop. I'll die if he stops.

"It's all right," he crooned, and returned to kissing forehead, cheeks, and chin. Using his hand behind her head to hold her for his depredations.

She moaned and yearned toward him. "Kiss me, Gideon." Her voice vibrated with longing.

"I forget . . ." He punctuated his speech with a scatter of kisses. He placed his mark on every inch of her face. Except her lips. Where she wanted him.

". . . how innocent . . ." More kisses.

". . . you are."

The hand she'd placed over his crazily hammering heart slid up to encircle his neck. Her fingers tangled in the hair that brushed his coat's high collar.

"You surprised me," she said shakily. "It wasn't that I didn't like it."

More glancing kisses. "What a sweet little wife."

"You're tormenting me," she accused, turning her head to try and catch his lips with hers.

"You've tormented me for days. I never thought I'd touch you like this."

"But you wanted to?" She knew the answer, but still she longed to hear him admit it.

"You're a fever in my blood," he said in a raw voice.

His hands shifted down her back, and he lifted her toward him. He parted his lips over hers. More gently than before. This time she was ready for the penetration of his tongue.

One brief foray. Retreat. A more thorough exploration.

Heat exploded behind her eyes. Searing pleasure flowed through her veins. She knew nothing but the scorching possession of his mouth. She gasped and pressed closer, opening her lips wider.

He stroked his hands up and down her back, tracing her spine. Everywhere he touched, he set up another hot whirlpool. Flame licked at her skin. Still, his mouth plundered hers with endless dark delight.

Tentatively, she slid her tongue against his. He made a growling sound of approval, and his hands tightened.

More bravely, she moved her tongue until the kiss was no longer invasion but ecstatic dance.

She made an inarticulate sound and edged closer, sliding awkwardly on the seat. He ripped his mouth from hers. He breathed in great gusts, and his eyes were blacker than ebony. He released a startled laugh and pulled her up against him.

"A curricle's not designed for lovemaking," he said unsteadily.

Charis was still dazed. Joy resonated through her like music. "I don't care. It was wonderful."

She sounded like a besotted ninnyhammer. What matter? She was a besotted ninnyhammer.

He loved her.

He touched her cheek with a gesture that split her vulnerable heart open. She'd loved him from the first, but until now she'd had no idea how physical pleasure turned love into something so vivid, it became a living entity.

"Shall we go back to the inn?" His voice was velvety with anticipation.

She curved into his side. For the first time, his arm circled her shoulders. She basked in the closeness. Her lips tingled with the memory of his kiss. Strangely, that kiss had changed things between them more than either time he'd used her body.

Hope poured into her brimming heart.

He loved her. She loved him. What could defeat them?

Eighteen

cross the remains of the meal he'd ordered in their rooms, Gideon watched his wife. The hostelry was famous for its cuisine. For all the attention he'd paid to the elaborate fare, it might have been sawdust.

Instead, his heart, his mind, his soul were full of his bride.

Charis.

Beautiful, beautiful Charis. His delight and his despair.

She'd been quiet on the drive back from the countryside. Nor had she spoken much during dinner. Like him, she'd toyed with her food. Now she looked up. Doubt swam in her hazel eyes like sharks in a clear sea.

She set down her fork with a decided click. Her slender hand clenched against the table. "What made you change your mind?"

Gideon didn't pretend to misunderstand. She was too clever to let his new attitude go unremarked and too brave to avoid the subject.

After a moment's thought, he gave her a frank answer. "I'm not sure I have."

He was guiltily aware that he played dangerous games with their future here. He still believed her best chance for happiness lay in a life separate from his.

But it was more than mortal flesh could stand to share a bed with his delectable wife and not touch her. Especially after the desolate hell he'd subsisted in since Rangapindhi. Charis thought because they loved each other, they had a chance. Gideon knew in his bones that love only made the price they'd both pay for their current indulgence more excruciating.

He should stay away from her. But he couldn't.

Of all his many sins, perhaps this was his greatest.

Her lips compressed with impatience, and she fiddled with the stem of her wineglass. "You're happy to touch me now."

He remembered this afternoon's delicious kisses, and he couldn't suppress a reminiscent smile. "More than happy."

His reply didn't mollify her. Her color rose, but her regard didn't waver. "What changed?"

He briefly studied the white damask tablecloth, then glanced up. "Well, there's the fact that I *can* touch you."

She blushed more furiously. "So you're reconciled to living as my husband?" He heard her difficulty forcing the question out.

He sighed, and his voice deepened into gravity as he answered with equal difficulty. "Charis, I'm not doing you any favors with what's happened. If I had a scrap of decency, I'd leave you alone."

Yes, he could touch her without turning into a beast. This morning hadn't proven that, but this afternoon had. He loved her, if anything, more than ever. If she asked him, he'd catch the stars from the sky for her.

But the factors that made him an unsuitable consort for this glorious girl remained as stark as ever.

Whatever private bliss life with his wife now promised, he was still a physical and mental wreck. His immediate strained reaction today to St. Helier's bustle confirmed that. The frail seedling of hope that had uncurled inside him this morning had shriveled as he'd felt the old, crushing, sick reaction to the crowd. Painful reality had crashed down upon him in all its inexorable grimness.

What a fool he'd been to believe this temporary reprieve meant a permanent cure to his ills. He'd never lead a normal life, he'd always have to hold himself apart, isolated. He couldn't lock someone like Charis away from the world and hoard her like a miser hoarded his gold. It wasn't fair, and eventually, he knew, she'd chafe at the restrictions of life with a recluse. He couldn't bear to see her bright spirit flicker and go out.

She said she loved him. But for all her sweet passion and determination, he wasn't convinced she suffered anything more than a particularly virulent case of hero worship. What he was firmly convinced of was his complete unworthiness. He'd failed so many times. He couldn't bear to contemplate failing her. As he surely would. Better he set her free to find the man she deserved.

He bit back his agony at the idea of her falling in love with someone else. He had to think of her future and not his own selfish desires.

Except that right now, his own selfish desires were paramount, unstoppable. He should leave her to sleep alone, but he already knew he wouldn't. The astonishing joy he'd found in her arms, when he'd thought any joy at all lost forever, made restraint impossible.

St. Augustine's self-serving prayer flickered through his mind. *Lord, grant me chastity and continence. But not yet.*

Charis lifted her wine but didn't drink; instead, she stared into the red depths with a troubled expression. "If you're sure it's an almighty mistake, why did you kiss me?"

Ah, smart girl, to pick the kiss as the betrayal of his principles rather than this morning's volcanic lovemaking. He told her the simple, incontrovertible truth. "Because, God help me, I can't resist you."

Startled, she looked up, and a smile of utter delight curved her full lips. "Really?"

She was so pleased with herself, he couldn't help laughing. Although he was a villain to encourage her belief that they could find happiness. It was a role he suspected he'd become accustomed to in coming days. Because, having tasted her, there was no way on this earth he could keep his hands off her while they shared these rooms.

Still, even as he acknowledged her power, his reply held an edge. "Yes, damn you, really."

"Well, that's all right, then." She put down her wine, stood, and rang for the servants.

Surprised, he turned in his chair to watch her. "Is that it? No more inquisition?"

"For the moment."

He heaved a sigh of masculine relief although he didn't trust this sudden docility.

As the maids cleared dinner, tidied the room, built up the fire, prepared the bedroom, he stood beside the mantel, holding himself apart. Just this much activity around him, and his sinews tightened with revulsion.

No, he was far from cured, God damn it to hell.

The chilling knowledge seeped into his bones. Briefly, he closed his eyes, trying to summon will to deny Charis—and himself. But will was putty against the potent lure of desire.

He and his wife would make love tonight. Anticipation fizzed in his veins. He sipped at his claret, wondering when he'd last spent an evening with a lovely woman, knowing they'd end up in bed.

She looked across from where she sat, pretending to read a book, and sent him a secret smile. She knew how the night would end too.

Gideon drew a deep breath as the door closed behind the last servant. Now just he and Charis remained, and the air suddenly seemed clearer, cleaner. He ignored the howl from his conscience that he had no right to touch his wife when he was such a disaster.

His eyes fastened on Charis as she set aside her book. He stayed where he was, enjoying the crescendo of expectation. His hands itched to drag her close for a drugging kiss. To discover what marvels lay under her lovely red gown.

She stepped up to him and took his wineglass away, her fingers brushing his gloved hand. Even that much contact would have once set him shaking and sweating. Now it just aroused sizzling need. Her carnation scent drifted out to whisper promises of paradise.

"Will you do something for me, Gideon?" she asked softly.

A dim warning sounded. In his besotted daze, he hardly heeded it. "It depends."

Her lips tilted upward as she placed the glass on the mantel. "That's hardly gallant. A true gentleman would obey my slightest whim."

"I'd say that gentleman didn't know you very well."

She laughed softly, and the husky sound made his gut churn with longing. For all his brave words, he'd lie down and die if she asked him.

"So suspicious."

"Suspicion has kept me alive on numerous occasions. It's a highly underrated characteristic." He sent her a searching look. "What do you want, Charis?"

She sucked in a steadying breath, and he realized that beneath the flirtatious humor, she was nervous. The warning clang became more insistent. "I want you to allow me to do with you what I will."

Charis resisted the urge to twine her hands together. She needed to convince Gideon she was a confident, self-aware woman, not a silly girl. Acting as jittery as a canary in front of a hungry cat wouldn't advance her cause.

He angled one black eyebrow. "Which involves what?"

She bit her lip before she remembered she meant to appear nonchalantly assured. Raising her chin, she forced herself to meet his wary dark eyes. "Well, undressing you, for a start."

Hot color seeped under her skin. Nonchalant assurance had never been likely. Even coherent speech seemed an unachievable goal. Surreptitiously, she wiped her palms on her skirts.

"I . . . see," he said slowly.

She waited for more. Anger. Protest. A resounding no. But he remained silent. She rushed into speech. "It's not salacious curiosity."

His lips twitched slightly although she read growing resistance in his eyes. "I'm pleased to hear it."

"This isn't a joke, Gideon," she said in a low urgent voice. "It's important that you've kept your clothes on whenever we've . . ."

"Made love?"

"Yes," she responded on a thread of sound. Her heart fluttered like a trapped bird against her ribs. Not a sparrow. Something big and fierce like a vulture.

He leaned on the mantel, his long body elegant and powerful. The flames from the grate cast strange, flickering shadows over his face. For a moment, he looked devilish. She licked lips dry with nerves. His eyes fastened on the movement. The blatant interest reminded her she wasn't completely powerless in this war. She stiffened her spine.

One gloved hand fisted on the mantel. His voice was silky with control. "So I hand myself over to your tender mercies? Do I have a choice?"

She knew he resented the way she undermined his defenses. She pressed her palms deeper into her skirts to hide their trembling. "You can say no."

"Then you won't share my bed tonight," he said grimly.

Her heart somersaulted with astonishment. Did he know just what he admitted? "I won't stay out of your bed to gain my way." She licked her lips again. "You see, I can't resist you either."

His appearance of tranquility abruptly shattered. With a furious movement, he jerked away from the hearth. He was visibly shaking. For one horrified instant, she wondered if his affliction was returning. He grabbed the back of a chair, gripping it with hard fingers. "In Rangapindhi, I was tortured."

"I know."

She saw his throat move as he swallowed. "You'll find my scars repulsive."

She blinked with shock. This hadn't occurred to her. Although if she'd thought, it should have. Spreading her hands, she spoke the truth in her heart. "I think you're beautiful. A few marks on your skin won't change that."

His brief laugh held no amusement. "You don't know what you're talking about."

She stepped close enough to touch him. "Let me see."

He released the chair. She recognized the gesture as a sign of reluctant acquiescence.

Very carefully she reached for the lapels of his black coat. The wool was warm from his skin. He braced under her touch although he didn't retreat. She took this as tacit permission to continue.

Slowly, she slid the coat from his shoulders and down his arms, then lifted it away. His jaw was set as if she tortured him. He was rigid as an oak board.

Dear heaven, let her instincts lead her right. If Gideon endured this suffering for nothing, she'd never forgive herself.

She tamped down guilt and fear as she turned to lay the coat over the chair. Something deeper than dread or compassion told her that until he let her see him without the armor of clothing, his essential self would stay hidden.

Her heart careening in a mad race, she steeled herself to face him. He'd dressed more formally than usual tonight. He stood before her in an exquisite white waistcoat, embroidered with silver vines. A snowy neckcloth. Shirt. Biscuit trousers. His hands, as always, were encased in gloves. Tonight, white evening gloves like the ones a dandy wore to a ball.

The betraying muscle flickered in his lean cheek, and he breathed unsteadily. The soft, broken hiss was the only sound apart from the flames crackling in the grate. When she lifted her hands to his waistcoat buttons, she felt the ragged rise and fall of his chest.

She flicked open one button. Two. Three. The beautiful garment sagged open.

She slid her hands under the brocade to slip it off. Now only the fine material of his shirt separated her from his skin. He was hot as a blazing fire and so tense she feared he might shatter.

Before she thought to censor herself, her gaze dropped. His arousal swelled against the front of his trousers in unmistakable demand.

"You know I want you," he said flatly. "You use it against me."

She shook her head, setting the waistcoat over his coat. With every garment she removed, she felt like she seized enemy colors in a battle.

"I use it *for* you." If she didn't believe that, she couldn't summon courage to persist. She gathered that courage and placed her hand over the bulge in his trousers.

Her breath caught. He made a strangled sound deep in his throat. She'd never touched him there before. Through his clothing, she felt the tensile power. The life. The vigor. Automatically, she shaped her fingers to the hard length. His flesh surged into her palm as if it had a will of its own.

Gideon closed his eyes. "Charis . . ."

She bit her lip and lifted her hand away. She shook as she reached for his neckcloth. Her fingers were clumsy, and the length of linen seemed impossible to untangle.

She sucked in a deep breath, redolent of Gideon, and forced herself to concentrate. Eventually, she managed to tug the neckcloth free. His shirt gaped. His pulse beat wildly at the base of his throat.

He breathed rapidly. So did she. The room felt close, confined, stifling. Need settled low and heavy in her belly.

She hadn't set out to titillate him. Or herself. But the act of undressing this big strong man—and him standing quiveringly still as she disrobed him—made heat well between her legs.

The air was sharp with arousal. Male and female. She wasn't touching him, but his desire surrounded her like sheets of flame.

He closed his eyes as if he couldn't bear to witness what she did. His tension was a vibrant, writhing force. Air scraped in and out of his lungs.

Doubt assailed her. Held her paralyzed.

Could she do this? Should she do this? What if her actions pushed him deeper into purgatory?

She braced her shoulders and reached forward to pull his shirt free of his trousers. Her heart banged against her ribs. Her hands shook.

He opened his eyes and snatched the hem of his shirt. "Here, damn you," he grated out. He tore the garment in two, shucked the ragged pieces, and dropped them to the floor.

Anything Charis might have said lodged unspoken in her tight throat. Her hands fisted at her sides. Her eyes flew up to meet Gideon's glassy gaze, then dropped to convulsively trace every line of his torso.

She'd known he'd be beautiful. But his virile splendor left her speechless. His pale skin stretched tight over ridges of hard muscle. Feathery dark hair covered the broad plane of his chest.

Scars patterned his chest and arms. Long lines that she guessed came from a whipping. Pale satiny welts that looked like burns. Round marks that could be bullet holes. A tangible history of unrelenting pain.

Her attention returned to his face. His jaw set like stone with stoic endurance.

He loathed this. He loathed this to the depths of his being.

Oh, Gideon, I'm so sorry. Forgive me.

She reached out and placed a gentle hand on one powerful arm. He flinched away. Just like he used to. Fear scored her heart. Would tonight hurl him back into his nightmare isolation?

She straightened. She'd set out on this path. For good or ill, she must follow it to the end.

Steeling herself for what she'd see, she slowly stepped behind him. He held himself so still, she couldn't hear his breathing anymore.

His back was long. Leanly muscled. Graceful in its strength.

Marred with scars upon scars upon scars.

How had anyone borne such torture and lived?

Scalding tears stung her eyes, but she forced them back. A sob jammed behind her lips. She must be strong, just as Gideon had been strong.

Her horrified gaze clung to the pattern of cicatrices across his flesh. Every inch of his back carried the mark of violence. His captors must have beaten him again and again. They must have stabbed him and burned him. Her imagination failed as she sought to measure his torment.

With one trembling hand, she touched a thick puckered line that snaked around his ribs. He flinched again, although the wound had long since healed.

"Have you had enough?" he asked cuttingly.

"Oh, Gideon, what did they do to you?" she whispered.

"I warned you."

She traced the scar, feeling where other scars intersected it. The raised flesh under her touch was unnaturally smooth. "I still think you're beautiful," she choked out.

His muscles tensed, then he jerked away from her tentative exploration.

"Do you indeed, sweet Charis?" he snarled, whirling to face her. "What about this?"

With savage swiftness, he ripped the gloves from his hands and flung them to the floor.

Nineteen

Charis's heart crashed to a halt. At last she saw what Gideon had hidden all this time. She saw and yet could hardly believe it.

She thought viewing the scars on his back had tested the limits of her courage. But this, this went beyond anything she could conceive.

Her appalled gaze clung to the ruined hands he spread out before her as if he taunted her with their shattered elegance. "Oh, Gideon," she whispered, the words lacerating her throat.

"Quite a sight, aren't they? At least they work. After the torture, I wasn't sure they would." His tone stung. He lifted his right hand and held it so close in front of her face that the tangled network of scars blurred. "Do you want these touching your skin? Do you?"

She jerked back, mainly at the corrosive pain in his voice, then made herself stand still and look without flinching. He wanted her to recoil, she knew. He wanted her to confirm he was as repulsive as he believed.

"Don't," she begged. Shaking, she reached out to catch his hand, but he wrenched free to stand in front of the grate.

Apart from hectic streaks of color lining his prominent cheekbones, his face was drawn and gaunt. His mouth was a white gash of anger. His black eyes were brilliant with humiliation and self-loathing.

"Don't touch you?" His bitter laugh made her cringe. "I wouldn't dream of desecrating your body with these claws."

"No . . ." He'd misunderstood her. Deliberately, she guessed. Her belly clenched in sick misery. She raised unsteady hands to her face and discovered it wet with tears.

He had so much pride. His pride was part of his extraordinary strength. But that also meant he'd hate her to cry over him. She should stop.

If only she could.

He sent her a blistering glare, then stalked toward the door, snatching up his coat on the way. "I've had enough of this. Find some other damned charity case."

"Gideon, please don't go," she forced through a throat thick with churning emotion.

"I'll see you in the morning," he grated out without looking at her. On the hand that clutched his coat, his broken knuckles shone white.

She couldn't let him leave like this, believing she despised him for his injuries. Lunging forward, she grabbed his bare arm with both hands. "No!"

"Let me go, madam," he said stiffly, although at least he curtailed his headlong retreat.

She expected him to shove her away and make his escape. But he stood facing the door, his back to her, quivering as he did in the grip of his affliction.

"Never," she vowed, her voice fracturing. She slid one hand down his arm to cup his poor, damaged hand between hers. "Never, never, never."

Dear Lord, she had to stop crying. She sucked in a broken breath and struggled for control.

He was as taut as a drawn wire. On edge. Furious. Grieving. Likely to lash out at the least provocation. Perhaps she pushed him too far, risked another attack. She muffled a sob and stroked his hand with trembling fingers as if touch alone could mend what could never be mended.

His other hand opened, and the coat dropped to the floor, tacit admission that he wasn't going anywhere. His glossy dark head lowered until his forehead rested against the door.

In the unnatural contours of the hand she held, she felt what his captors had done. The tracery of scars. The spurs and welts. The jagged knitting of the bones. Bones that had been smashed over and over. The knuckles were swollen. The fingernails were jagged and misshapen.

What had happened to him was obscene, unspeakable, barbaric. The damage made her want to scream and claw and fight. But all she could do was cry.

Heaven help me, I need to dam these endless tears.

"Charis, I don't want your pity." His voice was so deep, it was a subterranean growl.

He was wrong about her reaction. Pity was too weak a response to the horrors perpetrated on him. What he'd withstood beggared imagination. She felt like an ax cleaved her heart, and nothing would ever weld it whole again.

"I don't pity you." The words emerged as a choked murmur.

Still Gideon didn't look at her. "I don't believe you."

With a jerky movement, he laid his other hand flat against the dark wood of the door. It had been as tortured as its twin. But staring at his hand against the timber, she saw the grace and beauty it must once have possessed.

"My love . . ." Curse these tears, nothing stopped them. "I'm so sorry."

Words failed her. What could she say? Nothing was equal to what he'd been through. Instead, she followed where her heart dictated. Holding his shattered hand tenderly between hers, she raised it to her lips.

She placed a fervent kiss on the uneven knuckles. It was

an act of homage for all he'd borne. It was an act of over-whelming anguish. It was an act of gratitude that he'd survived so she could fall in love with him.

Under her lips, his flesh was warm. His hands looked like they belonged to a monster. The skin she kissed was unquestionably a man's.

He went utterly still. His shaking quieted. He didn't breathe. He didn't speak. His back was stiff with tension. If his living hand hadn't rested between hers, she'd almost wonder if he'd turned to stone.

In the brittle silence, she finally heard him take a shuddering breath. The hand she held curled into a fist. He drew another of those long, difficult breaths.

"I hate what they did to me." His voice was so low, she strained to hear him. He spoke toward the door. "I hate that I have to live with Rangapindhi forever."

Oh, my dear.

She recognized his shame and pain. Without thinking, she shifted, pressing herself hard against his back with its interlocking network of scars. She turned her hot sticky cheek against his skin, feeling the tight muscles, the lines of raised flesh.

His shoulders bent forward. He was so rigid, it was as if he kept himself upright through will alone. Compassion, all the more poignant because she couldn't express it, stabbed her. She waited in painful suspense for him to push her away, berate her, walk out. But he didn't move.

Without releasing the hand she'd kissed, she raised her other hand to cover his where it flattened against the door. He jerked infinitesimally under her touch, then subsided into stillness. She tried to infuse him with every ounce of her love. Physically. Through the human warmth he'd thought denied to him forever.

She didn't know how long she sprawled against him in wordless communion. She closed her eyes and let darkness take her.

After a long while, she felt him shift. She opened her eyes and straightened.

Finally, he turned to face her, forcing her to free one of his hands although she kept her clasp on the other. She steeled herself to look into his face as fear sent icy tendrils along her spine.

What would his expression reveal? Anger? Disdain? Coldness, as he rebuilt barriers of pride and detachment that had crumbled tonight?

His face was stark with some deep emotion she couldn't identify. She stared into his burning eyes.

"Charis . . ."

He looked as though he'd lost his soul. The stony desolation in his eyes cut her to the quick.

"It's all right, my love." She curled her arms around him, anything to assuage his cruel isolation. His muscles tensed as he resisted her. She tightened her embrace. "It's over. It's over."

For a long moment, Gideon stood unresponsive, unmoving. Then she felt him tense. Was he finally going to spurn her? She was astonished he'd endured her touch as long as he had. She was astonished he'd revealed his scars and his suffering. However he treated her now, the bond between them had become unbreakable.

Which wouldn't ease her hurt if he rebuffed her after all they'd shared in the last half hour.

He made a choked sound deep in his throat. She felt his chest expand as he sucked in a massive breath.

"Oh, dear God in heaven," he forced out in a cracked groan.

Shaking, he lashed his arms around her and tugged her roughly into his chest. His shoulders heaved convulsively as he buried his face in her neck. She felt the heat of his breath, the bruising power of his arms, the frantic race of his heart.

"I want to give you peace," she whispered into his thick

dark hair. Painful tears welled again. She loved him so much, it was agony.

"You have. You do," he said urgently, but the hands that clutched her so hard spoke of desperation, not rest.

This wasn't peace. Perhaps peace and he were such strangers, he no longer recognized it. "Oh, Gideon, I wish that were so," she said sadly.

He held her so close, he crushed her breasts against his chest. She drew a shallow breath, all his stranglehold allowed her. His head was heavy on her shoulder. His hair tickled her neck the way it had after he'd shared her bed for the first time.

"Whenever I look at my hands, it all comes back." His voice was thick, hesitant as he spoke into her skin. "The stink. The heat. The cold. The hunger and thirst. The unending pain."

With a hand that trembled with horror at all he'd suffered, she stroked his disheveled hair. The caress seemed so natural. How curious to think before this morning she couldn't have made it. Just as only a day ago it would have been unthinkable to cradle him in her arms and infuse his cold loneliness with her love.

So much had changed since they'd left Penrhyn.

"I don't know how you endured it," she said softly.

He tautened, and the muscles across his back became as unrelenting as steel. "I didn't endure. Before they finished with me, I screamed for mercy."

He was so hard on himself. If only he could spare some of the generosity he'd shown her to stanch his own wounds. "You didn't betray your comrades or your country," she said in a quiet but implacable voice. "You stood up to over a year of torture and didn't break. You're too brave for your own good."

"You wouldn't think that if you'd seen the pathetic fool I made of myself when they started on my hands." He rubbed his head against her neck in a desultory caress. The unforced gesture sent warmth spiraling through her. She could hardly comprehend he trusted her enough to stay in her arms.

"Oh, my love," she said in a low voice throbbing with emotion. She ran her hand in comforting trails over his powerful back. Under her hand, his scars created a bumpy tapestry, a map of the intolerable tribute his years in India had claimed. She couldn't see his ruined hands. She didn't need to. The sight would haunt her forever.

"You have to forgive yourself, or you'll go mad. Good Lord, Gideon. You're covered in scars. You hardly sleep. You flinch if anyone comes within reach." Her voice softened into persuasion. "You gave all anyone could ask. More. Much more. Everybody in the world sees that but you."

Charis turned her head and glanced a kiss across his cheek. The poignant tenderness inside her demanded some expression. She felt his breath catch. She suspected acts of uncomplicated affection had been rare in his life.

Because she ached for his solitude, because it was all too easy to picture a clever little boy happier with his books than any companions, she kissed him again. A glance of the lips that caught him on the rim of one ear.

Again the hitch in his breath. Slowly, he straightened and stared at her with a wariness that pierced her heart. Surely by now he must know she wanted only his good. But he'd been so hurt, he shied away from anything that smacked of love. For all the barriers she'd crashed through in the last days, she didn't fool herself that he was near to accepting he was worthy of her adoration.

The scars of Rangapindhi cut too deep for any simple remedy.

For now, he was with her and showed no signs of wanting to go. She intended to take what advantage she could. Rising on her toes, she kissed one side of his neck, then the other. She still held him, but loosely, easily, without the quaking desperation. He shifted restlessly, and his hands slid to span her waist.

She traced a line of kisses along one sinewy shoulder. Pausing when she reached the top of his arm.

A strangled sound emerged from his throat. She wasn't

sure whether it was encouragement or protest. She dropped another kiss on the ball of his shoulder.

The kisses were quick, soft, playful. Like those she'd give a crying child to coax it from a fit of sullens.

Except she knew to the depths of her soul that Gideon was no child.

He was a full-grown man. Potent. Passionate. Predatory.

A thrill shivered through her. More purposefully, she grazed her lips along the vein down the side of his neck. Feeling the powerful life thundering through him.

His breath caught again. Then he shifted and pressed his lips to the collarbone revealed under her red gown's square neckline.

Her heart stuttered. He became a participant at last. She closed her eyes and forced herself to breathe. Her hands settled loosely on his hips.

She pressed a kiss to his other ear.

He kissed her chin, his lips warm and firm.

She brushed her lips over his jaw.

He caught one earlobe in his teeth and bit down gently.

Response burned down to her toes, and a strangled moan escaped her. As he bent to kiss her shoulder, she caught a flash of masculine triumph in his face.

They no longer clung to each other like the survivors of a shipwreck. She'd kissed him to comfort, but somewhere the game had changed into a duel of kisses.

She angled her head and kissed the hammering pulse at the base of his throat. Instinct made her lick him there. His skin was warm and salty. Delicious.

She forgot the playful battle and licked him again. Slowly. Luxuriously. His flavor filled her senses. His low rumbling growl vibrated against her lips.

Dazed, she lifted her head and stared at him. The humor seeped from his expression. Replaced by an intense concentration that sent a sizzle of anticipation down her spine.

The innocent games were over.

Danger hovered.

Danger and passion.

Time stopped. Along with her heart and breath. She felt as though she poised on the brink of one of Penrhyn's craggy cliffs. Would she plummet to her death? Or would he catch her, as he always had?

As slowly as if he waded through deep water, Gideon raised his ruined hands. He set them on either side of her head and tipped her face up.

The moment held untold importance. It was as if he'd never touched her before. The brush of his scarred palms on her cheeks made her shiver with pleasure. He stared at her, flicking back stray tendrils of her hair with his thumbs.

With spine-tingling attention, his gaze traced her features. His black eyes glowed as if he looked upon his soul's desire. Deep in her bones, she finally recognized that he loved her and always would. He didn't want to love her, but he did. Perhaps he'd never say the words again, but the awe and worship on his face crushed any lingering doubts to dust.

A shaky sigh escaped her. His eyes focused on her parted lips. She grew taut with uncontrollable longing. Surely he'd kiss her like he'd kissed her this afternoon. She desperately wanted him to kiss her again. Her hands curled into his hips to urge him closer.

"You're so beautiful, you break my heart," he murmured.

"Gideon . . ." she choked out.

Any further response to that astonishing declaration was lost as with sudden decisiveness, he lowered his head and pressed his lips to hers.

Gideon felt the moist cushion of her lips flatten against her teeth. Then, sweet moment indeed, she sighed and parted to let him in. He thrust his tongue inside, testing the hard smoothness of her teeth, the hot honey of the interior. His heart raised a paean of rejoicing as her tongue fluttered, re-treated, returned to stroke and caress.

She learned fast, his darling wife. Only this afternoon, his deep kiss had shocked her. Only yesterday, he would have been incapable of touching her, let alone sharing this astonishingly sensual kiss.

Every second he held Charis in his arms felt like a miracle.

Very deliberately, he licked the roof of her mouth, the insides of her cheeks, delighting in the contrasting textures. Delighting in her response as her tongue brushed the sensitive underside of his.

She moaned and pressed her mouth harder against his. He sank into hot, succulent blackness.

He lifted his head and rested his forehead against hers. They panted, sharing the small space of air between them. The act felt as intimate as that extraordinary kiss. As if one life united them.

Feverishly, he slid his hand up her rib cage to where her breasts strained against her bodice. He slid his hand under the neckline, found a pebbled nipple, and pulled gently.

"Yes," she sighed, and traced the line of his mouth with her tongue.

Hunger slammed through him. Drowning out all other sound, his blood thundered. He leaned forward and bit her lower lip. She shivered with excitement, her hips jerking against him.

"If you want that dress to stay in one piece, take it off," he said unsteadily.

She gave a breathless gust of laughter. She hooked her hand around his neck and sent him a scorching glance under her eyelashes. "You'll have to help. It laces up the back."

"Damn fool fashion," he grunted.

Her face was flushed with need. Her lips were swollen and red with their frantic kisses. Her eyes were a deep and mysterious green. Tarns in the Penrhyn woods. He moved his thumb against her cheek, feeling the warm smoothness of her skin, the sticky remnants of tears.

She pressed her cheek into his ravaged hand. How quickly he'd accepted that his injuries didn't repulse her. Odd when he'd nearly died of shame revealing them.

He'd intended the searing honesty to break the connection between them, destroy her foolish infatuation at last. Instead, uncovering his secrets forced him to admit he was her slave and always would be.

"I don't want you to see anyone but me," she said huskily. Her voice was thick with the tears she'd shed. He wished he could promise there would be no more sorrow, but even at this joyful moment, he knew that would be a lie.

"I don't." He swallowed to dislodge the painful constriction in his throat. "I won't."

Gideon kissed her again. The desperate urge to possess faded, and his mouth moved with piercing tenderness. He raised his head and looked deep into her eyes. Her spirit shone clear for him to see. Brave. Generous. Honest. So full of love, it left him humbled.

He gently turned her around and began to undo the pretty red dress. Inch by inch, clumsy as a lad with his first woman, he revealed the smooth skin of her back. He pushed apart the edges and traced a line of kisses between her shoulder blades. Her breath faltered, then quickened. She lowered her head. He accepted the unspoken invitation and kissed a path up to her hairline. Her scent was stronger there. Carnations. Warm skin. Woman. *Charis.*

He buried his nose in the soft mass of hair and breathed deep, drawing her essence into his lungs. Into his heart.

He returned to unhooking her dress. "I'll need all night to get you out of this confounded rag," he growled in frustration, as yet another fiddly attachment refused to cooperate.

"Are you in such a hurry?"

The wench laughed at him. God help him, he liked it. "Yes."

Finally, the hook released. He turned his attention to the next one down. The line stretched endlessly.

She flexed her shoulders, and he fought the urge to bend

her over the nearest chair and take her from behind. This morning he'd leaped on her with a passion unlike any he'd ever known. The need to thrust his aching cock into her tonight made this morning's passion seem a mere milk-and-water fancy.

Patience, Trevithick. Calm down. She deserves better than a quick tumble. She deserves every ounce of skill you can muster.

He sucked in a breath and spoke more steadily as he reconsidered his earlier answer. "No. I want to show you everything you've missed."

Another of those voluptuous shivers rippled through her. Dear God, when she did that, he threatened to explode.

He rode the surge of desire and concentrated on the next hook. After spending the last week in rags, he could understand she didn't want to ruin the dress. But if the damned thing didn't come off soon, he'd shred it.

"Show me everything?"

Her overt curiosity made him smile. "Well, everything might require more than one night."

Her quivering sigh was answer in itself.

As though he unveiled something sacred, he slid the dress down her slender body.

Gideon's breath stopped.

She still wore corset, shift, petticoats. The sheer covering did little to hide the glories beneath. His rod throbbed, but he ignored its greedy insistence.

His eyes traveled down her straight spine to the firm bottom, pressing enticingly against the white lawn. With shaking hands, he released the tapes holding her petticoats. They fell with a whisper.

He'd never undressed an Englishwoman. Never dealt with such complicated garments. His Indian lovers had worn the graceful native costume. He had a sudden yen to see Charis in exotic silks.

One day . . .

He stepped in front of his bride. She was slender and graceful as a young willow. His gaze traced the lovely curves, returned to her breasts, pushed up by the corset to press against the chemise.

She raised her arms with a gesture of such natural sensuality, his heart jammed in his throat. A few deft tugs, and her hair fell in a curtain of shimmering bronze. Her scent filled the air so thickly, he thought he could touch it.

She blushed under his fiery regard. It surprised him how she suddenly became the shy, inexperienced girl.

She was a shy, inexperienced girl.

He must remember that. The unfettered passion in her kisses was deceptive. He turned her around again and tugged at the corset laces. "Infernal contraption."

She laughed softly as he finally found the knack of it. Desperation lent his fingers a deftness they'd lacked earlier. He burned to see her body without all these confounded draperies spoiling his view.

Swiftly, he slipped the corset off and draped it over the chair he'd fantasized bending her across. Cold sweat covered his skin. If he didn't control himself, he wouldn't survive this interminable disrobing. "Why do Englishwomen wear so many clothes?"

"Perhaps to torment Englishmen?" She turned to face him.

"You're wearing nothing for the rest of the week."

She gave a throaty giggle that made his gut clench with desire. "You'll shock the servants."

"The servants can go to Hades." He tugged the delicate shift over her head. With a satisfied gesture, he tossed it to the side, not caring where it landed.

Charis's color mounted, and she raised shaking hands to cover her bosom. He bit back a groan and drew her close for a long, openmouthed kiss. She kissed him back with gratifying enthusiasm, her brief shyness fading.

Again, he reminded himself to be careful, considerate, controlled.

Difficult to remember restraint when her hands ran up and down his back in a wild dance of desire. Or when her mouth clung to his as if she'd die if he stopped kissing her.

Slowly, he slid his hands up to cup her breasts. Her white flesh was exquisite, the nipples firm and dark. He couldn't resist sucking one sweet point into his mouth. She cried out and arched closer.

He licked and suckled, following the broken pattern of her breath to test her arousal. When she moaned and trembled in his arms as though tossed in a storm, only then did he turn his attention to her other nipple.

His patience with her clothing had vanished long ago. With one ruthless movement, he ripped her drawers away. Now nothing separated him from her body. She gasped with shock and tugged at his hair. The fleeting pain only built his arousal.

He continued feasting on her breasts while one hand fell to the curls at the base of her belly. For a moment of delicate suspense, his fingers tangled in the damp softness.

He drew on her puckered nipple and slid his hand between her legs. She moaned, and a shudder ran through her. Her hand curled against the bare skin of his back. Parting her, he explored her folds. He took his time, savoring the delight.

She thrust her hips forward. He twisted his fingers, seeking. He stroked sleek petals.

And found his goal.

Very carefully, he touched her, teasing without initiating climax. Even so, her body tightened in immediate, uncontrollable response. Her soft, guttural cry alerted him to how close she was.

He raised his head from her breasts. More than he wanted to live another day, he wanted to watch her face during her first orgasm. To his shame, she hadn't come close to her peak when he'd taken her before.

By God, she'd come tonight. Over and over. Until neither of them saw straight.

Her head tilted back, her breasts jutted forward, her eyes

flickered closed, her lips parted on a raw moan as he touched her again, with greater purpose. He increased the pressure. She shivered, and he felt a sharp sting as her nails dug into his back.

She stiffened on a cry, and he felt her cross the barrier. Sensual pleasure roared through his veins as he watched her find bliss. Her trembling thighs clamped around his hand, her body quivered as though she had a fever. Hot female moisture drenched his fingers. Her heady scent was rich in his nostrils.

She'd never looked more beautiful. He'd remember this sight till the day he died. He'd remember it with gratitude and love.

After a long, shuddering moment, Charis opened misty eyes and stared at him in bewildered astonishment. "Gideon?" Her voice was hoarse and low.

Reluctantly he withdrew his hand. "Are you all right?"

"I . . . I think so." She sounded more surprised than ecstatic. "What was that?"

He laughed softly. "A taste of what's to come, my darling."

Before she could question him further, he snatched her up for another kiss. After what she'd just experienced, her response was deliriously uninhibited. For the first time, her tongue invaded his mouth. The kiss became aggressive. She strained against him. Her nipples pressed into his chest, her arms encircled his neck, her hips thrust into his with an evocative rhythm.

Need surged like a tidal wave. But unlike this morning, it was need tempered by care. He intended to find joy tonight, but more than that, he intended Charis to find joy.

He swung her into his arms and carried her toward the bedroom. In graceful surrender, she rested her head in the crook of his shoulder.

"It's time, my wife."

He staked a claim he knew he had no right to make. But neither God nor the devil would stop him now. The world had stolen so much from him. It wouldn't steal this.

He kicked open the door. It crashed against the wall. Overwhelmingly conscious of her naked body and the moist brush of her breath against his skin, he strode across to the bed.

He laid his precious burden upon the sheets. He waited for her to cover her breasts or her sex, but she lay motionless, open to his gaze.

Perfect.

Time halted while he drank in her beauty. She still wore stockings and slippers, tied with ribbons around her neat ankles.

"Why are you smiling?"

He hadn't realized he was. "There's no end to an Englishwoman's armor. I'd forgotten your blasted shoes."

To his surprise and delight, she raised one leg and pointed her toes in his direction. He caught a tantalizing glimpse of the dark mysteries between her thighs. The sight made his cock swell and strain with agonizing need. He locked his teeth and fought back the rip of desire. He was going to do this right. And that meant maintaining at least a shred of control.

"Why don't you take them off?" she asked in a sultry voice he'd never heard from her before.

He wasn't giving her everything her own way. He let his smile broaden, become knowing. "Later."

His hands dropped to his waistband, and he roughly tugged his trousers open. Her eyes rounded. She licked her lips. His arousal built another notch, bathing his body in sweat. His heart raced with excitement.

Swiftly, he tugged off the rest of his clothes. He hadn't undressed in front of a woman since well before Rangapindhi. He'd imagined if he ever did, it would be an occasion of embarrassment and concealment.

But the light in Charis's brilliant eyes as she watched him looked like admiration.

How could that be? He was hardly a young girl's dream, with his scars and grotesque hands. But the familiar self-loathing couldn't sink its teeth into him when the woman he loved gazed at him as though he made the sun rise in the sky.

She slid up against the pillows, and her lush lips curved into a breathtaking smile of welcome. Her eyes were clear and burning with light.

She extended one hand toward him. "Come to bed, Gideon."

Twenty

Gideon's guarded expression as he stared at her out-stretched hand harrowed Charis's heart.

He'd been so hurt. Even now, when it couldn't be clearer how she loved and wanted him, he didn't trust his welcome.

The candlelight softened his terrible scarring. Instead, it emphasized the lean, muscled strength, the grace, the height. For all their vile tortures, the Nawab and his thugs couldn't destroy his essential beauty. Her gaze fell to his powerful thighs and the hard, seeking flesh rising between them. His virility filled her with shivery excitement.

"Come to me, my darling," she said on a breath.

His hesitation splintered. He surged onto the bed, bracing himself over her. She strained up and pressed her mouth to his. He groaned and kissed her back, soon taking charge.

His kisses were still so new, so startling in their delight. Perhaps one day, she'd become inured to the magic of his mouth on hers. In about a thousand years. Perhaps.

The rapacious hunger of his lips sent desire rippling

through her. Heat trawled along her veins, arrowed between her legs, made her move restlessly against the sheets. Tentatively, she ran her hands down his back. For all the burning need that now scorched the air, he'd withdrawn too often for her to trust no barrier remained.

"Yes, touch me," he groaned against her lips, and kissed her again. "Touch me, Charis."

The yearning in his voice convinced her that at last she could discover his body as she longed to do. As he rained ravenous, ravishing kisses across her face and neck and shoulders, she tightened her hands. She felt the shifting of muscle, the ridges of scarring under her palms. Poignant reminder of how near she'd come to never knowing him, loving him.

Her hands drifted lower, trailed across his firm buttocks. His breath caught on a strangled gasp, and his hips jerked forward, pushing hot hardness into her belly.

Automatically, Charis curved closer. After this morning, she should be used to what happened to her husband's body when he wanted her. But the heat and weight of that part of him pulsing against her made her toes curl with excitement.

"Oh," she gasped, her fingers digging into his buttocks.

"Yes," he hissed, and bit down on her neck.

She gave a delighted shudder, and her nipples tightened with a longing that was like pain. When he'd taken her breast into his mouth, she'd nearly shattered with rapture. She trembled for him to do that again.

As if she spoke her wish aloud, his lips closed over one aching crest. She tangled her hands in his thick black hair, cradling his head against her. As his teeth scraped the sensitive tip, blinding pleasure gripped her. A sharp cry escaped, and she bowed up closer to that sweet torment.

This morning's passion had been unforgettable but over too soon. Tonight, Gideon was stubbornly determined to take his time. With a piquant shiver, Charis remembered him saying he wanted to show her everything.

Everything?

Recollections of that astounding earthquake he'd set off

made her dizzy. The world had dissolved into molten ecstasy. She'd never imagined such sensations existed.

Could Gideon do that again? Her heart leaped with anticipation. Good Lord, was there *more*?

He moved to her other nipple, tonguing it, sucking, biting, so she shook with a tingling mix of pleasure and pain. She wanted him to worship her like this forever. She wanted him to fill her body with his.

"Gideon, don't make me wait," she begged, when desire threatened to incinerate her. She loved what he did, but the roaring need to have him inside her drove her insane. With every touch, frantic craving spiraled higher. She felt lost, empty, needy. "Please."

He raised his head and stared at her, his black eyes glittering. He looked like a pirate. A pirate of pleasure.

"You'll like what happens next." The current of warm laughter in his voice made her blood thicken to honey. "I promise."

His kisses this afternoon had hinted that the darkness that marked their lovemaking so far wasn't the whole story. Now the tormented, angry man who had burned with shame when he revealed his scars turned into a dream lover. Ardent. Commanding. Mindful of her pleasure.

Her heart overflowed with agonizing love, but she smothered the fatal words. Even now, she knew he didn't want declarations, commitments, vows.

"I like all of it," she admitted, praying what they did banished his shadows, even if only for a fleeting moment. "But please hurry."

He laughed softly and trailed a line of kisses between her breasts and across her rib cage. "Never."

She made an impatient sound, a sound transformed into a moan when he nipped the soft skin of her stomach. Her whole body was alive with sensation.

He kissed where he'd bitten her, as if to soothe the sting. But she'd reached such a pitch of arousal that nothing short of possession would satisfy her clamoring need.

"Gideon!" Her protest at his teasing faded on a gasp as he parted her legs with his hands and placed his lips . . . there.

Horrified shock paralyzed her. Surely this wasn't something a man did to a woman. Surely it couldn't be . . .

Thought disintegrated to ash as his mouth moved. She felt moisture, heat, suction. The soft friction of his hair between her thighs. The scrape of stubble on tender skin.

His mouth was hot. So hot.

Dear God, was that his tongue? There? She should pull away, demand he stop. Her shaking hands formed talons in the sheets on either side of her. No virtuous woman would suffer such unnatural attentions without protest. Was this some obscure Indian perversion?

She must insist he stopped.

Not yet.

The sheer strangeness of what he did held her unmoving under his predations. And now her astonishment was tempered by curiosity, even a curl of something that might have been pleasure.

No! She couldn't enjoy this bizarre act. It was too far outside anything she'd thought possible. Feverishly, she writhed under his mouth, trying to escape, but his hands on her hips were implacable.

"Gideon, stop," she said in a choked voice, as a fugitive bolt of response sizzled through her.

With reluctance she could feel, he withdrew from the astoundingly sensitive place he'd found. He dropped a kiss on the quivering flesh of her thigh.

At last he heeded her. That couldn't be disappointment spearing through her, could it? If it was, she was as depraved as he.

"Shh," he whispered, without looking up. No, he was too busy looking at her . . . down there. The realization should disgust her, but instead a forbidden thrill scorched its way down her spine. "Trust me, Charis."

He didn't wait for her answer. She wasn't even sure she

could muster a reply. Instead, he lowered his head once more. His tongue flicked more purposefully.

Charis's belly clenched with hot longing as he drew powerfully on that place. A warm melting sensation flooded her, and, to her embarrassment, she felt moisture well between her thighs. She tried to close her legs, but somehow that just trapped Gideon more tightly against her.

He didn't seem to mind her body's uncontrollable reaction although he must taste her body's juices against his seeking lips. Such intimacy was frightening, so much more alien than the times he'd thrust himself inside her. But she couldn't summon the will to move away, to demand he leave her alone.

A satisfied growl emerged from deep in his throat as he licked her. It was the most salacious sound she'd ever heard. Her throat closed on another protest as heat coiled deep inside her.

After what happened earlier, she had some inkling where this led. But how could he do that to her using just his mouth? It seemed extraordinary, outlandish, impossible. Still, the tension built. Dear heaven, he must cease this indecency before she exploded into a million pieces. With shaking hands, she reached down to push him away. But somehow her fingers ended up tangling in his damp, disheveled hair.

His mouth played endlessly against her, setting off explosions of reaction. She closed her eyes and hoped she'd survive this sinful pleasure. Broken moans emerged from her lips. Sounds she didn't recognize as hers.

As tension twisted tighter and tighter, she undulated toward his mouth. She no longer pretended she wanted him to stop. If he stopped, she'd die of frustration, sizzle away to nothing. A string of rhythmic sighs escaped her, and she gripped his head as if she'd fly into space if she released him.

At the point where she thought he'd either destroy her or fling her into a new heaven, he kissed her hard and long between her legs. White light erupted behind her eyes, and a jagged scream burst free.

The world retreated on a wave of hot delight. Her hands clenched hard in his hair, and she shivered wildly. It was devilish, wrong, profane, what he did. But she'd never felt pleasure like it.

Vaguely through her quivering daze, she felt him shift. Then the sweet benediction of his lips kissing her belly.

"You . . ." She paused and cleared her throat. After that life-altering experience, it was so difficult to speak. "You're wicked."

He laughed softly and rolled to the side, raising himself on one elbow so he could see her. "I'm sure you forgive me."

He cast one devastating glance down her naked body, and his lips, glistening and reddened with what he'd just done, curved upward in a sensual smile. She felt every sinew tighten with a renewal of arousal. In spite of the ecstasy he'd just given her, she burned for that most intimate of connections.

The ghost of his smile remained as he lifted a lock of her hair and toyed with it. Still trembling, she watched him. The sight of his broken hands made her ache with compassion. He deserved a lifetime of happiness for what he'd suffered.

She reached out to touch his face, needing to convey how she loved him. It still amazed her that she could make such gestures without him flinching away in horror. She trailed her fingers down his cheek, feeling the faint roughness of his beard.

Gideon stared at her with a savage concentration that stirred excitement low in her belly. Beneath his humor, his face was taut with barely-reined-in desire. A shy glance confirmed he was still hard and ready.

"I might forgive you," she said huskily, brushing his ruffled hair back from his forehead. To think he'd believed he was denied human touch forever. After what she'd discovered tonight, that fate seemed cruel beyond imagination.

His eyes didn't waver, and his voice became considering. "One day soon, I hope you'll do the same for me."

"What . . ." Shock made her lift her hand and sit up. Shock and wanton, uncontrollable curiosity.

Abruptly, the quiet moment of tenderness shattered.

"Next time," he said, ruthlessly pushing her back onto the mattress.

His face was intent, flushed with hunger. Heat sparked along her veins, and she waited in an agony of suspense for what came next. Her heart galloped with anticipation. She couldn't mistake how close to the edge he was. His desperation fed hers.

He reared over her, big, powerful, dominating. She raised her knees to frame his narrow hips. He kissed her with a fierceness that made her arch against him. His hardness pressed into her stomach. Soon, all that masculine power would be inside her.

She could hardly wait.

"Hold on to my shoulders," he said in a thick voice.

Wordlessly, she obeyed. His muscles tensed. His shoulders were as unrelenting as stone, as sleek as satin under her clinging hands.

Her heart thundering, she prepared to be conquered as he'd conquered her this morning. Only to discover he meant to woo her to rapture.

He tilted his hips forward. She felt sliding heat against her moist cleft. Then slow, delicious pressure.

At last . . .

She caught her breath and flexed her fingers against his damp skin. He breathed harshly, and a lock of hair tumbled over his forehead. The veins in his arms stood out in stark relief. She couldn't doubt control cost every ounce of concentration.

There was something viscerally satisfying about being the object of that unwavering focus. Last time they'd made love, he'd been lost to passion. That had been exciting. This was deeper, purer, sweeter.

He penetrated farther. She gasped as still-tender flesh stretched to accommodate him.

Of course he heard her. He paused in his tormentingly gradual invasion.

"Am I hurting you?" he asked in a gravelly voice.

She raised her head and kissed him briefly, then returned for a longer foray. This morning she'd felt desired, and the knowledge had been heady. Tonight, she felt cherished.

"Charis?"

"Don't stop," she whispered, and dug her fingers harder into his shoulders.

He pushed forward. The feeling was strange. Uncomfortable. Exciting. With every incremental incursion, he took over her body. With her body, her soul.

She moaned and moved to ease the blinding pressure. He went deeper. She gasped for air as if she drowned. His shoulders under her hands were slick and his face was gaunt, the skin stretched over his bones.

The ferocious expression in his black eyes as they burned into hers should frighten her. Instead, it made her belly knot with arousal. He edged farther. Paused.

Had he reached his limit? She braced against him. Then something inside her relaxed, opened with sudden welcome.

The tension drained from his back. His muscles bunched again. And. with a deep groan, he seated himself fully.

The sensation was extraordinary. Indescribable. It was like her love took on solid expression, breath, life.

Time stretched to eternity before her. For all their previous lovemaking, she'd never felt so close to another person. The dark intimacy was all-encompassing.

His breathing was ragged. The eyes that met hers were glazed with passion. He withdrew in one smooth movement and plunged back. Heat streaked through her, brilliant as lightning.

As he changed the angle, her passage closed hard around him. The fresh sensation made her jerk and tremble. Twice tonight he'd shown her bliss. But what he did now was prelude to something infinitely more powerful.

He thrust again, and she clenched in barbaric possession. Every parting and joining jolted her body. Vaguely through the gathering storm, she felt him dip one hand between them. Then the press of his palm at the juncture of her legs, the flick of his fingers.

Her eyes fluttered shut as fire engulfed her world.

Consuming flame rushed along her veins. Every muscle tightened to an agony that was the greatest pleasure she'd ever known. Nothing existed except the roaring inferno.

Through it all, one thing alone anchored her. The man who thundered into her as she convulsed with ecstasy. She held on to Gideon while unshakable love filled her. Indelibly part of the shining bliss, but somehow separate, immortal, and immovable like the sun.

Gideon was her sun. Her moon. Her sky. He created her anew in the fiery kiln of his passion.

Love flooded every particle of her body with liquid gold. The connection was transcendent, eternal, unbreakable.

Gradually, her shuddering calmed. Reality slowly returned. The earth became the place she lived in instead of a mere memory to someone lost in the stars. But radiance lingered like the last glow of light on the horizon after a perfect summer day.

Opening dazed eyes, she found Gideon staring down at her in wonder. His lips tilted in a smile that, did he but know it, told her he loved her as she loved him.

She was exhausted, spent, lost in languorous joy. Her joints were so loose, she felt like a rag doll. He could pound her into oblivion now, and she wouldn't utter a squeak of protest.

He looked equally strained. She suddenly realized he hadn't yet found relief. Shocked, she made an almighty effort and reached out to touch his chest. One glancing contact, and her hand flopped back to her side. Her muscles had the resistance of woolen stuffing.

She quivered from the extraordinary conflagration that had swept her up into blissful oblivion. She'd had no idea. Nothing in her life had prepared her for those transforming moments in his arms.

Gideon released a shaky breath and began to shift in and

out of her body in a leisurely glide. The soft friction soothed. He bent to lick the peak of one breast.

"I can't . . ." she protested on a dying whisper.

"I know," he soothed, drawing her nipple between his lips.

Sluggish response trickled down to where his body joined hers. He slid out and, with excruciating slowness, slid back in. He bit down softly on the pebbled peak.

She sighed, and this time when he moved, she rose to meet him. Immediately she felt new heat. The joining was deep and essential. An expression of love as much as desire.

Again, she stifled words he didn't want to hear. But her every heartbeat declared she loved him.

Instinctively, she rolled her hips, testing the sensation. He groaned against her breast and released her nipple to trace kisses across her collarbone. She laced her fingers in his thick hair, then gasped as he dragged her up to sit before him, still joined flesh to flesh.

He gazed into her face with the fixed concentration that was now familiar. A premonitory thrill shook her, made interior muscles tighten. His hands were ruthless, demanding, as he grabbed her hips and began to slide her up and down.

Her fog of satiated exhaustion, so overwhelming only minutes ago, vanished in an electric instant. Her legs automatically curled around him. She gripped his arms for balance. Desire bloomed in her belly.

She soon caught the rhythm. With a velvety laugh, he let her have her way. He leaned back on his hands, yielding to the summons of her pleasure.

The pleasure was astonishing.

Until now, it had never occurred to her that she could control what happened between them. The power, the delight made her head swim. She arched back, relishing the push and release inside her. He made her feel like a goddess. He made her feel like a woman in love.

Her breath escaped in broken gasps. She edged closer to another of those extraordinary peaks. Closer but not there. She sobbed and twisted, struggling to reach what she wanted.

"Not yet, my darling," he whispered. He rolled and pressed her down into the mattress. She cried out and twined her legs around his hips. Still, he moved in and out of her body. Relentless as the tide.

His bare, scarred skin was hot, slippery under her clinging hands. He groaned and trembled.

For her.

That knowledge shuddered through her like a cannon blast. With every thrust, he stole another inch of her soul.

Except he'd owned her soul from the first.

Soon, his movements became faster, wilder, less controlled. His chest heaved as he fought for breath.

Charis lost contact with everything but the hard male body that ruled her. Tension wound around her until it was unendurable.

Tighter and tighter.

Still he plunged in and out. Her fingers dug into his arms so deeply that they hurt.

Blackness pressed down. Surely it must end. Yet still the need built higher, red-hot copper wires that stretched every sinew.

She gasped for air. Her lungs ceased to function. Blindly, she pressed toward Gideon, the source of her agony, her only hope of release.

This was stronger, deeper, more overwhelming than what had happened before.

Could she survive this?

Her breath escaped in a long, tortured moan.

"Please, Gideon, please . . ."

Did he reply? Her ears were deaf to all but the endless clamor of desire.

Still, he moved inside her.

She whimpered and bit down on her lip until she tasted blood. She closed her eyes, helplessly seeking refuge in hot darkness.

The pressure climbed higher. She felt like she burst out of her skin. She felt like her bones crumbled to dust. She felt as if the world must end any second. In a blinding, endless cataclysm.

The unceasing friction between her legs was maddening. She shifted, seeking freedom from torment.

She opened blurred eyes and saw his face change.

"Now," he growled.

One mighty thrust, and the ceaseless anticipation peaked, broke, scattered in shards of flaming rapture. She dived through darkness into a landscape of shimmering light.

Her body spasmed in an unbearable wave. She screamed as pleasure threatened to crush her. Vaguely, through her crisis, she was aware of Gideon's groaning release.

For an eternity, she remained suspended, stretched on a rack of infinite joy. Doused with unearthly pleasure that made her cry aloud in delight. Her nails dug hard into his back as she clung to him like a rock in a sea of fire.

Dazed, changed, amazed, she returned to the world to find Gideon kissing her face, her neck, her shoulders. Tenderly. Sweetly. The sweetness all the more poignant for the violent storm they'd passed through.

"You're so beautiful," he whispered, glancing kisses across her cheeks and nose and forehead. Kisses like the enchanting ones he'd given her this afternoon.

For a long moment, she lay acquiescent. Her chest heaved as she sucked great breaths into empty lungs. Her muscles trembled with reaction.

Then she lifted her face toward him for more kisses. The innocence pleased her, warmed her to the heart. Even as his body rested in hers, and she quaked after that earth-shattering climax.

Gideon rolled to the side, taking her with him, still kissing her. Softly, he separated from her. She stifled a whimper of discomfort. After the uninhibited passion, she ached. Every muscle was tired, tested to its limit.

She'd never felt so good.

"Are you all right?" he murmured against her neck. His arms encircled her loosely, and his hands rubbed lazy circles on her bare back.

How could she describe the wonders she'd discovered? Words were inadequate to convey the glory. When he raised his head, she kissed his mouth very gently, trying to say with action what speech could not.

Oh, such joy to touch him freely, naturally.

His mouth moved upon hers. The kiss was warm, comforting. A thousand miles from his turbulent lovemaking.

Slowly, reluctantly, she drew away. "It was beyond anything I imagined."

His fingers combed through her tangled hair. Like every gesture in this glowing aftermath, his touch was tender.

His expression became serious, and his hand cupped her face. For a long moment, he stared into her eyes. "It's not always like this, Charis." He paused, and she saw him swallow. "I've never known anything to match what we just shared."

She blinked away tears. Her heart was so full, she thought it must burst. "I'm glad," she said in a thick voice. "I want you to be mine forever."

A shadow crossed his face, and with it, a hairline crack appeared on the shining surface of Charis's satisfaction. "Let's not tempt fate."

He bent to nuzzle her neck. Heat flared as he bit down on a sensitive nerve running up from her shoulder. She closed her eyes in willing surrender. But even as need surged, his answer troubled her heart.

Twenty-one

I t's midnight," Gideon said softly, his breath ruffling the hair on Charis's crown and disturbing her from her warm half doze.

They shared the settle before the blazing parlor fire. She curled into him, one arm loosely around his waist, one resting across his chest. Her palm lay flat over his heart. She loved to feel its steady beating, as though she connected directly to his life force.

"Do you want to go to bed?" she asked huskily, rubbing her cheek against his shoulder. This physical closeness still seemed a precious miracle. She never took it for granted.

His sleepy laugh was a deep rumble under her hand, and the arm he draped around her tightened. "I always want to go to bed."

After so many days of unbridled debauchery, a girl should lose the ability to blush. Nonetheless, heat rose in her cheeks. "You're insatiable."

"At least where you're concerned." He raised her hand

from his chest and brushed a kiss across her knuckles. She couldn't help shivering with response.

Over recent days, she'd watched the strain fade from Gideon's features. He looked younger, less haunted. Perhaps because when not making passionate love to her, he'd slept. Deep, undisturbed rest that she guessed he hadn't enjoyed for years. His dangerous life had worn him down long before he fell into the Nawab's clutches.

But while he smiled more often and more willingly, shadows lingered in his eyes. With a pang of sorrow, she realized they probably always would.

Since the night Gideon had shown her the pleasure a man and woman could find together, they'd rarely left their rooms. Sometimes Charis forgot the outside world with its demands and dangers existed. There had been no sign of Felix or Hubert and no warning about trouble at Penrhyn. The hotel servants tidied and brought meals or bathwater. The rest of her modish new wardrobe arrived. Gideon summoned a notary and set out legal safeguards against her stepbrothers. Her fortune was now officially his, at least until the end of June, when it reverted to her.

She'd hoped the change in Gideon would extend to an easier relationship with humanity. So far, she had witnessed no such merciful amnesty. To her sorrow, Gideon's immediate tension was visible whenever strangers set foot in this private kingdom. Her brief optimism that she'd found a remedy to his affliction faded further every time she saw him pale and recoil from other people.

He wasn't cured. Not by a long way. She fervently thanked heaven every day that he could touch her. But so far, his recovery advanced no further than that.

She knew when she looked into his eyes that he believed it never would.

That wasn't the only trouble nicking at the skein of sensual delight entwining her. For all its myriad pleasures, her new life was hollow at its center. The unspoken pain bit most at moments of purest happiness. Like now.

Gideon told her she was beautiful. He told her how much he wanted her. She had no doubts he desired her with endless hunger. But even when she felt they united into one being, words of love never escaped her husband's lips. She knew him well enough to interpret his silence as deliberate.

Nor did he mention his plans for when they left Jersey. It was as though these weeks they shared now existed outside time.

Coward that she was, she let him get away with avoiding the subject. She'd exhausted her store of courage standing up to him after their marriage. Now she was terrified that too many awkward questions would shatter their delicate bliss. Perhaps because with every day, the threat of leaving him plowed deeper furrows in her heart. She couldn't bear to hear him say he still meant them to separate. Although his silence on the matter indicated he hadn't relinquished his original scheme.

Her arm firmed around his waist as she laid an unspoken claim, defying his right to forsake her. But the words insisting he tell her what he intended crammed in her throat.

"Charis, it's midnight," he said with greater emphasis, then glanced at the clock. "Five past."

His unusual obsession with the time pierced her troubled reflections. She looked up in puzzlement. "Is that important?"

He kissed her quickly on the mouth. "You've lost track of the days, haven't you?"

"Lost track . . ." Perplexed, she blinked at him. Hard to marshal coherent thought when his kisses sent her spinning into dazzling Elysium.

His lips curved in the tender smile that always made her poor adoring heart somersault. "It's the first of March. Happy birthday, my darling."

Her birthday . . .

Stiffening, she drew away. She forced her befuddled mind to calculate back. So difficult to count paradise in minutes and hours. She'd barely been aware whether it was day or night. Gideon lit her life like the sun. She needed no other fire in her heavens.

"You have possession of your fortune." She couldn't define his tone. He didn't sound particularly triumphant. He kissed her again, more gently this time. "We won, Charis."

They'd vanquished her stepbrothers. She was safe. Relief filtered through her. And fear that now the threat passed, everything would change between her and Gideon.

She forced herself to speak though she knew he wouldn't want to hear what she said. "Because of you." She swallowed and continued in a voice that vibrated with emotion. "I owe you everything."

"I don't want your gratitude." His expression hardened, and he sat up. His arm slid away from her. Worse, his emotional withdrawal was unmistakable as frost in the air.

"Well, you've got it. Forever." She mustered the courage that lately had been so sadly lacking. The murky currents swirling beneath the bright surface would no longer be denied. Her tone developed an edge. "I can be grateful to you and love you. The two aren't mutually exclusive."

She hadn't mentioned love since the morning he'd surrendered to lust and leaped on her. Always, even at the peak of sexual pleasure when her whole world was Gideon, she'd bitten back the words. His silence had fed hers.

Her wisdom in restraining any declaration became abundantly clear. He surged to his feet and regarded her with the wary expression she'd hoped never to see again. The hollow in her heart resonated as if a huge mourning bell clanged inside it.

"Charis, it's our last night on Jersey," he said somberly, ignoring her challenge. Although his guarded eyes told her he'd heard her. "Tomorrow we sail for Penrhyn,"

No, no, no, no, no.

"We're leaving?" Her question rang with dismay.

Could the tenuous bond she'd established with him outlast a return to daily life? Here she was the center of his existence. She wasn't vain enough to expect that to continue forever. But she needed longer to make him completely hers.

Did he even intend to keep her with him?

Grim foreboding swamped her. Was this her ration of joy, these few glorious days on Jersey?

Reluctant amusement quirked his lips. "We have to go at some point, you know."

Blindly, she lurched up and turned away, fisting her shaking hands in her skirts. His attempt at lightness grated, hurt. He treated her like an easily distracted child. "Not yet."

She heard him approach, then his hand curved around her arm. She felt the roughness of his scars against her bare skin. His touch reminded her of his suffering and how far he'd come since they'd married.

Had he come far enough?

His voice was warm, encouraging. "There's no need to be frightened. You've reached your majority. The Farrells can't harm you. We're free."

He misunderstood her reaction. Of course the threat of Felix and Hubert had darkened her days. But more important by far was her endless battle for a future with Gideon.

"We're not free. We're married," Charis said in a muffled voice, bending her head.

He released her with an abrupt gesture and stepped away. She felt the distance like the blow of an ax. "If I could have devised another way to save you, I wouldn't have forced you into such drastic action," he said curtly.

The sweet concord of minutes ago was only a bitter memory. The suddenness of the change left her staggering in its wake. She turned to face him, knowing her pain was naked in her face. "You know I'm always grateful for . . ."

"Enough!" One ruined hand sliced the tense air. "If I hear the word *grateful* once more, I won't be responsible for the consequences."

"But, Gideon . . ."

"Devil take you, Charis, stop!" He paused, visibly fighting for composure. Bitterness frayed his voice, and his shoulders were ruler straight with tension. "Really, you shouldn't thank me. As it's turned out, our marriage was precipitate. Your stepbrothers haven't traced us. We didn't need to take such permanent measures. I can only offer my profoundest regrets."

The sharp slap resounded like the report of a bullet.

Gideon's head whipped back, and his expression registered shock rather than anger. The red imprint of her hand darkened his cheek.

The grim, echoing silence extended. And extended.

Shaking, Charis lowered her arm and backed away on unsteady legs. She wasn't frightened. She was so furious, her vision turned black.

"How dare you?" Her voice lowered to trembling vehemence. "You've had me in your bed. You've been so deep inside me, you've touched my soul. Yet you have the gall to talk about regret?"

"What I've done to you is unforgivable," he said harshly. As shock receded, rage lit his black eyes. "And yes, I do regret that I've hurt you."

Her fragile happiness shattered around her with a sharp crack that sounded like a heart breaking. Her lips felt stiff as she voiced her worst fears. "You can't mean to follow your original plan, that we should lead separate lives?"

His jaw set like stone. "The basic difficulties remain. It still seems the best solution."

Agony stabbed her, stole her breath, made her stumble back a step. She felt betrayed, devastated, lost. Somewhere, she found strength to speak. "Is that what you want?"

"It doesn't matter what I want. I'm trying to do what's best for you."

She clenched her fists at her sides. Either that or batter at him like a madwoman. She loved him more than her life. And at this moment, if one of his pistols had been in reach, she'd happily have put a bullet through his thick skull. "So these last days mean nothing? You can't expect me to believe that. You've found happiness in my arms, Gideon. Don't ever lie about that."

The skin on his face tightened. She braced to hear him say the words that turned her dream of love into a travesty.

His throat worked as he swallowed and he avoided her gaze. "I should never have touched you. It was wrong. It was cruel. The fact that I can't stay away from you is no excuse. It's only an indictment of my own damnable weakness. You should curse me with your every breath. One day you will. Even if we take the sensible course and part now."

He blamed himself for what happened but couldn't deny the bond between them. She should find that reassuring, but she knew how obstinate he was. Obstinacy had kept him alive in India. How tragic that obstinacy now made him surrender his chance of happiness. And hers. He tried to do the right thing, the noble thing, but all he did was condemn them both to a lifetime of loneliness.

Charis had prayed love would wash away the poison of Rangapindhi. She saw now her prayers hadn't been answered.

Her voice rang with resentment. "You're such a fool, Gideon."

"One of us has to keep a clear head without getting lost in the romance of it all," he said with wounding sarcasm.

He wanted her to let him go to perdition in peace. Well, he'd picked the wrong wife if he expected her consent to that. Still, only the knowledge that he loved her, however much he wished he didn't, kept her fighting. This battle was dangerous—it could destroy both of them.

Her nails dug deep into her palms, the slight sting nothing compared to the way he lacerated her heart with his stubborn rejection. He was the cleverest man she knew. And when it came to her, the stupidest. "We desire each other."

She saw him consider sidestepping the statement. After these days of passion, she knew him so well. Why didn't he know her in return?

Something in her face must have convinced him evading the issue wasn't an option. His lips lengthened in a grim smile. "Yes, there is desire. Enough to set the world on fire. But desire isn't enough."

As her false paradise disintegrated around her, she stopped lying to him and to herself. "And there's love. I love you, and you love me. You told me once."

A compressed line of guilt and sorrow replaced his smile. "I had no right to say that. I hoped you'd forgotten."

In a different universe, she would have laughed. Forgotten? Those words were permanently carved on her heart, even if he never said them again. "No chance."

He looked ill and tired and tense. He looked like a man contemplating the end of the world. "I've wronged you so deeply, I can never make recompense."

Her temper spiked. "How have you wronged me? By showing me a man can be more than a selfish brute? By saving me from rape? By teaching me about ecstasy?"

He was so pale, the mark on his cheek where she'd hit him stood out like a beacon. "By making you believe we could have a life together. By coming to your bed night after night when every principle dictated that I stay away. By tying you with bonds of *gratitude* . . ." He spat out the word like a curse. ". . . you'll never break, even when you realize what you feel now is illusion."

She flinched. Surely he didn't still think her love was sickly hero worship? Not after all they'd shared. The accusation hurt more than acid flung in her face.

She drew a shaky breath and reminded herself that he loved her, hard as it was to believe when she confronted his anger and derision. She fought for her life here. She couldn't let him defeat her.

"I forget you're so much older and wiser than I." Gideon wasn't the only one with sarcasm in his arsenal.

His expression closed. Once, she'd have retreated from his bristling hauteur. But she'd held him gasping with release too often for the mask of control to dupe her. He wasn't controlled. He was anguished and angry and desperate.

"After Rangapindhi, I feel a thousand years old." He spoke sadly, so sadly her heart clenched.

Pity almost made her step down. Almost.

"Gideon, I don't discount what happened to you." Her voice became less strident. "I don't blind myself to what your ordeal cost you. Still costs you. That doesn't mean your decisions are always correct. Right now, you're disastrously wrong."

"You force me to be frank." A muscle jerked spasmodically in his cheek. He turned and prowled toward the window, where he curled one hand in the curtains. "Let me lay out some facts. If you can bear to contemplate mundane reality."

"I'm more aware of facts than you are," she said through tight lips. His mockery stung. "But pray, dazzle me. I wait in humble anticipation."

Even in profile, she didn't miss the way his mouth flattened with annoyance. "Very well," he bit out, every word as precisely cut as a diamond. And just as sharp. "I'm going back to Penrhyn to an arduous, frugal future. Isolated. Lonely. You are the kingdom's greatest heiress. I'm physically and emotionally incapable of offering you the life you deserve."

Disbelief rose to choke her. "You reject me because you're worried I'll pine for the occasional party?" Her voice began to shake. "You truly believe I'm irreparably shallow, don't you?"

He ran his hand through his hair, mussing it to wildness, and whirled to confront her. "Damn it, Charis!"

He sucked in an audible breath as he struggled for control. "I'm a freak, a poltroon, one step off being a lunatic. I can't bear people around me, touching me. You know my affliction. In spite of my insatiable hunger for you, you know essentially I haven't changed. Why can't you see what you want is impossible?"

Stepping closer, she replied with matching heat. "Because of that insatiable hunger. Because you can bear my touch. Because I don't care about other people. I only care about you."

"You say that now. How will you feel in twenty years when you've wasted your youth on a man who only exists in your imagination?"

She couldn't doubt his sincerity. No matter how mistaken he was. She made an angry sound in her throat. "And if I'm pregnant?"

He'd been pale. Now he went stark white. His eyes sparked like burning coals. "Don't you want to bear my child?"

"I want it more than I can say." Almost as much as she wanted to stake her place in his closed heart. Strange to recognize that need so powerfully and so immediately. She placed a trembling hand on her belly. Could a new life already grow inside her? The idea was overwhelming. Frightening. Exciting.

Gideon's blazing eyes fastened on her gesture, and a savage expression crossed his face. "Dear God, are you pregnant?"

Was she? With all that had happened, she'd lost count of the days. And she'd been so focused on Gideon, she'd hardly considered consequences. "It's too early to say. Do you still mean to send me away if I carry your child?"

He looked like he reeled at the prospect of fatherhood. "I don't know."

An ounce of her earlier sarcasm crept into her voice. "Why are you so shocked? The natural result of what we've done for the last two weeks is a baby. Surely you gave some thought to the matter."

He slumped against the wall, his face ravaged with despair. "Yes." He hesitated and shook his head with bleak incomprehension. "No."

There was a charged silence, then he continued in a dull voice. "Of course I knew I took risks. If I thought beyond how much I wanted you, it was to say we'd deal with any complications when the time came."

She twined her arms around herself as ice congealed in her blood. Her momentary hope shrank to a cold kernel the size of a pebble. "Risks? Complications? Don't you want a baby?"

He tensed. "If I'm not fit to be a husband, I'm certainly not fit to be a father. If we have a child, it . . ." He must have interpreted her expression correctly because he paused. ". . . he or she must go with you."

She raised her chin although she was so deathly tired of battling him. He loved her, she reminded herself. But the words lost their power with every repetition. "Why does anyone have to go anywhere?"

"Aren't you listening?"

"All I've heard is a lot of nonsense." She turned away and stalked toward the bedroom. She was disheartened, angry, exhausted. Trying to get Gideon to see sense was like flinging herself over and over against a mountain.

For one electric moment, she'd wondered if she'd shaken his certainty. She hadn't mistaken what she'd seen in his face when he asked if she was with child. He'd been furious with himself. And her.

But she'd seen more in his ferocious black gaze.

She'd seen longing.

He wasn't nearly as implacably set upon his desolate future as he wanted her to think. If she had his baby, he wouldn't desert her. She knew that in her bones.

Dear God, let me be pregnant.

As she reached the doorway, he spoke in a grave voice. When she turned to face him, he looked weary and curiously defeated, although he'd withstood her every attack. "I know you believe I'm cruel and capricious and pigheaded. But I swear I'm acting in your best interests."

"I wish you'd think of yourself for once. Ask yourself what you want and seize it." Blinking back acrid, painful tears, she left him alone.

Twenty-two

G ideon turned the hired gig onto the lonely road that snaked across the moor to Penrhyn. At his side, Charis remained bundled away from him in her new blue pelisse and matching bonnet.

She'd been broodingly quiet since before they'd left Jersey yesterday. On the storm-tossed boat that finally reached the mainland south of Penrhyn this morning. During this jolting carriage ride in a shabby, ill-sprung vehicle over potholed roads.

It was well into the afternoon, and still she remained locked away as securely as if a wall of bricks and mortar separated them. She'd rebuffed his stilted attempts at conversation, seemingly content to stare at the rough countryside.

She'd never been a chatterer. Her ability to maintain a restful silence was one of the many things he admired.

This silence wasn't restful. It seethed. With every mile, the tension twisted tighter.

They hadn't resolved their acrimonious argument. How

could they? She wanted what he couldn't in conscience give her. Tying a beautiful, vital girl like Charis to a physical and mental wreck like him was a sin against nature. He'd always recognized that. His pride wouldn't countenance it. His heart couldn't endure it. All the passion in the world didn't change that one bleak reality.

How the devil was he going to live without her?

The memory of the last, radiant days should fill him with regret. His passion had misled Charis into believing they had a chance together. He'd glimpsed a bright heaven that only mocked him now.

But selfish bastard he was, he couldn't repent what he'd done in Jersey. Not when desolate solitude beckoned ahead.

After their quarrel, they'd slept apart for the first time in over a week. Not that he'd slept. Instead, he'd sat in the parlor, watching night change to grim day. He'd felt like a mongrel cur tossed into the gutter to starve. He still did. Dear God, was this how the rest of his life was going to be?

He beat back the questions, the guilt, the anguish that plagued him. His gloved hands hardened on the reins, and he urged the ungainly pony to a faster pace. The gig bounced along the rocky track. He couldn't risk slowing down. The clouds closed in, and they'd be soaked if rain caught them on this heath.

Charis's gloved hand clenched on the edge of the lurching carriage. It had been the only vehicle available in the small fishing village where they'd found safe harbor this morning. They'd tried to land at Penrhyn Cove, but the seas made it too dangerous.

With every second, the weather worsened. A biting wind howled. The sky loured, black and menacing, and thunder rumbled in the distance. He needed to get his wife to warmth and safety. Where she could ignore him in comfort.

He slapped the reins against the pony's fat rump. They were still several miles from the house. He made a frustrated sound and looked at Charis.

She studied him, her eyes more brown than green, under-lined with dark circles. She looked proud, distant, unhappy . . . *beautiful.*

In the strange gray light, her fine brows arched with what he read as disdainful curiosity. "Are you quite well, Gideon?"

"Yes, of course," he said curtly.

Her lips lengthened with irritation. "You're very restless, and you're making bizarre noises."

"I'm worried about the weather."

She looked around the open plateau. High in the sky, birds streaked to escape the coming tempest. The wind competed with the gig's rattle and the clop of the pony's hooves.

Her hand shifted to touch the necklace he'd given her the morning they left Jersey. England's greatest heiress must own bank vaults full of spectacular parures. But when he'd seen the amber-and-gold circlet in the jeweler's window in St. Helier a week ago, he'd immediately thought of Charis. The unusual intensity of the yellow stones reminded him of the light in her eyes when she was happy.

A light noticeably absent today, damn it.

Although her thanks were subdued, she'd seemed to like the trifle. At least she wore it.

Not for the first time, Gideon felt all at sea with his wife. Marriage was a difficult and complicated endeavor. Perhaps it was a good thing that his would be so short-lived, at least in any meaningful sense.

And didn't that cheer him up no end?

Dourly, he stared past the pony's ears at the rutted path. It was difficult not to view the surrounding wasteland and threatening sky as omens of his future.

"We're not far from home, are we?" she asked, without looking at him.

Home. Gideon supposed she must consider Penrhyn her home. Lord knows she'd been exiled from anywhere else she rightfully belonged. Now he prepared to exile her again. He knew he did the right thing in setting her free. But at this moment, it didn't feel like it.

"Not far. Pray God we beat the rain."

The road dipped into a tree-filled dell. Interlacing branches turned the gloomy afternoon into night. Away from the wind, the gig's creak seemed unnaturally loud.

Then the ambush came.

When the tree crashed in front of them, at first, stupidly, Charis thought the wind caused the accident.

Then she realized there was no wind in this hidden hollow.

"Damn it." His powerful shoulders bunching, Gideon struggled to control the rearing, squealing pony. The tree had missed the animal by inches. "Whoa there! Settle down!"

Charis clung trembling to the rocking gig as the maddened horse bucked and fought. Gideon fought to enforce obedience. Finally, recognizing the hand of authority, the pony stood quivering between the shafts with its head lowered.

Gideon cast her an urgent glance. "Jump, Charis, and run!"

But it was too late. Charis hardly drew breath before a roughly dressed man appeared from the underbrush. He snatched the halter with cruel force, wrenching the skittish pony's head up.

"Sir Gideon, what a pleasure." The oily self-satisfied voice oozed down Charis's spine and held her paralyzed on the seat. A terrifyingly familiar voice.

Across the pony's heaving back, she met Felix's gelid gray regard. Her every muscle tensed. Choking fear set like stone in her belly. Dear Lord, they were trapped.

Felix looked so pleased with himself, rage boiled up to drown her fear. With just such an expression, he'd watched Hubert beat her black-and-blue. She invested every ounce of the contempt she felt into her glare. "Felix. Still a sneaking little worm, I see."

Her stepbrother's hands clenched on the halter, so the frightened pony whinnied and tossed its head in protest. "Shut up, you little bitch!"

"And eloquent as ever. I'm impressed." Her voice lowered into irony. "I find myself less impressed with your appearance. Have you given up bathing for Lent?"

"Stay quiet, for God's sake," Gideon hissed, dragging her to his side with one strong arm. With his other hand he reached into the pocket of his greatcoat, she guessed for his pistol. "What in Hades are you about, Farrell?"

He didn't shift his attention from Felix, and his voice was sharp and lordly, as it had been when he spoke to the brothers at Penrhyn. Charis pressed closer, her brief defiance fading beneath growing awareness of their terrible danger.

"I wouldn't do anything too impulsive, if I were you, Trevithick." Felix drew himself up and made a dismissive gesture. "You're expendable, and I'm sure you won't wish to leave my sister undefended."

He nodded to someone behind the gig, and Charis heard the unmistakable sound of a gun cocking. She didn't need to see who it was. The two brothers rarely acted apart.

Her pulses raced, and sweat prickled her palms, but Gideon's heartbeat remained steady and sure under her cheek. The unhurried, regular sound bolstered her courage. Even as he lifted his hand away from his pocket.

"Lady Charis is now my wife," Gideon said calmly, his arm tightening around her in a silent promise of protection. But how could he keep her safe when the brothers had them at such disadvantage?

"The devil she is," Hubert snarled, stamping into view and brandishing two large horse pistols.

The brothers' fortunes had clearly worsened in recent weeks. They were unshaven, their clothing was creased and stained, and their linen was gray. The Farrells' unkempt state hinted they'd been sleeping rough. With sudden spite, Charis hoped it had rained every night. She hoped it had *snowed*.

"We've ridden to Gretna and back. We know you haven't married the slut," Felix snapped, snatching one of the guns from Hubert and aiming it squarely at the pair in the gig.

Gideon didn't flinch although she felt him subtly shift so his body shielded her from the pistol. Foolish, heroic man. The rusty taste of regret flooded her mouth as she remembered how angry she'd been with him all day.

"I have indeed wed this *lady*." Gideon bit out the last word. His sangfroid stirred Charis's admiration even as acid dread rushed through her veins. "In Jersey a fortnight ago. For confirmation, apply to the Reverend Thomas Briggs of St. Helier. Lady Charis's person and fortune are now at my disposal."

Stupid Hubert lowered his pistol. Felix cast him an irritated glance. "What the hell are you doing, man?"

"They're married," Hubert spluttered. "The game's up."

"For God's sake, keep them in your sights!" Felix whipped around to face Gideon and Charis. The feral light in his eyes indicated this was his last desperate throw of the dice, and he intended to win. "It's not as simple as that, Trevithick."

"No?" Gideon still sounded nonchalant. "Any harm gets you no closer to the money—and garners you a hanging when the law catches up with you. Make no mistake. You and your brute of a brother are identified as likely culprits should mischief befall us."

"You have it all wrong." Felix's smile took on a smug curve that sent a shiver down Charis's backbone. "I mean everyone to walk away safe and sound, Hubert and I considerably richer and you, sadly, considerably poorer."

Gideon's soft laugh lifted the hairs on the back of Charis's neck. He sounded utterly powerful. As if he hadn't a care in the world, for all that they were held at gunpoint without hope of outside aid in this wild woodland. "I wouldn't toss you a farthing after what you did to her, you bastard."

Felix's lip curled in scorn. "Brave words." Without shifting his attention from the gig, Felix tilted his head toward Hubert. "Get the jade."

Hubert stepped toward them, then hesitated as Gideon spoke with a cold savagery that made Charis's heart skip a beat. "Touch her, and you're dead."

Felix's face hardened. Most people considered him a handsome man, but for a moment, he looked uglier than a hobgoblin. Charis suppressed another shiver. "We'll hold the chit until you transfer every penny of her fortune to me."

Charis bit back a gasp, and her hands clenched in Gideon's coat as if that would save her from being dragged away. She should have expected this. She knew from bitter experience that Felix hated to be bested. He'd never allow her money to slip through his fingers.

"Don't worry." Gideon looked down at her and his arm firmed around her shoulders. "I won't let them take you."

"Can't we fight?" Charis's voice shook with distress.

Regretfully, Gideon shook his head. "They're armed. The risk of your getting hurt is too great." He turned his unblinking gaze to Felix. "Take me instead."

Gideon's easy tone momentarily deceived Charis. Then, with disbelieving shock, she realized what he offered. On a strangled cry, she straightened and stared at him in horror.

You will not do this, my love. I won't let you.

Felix gave an unimpressed grunt. "What purpose will that serve?"

"It keeps her out of your filthy paws." Gideon's tone dripped derision.

Felix sent him a hate-filled glare. "Sadly, because of your machinations, it's your signature we require, not hers."

"My man of business is at Penrhyn to advise her how to get the money. Charis can contact the trustees and the bank, organize the papers. Until then, I place myself at your disposal."

Her belly twisted in denial, and her hands clawed at his coat as if she'd restrain him by main force if she must. "No, Gideon, this is unthinkable. You can't."

The broken protest faltered into silence. She couldn't risk Felix and Hubert discovering his vulnerability. If they knew what Gideon risked by becoming their hostage, they'd torture him to insanity.

"You can't," she repeated in a shaking voice, wishing they

were alone, wishing she'd never met him and put him in this danger. Better she'd married Desaye weeks ago. What she'd always feared had finally come to pass. Her dilemma threatened to destroy the man she loved.

Through glazed eyes, she saw Gideon register her terror and rise above it. His black gaze as it probed hers was certain, unafraid. "I'm not letting them within a yard of you, my darling."

It was the same voice he'd used when he'd stubbornly insisted they had no future together. Her instincts told her he was determined on this course, and nothing she said would shift him.

She had to do something. She had to stop him. He confronted his vilest nightmares for her, and she wasn't worth it.

She swallowed the lump of furious emotion in her throat, only to have words fail her again as Gideon raised her gloved hand and brushed a fleeting kiss across her knuckles. Scalding tears prickled her eyes.

Felix and Hubert were ruthless, violent bullies. They'd work out their frustrations on their captive. Even without his affliction, Gideon faced pain and humiliation at their hands. With his affliction, the consequences could be catastrophic.

"No . . ."

Gideon's jaw took on the familiar implacable line. "I swore these dogs would never touch you again."

"Dear me, your gallantry touches my heart," Felix said sarcastically as he moved closer in unmistakable threat. "But I do believe we're better keeping the jade."

"Completely unacceptable." Gideon didn't look at Felix, and he spoke as if he held the upper hand in this ugly scene.

Felix emitted a harsh laugh. "By God, you're a cool one. What's to stop us taking her?"

"I'll stop you."

"You forget who has the gun." Even so Felix paused.

Gideon's smile was superior as he turned to her stepbrother. "Kill either of us, you lose your chance at the money."

"You'd still be dead," Felix said grimly, raising the pistol.

Gideon shrugged off the jibe. "Frankly, I don't know why you expect to get away with this. We'll lay the facts before the law at the first opportunity."

How could he sound so confident when he must know what was likely to happen? His reckless courage made Charis's belly lurch with nausea.

"We're not fool enough to wait around like sitting ducks. Hubert and I are for the Continent."

"While you're welcome to the slut," Hubert said. "Even if you'd managed to keep her fortune, you'd soon find you made a poor bargain."

Charis hardly noticed the insults. Her mind worked too frantically to find something to persuade Gideon against this perilous course. He'd sacrificed so much for her, but this went beyond what anyone could ask. It would be like facing Rangapindhi all over again.

Gideon didn't look at the brothers but spoke directly to her. His voice rang deep and sincere. "My wife is more precious than rubies. If she came to me wearing only her shift, I'd still be rich beyond measure."

He made the extraordinary declaration for her sake in case things went wrong. Charis's heart twisted with overwhelming love.

Oh, dear God, whatever happens, let him live through this.

"I can't leave you," she said unsteadily. Blind fear dug icy talons into her. "Don't make me."

"I must." He released her hand and his voice lowered. "Akash and Tulliver are at the house. They'll know what to do."

"Gideon . . ." His name was a ragged plea. She watched his expression close against her. His purpose was clearly unshakable.

Gideon faced Felix, his face set with disdain. "So you agree? I place myself in your charge, and Charis goes free?"

No, this must not be. In blind distress, she turned to Felix. "Take me." She was mortified that her voice broke.

"Both so eager to sample our hospitality." Felix's laugh

was cutting. "Make up your minds. One of you needs to get the money."

Gideon sent her stepbrother a flinty look. It was as if she'd never made the offer to stay in his place. "I assume you have a mount for Lady Charis. Unless you intend to shift the tree."

Gideon's continued calmness astounded her even through her dread. He wasn't shaking or sweating or pale. He looked like the invincible man who'd come to her rescue in Winchester.

Hubert's piglike eyes darted between Gideon and Felix as he tracked the shifts of power. "She can have my nag."

Gideon turned to her and gently cupped her face. His smile, like his touch, was poignantly tender. She searched his eyes for the fatalistic resignation she'd seen so often when he faced down his demons. All she read in the glowing black depths was strength, serenity, resolve.

And love, like a single star shining over a dark sea.

"Trust me, my darling," he said softly. "If you love me, trust me."

He knew he defeated her with that last demand. Gathering her ragged courage, she swallowed another furious protest and raised her chin.

Agreeing to what he asked was the hardest thing she'd ever done. Harder by far than defying Felix and Hubert or confronting the vile sailors in Portsmouth. Harder even than fighting Gideon for the chance to create a life together.

Fear coiled like an angry snake in her belly. For all Gideon's bravery, she abandoned him to an ordeal that could break him. But she couldn't let him down. Or succumb to pathetic, immature hysterics. She was the daughter of Hugh Davenport Weston. She was the wife of Gideon Trevithick. She wouldn't shame either valiant hero by failing now.

"I'll go," she muttered reluctantly.

She closed her eyes in despair as Gideon pressed his lips to hers. The kiss was sweet, passionate, heartbreakingly brief.

As he slowly drew away, she looked into his eyes. The star was still there. More radiant than ever.

"I love you." She could no longer hold back the words.

"I love you." He spoke without reluctance or equivocation. She snatched the vow close and locked it in her heart, never to let it go. Surely if they loved each other, Felix and Hubert couldn't defeat them.

Such hope rang false when she forsook her beloved to torture and imprisonment.

"Oh, for God's sake, get a move on," Felix said in a theatrically bored voice.

She ignored her stepbrother's jeering. She clung to Gideon's hand as she climbed down from the carriage. Her knees felt like custard as she reached the road.

Summoning all her courage, she released Gideon and braced her shoulders. Standing straight, she faced Felix. A scatter of cold raindrops hit her. The storm wasn't far off. A crack of thunder made the pony start and neigh.

The gig creaked as Gideon jumped to the road behind her. He towered over her, and his gloved hand closed firm and possessive around her arm. "She leaves unharmed. Otherwise, we have no agreement."

Felix gestured Hubert toward Gideon. "She'll leave unharmed, all right. But only when we've got you trussed nice and tight."

Charis waited for Gideon to object, but he merely said, "Let me give Lady Charis my coat. The weather's about to break."

Felix nodded briefly. "No tricks. I can hurt you without killing you."

"I'll keep that in mind," Gideon said dryly.

He released Charis and quickly divested himself of his coat. As he dropped it over her shoulders, it swamped her. Immediate warmth surrounded her. And Gideon's scent. Such an absurd thing to bolster her unsteady resolve.

Gideon brushed one gloved finger across her cheek and smiled. "It's like old times."

Her skin tingled under his touch. His words reminded her they shared a history of danger and survival. She wished she could draw comfort from the fact. "Be careful, Gideon," she whispered, her throat thick with anxiety and love.

He stepped past her. Charis bit back a protest as Hubert grabbed Gideon's hands and roughly wrenched them behind his back. Her husband stood stiffly, but he presented no resistance. Could the touch of Hubert's hand spark an attack? Please, no.

How could Gideon bear this? He must know what the brothers had in store. His unflinching bravery threatened her fragile control. Her belly knotted with sick anguish. He gave himself over to torment for her sake. She felt like she pushed him back into the pit in Rangapindhi with her own hands.

When Gideon looked at her, he must have read her faltering purpose. "Put the coat on properly. You've got some tough riding ahead." He sounded as if he sent her off on a morning's canter. She remembered she owed it to him to reach Penrhyn and save him. No matter how she wanted to scream and cry against what happened now.

She stiffened her spine. Her gaze clung to his face as she memorized every beloved feature. His burning eyes, the proud blade of his nose, his passionate mouth, taut with controlled anger. Beneath his composure, she knew he was fuming. She wanted him to stay furious. The fierce emotion might keep his ghosts at bay.

"Good-bye, my love," she said huskily.

He stared back. "Godspeed, Charis."

"Come on." Felix snapped, snatching her arm. His touch bruised, even through the thick woolen sleeve. "All hell's about to break loose."

"Let her go," Gideon said in a low, dangerous tone.

For all that the brothers were armed and Gideon was bound, Felix's hand automatically dropped away from her. Charis sent Gideon a grateful glance, then picked up her skirts and followed Felix.

There was nothing more she could do for Gideon here. Pray heaven, she could help him once she was free.

In spite of her urgency to reach Penrhyn, Charis took one last lingering look at her husband as she climbed the steep bank to bypass the fallen tree. Dwarfing Hubert, he stood tall and proud and undefeated. No trace of fear or weakness showed in his set features.

Stay safe, my love. Stay safe until I come for you.

She sent him a burning glance, a message to be strong, a promise to save him as he'd saved her so often. Then she dropped below the tree's branches, and he disappeared from view.

Two horses were tethered in the underbrush. Neither with a sidesaddle. She hadn't ridden astride since she was a girl at Marley Place. It would be difficult in skirts and on a mount she didn't know. Especially in weather that intensified with every second.

The rain fell in sheets now. Felix was soaked through, and Charis shivered as freezing water trickled down her neck. Her bonnet was a useless, sodden mess. With shaking hands, she ripped at the ribbons and tugged it off.

"How will you know when the papers are ready?" she asked in a frigid voice. If Gideon could be strong, so could she.

"I'll send a message." Felix grabbed one of the horses and hauled it into the open. The stocky bay snorted and fought at leaving the shelter of the trees. "Let me give you a hand up."

"Don't touch me," she snapped.

"Suit yourself, my lady." He presented the reins with an ironic gesture.

Snatching them out of his hand, she spoke soothingly to the nervous animal. She scrambled onto its back, swathing the greatcoat around her. The storm was bad enough in this hollow. She dreaded to think what she'd face on the open moor.

The horse curveted at having a rider, but Charis quickly brought it under control. She glared through the downpour at Felix. "If you hurt my husband, I'll hunt you down and kill you."

Felix gave a harsh laugh. "You always were an unnatural chit. Once I get the money, I have no further interest in either of you. Although I'll wager Trevithick will curse the day he tangled with the Earl of Marley's termagant daughter."

She ignored his jibes. "Remember what I said. I know you and Hubert are eager to prove your prowess on a defenseless man."

Kicking the horse into a gallop, she forced it up the slippery path out of the dell. As she bent forward over the beast's neck, her heart pounded out a single message. *Gideon, wait for me.*

Twenty-three

Up on the moor, the wind roared like an angry monster. It turned the driving rain into knives that pierced the thick greatcoat like muslin. Fierce cold sliced through Charis's bones. But nothing made her colder than her fear for Gideon.

Her mount neighed and fought as she battled to turn it onto the faint path toward Penrhyn. She sawed furiously at the bit, but the animal was too frightened to settle.

"Please, please, behave for me," she sobbed, tightening her thighs to keep her seat on the twisting horse. Her arms ached with stopping it bolting back the way they'd come.

Gideon needed her. Every second counted. Hunkering down in the saddle, she grimly set to gaining control over the beast.

Eventually, the animal began to splash its way westward at an unsteady gallop. Charis's shoulders knotted with strain, and she panted for breath. She leaned over the horse's neck, calling encouragement although she knew the gale whipped her words to oblivion.

All the time, her heart pounded out a silent message to Gideon.

Wait for me, my love. Wait for me. Wait for me.

Dread created its own swirling storm inside her. Not dread for herself, dread for her husband. Had he kept his ghosts away? What were Felix and Hubert doing to him? Where did they mean to keep him? Dear Lord, don't let it be somewhere dark and constricted like the pit at Rangapindhi.

She blundered on. The rain turned her clothes to heavy wet ice. Her sodden braids collapsed and tumbled down, blinding her. With one shaking hand, she hurriedly dashed her dripping hair away from her eyes. The storm transformed the afternoon into night, lit by jagged flashes of lightning, punctuated by rolling thunder.

The horse released a high-pitched neigh and balked at a swollen stream. Ruthlessly, Charis kicked it until it launched into an ungainly jump. "Come on!"

The animal stumbled when it reached the crumbling bank. Charis slid dangerously, nearly fell into the raging flood. After a terrifying, breathless pause, the flagging horse found its feet, slipping in the mud.

She hoped to heaven she followed the right path. Or any path. Either she'd missed Penrhyn's gateposts in the squall, or she was yet to reach them. Or she was hopelessly lost. Gideon said it was only a couple of miles to the house, but she felt she'd been riding forever.

"Stay with me." Her frozen hands closed clumsily on the reins.

The weather worsened. The wind became a malevolent, deadly force. She wondered how the plucky little horse kept going.

"There's a warm stable ahead. Oats. Hot bran mash. Soft straw for your bed."

She repeated the promises over and over. She didn't know if the gallant beast heard. The words were for her benefit as much as the horse's. She kept talking until her voice scraped over her throat.

All the time, she struggled to hold on to hope. Hope that Gideon was safe. Hope that Akash and Tulliver would rescue her husband. Hope that she'd find her way home. If she was caught on the moor when night fell, what could she do?

Keep going.

What choice did she have?

Fatigue made her muscles burn like fire. Her arms felt like iron weights. Cold stole the strength from her legs. Her eyes stung with staring into the arctic blast. Anxiety for Gideon was an evil, black, roiling mass in her belly.

The horse stumbled again, and this time was slower to find his feet. After his initial reluctance, he'd proven a valiant companion.

"Not far now, I promise. Just one more effort. One more." Her voice cracked, and tears she'd fought for so long rose to her eyes. Her teeth chattered so fast, she could barely speak. "It's for Gideon, you see. We have to save him. He's so good, and I love him more than life. And he's suffered too much."

The horse hung his head, his sides heaving with exhaustion, as the rain poured off him. Still crooning a fortifying litany, Charis slipped to the ground, landing with a splash. Icy water flooded her half boots. Her numb legs bent under her. She cried out sharply and grabbed the stirrup, just saving herself from hitting the ground. Her arms screamed in protest as she inched herself up. Her heart thudded furiously, her breath emerged in ragged gasps.

"Oh, Gideon, please be alive," she sobbed in despair, burying her face in the horse's saturated coat.

For a few seconds, she stood with the rain pounding down on her bare head. Stray pictures drifted into her mind, then dissolved. Coherent thought faded to a gray mist.

One idea remained clear. Gideon. She must save Gideon.

She blinked, forced her eyes to focus, her mind to function. Gideon needed her. She locked her knees until they held her upright. For a groggy moment, she clutched the slick leather stirrup. Then she released it and stood as the wind whipped around her.

She could do this. She could go on.

But her horse had reached the end of his endurance.

She forced words past lips that felt like solid ice. "We're nearly home. Not far now." God help both of them if she lied.

She fumbled for the reins and staggered ahead on foot. The horse followed docilely, too tired to resist, wading through dirty water that lapped over his fetlocks.

Eventually, she dragged the sodden greatcoat off and dropped it beside the path. Wet, it was heavier than lead, and it offered no protection. Or so she thought until she confronted the full force of the wind. The blue merino pelisse had been snug and warm on Jersey. Here, on a freezing Cornish moor in the middle of a deluge, she might as well have been naked.

Still she stumbled on. Her legs stung as if a thousand blades nicked at them. She shivered so badly, her muscles cramped to agony. She could no longer feel her feet.

The darkness now was nearly impenetrable. Devils in her head whispered that she'd die out on this moor and nobody would ever know Gideon was in trouble.

She strove to muffle the cruel voices, but with every footstep, their howls grew louder.

Then over the wail of the wind, the slap of the rain, she heard a dull pounding. It came closer and closer.

Her sluggish brain puzzled over the sound. Was it blood beating in her ears? Thunder? Gunfire? But who could fire a gun in this wet?

When the big black horse cantered out of the rain, like something risen from the mouth of hell, Charis stopped stock-still. Her dazed mind couldn't comprehend she was no longer alone. Or whether this new arrival signaled danger or rescue.

"Lady Charis?"

The rider drew to a rearing halt in front of her. The risk she took standing in the middle of a road in Stygian darkness vaguely registered. Her horse tugged listlessly at the reins but was too weary to pull free.

Stupidly, she blinked up at the man looming above her in the saddle. Water cascaded down her face and obstructed her sight. She swallowed, trying to summon a greeting. Nothing emerged apart from a broken whimper.

"Lady Charis?" He dismounted in one easy move and stepped forward. "Lady Charis, it's Akash."

"Akash . . ." she croaked without moving.

"Gideon wrote from Jersey and told me to expect you this evening at the latest."

"The weather . . ." Then the significance of his arrival struck so hard she staggered with dizzy relief. Sudden energy buzzed through her. Blood that had frozen abruptly began to flow again. Her mind churned with new hope and determination. "Akash, we have to help Gideon. My stepbrothers have him."

She turned back the way she'd come. Akash would help. Akash would save Gideon. Everything would be all right.

"Wait." Akash grabbed her arm. She was so cold, she hardly felt it. "You can't go like this."

Confused, she turned to stare at him. This didn't make sense. Akash was Gideon's friend. He'd saved him before. He'd save him now.

"Didn't you hear me? Gideon's in trouble." Her voice became stronger as she strove to speak above the shrieking wind. "There's no time to delay."

He swept his hand across his face in a futile attempt to clear the rain from his eyes. "Charis, Penrhyn is only minutes away. At least come back and get dry. We'll make plans there."

Had she almost made it home? It seemed too good to be true. Reaction hit like an avalanche. Her knees threatened to fold under her. She glanced back to her brave little horse. He'd carried her this far, but he'd carry her no farther tonight.

She drew a sobbing breath, and the fight drained out of her. As she was, she was no use to Gideon. If she was to help him, first she needed warmth and food and a chance to recover her strength.

But how it tortured her to delay his rescue. Even when she recognized the necessity of finding shelter before she collapsed.

"Yes, take me home," she said dully, and stood in shivering acquiescence as Akash wrapped his own much dryer coat around her.

Her heart in her throat, Charis crouched in the brown winter bracken and studied the overgrown entrance to the disused tin mine. It had stopped raining a couple of hours ago, and a cold gray dawn had broken.

She wore one of Gideon's mother's riding habits, and the ground under her was wet and muddy. At her side, Akash held a pair of beautifully chased silver pistols and watched the mine just as avidly. Hidden around them in the bracken were ten stalwart Penrhyn men. The same men who had unhesitatingly raced out into the foul night to locate Gideon.

The sight of the mine made her feel sick. She still reeled from discovering that her stepbrothers kept her husband in an underground tunnel. When the searchers returned to Penrhyn with the news, she'd barely been able to control her rising gorge. Fear remained a sour, bilious taste in her mouth.

In such a place, memories of Rangapindhi would be inevitable. Was it also inevitable that Gideon must succumb to his ghosts? Perhaps they'd steal him forever this time. With horror, she remembered his shaking, debilitating illness after Portsmouth. This fresh torture must test his limits, no matter how strong he was.

Let him be all right.

She bit back rising panic. She'd promised herself she'd

be brave for Gideon's sake. But, sweet God, it was difficult when she imagined her husband trapped in suffocating darkness.

What if she managed to save his body yet couldn't save his sanity? The prospect didn't bear contemplation. Although her mind did nothing but play grim scenarios.

Courage, Charis.

She tightened her grip on her pearl-handled pistol. Her eyes were scratchy from lack of sleep, and her pulse thundered in her ears. The hairs on the back of her neck prickled. She knew Gideon was close. She felt it in her blood, the way an animal recognized the approach of its mate.

"Gideon will have my guts for garters when he finds out I brought you on this escapade," Akash muttered in a voice so low only she heard it.

"I gave you no choice."

The only way he could have kept her away was by locking her in the attics. Even then, she'd have done her best to climb out. Akash had been determined to leave her safely at the manor, but her obstinacy had outlasted all argument. If Gideon's demons had conquered him, she needed to be there to fight them.

"He still won't like it," Akash said gloomily.

She prayed Gideon was alive not to like it. Strangely, Akash hadn't been overly concerned when she laid the whole story of the ambush before him last night. Yet surely Akash more than anyone knew what imprisonment meant to Gideon.

Tulliver appeared on top of the bank overhanging the entrance and waved before dropping out of sight. It was the arranged sign for movement within.

Purpose flowed through Charis in a reviving flood, and her heart took on a surer, steadier rhythm. She would save Gideon, no matter what forces ranged against her.

Not long now, my love. Wait for me . . .

Akash gestured behind him. With surreptitious rustling,

the men crawled forward. Charis was aware of the movement, but she didn't shift her attention from the mine.

Hubert emerged into the daylight, leading two horses. She immediately recognized the homely pony Gideon had hired to draw the gig.

Her stepbrother yawned and stretched, his lack of self-consciousness indicating he had no inkling he was observed. Hatred flared in Charis's belly as she watched him. He was about ten yards away, close enough for her to see he looked even worse than yesterday. Impossible to believe he held one of the kingdom's oldest titles. In his dirty, ragged clothes and with his greasy, overlong hair, he'd pass for a beggar.

Soundlessly, a wiry Cornishman rose from the bracken that grew toward the entrance. Another joined him. Using the undergrowth for cover, they'd circled behind Hubert, who stepped into the watery sun. A few silent steps, and one man covered Hubert's mouth to muffle any shout of warning. The other man quickly overpowered him.

The struggle was over in seconds. Hubert lay gagged and bound. He writhed as the men dragged him away from the cave. His muffled grunts of protest ceased abruptly when one of his assailants kicked him hard in the ribs.

There was no sign of Felix. A charged silence fell. Charis's gloved hand curled with painful force around her pistol. At her side, Akash tensed and raised his guns.

"Hubert? What the devil are you playing at?"

Felix's irritated question emerged as an eerie echo from inside the mine. One of the ponies snorted nervously and trotted toward the bracken, trailing its halter rope.

"For God's sake, stop messing about." Felix appeared at the entrance. Then, just as quickly, slipped back under cover.

Like a deadweight, foreboding settled in Charis's stomach. Any chance of another surprise attack was lost. And still she'd seen nothing of Gideon. Over and over, her mind chanted her desperate prayer. *Please, God, let him be all right.*

"Come out, man. The game's up." Akash stood, and his voice rang across the open area in front of the mine. "You don't have a hope of getting away with this."

Tulliver jumped down from his hiding place above the mine and hid from Felix's view beside the entrance. A wicked-looking knife jutted from his belt, and he held a pistol. For a heavyset man, he moved with incredible smoothness.

Felix called out from inside. "You forget—I have Trevithick."

Charis was sickeningly familiar with her stepbrother's defiant tone. For one surreal moment, it transported her back to their first meeting. He'd expressed his contempt for his new stepsister in just such a voice. And received a cuff from his hulking father in return. A cuff he'd returned with interest when he got Charis to himself.

He'd always been a sneaking, sadistic little bully. Bile filled her mouth as she imagined what state Gideon was in, bound and at Felix's mercy.

Akash strode toward the cave, his guns held ready, his body tall, straight, and reeking confidence. "We have your brother."

"You won't hurt Hubert. I, however, have no such scruples about my hostage."

Charis could wait no longer. She stumbled upright on shaking legs, her heart racing with a turbulent mixture of hope and trepidation. "Gideon, are you all right?"

There was a silence. Hope shriveled like an old walnut in her breast. Her heart faltered to a stop.

Were they too late? In a fever of anguish, she darted forward to stand beside Akash.

"Charis?" Gideon's voice was rusty, but the mere sound of it sent joy fizzing like newly opened champagne through her veins. She swayed briefly and closed her eyes as dizzying waves of relief battered her.

It was a miracle. She had no other explanation. He was alive. And aware.

And blisteringly angry. "What the devil are you doing here?"

In spite of the danger and his audible displeasure, she couldn't contain a choked laugh. She raised trembling fingers to dash burning tears of happiness from her eyes. "Saving you."

"Go back to the house. Now."

"I told you," Akash muttered.

"I want to negotiate," Felix shouted. "My freedom for Trevithick's release."

"Don't be a fool, man," Akash snapped, taking a step closer to the mine. "We've got you surrounded. You can't escape."

"Then there's no reason to keep Trevithick alive."

Charis's throat constricted with renewed terror. Her relief had been premature. The threat Felix posed was as real as ever.

"He'll kill Gideon if we push him too far," Charis said unsteadily. "He's not bluffing."

Akash frowned down at her. "A murder charge won't help his case."

"He's smart enough to know his case is hopeless." She raised her chin and stared unwaveringly into Akash's deep brown eyes. "I don't care what happens to Felix. Kill him, let him go free, whatever you have to do. Just as long as we save Gideon."

His eyes darkened as if he realized what it would cost her to let Felix get away with his crimes. Then he nodded and faced toward the mine, cocking his guns. "All right, Lord Felix. I'll come in."

"I'll go with you," Charis said quickly.

Akash cast her a glance that mingled astonishment and disapproval. "Out of the question."

Her jaw firmed. "Make me stay."

She saw him consider getting one of the Penrhyn men to restrain her, then clearly he thought better of it. Or perhaps he took pity on her frantic need to see her husband. His tone was low and adamant. "You are not to speak. You are not to move unless I give you the word."

"I promise." Her voice shook with gratitude. "Thank you."

"I hope I don't live to regret this," he said grimly. He raised his voice. "Don't try anything, Lord Felix."

"Drop your weapons first. And remember, any tricks and Trevithick's a dead man."

Akash glanced at Charis, who nodded. Both of them laid their guns on the ground, then approached the mine entrance.

With every step, her heart beat faster. Fear closed her throat and made her skin itch. If Felix decided to shoot them, they had no protection.

Surely he couldn't be so stupid. He wouldn't be able to kill every man here. Then she remembered his vanity and recklessness.

"Watch our backs," Akash hissed to Tulliver, as they passed under the heavy wooden beams that supported the entrance. Tulliver nodded while Charis and Akash edged inside.

Momentarily, the dimness blinded her. The dank tunnel was deathly cold. The air was rank with bats, stale air, and decay. Carefully, she moved forward, conscious of Akash as a silent, reassuring presence beside her.

"Damn you, Charis," Gideon cursed from farther along the tunnel. "Get out of here."

"No, she should stay," Felix said in a silky voice. "A foolish, but noble gesture, my dear stepsister. You've presented me with yet another hostage. I must thank you."

As her eyes adjusted to the gloom, lit by one lantern, she saw that Felix aimed his pistol squarely at her chest. It was one of the big clumsy horse pistols from yesterday. She glanced at him, long enough to read the desperation in his face. Then her attention flitted past him and settled on Gideon. He stood, hands bound behind his back, a few paces beyond Felix in the center of the brothers' makeshift camp.

He glared at her like he wanted to kill her. His black eyes

blazed in his pale face, and his mouth was a long line of displeasure. He should have appeared powerless. Instead, he looked indomitable, magnificent, undaunted.

There was blood on his jaw and bruises under his torn shirt. The visible evidence of Gideon's ordeal made her heart slam to a shocked halt.

"Gideon . . ." She took a shaky step toward him, only to come to a trembling halt as his eyes narrowed with temper.

To think she'd fretted about this man's ability to cope with captivity. He'd walk through a raging hurricane without turning a hair. His bruises and abrasions only emphasized his invincible spirit.

Gratitude punched the breath from her lungs, made her hands shake. She blinked back more tears. They weren't safe yet. She couldn't relax her guard.

"You spineless toad," she spat, turning on Felix. "How dare you beat a bound man?"

"Charis, I'm fine," Gideon snarled. "But you won't be when I get my hands on you. Akash, blast you, what were you thinking, bringing her here?"

"You're getting ahead of yourself, making plans for what you'll do once you're free," Felix said snidely. He backed against the wall, his gun still trained on Charis. "I have to ask myself if I really need three hostages. Perhaps I'm better off disposing of one of you."

"You must know this rash gamble has come to its end." Gideon's voice rang with authority. "Surrender while you have a chance at convincing a judge you deserve leniency."

Felix's expression hardened. Charis shivered as she thought of a rat caught in a trap. She didn't fool herself that this particular rat was harmless. He knew he'd lost, and he'd take them all down with him if he could.

"What I've done is a hanging matter," Felix snapped. "I'm not a fool. I won't offer myself up like a lamb to the slaughter. There's fight in me yet."

"That's lunatic." Akash stepped closer with unconcealed threat. "What can you hope to achieve?"

"Damn it, stay back!" Wildly, Felix swung the gun toward Akash.

Charis used Felix's momentary distraction to dash across the rubble-strewn floor to Gideon. With a broken sob, she threw her arms around him and buried her head in his chest. She drew in his familiar scent, felt the steady thud of his heart against her breast. Relief thundered through her.

He was alive. He was alive. They would come out of this yet.

His skin was chilled, and his tattered shirt was clammy from last night's downpour. He stood rigidly in her hold, his muscles taut. For one horrified moment, she wondered if his affliction had returned.

Then she realized he wasn't sick, he was angry. He vibrated with incandescent fury.

"How dare you put yourself in danger?" he growled, resisting her clinging hands.

"I've got a knife," she whispered, looking up at him.

At last he glanced at her. His jaw worked as he fought to master his temper. She read his anxiety for her, his rage. But more, she saw the mirror of her own longing in his black eyes.

"Oh, hell, Charis," he muttered, his mouth turning down with annoyance. He bent his head and kissed her, briefly but hard. She knew it was meant as punishment, but she felt the blazing love underlying the rebuke. "Now get out," he said softly but firmly.

"Not yet." She fumbled in her pocket for the small blade she'd taken from a display of arms at Penrhyn. It probably hadn't been used since Black Jack's day, but she'd tested its edge, and it was sharp.

She cast a quick glance across at Felix and took advantage of his focus on Akash to slide behind Gideon. Watching her stepbrother out of the corner of her eye, she sawed at the binding around Gideon's wrists. It was dark where she stood, but still light enough for her to see the broken skin under the coarse rope. Her anger at her stepbrothers hitched higher.

"She's not going anywhere." Felix sidled in Gideon's direction, keeping his pistol aimed at Akash. "She's my surety I'll get out of here."

"There's a dozen guns outside, more if the militia have arrived," Akash said dismissively. Charis wondered if he guessed what she was up to and kept Felix occupied deliberately. Biting her lips, she worked more furiously at the rope. "Even if you do kill us, you won't get far."

Felix gave a scornful grunt, his eyes darting around the mine as if he sought an escape route. "Oh, yes, I will. Nobody will risk hurting her."

"What about Lord Burkett? Do you intend to abandon him to his fate?" Contempt sizzled in Gideon's words.

Felix shrugged without shifting his gaze from Akash. "He can take his chances. He'll get to plead his case in the bloody House of Lords, whereas I'll be treated like a common criminal."

"You *are* a common criminal," Akash said coolly.

Felix took a menacing step toward Akash. "Shut your mouth, you black bastard."

"Give it up, Farrell," Gideon said steadily. "If you come quietly, I'll see what I can do about a lighter sentence. Transportation at least leaves you your life."

Felix flinched in horror. "To that filthy hole, Botany Bay? I'd rather be dead." He was considerably closer to Charis and Gideon than he had been. She applied the knife with renewed energy and prayed the shadows hid what she did.

"Keep this up, and you will be," Akash said grimly.

"You speak as though my defeat is a foregone conclusion."

"It is." Gideon bunched the muscles of his arms, jerked his wrists hard, and snapped the last threads of his bindings.

"Not when I've got Charis." Felix lunged, but Gideon moved faster than a striking cobra and grabbed him before he laid hands on her.

"Little slut untied you, did she?" Felix grunted, fighting to get purchase on the larger man.

For a sickening moment, the two men teetered, casting a dance of grotesque shadows onto the mine's walls. Then they fell and struck the ground with a thud that Charis felt in her bones. There was a sharp rattle as pebbles shot across the floor in all directions.

"Damn you, Trevithick!" Felix grunted, then finished on a loud exhalation as Gideon landed a hard punch to his stomach. The sickening sound made Charis flinch back.

She couldn't tear her eyes from the struggle. The fight was cruel, frantic. Over and over, they rolled in a clumsy, murderous battle. She desperately tried to see who gained the advantage, but darkness and constant movement made it impossible to tell.

A storm of punches and groans punctuated the ungainly violence. Charis's belly cramped with dread, and she backed on unsteady legs to press against the cold rock.

Felix fought dirty, and he was strong and wiry, for all his fashionable languor. Gideon was bigger, but he'd been bound and beaten. Heaven knew what injuries the brothers had inflicted on him during the night.

A pistol shot rang out, resounding as the noise ricocheted off the rock.

"Gideon!" Charis screamed, lurching forward. Her heart slammed against her ribs. Her eyes went blind.

Akash caught her around the waist and stopped her flinging herself on top of the combatants. "Charis, it's all right."

She hardly heard him through the clanging in her ears. If Gideon was dead, she didn't want to live. Without him, there was nothing in the world she wanted.

Akash spoke more sharply. "Charis, they're alive."

At last she heard and understood. She realized how tightly he gripped her against his chest. Her fingers dug into his arms with bruising force.

The bullet must have gone wild.

Her sight cleared, and her terrified gaze focused on Felix

and Gideon. She realized both men still moved, still struggled to best the other. Her aching heart started beating again. She sucked rancid air into starved lungs.

Dear heaven, thank you, thank you, thank you.

She trembled convulsively in Akash's grip. The tall body looming behind her bristled with silent tension. His support was welcome. She wasn't sure her legs would hold her. Her mouth was dry as cotton, and her heart pounded like a mallet wielded by a madman.

She stifled her urge to call encouragement to Gideon. He needed all his concentration to defeat Felix. The now-useless gun bumped across the floor as a wildly kicking leg sent it sliding. Gideon rolled over and kicked it more purposefully, propelling it out of reach.

She straightened, ashamed of her weakness. Akash must have realized she'd regained control of herself. He released her and edged around the fight to pick up the gun.

The men on the ground grunted and gasped and wrestled for dominance. They writhed across the rough floor. Felix flung out one leg and sent a tin kettle rattling against the rocks. The sharp metallic clatter made Charis jump. She raised one shaking hand to her mouth to hold back a scream.

The bone handle of the little knife she clutched in her other hand was slippery with sweat. If only she saw a chance to intervene. But all she could do was stand in agonized suspense on the conflict's edge.

Felix rolled on top of Gideon and clawed at his throat. For an endless moment, time hung suspended. Then Gideon twisted with what seemed impossible strength and dislodged his attacker.

The battle continued. Charis's hand dropped from her face to twine with painful tightness in her skirts. More thumps. More hoarse grunts and gasps. With a shuddering groan, Gideon jerked onto his knees, straddling Felix and gripping his neck.

"Die, you bastard!" Felix forced out. He flung Gideon

away to land with a sharp crack of bone on rock. Charis bit back another cry. Every muscle tensed to excruciating pain as she waited for Felix to surge up and land the decisive blow. But instead he lay winded and unmoving a few feet away.

"For God's sake, help Gideon," she begged Akash in a strained whisper as he returned to her side.

"He's better on his own," Akash said softly.

It seemed hours before Gideon stirred even though she knew it must only be a fraction of a second. As he sat up, he shook his head to clear his vision. He staggered upright at the same time as Felix found his feet.

Exhaustion and pain took their toll. Both men panted in jagged gasps as they circled one another, their fists upraised. Felix's left eye swelled, and his mouth was broken and bloody. Charis noticed that her stepbrother's gait was uneven, and he favored his left leg.

She drew another shuddering breath and stared at Gideon. He looked dirty and disheveled and bruised but otherwise blessedly whole, and his eyes were bright and alert. They focused on Felix with a glint of triumph. There had been some shift in the battle, and it had been in Gideon's favor.

"Give it up, Farrell. There's nowhere to go." He sounded calm, confident, like the man who had saved her life. He flexed his gloved hands and rolled his shoulders.

"I'll get out of this, Trevithick." Felix stumbled on the rough ground but didn't fall. "Damn well see if I don't."

Charis watched as he staggered farther into the tunnel. His eyes remained fixed on Gideon, who took a step after him.

"You won't escape that way, man. Didn't you explore your hideaway? The mine peters out in the hillside."

"Felix, he grew up here," Charis called, desperate to bring this ghastly scene to an end. "He knows every inch of the estate. You're trapped."

"Shut up, you little bitch." Felix sounded savage, furious, as he backed away on faltering feet. His voice resonated oddly as the tunnel narrowed. "We'll see who's trapped."

"Be careful. There's a mineshaft behind you." Gideon set out after him, his booted heels thudding sharply on the hard dirt floor. Charis broke away from Akash and followed, gripping her knife. She still didn't trust her stepbrother even though she could tell he had reached the end of his strength.

"Resorting to childish tricks now, Trevithick?" Felix's grating laugh sent a shiver down her spine. He retreated more quickly from the light.

"Take a look if you don't believe me." Gideon's voice roughened with urgency. "For God's sake, man, listen to me! Look behind!"

"And take my eyes off you? You must think I'm a damned half-wit."

"Farrell . . ."

Felix kept up his odd crablike shuffle, then suddenly tottered. His arms windmilled as he fought for balance. It was tragically clear Gideon's warning was sincere. Charis's stomach lurched with horror.

Gideon leaped forward. But even fast as he was, he was too late and too far away.

With a high-pitched scream of fury, Felix lost his footing and tumbled over the edge.

Twenty-four

There was a sickening, distant thud, then silence descended like an ax.

Shocked, unable to credit what had happened, Gideon stood on the edge of the shaft. He couldn't see anything in the darkness. It went down too far.

"Farrell?" he called. During his childhood, a miner had fallen down the shaft and died. It was one of the reasons the workings were abandoned.

He called again, recognizing the act as futile.

He'd despised Felix, wanted to make him pay in blood and suffering for hurting Charis. But all the same, this was a sorry end for anyone, even the most despicable cur.

Dizziness struck from nowhere, and he swayed. He ached from the beating and the fight. Through the buzzing in his ears, he heard Charis's husky cry as she launched herself after him.

Still reeling, he staggered to face her and caught her up against him, hiding the black chasm behind him from her sight. His shaking arms lashed around her slender softness with a desperation he only now let himself acknowledge.

She's here. She's unharmed. Thank You, God and all Your angels.

The still, cold watches of the night had tortured him with the devastating possibility that he'd never see her again. A prospect more agonizing than Hubert's punches or Felix's childish taunts. So much worse than his persistent fear that his demons would emerge from the dank darkness to claim him. His raw anguish made a mockery of his plans to send her away, even when he knew it was for her own good.

"Oh, my love, my love," he whispered, and buried his face in her thick, silky hair. He drew in a shuddering breath full of her scent. She smelled warm and alive. Clutching his back as if she never meant to let him go, she quivered in his arms.

For a long, glorious moment, he held her and luxuriated in the knowledge that they'd come through, that they were alive and together. Giddy relief swamped his rage that she put herself in danger. He should have known she'd never leave his rescue to others. Not his brave Charis.

"You're safe," she choked out against his skin. "You're safe and you're . . . you're well. Oh, Gideon, I was so afraid." She finished on a broken sob and pressed her hot face into his bare chest, above his furiously pounding heart.

He forced himself to relax his bruising grip. The reality slowly dawned on his dazed mind that the threat had passed. He drew far enough away to see her. Even in the dim light from the tunnel mouth, the strain she'd been under was apparent in the muddy brown of her eyes and the dark marks underneath them. But her face was aglow with relief and happiness. And love.

"My darling . . ." Words failed as love surged up as unstoppable as high tide into Penrhyn Cove. "Are you crying for Felix?"

"No." Then more strongly. "No! What happened to him is horrible. But I'm crying because . . . because we're free at last."

He smiled down at her, then winced when the expression tested his torn lip. "Happy tears?"

She gave a jerky nod. "Happy tears." Regret shadowed her eyes as carefully she touched the graze on his mouth. "They hurt you. I'm so sorry."

"It's nothing." Truly, it was nothing. In return for the joy of having her in his arms, he'd undergo a thousand beatings. He pressed her shaking hand against his cheek. With every minute, he breathed more easily. *The danger was over.* He could hardly believe it.

He heard footsteps approach and looked up to see Akash striding down the tunnel with a flaming torch. At his side, Tulliver carried the lantern from the brothers' camp. The extra lights were welcome although Gideon doubted they were strong enough to reveal the base of the shaft. The ominous silence behind him confirmed his immediate guess that Felix had perished in the fall.

"You heard what happened?" Gideon asked.

"Yes. Is there any chance he survived?" Akash raised the torch in Gideon's direction, clearly checking to see if he was all right.

"I doubt it. But we need to get him out. Tulliver, can you muster some men to climb down? I assume someone brought rope. If not, the Farrells had some." His arms tightened around Charis. He'd come so close to losing her, he wasn't ready to relinquish her yet, especially when she still trembled with reaction.

"Aye, guvnor." Tulliver cast Gideon and Charis a cryptic glance, then headed back outside.

Gideon stared over Charis's ruffled head to where Akash waited. Overwhelming gratitude flooded him. How could he thank this man for all he'd done? Through the years of danger in India, the rescue from Rangapindhi, and the care and loyalty since. Words were inadequate recompense, but they were all he had.

"Thank you, my friend," he said gruffly. He wanted to say so much, but he settled for, "Once again you've saved me."

"You're welcome. Life would be considerably less interesting without you." Smiling faintly, Akash inclined his dark head in acknowledgment. "The true gallantry was Lady Charis's. It was she who rode through the deluge to bring us word of what had happened."

Gideon smiled down at her. He didn't need Akash to point out how exceptional his darling was. What a wife he'd found for himself. Strong enough to defy the world for him. "I knew she wouldn't fail. I knew she'd rout her stepbrothers."

"You didn't say that at the time." Her voice was choked.

"I didn't have to."

Looking pensive, she glanced toward the ominously quiet mineshaft. "I'm not hypocritical enough to say I'm sorry."

"Yet . . ."

She cast him a quick, understanding smile. "Yes. Yet." She looked around the dark, cold passage and shivered. Four villagers passed them with respectful nods and began to organize the retrieval of Felix Farrell. "Let's get out of here."

"Capital notion." Akash stood back to let Gideon and Charis precede him. As Gideon passed, Akash reached out to clasp his shoulder in a brief gesture of affection.

After the mine, daylight dazzled. Gideon placed a steadying hand on Charis's arm. The day was fine, and sun sparkled on puddles and dripping foliage. The air smelt fresh and clean. He sucked in a deep breath, savoring the sea's salt tang.

The scent of Penrhyn. The scent of home.

The crowd outside made him brace for the familiar sick haze. He felt Charis's loving concern as she slid her arm around his waist.

But when he surveyed the welcoming faces turned toward him, he was only aware of open sky and clear air, the breeze against his skin, Charis's enticing warmth pressed to his side.

Had his wife spoken more truly than she realized? Was he finally free?

The shock was too much.

He staggered. His sight narrowed to a single beam of light.

"Gideon, what is it?" Charis's hold tightened. As ever, her

touch anchored him. His shaking arm twined around her slender shoulders, and he fought not to lean on her as his legs threatened to fold beneath him.

The wave of light-headedness passed, leaving him lost, bewildered. What had happened? Since Rangapindhi he'd been unable to endure people around him. So many defense mechanisms had become second nature.

Yet today he needed none of them.

His whirling mind struggled to make sense of it all. Now he thought about it, the demons should have tormented him long before this. Yet they'd been remarkably silent. Felix and Hubert's kidnapping hadn't sparked an attack. Nor, more significantly, had captivity in the dark tunnel.

But he'd been blisteringly angry when they took him. With the brothers and more, with himself, for placing his wife in danger.

The anger had passed, and still there were no screaming ghosts in his head. He stared at the villagers. He looked past them to Sir John Holland and the militia, surrounding a shackled Hubert. Then he sought and found the two men who had stood by him through so much. Tulliver watched expressionlessly from Akash's side. Akash's gaze as he surveyed Gideon and Charis was steady and unsurprised.

He knew the signs of Gideon's illness better than anyone. Gideon was sure he wouldn't have survived the worst attacks without Akash's arcane medical knowledge. What did his friend make of this abrupt change?

Then, with another shock, Gideon remembered that Akash had touched him without hesitation in the mine.

"You know, I think I'm all right," he said in a thick voice to Charis, who stared up at him with shining eyes. Did she too guess what had happened?

His dreams had been so humble yet so out of reach. Had heaven relented after all his pain? It seemed beyond belief.

"I need to talk to Hubert," Charis said quietly. "He shouldn't learn about Felix from a stranger."

"That's a consideration the cur hardly warrants," Gideon

said grimly. She was so strong. If she hadn't been, she'd have given up on her husband weeks ago.

"Nevertheless, I must do it."

Reluctantly, Gideon released her, immediately missing her nearness. He watched as she crossed to where a chained and guarded Hubert waited in sullen, fulminating silence. Even with Hubert shackled, Gideon fought the illogical urge to drag her back into his arms, where she was safe. Would this instinct to protect her ever fade? Not while he breathed.

Across the open area, Hubert let loose a broken groan. The bulky brute swiftly went from surly resistance to utter collapse. Tears poured down his face. Charis said something, and placed a hand on his shoulder. He accepted her comfort, much as he didn't deserve it. Gideon felt another surge of admiration for his wife's generosity. If the decision were left to him, he'd let the bastard suffer.

Sir John approached, smiling, extending his hand. Dazed, Gideon returned the handshake. How simple the gesture was. Only a day ago, it would have been a painful ordeal.

"Sir Gideon, rum doings indeed. I can't say how pleased I am to find you unharmed."

"Thank you, Sir John." Astonishment and wonder still gripped Gideon. The change was too sudden for him to trust although with every minute, it became more likely that the impossible had occurred.

"I take it the other villain is incapacitated inside the mine?"

Gideon forced himself to concentrate on immediate matters. So difficult when unfamiliar happiness bubbled up like a new stream. He gave the magistrate a short recounting of events from when he'd discovered Charis in Winchester.

Akash joined them. When Gideon performed introductions, Sir John, to give him credit, displayed only a moment's confusion at meeting Akash Stamford, the new Viscount Cranbourne.

"What happens now?" Gideon kept an eye on Charis and the distraught Hubert.

"We'll take Lord Burkett to London for trial. You'll likely

be called to appear." Sir John looked tired and troubled. "I can't see him escaping the noose. If you'll come with me now, we can . . ."

Akash smoothly interrupted. "I'll start the formalities. Sir Gideon was held overnight. His lady has ridden through a storm and managed no sleep since. Let the Trevithicks go home."

Looking abashed, Sir John cleared his throat and nodded. "Of course. Wasn't thinking. Nothing that can't wait. Appreciate your cooperation, my lord."

The Penrhyn men emerged from the mine, holding an unmoving, black-coated body. Gideon saw at a glance there was no hope for Felix. He met Charis's gaze across the clearing and shook his head. She nodded but remained dry-eyed. Hubert's painful, choked sobs intensified as the villagers carried Felix's limp form past him.

With each moment, Gideon became easier in his skin. He moved among the local men, thanking them. Nobody needed to tell him they'd braved the storm to find him. Hard to believe it had taken him twenty-five years to recognize the unbreakable bonds that tied him to this land and its people.

Tulliver came up, leading Khan. One mount for two riders, the sly dog. With a word of thanks, Gideon took the reins and rubbed the horse's nose in greeting. He'd missed the spirited thoroughbred over the last weeks.

With his usual impassivity, Tulliver handed over the coat he carried under his arm. "Here you are, guvnor. Thought you might need some extra covering"

Gratefully, Gideon pulled the garment over his ragged shirt. He must look a ruffian. He badly needed a bath and a change of clothes. He needed a shave and a hot meal. More than anything, he needed time alone with his wife. With relief, he watched Charis move away from Hubert and approach Sir John.

He turned his attention to Tulliver. Akash wasn't the only

one who deserved his undying gratitude. "I appreciate it. Just as I appreciate your rushing to my rescue today."

"I'm honored to serve you, sir." Tulliver's eyes held a hint of uncharacteristic softness. "Always have been. And I reckon gratitude goes both ways. You won't recall, but I was one of the soldiers who pulled you out of that pit in Ranga-pindhi, more dead than alive."

Astonishment gripped Gideon at this revelation. "By God, I never knew."

"My last assignment for the Company. Those heathens we locked up after the invasion talked like you was a god. They'd never seen such grit. Nothing they done could break you." Tulliver's voice deepened with feeling. "You kept your mouth shut and saved me and my chums from a bloodbath. When I heard you sailed home on the same packet as me, I set myself to enter your service."

Gideon tried to remember the exact moment he'd offered Tulliver a place. The details were hazy. When he'd been delirious with fever on the ship, Tulliver had turned up to help, and he'd been around ever since. Capable, resourceful, taciturn. In fact, that was the longest speech Gideon had ever heard the man make.

"I haven't been an easy master," he said with difficulty.

"Maybe not always, lad, but I knew you'd come right, given time and incentive. Gold always rings true."

Gideon swallowed a lump of emotion. He owed this man more than he could ever repay. "You know you've always got a home at Penrhyn." Shabby return for the selfless devotion.

Tulliver's wry smile appeared. "Aye, guvnor. I'd counted on that and all. A nice quiet life by the seaside in my old age suits me down to the ground. Although it's not exactly been quiet so far."

Gideon laughed with a lightheartedness he couldn't remember feeling for years and clapped Tulliver on the back. Another natural gesture unthinkable yesterday.

His pulse racing with a mixture of anticipation and trepidation, Gideon led Khan up to Charis. He felt like a nervous schoolboy. Absurd after all he'd been through with her. But recent events had created a new map between them, and he wasn't yet sure how to navigate it.

"I should get you back to Penrhyn." Before she could object, he caught her by the supple waist and tossed her up onto Khan's back.

She laughed breathlessly and found her balance with the confidence of a natural horsewoman. "Apparently I have no say in the matter."

"None at all." He ignored her startled eyes and turned to shake Sir John's hand again. "Come by the house tomorrow, and we'll sort everything out."

"I wish you good day, Sir Gideon, Lady Charis." The man's eyes held a spark of amusement. Obviously, he hadn't forgotten what it was to be young and newly married.

Gideon shoved one booted foot in the stirrup and flung his other leg across the saddle. The high-strung horse danced under the double weight, but Gideon quickly brought him under control.

Charis sat across the front of the saddle, her back against Gideon's arm, her skirts cascading down Khan's side. He relished her sweet warmth. She wasn't wearing a hat, and strands of soft bronze hair tickled his chin.

Raising a hand to Akash, who watched them with a faint smile, Gideon urged Khan to a canter along the path to Penrhyn.

"That was high-handed," Charis said in a neutral voice once they were away from the crowd. Gideon noted she made no great effort to wriggle away. No effort at all, really.

He laughed and tightened his hold on her. "Black Jack lives in my veins, remember?"

He slowed Khan to a walk. The need to get back to the

house and confirm she was his in the most basic way was a fever in his blood. But he wasn't a barbarian, much as he felt like one right now. They had to talk before he tumbled her into his bed.

She turned her face toward his. Her expression was unexpectedly grave. "Does all this mean you no longer want to send me away?"

Uncomfortable heat crawled up the back of his neck. "I never *wanted* to send you away."

"Nevertheless that was—is—your plan."

She wasn't letting him wriggle out of this. He knew he had to lay his heart before her like a tribute before a despotic queen. Good God, he owed it to her, after acting such a self-righteous clodpole.

"That's something we need to discuss."

She arched her eyebrows. Suddenly the *grande dame*. "Oh?"

"I think . . . I believe . . . I hope . . ."

He stopped. Damn, he made a hash of this. Drawing a deep breath, he strove to present his case with a modicum of address. "I seem to have overcome my . . . problem." At least it was a complete sentence, even if he stumbled over the last word.

He'd never settled on how to describe the creeping horror that suffocated him when the ghosts of Rangapindhi howled. In his mind, he'd always called his affliction the demons, but that seemed too melodramatic a description in the clear light of day.

Charis's eyes were unwavering. "I know."

He made a frustrated sound deep in his throat. "Curse you, you don't sound very pleased."

"Of course I'm pleased."

"Or surprised." He spoke over the top of her declaration.

"You forget I saw you in the mine. I've never beheld a man more in control of himself or circumstances. Even bound as you were." Her voice softened. "What happened, Gideon?"

"It's hard to explain." He paused, seeking the words. "It goes back to learning to touch you. That changed the world for me."

"And after all that, I nearly lost you when you handed yourself over to my stepbrothers." He couldn't mistake the anger in her voice or the furious gold sparks in her eyes.

"I'd die to keep you safe." He spoke from the depths of his heart. "You know that."

"Yet you say you're not a hero," she said bitterly.

"I'm just a man, Charis. But protecting you is part of who I am. You can't ask me to change that. I couldn't, even if I wanted to." His voice lowered to persuasion. "Come, sweetheart, let's make peace."

"I suppose I'll forgive you." There was a misty light in her eyes as she surveyed him. "Eventually."

The time had come. His gut clenched with nerves as he realized his happiness depended on the next few minutes. She wouldn't call him a hero if she knew the sheer unadulterated terror that closed his throat. He meant to offer her everything he was and everything he had. If she refused him, she'd cast him into darkness again.

"Walk with me. It's not far to the house." Over the next rise, they'd see the sea and Penrhyn. *Home*.

He drew Khan to a halt, slid to the ground, and lifted her down. His hands lingered at her slim waist, and again he fought the impulse to kiss her. They must settle everything first. Then, God help her, she'd spend the next week naked in his bed.

Hell, the next month.

They fell into step on the pale winter grass. The sun shone warm on his head, bright promise of a new spring.

For a few moments, they walked shoulder to shoulder, him leading a placid Khan. Gideon tugged off his gloves and grabbed her hand. He'd tried to resist touching her, but it was impossible. The memory of her, her voice, her face, her sweetness, were all that had sustained him through the long, dark night of captivity. He needed to have her near more than he needed air to breathe.

Her fingers twined around his bare scarred hand with a welcome that made his heart stumble to a lovesick halt. Despite his hunger for her, he found himself reluctant to shatter this sweet idyll. There had been so much strife and anguish between them, this serenity seemed a benediction.

Typically, Charis was the one to confront all that lay unspoken. "Gideon, what happened at the mine?"

"I found myself again." It was as close to the truth as he could manage. "You changed me. The memory of you kept me from losing my mind. And as the night went on, I discovered the dark was just the dark and people just people. The wild fancies of my imagination . . . vanished." He put a vague thought into words. It was as good an explanation as any for the glorious change that had overtaken him. "A miracle."

"No." Her voice sounded husky as it always did when she succumbed to deep emotion. "It's no miracle. Your own courage brought you clear of the storm. You faced your horrors when you surrendered yourself to my stepbrothers for my sake."

Was she right? Would he ever know? It didn't matter why he'd changed. What mattered was he *had* changed. "And being tied up in a mine gave me ample time for reflection."

Charis released a spurt of unwilling laughter. "You sound like you recommend a period of incarceration."

He gave a dismissive huff. "I wouldn't go that far." He sobered. He floundered for an explanation that made sense. Difficult, when none of it made sense to him. "I have to live with what happened in Rangapindhi. It wasn't my fault my colleagues died . . ."

"But your conscience lacerated you because you couldn't save them. It's that overdeveloped protective instinct again."

"I despised myself for living when they died."

The words hung stark in the air. Her hand tightened around

his. The silent communication crushed the seeds of self-hatred still lurking in his heart. Her voice vibrated with sincerity. "My love, if you hadn't lived, you couldn't have saved me. The workings of destiny are mysterious."

Her words echoed the odd moment of perception last night where he'd struggled to view himself as an outsider would. When he'd felt the shades of Parsons and Gerard hover uncannily close in the thick darkness, so reminiscent of the pit where his friends had died.

He'd always imagined his colleagues must hate him from beyond the grave for living when they'd perished in pain and humiliation. But the spirits that kept him company through the long hours of blackness in the mine had been benign, not angry at all. Ever since Rangapindhi, he'd remembered them as gruesome specters. Last night they'd visited him as they'd been in life. Fine, brave men who had sacrificed everything for duty.

Only then, blessed by his dead colleagues at last, had Gideon taken the most terrifying step of all.

He'd contemplated establishing a life at Penrhyn with Charis and, God willing, children. Trevithicks to fill the rambling old house with laughter and chaos and love. That hope had sustained him through the darkness and the violence and the incarceration. He wanted to build on the love that already grew between him and Charis and stoke it into a blazing, endless fire to light his days.

If she agreed.

His hand closed ruthlessly around hers. "And I thought about you."

"I should hope so," she said unsteadily. She looked up at him, and he caught the sparkle of tears in her hazel eyes.

"I thought how I love you and what an arrogant ass I've been." He paused and spoke with difficulty. "Last night, I realized I'd reached the limits of selflessness. I sat in that cave and imagined living without you. I couldn't bear to contemplate it."

She lifted her free hand to touch his face in a gesture that cut right to his aching heart. "Oh, my love, you don't have to live without me."

He came to a standstill. "Charis, I can't promise I'm cured, I can't promise anything beyond my eternal love. But you need to know I'll never willingly give you up. You're mine forever."

The radiant certainty in her eyes warmed him to his bones. "Gideon, I love you. You love me. That's all that matters." Her smile took on a hint of seduction that fired his blood. "Now take me back to Penrhyn and swive me silly."

Her gaze held no questions. She accepted him as her future just as he accepted her. More than accepted. Greeted with open arms. His doubts melted away like snow under the sun. He'd have time for explanations and apologies later. Or perhaps explanations and apologies would never be needed.

He dropped Khan's reins. "Come here, Charis. If I don't kiss you, I'll go mad."

Laughing, she fell against him. The kiss was an act of passionate gratitude for their survival, a wild melding of lips and tongues and teeth. It was a physical expression of a love that touched his soul. A love he knew would last the rest of his days. They were both breathless and trembling when they finally drew apart.

He lifted her up on Khan's back and leaped into the saddle behind her. "Hold on!" he shouted and headed for home at a breakneck gallop.

Khan came to a rearing stop in Penrhyn's front court, his hooves clattering on the stone paving. For Charis, the ride had passed in a rapturous blur of wind and color. She clung to Gideon, lost in a tumult of emotion. That extraordinary kiss still heated her blood, made her heart thunder.

A groom dashed out to hold the restive horse while Gideon jumped down and tugged Charis after him. Her feet fleetingly touched the ground before he swung her into his arms.

"Gideon!" she gasped, as he strode up the worn stone steps to the front door that opened as if by magic. Her heart swooped and skipped a beat. She felt like she was being kidnapped. It was incredibly exciting. "You make me breathless."

"I will before I'm finished," he promised in a low voice, marching into the house.

Ooh, yes, please.

She hooked one hand around the strong column of his neck as he passed the curtsying maid who had opened the door. The dark, cavernous hall flashed past, then they climbed the staircase. He turned at the landing and swept her into his room.

She'd never been in here. She had a momentary dazzling impression of light and casement windows opening onto a sparkling sea. Old carved furniture. A breeze smelling of the ocean.

Gideon started kissing her, and she didn't care where she was as long as he never let her go. She closed her eyes and gave herself up to the hungry predations of his lips.

"I love you," she said over and over in broken sentences, kissing his face and his neck and the skin revealed by his torn shirt. What exquisite freedom it was, finally to say the words without restraint.

He kicked the door so it banged shut behind him and carried her to the bed. He came down over her, kissing her as if he starved. The musky scent of his arousal filled her senses. Ruthlessly, he tugged his coat off and tossed it to the floor.

She'd long since known he wanted her. Their days in Jersey had been replete with sensual exploration. But the unfettered desire in his touch now was new. The barriers he'd always raised against her in his heart had dissolved to nothing.

She'd never felt claimed before. She felt claimed now.

And reveled in the possession because she knew he gave himself into her keeping with every touch, every kiss.

Shaking, she ripped at his shirt while he feverishly ran his hands over her body. Her breasts swelled and ached for his touch. She yearned to feel the glide of his skin against hers. She yearned to welcome him inside her in the most intimate touch of all.

Impatience made her clumsy. She ended up tearing the ruined shirt until it fell in shreds from his heaving shoulders.

He tugged her upright and struggled to undress her while she rained kisses across his bare torso. Fresh bruises and abrasions marked his scarred skin. Reminder of what he'd endured for her sake. She bit down delicately on one light brown nipple and felt fierce reaction shiver through him. She did it again, harder this time.

"Devil take it, Charis. I'm filthy. I need a shave." He clamped one powerful hand in her hair and drew her head back from his chest. His face was vivid with arousal. Color bloomed along his cheekbones and his eyes burned like black fire. "Do you want me like this?"

She laughed low in her throat and tore at his breeches. If he was a new, more dominating lover today, she'd transformed into an utterly shameless hussy. "Yes."

"So be it."

His face set with determination. Roughly, he wrenched open the jacket of her riding habit. Buttons flew through the air and bounced across the floor. He tore at the white shirt beneath. Within seconds, skirt, stays, and shift lay on the carpet.

The abrasion of his shadow beard on her naked skin made her cry out in delight. She arched so her breasts jutted forward, demanding attention. She fumbled at her hair, sliding pins free until it fell about her shoulders in an untidy mass.

"I love you," he groaned, burying his hands in the tumble of hair and bringing her up for a famished kiss. "How I love you."

"Tell me again," she said in a vibrating voice.

He did. Repeating the declaration, he pushed her back onto the silk bedcover. He kissed her breasts and belly and dragged boots, drawers, and stockings off until she lay before him bare, open and ready.

Soon he was naked too. He surged above her. No more

preliminaries. She didn't mind. She craved this joining as much as he.

He thrust hard, as if proclaiming her his kingdom.

Then he lifted his head and stared at her with such reverence, her heart cartwheeled. She drew him down for a deeply passionate kiss. Even as her tongue pushed into his mouth, his body moved in hers.

The rhythm, his weight, his spicy scent, the heat of his skin, all were familiar. All were utterly new.

As they spiraled into ecstasy, her soul expanded, took flight. The experience was unlike anything before, for all their desperate passion in St. Helier. It was as if he flung open every gateway and invited her in. And she entered victorious to blaring trumpets and fluttering banners.

The triumphal music reached a dazzling climax. She arched and cried out as her world erupted into blinding light. Bright angels chorused around her, repeating one phrase over and over in harmonies that made her skin sing.

I love you, Gideon. I love you, Gideon.

She quivered with wild delight, lost in the brilliance. She knew Gideon was with her. He'd be with her always.

She opened her eyes to find him raised on his arms above her, watching her intently. His black gaze glittered in unmistakable possession as he looked down at her.

"I've never . . ." Her voice trailed away.

He looked like a man who had conquered the world. He looked like a man who had fallen in love deeply and irrevocably.

"I know."

She raised one shaking hand to his cheek. His gaze was intent and told her he, like she, had been reborn in fire.

She'd never seen his eyes so clear, so unguarded, so full of love. Her heart overflowed with a happiness more precious because she'd believed it eternally out of reach.

"No shadows," she whispered, at last recognizing the difference in his face.

"No shadows," he echoed. He bent his head to kiss her, silent promise of a shining future.

RULES OF ENGAGEMENT

Rules . . . are made to be broken.

This fall, meet four ladies—who won't let a few wagging tongues stand in the way of happiness—and the handsome gents who are willing to help them break with convention.

Turn the page for a sneak preview at delicious new romances from Laura Lee Guhrke, Kathryn Caskie, and Anna Campbell, and a gorgeous repackaged classic from Rachel Gibson.

WITH SEDUCTION IN MIND

A Girl-Bachelor novel by
New York Times **Bestselling Author**
LAURA LEE GUHRKE

Infamous author Sebastian Grant, Earl of Avermore, has seen better days. His latest play opened to crippling reviews, his next novel is years overdue, and, to top it off, his editor assigned feisty, fire-haired beauty Daisy Merrick as his writing partner (never mind she's the critic who thrashed his play)! And yet, as frustration turns to desire, it seems the one place Sebastian can find relief is in the beguiling Daisy's arms . . .

Sebastian rolled down his cuffs and fastened them with his cuff links, then gave a tug to the hem of his slate-blue waistcoat, raked his fingers through his hair to put the unruly strands in some sort of order, and smoothed his dark blue necktie. He went down to the drawing room and paused beside the open doorway.

Miss Merrick's appearance, he noted as he took a peek around the doorjamb, was much the same as before. The same sort of plain, starched white shirtwaist, paired with a green skirt this time. Ribbons of darker green accented her collar and straw boater. She was seated at one end of the long yellow sofa, her hands resting on her thighs. Her fingers drummed against her knees and her toes tapped the floor in an agitated fashion, as if she was nervous. At her feet was a leather dispatch case.

He eyed the dispatch case, appalled. What if Harry wanted him to read her novel and give an endorsement? His publisher did have a perverse sense of humor. It would be just like Harry to pretend he was publishing the girl and blackmail Sebastian into reading eight hundred pages of bad prose before telling him it was all a joke. Or—and this was an even more nauseating possibility—she might actually be good, Harry did intend to publish her book, and they truly did want his endorsement.

Either way, he wasn't interested. Striving not to appear as grim as he felt, Sebastian pasted on a smile and entered the drawing room. "Miss Merrick, this is an unexpected pleasure."

She rose from the sofa as he crossed the room to greet her, and in response to his bow, she gave a curtsy. "Lord Avermore."

He glanced at the clock on the mantel, noting it was a quarter to five. Regardless of the fact that it was inappropriate for her to call upon a bachelor unchaperoned, the proper thing for any gentleman to do in these circumstances was to offer her tea. Sebastian's sense of civility, however, did not extend that far. "My butler tells me you have come at Lord Marlowe's request?"

"Yes. The viscount left London today for Torquay. He intends to spend the summer there with his family. Before he departed, however, he asked me to call upon you on his behalf regarding a matter of business."

So it was a request for an endorsement. "An author and his sternest critic meeting at the request of their mutual publisher to discuss business?" he murmured, keeping his smile in place even as he wondered how best to make the words "not a chance in hell" sound civil. "What an extraordinary notion."

"It is a bit unorthodox," she agreed.

He leaned closer to her, adopting a confidential, author-to-author sort of manner. "That's Marlowe all over. He's always been a bit eccentric. Perhaps he's gone off his onion at last."

"Lord Avermore, I know my review injured your feelings—"

"Your review and the seven others that came after it," he interrupted pleasantly. "They closed the play, you know."

"I heard that, yes." She bit her lip. "I'm sorry."

He shrugged as if the loss of at least ten thousand pounds was a thing of no consequence whatsoever. "It's quite all right, petal. I only contemplated hurling myself in front of a train once, before I came to my senses." He paused, but he couldn't resist adding, "Hauling you to Victoria Station, on the other hand, still holds a certain appeal, I must confess."

She gave a sigh, looking unhappy. As well she should. "I can appreciate that you are upset, but—"

"My dear girl, I am not in the least upset," he felt compelled to assure her. "I was being flippant. In all truth, I feel quite all right. You see, I have followed your advice."

"My advice?"

"Yes. I have chosen to be open-minded, to take your review in the proper spirit, and learn from your critique." He spread his hands, palms up in a gesture of goodwill. "After all," he added genially, "of what use to a writer is mere praise?"

She didn't seem to perceive the sarcasm. "Oh," she breathed and pressed one palm to her chest with a little laugh, "I am so relieved to hear you say that. When the viscount told me why he wanted me to come see you, I was concerned you would resent the situation, but your words give me hope that we will be able to work together in an amicable fashion."

Uneasiness flickered inside him. "Work together?" he echoed, his brows drawing together in bewilderment, though he forced himself to keep smiling.

"Yes. You see . . ." She paused, and her smile faded to a serious expression. She took a deep breath, as if readying herself to impart a difficult piece of news. "Lord Marlowe has employed me to assist you."

Sebastian's uneasiness deepened into dread as he stared into her upturned face, a face that shone with sincerity. He realized this was not one of Harry's jokes. He wanted to look away, but it was rather like watching a railway accident happen. One couldn't look away. "Assist me with what, in heaven's name?"

"With your work." She bent and grasped the handle of her dispatch case, and as she straightened, she met his astonishment with a rueful look. "I am here to help you write your next book."

THE MOST WICKED OF SINS

A Sinclair Family novel by
USA Today **Bestselling Author**
KATHRYN CASKIE

Lady Ivy Sinclair is used to getting her way. So
when an Irish beauty steals the attention of the
earl Ivy had claimed, she hatches a devious
plan: distract the chit with an irresistible actor
hired to impersonate a marquess. But can Ivy
resist Dominic Sheridan's sinful allure, or will she
fall victim to her own scheming?

D amn it all, answer me!" A deep voice cut
into her consciousness, rousing her from the
cocoon of darkness blanketing her. She could
feel herself being lifted, and then someone shouting
something about finding a physician.

She managed to flutter her lids open just as she felt
her back skim the seat cushion inside the carriage.

Blinking, she peered up at the dark silhouette of a
large man leaning over her.

"Oh, thank God, you are awake. I thought I killed
you when I coshed your head with the door." He
leaned back then, just enough that a flicker of light
touched his visage.

Ivy gasped at the sight of him.

He shoved his black hair away from eyes that

looked almost silver in the dimness. A cleft marked the center of his chin, and his angular jaw was defined by a dark sprinkling of stubble. His full lips parted in a relieved smile.

There was a distinct fluttering in Ivy's middle.

It was *him*. The perfect man . . . for the position.

"It's *you*," she whispered softly.

"I apologize, miss, but I didn't hear what you said." He leaned toward her. "Is there something more I can do to assist you?"

Ivy nodded and feebly beckoned him forward. He moved fully back inside the cab and sat next to her as she lay across the bench.

She gestured for him to come closer still.

It was wicked, what she was about to do, but she had to be sure. She had to know he was the right man. And there was only one way to truly know.

He turned his head so that his ear was just above her mouth. "Yes?"

"I assure you that I am quite well, sir," she whispered into his ear, "but there is indeed something you can do for me."

She didn't wait for him to respond. Ivy shoved her fingers through his thick hair and turned his face to her. Peering deeply into his eyes, she pressed her mouth to his, startling him. She immediately felt his fingers curl firmly around her wrist, and yet he didn't pull away.

Instead his lips moved over hers, making her yield to his own kiss. His mouth was warm and tasted faintly of brandy, and his lips parted slightly as he masterfully claimed her with his kiss.

Her heart pounded and her sudden breathlessness blocked out the sounds of carriages, whinnying horses, and theater patrons calling to their drivers on the street.

His tongue slid slowly along her top lip, somehow making her feel impossible things lower down. Then he nipped at her throbbing bottom lip, before urging her mouth wider and exploring the soft flesh inside with his probing tongue.

Hesitantly, she moved her tongue forward until it slid along his. At the moment their tongues touched, a soft groan welled up from the back of his throat and a surge of excitement shot through her.

Already she felt the tug of surrender. Of wanting to give herself over to the passion he somehow tapped within her.

And then—as if he knew what he made her feel, made her want—he suddenly pulled back from her.

She peered up at him through drowsy eyes.

"I fear, my lady, that you mistake me for someone else," he said, not looking the least bit disappointed or astounded by what she had done.

"No," Ivy replied, "no mistake." She wriggled, pulling herself to sit upright. "You are exactly who I thought you were." She straightened her back and looked quite earnestly into his eyes. "You are the Marquess Counterton . . . or rather you will be, if you accept my offer."

CAPTIVE OF SIN

**An eagerly anticipated new novel by
ANNA CAMPBELL**

Returning home to Cornwall after unspeakable tragedy, Sir Gideon Trevithick stumbles upon a defiant beauty in danger and vows to protect her—whatever the cost. Little does he know the waif is Lady Charis Weston, England's wealthiest heiress, and that to save her he must marry her himself! But can Charis accept a marriage of convenience, especially to a man who ignites her heart with a single touch?

Charis' eyes fastened on Sir Gideon, who waited outside. A cloud covered the moon, and the striking face became a mixture of shadows and light. Still beautiful but sinister.

She shivered. "Who are you?" she whispered, subsiding onto her seat.

"Who are you?" His dark gaze didn't waver from her as he resumed his place opposite, his back to the horses, as a gentleman would.

Charis wrapped the coat around her against the sharp early-morning chill and settled her injured arm more comfortably. "I asked first."

It was a childish response, and she knew he

recognized it as such from the twitch of his firm mouth. Like the rest of his face, his mouth was perfect. Sharply cut upper lip indicating character and integrity. A fuller lower lip indicating . . .

Something stirred and smoldered in her belly as she stared at him in the electric silence. What a time to realize she'd never before been alone with a man who wasn't a relative. The moment seemed dangerous in a way that had nothing to do with her quest to escape Felix and Hubert.

"My name is Gideon Trevithick." He paused as if expecting a response but the name meant nothing to her. "Of Penrhyn in Cornwall."

"Is that a famous house?" Perhaps that explained his watchful reaction.

Another wry smile. "No. That's two questions. My turn."

She stiffened although she should have expected this. And long before now.

"I'm tired." It was true, although a good meal and Akash's skills meant she didn't feel nearly as low as she had.

"It's a long journey to Portsmouth. Surely you can stay awake a few moments to entertain your fellow traveler."

She sighed. Her deceit made her sick with self-loathing. But what could she do? If she told the truth, he'd hand her over to the nearest magistrate.

"I've told you my name and where I live. I've told you the disaster that befell me today. I seek my aunt in Portsmouth." Her uninjured hand fiddled at the sling and betrayed her nervousness. With a shuddering breath, she pressed her palm flat on her lap. "We're chance-met travelers. What else can you need to know?" She knew she sounded churlish, but she hated telling lies.

In the uncertain light, his face was a gorgeous mask. She had no idea if he believed her or not. He paused as if winnowing her answers, then spoke in a somber voice. "I need to know why you're so frightened."

"The footpads . . ."

He made a slashing gesture with his gloved hand, silencing her. "If you truly had been set upon by thieves, you wouldn't have hidden in the stable. Won't you trust me, Sarah?" His soft request vibrated deep in her bones, and for one yearning moment, she almost told him the truth. Before she remembered what was at stake.

"I . . . I have trusted you," she said huskily. She swallowed nervously. His use of her Christian name, even a false one, established a new intimacy. It made her lies more heinous.

Disappointment shadowed his face as he sat back against the worn leather. "I can't help you if I don't know what trouble you flee."

"You are helping me." Charis blinked back the mist that appeared in front of her eyes. He deserved better return for his generosity than deceit.

She tried to tell herself he was a man, and, for that reason alone, she couldn't trust him. The insistence rang hollow. Her father had been a good man. Everything told her Sir Gideon Trevithick was a good man too.

She forced a stronger tone. "It's my turn for a question."

He folded his arms across his powerful chest and surveyed her from under lowered black brows. "Ask away."

TRUE CONFESSIONS

The classic novel by
***New York Times* Bestselling Author**
RACHEL GIBSON

Tabloid reporter Hope Spencer is in a rut. But when she flees her same-old LA life for the respite of Gospel, Idaho—she gets oh-so-much more than she bargained for. Sticking out like a sore thumb in her silver Porsche and designer duds, Hope isn't looking for any entanglements. But when a years-old murder mystery throws her together with Gospel's sexy sheriff Dylan Taber—she might not want to avoid this snag in her plan.

W hat in the hell is that?"
Dylan glanced across the top of the Chevy at Lewis, then turned his attention to the silver sports car driving toward him.

"He must have taken a wrong turn before he hit Sun Valley," Lewis guessed. "Must be lost."

In Gospel, where the color of a man's neck favored the color red and where pickup trucks and power rigs ruled the roads, a Porsche was about as inconspicuous as a gay rights parade marching toward the pearly gates.

"If he's lost, someone will tell him," Dylan said as

he shoved his hand into his pants pocket once more and found his keys. "Sooner or later," he added. In the resort town of Sun Valley, a Porsche wasn't that rare a sight, but in the wilderness area, it was damn unusual. A lot of the roads in Gospel weren't even paved. And some of those that weren't had potholes the size of basketballs. If that little car took a wrong turn, it was bound to lose an oil pan or an axle.

The car rolled slowly past, its tinted windows concealing whoever was inside. Dylan dropped his gaze to the iridescent vanity license plate with the seven blue letters spelling out MZBHAVN. If that wasn't bad enough, splashed across the top of the plate like a neon kick-me sign was the word "California" painted in red. Dylan hoped like hell the car pulled an illegal U and headed right back out of town.

Instead, the Porsche pulled into a space in front of the Blazer and the engine died. The driver's door swung open. One turquoise silver-toed Tony Lama hit the pavement and a slender bare arm reached out to grasp the top of the doorframe. Glimmers of light caught on a thin gold watch wrapped around a slim wrist. Then MZBHAVN stood, looking for all the world like she was stepping out of one of those women's glamour magazines that gave beauty tips.

"Holy shit," Lewis uttered.

Like her watch, sunlight shimmered like gold in her straight blond hair. From a side part, her glossy hair fell to her shoulders without so much as one unruly wave or curl. The ends so blunt they might have been cut with a carpenter's level. A pair of black cat's-eye sunglasses covered her eyes, but couldn't conceal the arch of her blond brows or her smooth, creamy complexion.

The car door shut, and Dylan watched MZBHAVN walk toward him. There was absolutely no over-looking those full lips. Her dewy red mouth drew his attenion like a bee to the brightest flower in the garden, and he wondered if she'd had fat injected into her lips.

The last time Dylan had seen his son's mother, Julie, she'd had that done, and her lips had just sort of lain there on her face when she talked. Real spooky.

Even if he hadn't seen the woman's California plates, and if she were dressed in a potato sack, he'd know she was big-city. It was all in the way she moved, straight forward, with purpose, and in a hurry. Big-city women were always in such a hurry. She looked like she belonged strolling down Rodeo Drive instead of in the Idaho wilderness. A stretchy white tank top covered the full curves of her breasts and a pair of equally tight jeans bonded to her like she was a seal-a-meal.

"Excuse me," she said as she came to stand by the hood of the Blazer. "I was hoping you might be able to help me." Her voice was as smooth as the rest of her, but impatient as hell.

"Are you lost, ma'am?" Lewis asked.

At Avon Books, we know your passion for romance—once you finish one of our novels, you find yourself wanting more.

May we tempt you with . . .

- **Excerpts** from our upcoming releases.

- Entertaining **extras**, including authors' personal photo albums and book lists.

- Behind-the-scenes **scoop** on your favorite characters and series.

- **Sweepstakes** for the chance to win free books, romantic getaways, and other fun prizes.

- Writing **tips** from our authors and editors.

- **Blog** with our authors and find out why they love to write romance.

- **Exclusive content** that's not contained within the pages of our novels.

Join us at
www.avonbooks.com

AVON

An Imprint of HarperCollins*Publishers*
www.avonromance.com